The Mysterium

THE MYSTERIUM

A Hugh Corbett Medieval Mystery

P. C. Doherty

Minotaur Books ⚎ New York

THE MYSTERIUM. Copyright © 2010 by Paul Doherty. All rights reserved.
Printed in the United States of America. For information, address St. Martin's Press, 175 Fifth Avenue, New York, N.Y. 10010.

www.minotaurbooks.com

Library of Congress Cataloging-in-Publication Data

Doherty, P. C.
  The Mysterium : a Hugh Corbett medieval mystery / P. C. Doherty.—1st U.S. ed.
     p. cm.
  First published in Great Britain by Headline Publishing Group, 2010.
  ISBN 978-0-312-67819-7 (hardcover)—ISBN 978-1-4299-4240-9 (e-book) 1. Corbett, Hugh (Fictitious character)—Fiction. 2. Great Britain—History—Edward I, 1272–1307—Fiction. 3. Serial murder investigation—England—London—Fiction. I. Title. II. Title: Hugh Corbett medieval mystery.
  PR6054.O37M97 2012
  823'.914—dc22

                                                                    2012003259

First published in Great Britain by HEADLINE PUBLISHING GROUP,
an Hachette UK Company

First U.S. Edition: April 2012

10 9 8 7 6 5 4 3 2 1

To Ida Margaret Barbero Terracino,
no mother more loved and lovely.
A true Christian lady and the best of teachers.
From the rising of the sun to its setting,
we shall never forget you.
(The Terracino family)

The Mysterium

Prologue

Soul-scot: the last payment of the dead . . .

A cold wind swept the Thames. The river, a broad ribbon of inky blackness lit here and there by the glow of lamp or candlelight, surged powerfully between its banks. The late winter rains had lashed the King's great city of London, drenching the thatched roofs of the poor and cascading down the dark red tiles of the stately Cheapside mansions. The year was turning. Spring was easing its way into the ice-bound countryside beyond the Tower. Soon the harsh rigour of Lent would be imposed, fasting, sack-cloth and penance. The shriving pews of London churches would become busy. Those seeking absolution would creep to the cross hoisted high on the rood screen to confess their sins: pride, avarice, greed, lust and, above all, murder.

The chroniclers, sitting in the scriptoria of their monasteries and abbeys, cowls pushed over shaven sculls, mittened, ink-stained fingers fluttering over plates of fiery coal, were strident in their judgement. Murder had made London its haunt. The Beast of the Apocalypse, begotten by Cain, prowled the sordid, spindle-thin alleys of the city. Murder lurked in the runnels of Cheapside and flittered like some darting shadow along the corridors of palaces, across the galleries of stately mansions and even through the paved cloister walks of their own houses. With the horned features of a babewyn or a gargoyle, it seemed to strike, strike and strike again. It battened fat, waxed strong on other sins, some fresh and bloody like hunks of meat sliced by a hunter: power, lust, greed, revenge, hatred or passions freed by too much ale or wine. It also nourished itself on ancient sins supposedly long forgotten, the roots of which had dug deep like weeds in a graveyard, stretching down to break through the coffin wood or the linen shroud to draw a morbid strength and vigour from the ill-named dead. The chroniclers listed such horrid deeds, as did the coroners' rolls at the Guildhall with their litany of 'death other than their natural death'. Murder erupted from the dark on Fleet Street, on the highway through Holborn, outside the gates of the Temple, in the shadow of Aldgate and Cripplegate, within bowshot of the Tower and on the approaches to London Bridge.

On 6 March, the year of Our Lord 1304, the thirty-second year of King Edward I, the eve of the Feast of St Perpetua and Felicitas, who died as martyrs in the Roman arena, murder unfolded its standard on the banks of the Thames at Queenshithe close to the small Chapel of the Oak. Its victim, Ignacio Engleat, lying bound and gagged against the slime-covered wall of an alleyway, faced the soul-cutting terror of his own swift-approaching violent death. He stared in terror at the dark shape busy about him, all hooded and visored, humming a Goliard song about a scholar walking a flower-fringed lane to meet his love-sweet. Ignacio wanted to live, but if he was to die, he must be shriven, confess his many sins, his cloying lusts, his deep thirst for the glee cup of the richest Bordeaux. He had sinned that very evening, visiting the whorehouse the Comfort of Bathsheba, doing business with the strumpet-mongers and lying with a maid soft and tender, her skin smooth as silk and white as milk, hair as red as the sun, lips sweeter than the honeycomb. Afterwards he'd gone downstairs to the tavern next door, the Halls of Purgatory, where he'd demanded and drunk a goblet of the best claret. He had fallen asleep and woken here in this freezing, filthy antechamber of hell. He could not remember how. He must have been drugged with some malignant potion mingled with his wine.

Ignacio watched in horror: that shifting shape, breathing heavily, was dragging a corpse towards him, the decaying cadaver of a river pirate hanged and left on the banks of the Thames for three turns of the tide. A corpse washed by the river but still slimed with corruption. In those few heartbeats after he had woken, the moon had bathed the horrid sight in its ghostly light – the scaffold arm, the dangling corpse, the flitting shape of his attacker humming that damnable song as he'd crept across and cut the corpse down – and he had realised immediately what was about to happen. After all, he was a *clericus peritus lege* – a clerk skilled in the law. Hadn't he sat in Westminster Hall as scribe to the Court of King's Bench? Hadn't he been out on assize in the shires? Hadn't he been sworn as a commissioner of oyer and terminer, 'to hear and decide'? Wasn't he an experienced jurist, close friend and servant of Chief Justice Walter Evesham, appointed directly by the King? So why was he here? Why was he going to be punished in such a heinous way? He strained against the gag and bonds that

3

held him tight. He should have known. He should have read the signs when Justice Evesham fell like Lucifer, never to rise again. All this for what? Justice Evesham now sheltered in the Abbey of Syon on Thames, a recluse, a sanctuary seeker from the law he had once exercised so imperiously. And he, Ignacio Engleat, Evesham's clerk, was bound and gagged like a malefactor in this fetid runnel.

Ignacio blinked away the rain and sweat running down his balding brow. The shadowy assassin hovered over him. Ignacio tried to plead, but it was to no avail. He was seized and stretched out along the ground, the stinking corpse of the river pirate placed on top of him. He turned his head from the putrid stench, that horrid face, eyes all pecked by the gulls, the scabby skin hanging in shreds, the flesh nothing but the seeping softness of corruption. He tried to beg, but the assassin, still humming, tightened the cords around him. Ignacio, terror-stricken, tried to move, but both he and the dead pirate, lashed to him, his rottenness now clinging to him like a cloak, were dragged across the rutted trackway, its sharp cobbles cutting his flesh.

The assassin paused. Ignacio blinked and screamed silently as his assailant dug the tip of the knife into his forehead, etching a symbol. Now, at the moment of death, Ignacio abruptly recalled the morbid memories of his own past. The Angel of Death had singled him out. Justice had recalled ancient sins. The Mysterium! Hadn't he marked his victims in such a way? Hadn't he, Ignacio Engleat, Evesham's personal clerk and scribe, listed the macabre details of such ghastly killings? But the Mysterium was gone, surely? Boniface Ippegrave had been exposed and disgraced by no less a person than Walter Evesham. Of course, like all Evesham had done, that was a lie. Now the ghost of Boniface Ippegrave had returned to carry out vengeance. Ignacio whimpered. He tried to recall the opening verse of Psalm 50, but all he could remember as, lashed to that corpse, he was pulled like a sledge across the cobbles were the words of scripture: 'Israel prepare to meet your God.' That was Ignacio Engleat's last conscious thought as he and his dead companion were tipped over the edge of the quayside into the freezing black river.

A few hours later, Abbot Serlo of Syon on Thames finished his dawn Mass in honour of St Perpetua and Felicitas in the chantry chapel of St Patrick. He thanked the lay brother who'd acted as server, then took off the red robes of the liturgy for that feast. As he did so, his keen blue eyes made out St Patrick's prayer inscribed in gold on a black panel against the chantry wall to the right of the altar. 'I bind unto myself this day, the strong name of the Trinity by invocation of the same, Three in One and One in Three. From the snares of demons, from the sedition of vice and any man who plots against me near and far . . .'

Abbot Serlo scratched his tonsure and wondered if that was a warning. As if in answer, Brother Cuthbert, brown robe fluttering, hobbled into the chapel as fast as his aching limbs would let him, hard sandals rapping the paved floor.

'Father Abbot, Father Abbot.' Cuthbert leaned against the entrance to the chantry chapel, gasping for breath. 'Father Abbot,' he repeated, 'you'd best come. Walter Evesham, he cannot be roused. I cannot wake him; there's no—'

Abbot Serlo whispered to his altar server, who hurried off, whilst the abbot followed Cuthbert out of the abbey church. It was a crisp, icy morning, the sky greying, the last stars disappearing, in the east a red glow. Serlo closed his eyes.

'*Deo Gratias*,' he whispered. The earth would dry and the brothers could break the soil, but first this . . .

The abbey buildings rose black against the sky. Already members of the community were busy. Brother Odo the sacristan, with his great bunch of keys, was leading a line of novices, each with a shuttered lantern, around the abbey. Candles, lamps and tapers were to be lit, chains unlocked, gates opened and treasures checked. As Father Abbot passed, the brothers, heads bowed, whispered, '*Pax tecum*' – peace be with you. Abbot Serlo replied, his eyes still on the hobbling figure of Cuthbert, busy leading him through the cloisters where the gargoyles grinned evilly in the murky light. They went out across the herb and flower plots into the Paradise of Benedict, the main garden of the abbey, its hoed banks greening with the first show of spring. As they reached Goose Meadow, stretching down to the curtain wall of the abbey and the Chapel of St Lazarus, which now served as the abbey's corpse house or coffin chamber, the wet grass chilled Abbot Serlo's feet, the water seeping over the thick leather soles of his sandals in between the sturdy thongs. Serlo hid his irritation. Cuthbert would not have come unless this was serious. Not for the first time he quietly wished that the disgraced Chief Justice Walter Evesham had chosen another abbey or monastery in which to seek sanctuary and withdraw from the world.

They passed a copse of trees and stepped on to the path leading down to St Lazarus' chapel, which had stood here long before the abbey was ever built. According to Brother Cornelius the chronicler, it had been built by the Saxons. A previous abbot had tiled the roof with costly red slate and replaced the main door, yet it still remained an ancient place, its nave of coarse grey ragstone, windows mere arrow-loops, protected by shutters. Serlo paused to catch his breath and take in the view. He had always wanted to do something about this forbidding, sombre place built close to the curtain wall overlooking the river. Cornelius claimed the ancient chapel had once been called 'the Church of the Drowned', a place where corpses dragged from the nearby Thames could be brought. Stories and legends swirled of how the chapel was still haunted by the earthbound souls of those who'd drowned, either by suicide or the victims of accident or murder.

'Father Abbot?'

Serlo broke from his reverie. Cuthbert was looking strangely at him.

'Father Abbot?' he repeated.

'Of course.' Serlo smiled. He followed Cuthbert, the *custos mortuorum* – the keeper of the dead – off the grass and along the narrow, pebble-dashed path. Near the main door lounged Ogadon, Cuthbert's guard dog. As the two robed figures approached, the great mastiff lumbered to his feet and walked as far as his clinking chain would permit. Serlo patted the the dog's black head and followed Cuthbert into the church.

It was a grim place, Serlo reflected, with its squat drum-like pillars and narrow windows through which slivers of morning light pierced. Torches flickered at the far end. Above the stark altar on its dais rose a huge bronze crucifix flanked by thick purple candles, their flames dancing in the breeze. Charcoal casks spluttered, their smoke perfumed with sprinkled incense. Pots and jars of crushed herbs were ranged along the walls in a futile attempt to hide the cloying smell of decay. Down the nave of the little chapel stood nine great tables in rows of three. On two lay corpses draped in black and gold cloths with a red cross sewn in the centre. Serlo recalled that one of these was old Brother Edmund who used to work in the infirmary; the second was a beggar found near the great gatehouse. He took the proffered pomander, and Cuthbert led him across the gloomy nave and down steep steps to the cellar beneath, where a paved passageway, lit by torches, stretched past three cells into the darkness. Two had their doors open; the third, at the far end, was heavily barred by a wooden beam held firmly in the iron clasps fixed to the oaken lintel on either side. Cuthbert led him to this.

'I just knocked,' the old lay brother whispered. 'Father Abbot, I just knocked, but no sound. I looked through the grille, but the light is poor.'

Helped by Cuthbert, Serlo climbed on to a wooden tub and peered through the iron grille fixed into the top of the door. Inside the cell it was dark; there were no windows, only a small slit high in the wall, wafer thin, no broader than a man's finger, allowing a crack of light through the limestone brick at the base of the chapel wall. No lamp or candle burned, the murky darkness betrayed nothing except a shape sitting at a table.

'Lord Walter,' Serlo called. 'Lord Walter!' He banged on the door.

'My lord abbot, perhaps he's suffered a seizure?' Cuthbert whispered. 'His humours were much disturbed.'

'He's no prisoner, brother, despite what the King says.' Serlo breathed heavily, stepping down from the tub. He kicked this away just as other lay brothers, summoned by the altar server, hurried down the steps shouting greetings to Brother Ogadon to quieten his grumbling bark. They crowded into the narrow passageway even as their abbot removed the outside bar and tried the door.

'It is also secured from within,' whispered Cuthbert. 'My lord Walter always insisted on that. A bar is fastened to the inside lintel; it can be swung down. I don't know why . . .'

'Break it down!' Serlo ordered.

Cuthbert stood away.

'Fetch what you have to.' Serlo gestured at the door. 'Just break it down.'

The lay brothers organised themselves. Stout logs were brought. Abbot Serlo went up and knelt before the bleak altar in the corpse chapel. He recited the requiem for those who lay there and tried to suppress a deep chill of apprehension. Something was wrong. The King would not be pleased. Lord Walter Evesham had been a high and mighty justice, the terror of outlaws and wolfsheads, be it in the cavernous darkness of Westminster Hall or out on commissions of eyre, delivering jails and decorating scaffolds and gibbets the length and breath of the kingdom. Then he had fallen like a shooting star. The King had returned from Scotland to investigate matters in the city. Lord Walter had been weighed in the balance and found very much wanting. Serlo lowered his head, listening to the battering against the door below. Walter Evesham had fled here seeking sanctuary. He'd proclaimed that he was tired of the world, exchanging his silk and samite robes for the coarse hair shirt and rough sacking of a Benedictine recluse and demanding shelter and protection. Edward of England had openly jeered at this so-called conversion, but allowed his former justice to stay on one condition: that he never left the grounds or precincts of the Abbey of Syon. That had been two weeks ago . . .

The crashing below and the sounds of ripping wood brought Serlo to his feet. Brother Cuthbert clattered up the steps.

'Father Abbot, Father Abbot, you'd best come.'

Serlo hurried to join him. Down in the eerie vaulted passageway, the lay brothers clustered together like frightened children. The door to the former justice's cell had been ripped off its leather hinges and lay to one side, the wood around it much damaged where the inside bar had been torn away. The abbot stood on the threshold. A former soldier, a knight who'd served in Wales and along the Scottish march, he recognised, as he would an old enemy, the reek of violent death and spilt blood. He took the lantern horn from Cuthbert's rheumatic hands, and walked through the shattered doorway and across to the table. The pool of dancing lanternlight picked out all the gory horror. Walter Evesham, former Chief Justice in the Court of King's Bench and Lord of the Manor of Ingachin, lay slumped, head slightly to one side, his throat cut so deep it seemed like a second mouth. Blood caked Evesham's dead face and drenched the top of his jerkin, forming a dark crust over the table and the pieces of jewellery littered there.

I

Botleas: a crime so serious,
there can be no financial compensation

'Archers forward, notch!' Ranulf-atte-Newgate, Clerk in the Chancery of Green Wax, raised his sword and stared across the sprawling cemetery that ringed the ancient church of St Botulph's Cripplegate in the King's own city of London. Ranulf was in armour, a mailed clerk, hauberked and helmeted. In one hand a kite-shaped shield was raised against the bowmen peering from those arrow-slit windows in St Botulph's tower. This full-square, sturdy donjon towered over the cemetery, an ideal refuge for the miscreants who had escaped from nearby Newgate. Ranulf felt exhausted. The chain-mail coat weighed heavy, his arms ached and the cold morning breeze was chilling his sweaty body. The helmet with its broad nose guard pressed down tightly and his cropped red hair itched. He stared across at his master Sir Hugh Corbett, Keeper of the Secret Seal, who was similarly armed, though he had not yet donned his helmet. Corbett's olive-skinned face was drawn, dark shadows circled his deep-set eyes and his black hair was streaked with glistening grey. He was so sweat-soaked he had pulled back his chain-mail coif, and was staring fixedly at the church.

'Sir Hugh, on your mark?'

Corbett gripped his sword and stared around what used to be God's acre at St Botulph's but was now a battlefield. The dead sprawled under rough sacking that hid the gruesome sword and axe wounds to face, neck, chest and belly. Corbett closed his eyes and muttered a requiem for the dead. He should not be here in this slaughter yard. On this mist-hung morning he should be in his own manor at Leighton, sitting in his chancery chamber with his beloved books or walking out with the Lady Maeve. He opened his eyes and stared at the Welsh archers in their brown leggings, their Lincoln-green jerkins now covered in blue, red and gold royal tabards.

'Archers, on my mark!' he shouted.

They thronged forward, longbows notched, bearded faces beneath their steel sallets tense and watchful. Behind the row of bowmen stood a huge cartload of straw and oil waiting to be torched. From beyond the cemetery walls rose the muffled clatter of the citizens of London who had thronged to watch this deadly confrontation reach its bloody climax.

'Sir Hugh, Sir Hugh Corbett?' called a clear voice.

Corbett lowered his sword and groaned as Parson John, vicar of the parish, pushed his way through the thronging archers, holding a crucifix.

'Sir Hugh, I beg you wait.' Parson John grasped the wooden pole of the cross more tightly and knelt before the Keeper of the King's Secret Seal. 'I beg you.' He lifted his unshaven face. It was thin, haggard, the green eyes red-rimmed. 'No more of this. Let me talk to these malefactors.' He paused and ran a hand through his cropped blond hair. Corbett noticed how the tonsure was neatly cut, the fringe over the broad brow laced with sweat, the furrowed cheeks stained with dust.

'Father,' Corbett crouched down to face him squarely, 'look around you. Sixteen dead here, more in the church, your own people cruelly slain. These felons are condemned men, rifflers who broke out of Newgate. They have slaughtered again and again, not only here, but yesterday in Cheapside, along the streets of Cripplegate and more elsewhere. Then there are the women they abducted.' He swallowed hard. 'At least their screams have stopped. The church is now encircled, it has to be stormed.' He saw tears in Parson John's eyes. 'I know,' whispered Corbett. 'These are hard times for you. Your own father's fall—'

'My father has nothing to do with this.'

'I don't agree,' hissed Corbett, his voice turning hard. 'Your father may well have something to do with it. My orders are explicit. Sir Ralph Sandewic has now retaken Newgate. I will storm the church, your church, and bring this bloody mayhem to an end.'

'Sir Hugh.' Ranulf was pointing to the top of the church tower. Figures could be seen darting between the crenellations; similar ominous movements could be glimpsed at the narrow windows. Corbett followed Ranulf and put on his helmet, he then stood up, ignoring the priest, who still knelt grasping his cross.

'Mark!' Ranulf screamed. The mass of Welsh archers obeyed; their great yew bows, primed and curved, swung up. 'Aim,' Ranulf bellowed, 'loose.' A shower of barbed shafts, a cloud of feather-winged death, streaked into the sky. Most of the arrows clattered against the rough stone of the church, but screams and a body toppling from the tower top showed that some of the archers had found their mark. At Ranulf's orders more volleys were loosed, driving the defenders from the parapet and the various windows. The bowmen advanced. Fresh clouds of arrows shattered against the stonework. The great war cart was dragged forward, its pointed battering ram jutting out. The combustibles were fired, the oil, tar and ancient kindling roaring like a furnace as a group of sweating archers, protected by their comrades, pushed at the long poles, driving the cart down the slight incline towards the great double doors of the church. Corbett flinched as an arrow whipped by his face. He screamed at the archers to push harder. The cart lurched forward, flames and smoke billowing up. He roared at the men to let go and retreat from the few enemy bowmen who still manned the windows. The cart held true, trundling down the slope and crashing into the main door. As the sharpened battering ram wedged deep into the wood, flames roared along it.

Corbett and Ranulf, protected by a screed of archers, now retreated out of bowshot. The Welsh kept up their arrow storm as the two man took off their helmets, pushed back their coifs and gratefully washed hands and faces in a bucket of rather dirty water. The captain of archers, Ap Ythel, brought blackjacks of ale and a platter of hard bread from a nearby tavern. As Ranulf chattered to the master bowman, Corbett ate and drank greedily, staring at the conflagration around the main door. He felt exhausted. He'd been in his chancery chamber at the exchequer in Westminster when the royal courier had arrived. The riffler leaders Giles Waldene and Hubert the Monk had been consigned to Newgate with at least two dozen of their coven, all victims of the sudden fall from grace of Walter Evesham, the chief justice. Corbett ruefully wished they'd been lodged in the Tower. Waldene and the Monk had been committed to the infamous pits, their followers left in the common yard, where Waldene's gang had clashed with Hubert's. The fighting had spread, other prisoners becoming involved. The Keeper of Newgate and his guards had proved woefully inadequate. The great prison yard had been reached and its gates stormed. The King's chancery had dispatched urgent writs to the Constable of the Tower Sir Ralph Sandewic, a veteran experienced in crushing riots in Newgate and the Marshalsea. He in turn had called on Corbett as senior chancery clerk, who had summoned Welsh archers camped near the Bishop of Ely's Inn.

The escaped prisoners, ruthless and merciless, had fought their way along Cripplegate or escaped out on to the wild heathland beyond the walls, where Sandewic was waiting with his men-at-arms. The old constable had shown no mercy. Any prisoner caught was asked one question: 'Are you from the Land of Cockaigne?' Sir Hugh Corbett, for his own mysterious purposes, had insisted on this. A blank look or a refusal meant immediate decapitation. The severed heads of the fugitives, tarred and pickled, already decorated the spikes along London Bridge. Other felons had fought their way into St Botulph's yesterday evening, just as the compline bell tolled. Parson John had been surpliced, ready to chant the day's last praises to God, when they had burst in. The priest had escaped; others were not so fortunate. Robbed and slain, they were tossed through the open door before this was sealed and blocked. Several women had been taken prisoner, and when Corbett and his archers reached St Botulph's, they could hear the screams of the unfortunates who were being raped time and time again. Eventually the terrible screaming had ceased, and Corbett believed the women were dead. Once organised, he'd launched an assault, which was savagely repulsed; only then did he learn that the escaped prisoners had also pillaged the barbican tower at Newgate and seized bows, arrows and all the armour of battle.

'Sir Hugh?' Ranulf, red hair damp, green eyes in his white face bright with the fury of battle, was eager to finish this. 'Soon?' he demanded. 'Soon we'll attack?'

Corbett nodded. Ranulf saw this as an opportunity to excel, to prove that he, a chancery scribe, was as valiant as any knight in battle. Corbett looked beyond Ranulf at the cart, which was now a blazing bonfire.

'It's caught the door,' Ranulf murmured. 'Master, we are ready.'

Corbett rose and followed Ranulf out into the cemetery, keeping to the trees and crumbling crosses of the headstones. They moved down the side of the church, where a group of men-at-arms stood waiting with a makeshift battering ram, a long sharpened log swung by chains from a wooden framework. Corbett stared at the narrow corpse door. It was undoubtedly blocked, but it was still vulnerable.

'Listen.' He pulled the chain-mail coif over his head. 'Bring the ram up as quickly as possible. The felons will be gathering near the main entrance. There are no windows above the corpse door, and those to the side are narrow. We must force that entrance as quickly as possible.' The men-at-arms, all liveried in the arms of the royal household, grunted their assent.

Corbett and Ranulf helped lumber the ram across the broken ground, squeezing past the funeral monuments. They reached the church without trouble. Immediately the ram was swung back, crashing into the corpse door so hard it began to buckle. Corbett quietly prayed that the felons would remain massed near the main entrance. The pounding continued. Welsh archers began to feed their way across, bows at the ready; others armed with round shields and short stabbing swords followed. The pounding hammered on remorselessly. An ear-splitting crack and the corpse door snapped back on its hinges. An arrow whipped through the air, skimming over their heads. In reply, the Welsh archers loosed a shower of shafts. Screams and yells echoed. Ranulf, helmet on, followed Corbett into the darkness of the church. Shadows emerged. Corbett parried and thrust with a hulking brute garbed in a woman's dress, his painted face all bloodied. The stink from his body was foul. Corbett drove the monstrosity back, fending off the huge mallet his opponent whirled. An arrow cut through the air, taking the felon full in the face, and he toppled to the ground, writhing in his death throes.

Corbett wiped the sweat from his face. Smoke from the main door seeped through the nave, which was now riven with the clash of steel, the hiss of arrows, groans and screams. Men staggered away clutching blood-bubbling wounds. As the burning door at the main entrance began to crumble, the ram that pierced it, still smouldering and licked by dying flames, was pushed deeper into the nave. The door finally collapsed, and archers, braving the fire flickering around the lintel, clambered over the smoking wood and poured into the church. The battle was over.

Some of the prisoners tried to escape, only to be cut down or forced back. A few attempted to hold out in the tower; they were pushed to the top, but none chose to jump, as Ranulf remarked, and resistance faded. Corbett ordered chains and ropes to be brought. At last a long line of felons, about twenty in number, lay shackled in one of the darkening aisles, kicked and cursed by the archers. Corbett, joined by Parson John and Ranulf, watched as the bodies of the victims, men and women, some very young, were brought out. They had all been stripped, horribly abused and tortured, their skins scorched by candle flame. Corbett ordered them to be decently tended, and Parson John had all the corpses, including two archers, laid out along the centre of the nave. Corbett had wandered many a battlefield, but this sight was truly piteous. Some of the victims had perished quickly from arrows embedded deep in their chests, others had taken time to die.

'Harrowing and hideous!' Corbett crossed himself and stared around. The church was like a flesher's stall, awash with blood, littered with the detritus of battle. Sheets were brought out and flung over the corpses. Master Fleschner, the parish clerk, was summoned. He first retched and vomited, then began the grisly task of listing those killed: Margaret-atte-Wood, spinster of Jewry, Aegidius Markell, vintner of Moletrap Alley, along with all the other innocent victims of the murderous anarchy.

The archers, with stronger bellies, complained of being hungry. Ranulf, who'd walked the length of the long line of gruesome corpses, ordered their captain to requisition food and drink from nearby taverns and cook shops. Corbett just stared at a wall painting of a demon with bat-like ears, the torso and cloven feet of a goat, its eyes grisly black in a fiery red face.

'There are demons and there are demons,' Ranulf remarked, coming up behind him. 'Those in the flesh are worse.'

'Much worse,' Corbett whispered. 'See what they did, Ranulf? God knows why. Some souls like nothing better than to see the world crack and collapse in a welter of killing.'

'I have to anoint the dead.'

Corbett looked over his shoulder at Parson John, eyes staring in a pallid face.

'I'll give them general absolution but I want to anoint each one. I think I should do that, and afterwards . . .' The parson gestured round. 'This church is polluted; it will have to be re-consecrated. It happened so quickly, Sir Hugh. Early yesterday evening we had gathered, as we always do, the Guild of St Botulph's, to sing compline . . .'

'Father, go home.' Corbett beckoned an archer across. 'Take Parson John to the priest's house,' he ordered quietly. 'Make sure he drinks a deep cup of claret. Only then let him come back and do what he wants.'

Parson John looked as if he was going to object, then he shrugged and walked off. Screams and groans echoed from the shadowy transepts where the prisoners lay huddled. Ranulf had gone amongst them, kicking and lashing out with the flat of his sword. Corbett went and grasped his arm. Ranulf turned, fist raised, his lean face tense with anger. His green eyes seemed larger, red hair fanned his face like a halo of flame, spittle frothed at the corner of his mouth.

'Leave it,' Corbett ordered. He stared Ranulf down, gripping him by the wrist. 'Leave it, Ranulf. We'll try them by due process of law, then,' he glanced down at the prisoners, 'we'll send them to God's tribunal.'

'Aye, and I'll join you in that.'

Corbett looked round. Sir Ralph Sandewic, Constable of the Tower, emerged from the shadows, his craggy face wreathed in a smile, his snow-white hair, parted along the middle, tumbling down to his shoulders. Dressed in half-armour, he stood fingering the hilt of his great sword, then he raised a hand and snapped his fingers. Two men-at-arms wheeled their barrow forward. Corbett stared down at the severed heads piled there: the jagged necks, half-closed eyes popping out, mouths and noses encrusted in blood. Flies and insects crawled over the mottled skin of the dead faces. Corbett swallowed hard. He'd seen too much. He walked away even as Ranulf helped Sandewic push the barrow in amongst the chained prisoners so that they could stare, as Sandewic put it, on their own future.

Corbett went outside. The cemetery was now being cleared, all the corpses removed, only black stains on the icy grass showing where they had sprawled. Archers were collecting spears and arrows, scraps of clothing and armour. The fire at the great door had been doused, the half-charred battering ram pulled away. An archer brought across a tankard of ale. Corbett thanked him and gulped it to clear the smoke and dirt from his mouth. He breathed in deeply, then summoned an archer and sent him out of the cemetery beyond the lychgate, where a horde of city bailiffs and men-at-arms kept the curious at bay. A short while later the archer returned with a Friar of the Sack he'd found preaching from a cart on the approaches to Cripplegate. A beanpole of a man, the friar's lugubrious face was redeemed by merry eyes. Corbett fished in his purse and brought out a coin.

'For the poor. Brother, you are an ordained priest?'

'Fifteen years in all,' quipped the friar, blessing Corbett. 'I carry my licence if you want—'

'No,' Corbett breathed, 'I do not want to see it.' He licked his lips. 'I am Sir Hugh Corbett, Keeper of the Secret Seal. I am also the King's commissioner in these parts, with the power of oyer and terminer.'

'To hear and to finish,' the Franciscan translated. 'And I,' he extended a hand for Corbett to clasp, 'am Brother Ambrose of the Order of the Sack, summoned I suppose to attend the dead?'

'Or those about to die,' Corbett replied wearily. 'I've taken prisoners. You'll shrive them if that's what they want, yes?'

The friar pulled a face, then looked over his shoulder. Sandewic had emerged from behind the church, a two-headed axe over his shoulder. The men-at-arms beside him carried a blackened block, scarred and bloodstained.

'I see.' The friar rubbed his face. 'Yes,' he continued as the block was set down with the axe beside it. 'Death has truly set up camp in God's acre.'

Corbett stared up at the sky. The day was drawing on, the sun was strengthening; the mist that had swirled over this cemetery had gone, as had the silence. The sounds of the city echoed clearly across the wall: the rattle of carts, the furious shouts of traders, the cries of children and the clop of horses. Corbett smelt the fragrance of the still damp grass, then that other, more pervasive tang, of spilt blood and rent flesh. He crossed himself and went back through the corpse door into the nave.

Ranulf had prepared everything. The offertory table had been moved just before the entrance to the beautifully carved rood screen, three stools behind it. On the table, now draped with a purple altar covering, stood two lighted candles, a book of the Gospels and a drawn sword. Corbett nodded at Sandewic and took the stool in the centre. Master Fleschner, the parish clerk, would serve as scribe, leaving the dead to Parson John, who was moving from corpse to corpse, a stole around his neck, a phial of holy oils in his hands. Every so often Corbett would capture the words of the swiftly whispered prayer: 'Go forth, Christian soul . . .'

Corbett blessed himself, then stood up. The church was now silent except for the muttering of the priest and the groans and cries from the prisoners. Welsh archers, bows notched, stood guard at all doors and in the sanctuary, whilst on either side of the nave thronged Sandewic's men-at-arms. Corbett, one hand on the Gospels, the other grasping the hilt of his sword, loudly proclaimed how, by the terms of his commission, Edward, 'by the grace of God, King of England, Lord of Ireland, Duke of Aquitaine, demands that all mayors and bailiffs et cetera recognise Sir Hugh Corbett as the King's Commissioner of Oyer and Terminer, to hear and determine all cases . . .' Once finished, he sat down.

'You know,' he declared to his two companions, 'these are

adjudged felons taken in arms against the King. They are guilty of murder, rape and pillage. Each will face the same charges and be asked to reply. I have one question for each of them: are you from the Land of Cockaigne?'

'What is this?'

Sandewic and Ranulf spoke almost together.

'You ordered me to ask those taken out on the heath the same question,' the constable declared. 'The Land of Cockaigne? What is that to these felons?'

'Cockaigne,' Corbett replied, 'is a fool's version of life: a glutton's kingdom where food and drink present themselves already prepared. Pigs trot up fully roasted, a carving knife deep in their flanks. Geese fly but they are already spitted and cooked. Larks, grilled to crispness, swoop into your mouth. Buildings are made of food; the roofs are pancakes, the fences sausages, dripping on the floor.' He smiled at his companions' puzzlement. 'That is all I can say for the moment. It's a place of nonsense where ducks are shoed and the hare chases the fox. Apparently it's a cipher used by one of the King's spies,' he whispered. 'God knows who he or she is, but,' he stared into the darkness, 'it's quite apposite, eh?' He pointed to the sheeted corpses. 'A world turned topsy-turvy, where the innocent suffer and the guilty escape.'

'Not now,' Ranulf murmured.

'I am not talking about those waiting to die,' Corbett observed, 'but Giles Waldene, the King of Ribauds, and Hubert the Monk. They both lie in the pits at Newgate. They did not join this affray. They'll claim no knowledge of it and demand to be tried by their peers. I wonder.' He pointed across the nave to where the captain of archers and his company were pulling the prisoners to their feet. 'Did any of those suspect?'

'What?' Sandewic grated.

'That in their midst was a traitor who would sell them body and soul to the King's justice? Someone who, for profit perhaps, would turn King's Approver and become their destroyer. God knows why that riot took place and who caused it. We may be doing God's work, perhaps the King's, but,' Corbett added grimly, 'the devil's also! He must be ravenous for the souls of those we are going to judge.'

'Such is life,' Sandewic retorted. 'Sometimes it's hard to tell the difference between good and bad.' He pointed across the nave. 'Let's not keep the demons waiting.'

The trials began. According to law, the felons had no real defence. Indicted already, they'd then 'broken from the King's jail to carry out hideous depredations against the Crown's good and faithful servants, as well as horrid blasphemy against Holy Mother Church'. Each of the prisoners gave his name to the parish clerk, who was sitting at the end of the table, busy keeping a record. The accused was then faced with a list of gravimina, or charges, and invited to reply, which was usually in the form of a curse or a mouthful of spit. When the question about the Land of Cockaigne was first asked, the parish clerk glanced up in surprise; thereafter each prisoner shook his head and continued with the usual tirade of abuse.

Sentencing was a foregone conclusion: 'Guilty!' Corbett declared. 'Proven as charged with no defence.' Once sentence was passed, the condemned were hustled out into the cemetery.

The Friar of the Sack, seated in the shadow of a buttress, offered to shrive them; some accepted, others refused. All were eventually dragged to the block, hands tied behind them. Two archers made each of them kneel, forcing the condemned man's head to one side against the block whilst the executioner, with unerring accuracy, brought down the heavy double-headed axe. Its hard, chilling thud echoed through the opened corpse door, as Sandewic murmured, like the sound of hell's gate slamming shut. Sometimes the prisoner protested and struggled, only to be knocked senseless.

Corbett, mouth dry, continued. The line of prisoners shortened. Parson John, further down the nave, finished his ministrations and sat with his back to a pillar, watching the grim process of law being carried out. Corbett called a brief halt as the bells of other churches rang out the Angelus. From the nearby streets the market horns brayed, the signal for trading to cease so that the guildsmen and stallholders, as well as their customers, could adjourn to the taverns, wine booths, cookshops and pastry houses to break their morning fast. Corbett asked for watered wine and stood in the Lady Chapel. He drained his cup, then knelt at the prie-dieu. Parson John came up, asking in a whisper when this would all be over. Corbett just knelt, staring up at the statue, and shook his head. The parson repeated his question. Corbett turned.

'It's never over, priest,' he murmured. 'Don't you see?' He pointed to a wall painting to his left, Cain slaying his brother with the jawbone of an ass. 'That's what we are, Father, killers to the bone, all of us, sons and daughters of Cain.'

'Not all of us!'

'Aren't we?' Corbett asked hoarsely. 'If not with knives and clubs, don't we slay each other in our souls? Aren't such thoughts the dreadful parents of our deeds?'

The priest stepped back, face shocked. He stared open-mouthed at Corbett, then, spinning on his heel, walked off into the gloom of the church.

'Master, Master.' Ranulf approached softer than a cat, beckoning with his hand. 'Sandewic has been out to see the heads piled in their baskets. He's like a farmer with choice plums. He says he'll decorate the bridge, the Tower and every wall spike in Newgate. By the way, where is Chanson?' he continued. 'Our Clerk of the Stables appears to have—'

'Our Clerk of the Stables,' Corbett retorted, coming out of the Lady Chapel, 'is carrying documents to the King, who, I believe, is flying his hawks in the woods outside Sheen. There's been trouble in the Narrow Seas. French privateers—'

'Sir Hugh,' Sandewic called, 'we should begin again.'

'And again, and again . . .' Corbett murmured.

It was late afternoon by the time they were finished and the last ominous thud echoed through the church. All the felons bar one had been tried and executed. The sole survivor was Thomas Brokenhale, alias John Chamoys, alias Reginald Clatterhouse, alias Richard Draper, also known as Lapwing. Sandewic reported how Lapwing had been seen in the company of the prisoners at Newgate early the previous afternoon. He had then disappeared, but returned mid-morning to watch events from near the lych-gate. One of the Newgate gaolers had recognised him as a visitor to Waldene's coven in prison. Lapwing had been held fast in the cellar of a nearby tavern before being dragged across for investigation. A young, cheery-faced rogue, he confessed to having some knowledge of both Waldene and Hubert the Monk. He had not, however, so he claimed, raised a hand against man or maid. No, he knew nothing about the Land of Cockaigne, but he did know his rights. 'I'm a clerk,' he protested, showing the faint tonsure almost overgrown by his dirty reddish hair. More importantly, he could recite the first verse of Psalm 50. *Have mercy on me oh God in your kindness, in your compassion blot out my offence.*

'I'm a clerk,' he repeated. 'I demand to be tried by Holy Mother Church. I am not subject—'

'Shut up!' Sandewic bawled. 'You're guilty and you'll die with your coven.'

Corbett intervened. Lapwing, whoever he was, had pleaded the law. More importantly, Corbett sensed the man was telling the truth. He was not like the rest of the rifflers and ribauds, who lived for the day and certainly didn't care for the next. Sandewic, however, proved obdurate. Offended by Lapwing's insolence, the constable wanted the accused's head, and bellowed that he'd even risk excommunication by the bishops. They had cursed him before and they'd certainly do it again. He didn't give a demon's fart for their arrogance.

Sandewic's shouting attracted the attention of his men-at-arms, who thronged across the nave. Corbett became uneasy. Ranulf rested his hand on the hilt of his dagger. Sandewic bawled for his sword. Lapwing's smile faded, and he hastily scrabbled at a secret pocket in his jerkin, brought out a thin scroll and handed this to

Corbett. The Keeper of the Secret Seal unrolled it, read the contents, smiled and looked at Sandewic.

'Listen to this, Master Constable!' he said. '"The King to all faithful subjects. Know you that Stephen Escolier (also calling himself Lapwing) of Mitre Street, Cripplegate, is a faithful servant of the Crown, a clerk of this city. Know you that whatever he has done, he has done for the good of the Crown and the safety of this Realm."' The writ was witnessed by a leading judge, Hervey Staunton, and his henchman Roger Blandeford, and sealed with the King's personal signet. Corbett handed it back to Lapwing, who smiled, winked at Sandewic and swaggered out of the church.

Corbett wearily declared he was finished. 'What had to be done,' he declared, 'has been done.'

He left the church, going across the busy street into the Burning Bush tavern, where he and Ranulf had stabled their horses. He was washing his hands and face in a bowl at the lavarium when he heard Ranulf groan. He glanced back at the door. Chanson stood there, hopping from foot to foot.

'The King wants us?' Corbett breathed.

'Yes, Sir Hugh, he does,' Chanson called back. 'He is waiting at the Abbey of Syon on Thames. Lord Walter Evesham has been horribly murdered.'

2

Nithing: to be adjudged truly wicked

Today, reflected Corbett, the Feast of St Perpetua and Felicitas, I shall certainly not forget. He pressed a pomander soaked in a mixture of fennel and lavender against his face and walked around the mortuary tables in the corpse chapel at Syon Abbey. He fought his weariness and ignored the hum of conversation as Ranulf informed the King and his entourage about what had happened at St Botulph's. He wanted to climb the steps, go out and embrace the last of the evening, capture the essence of that sunset when the western sky turns to a glorious band of blue and fiery gold. He wanted to feel the breeze, heavy with the promise of spring, cool against his face and to catch the last birdsong of the day.

'What did the poet write – ah yes,' he murmured. 'The bird-song of each day is totally unique. In all creation it has never been heard before and never will return.' He'd love to be free of this coat of mail, wrapped in a cloak instead; to sit by his hall fire, crackling and merry, contemplating the day with Maeve, or stand with her in that lovely bower overlooking their herb garden. In a word, he wanted to go home.

'Sir Hugh?'

The King was demanding he inspect those three cadavers. Corbett took a deep breath and stared down at the corpse of Walter Evesham, former Chief Justice in the Court of King's Bench.

'I never liked you in life,' he whispered, 'and death has not changed that.' He breathed a prayer and studied the grisly remains of that old hypocrite garbed in the brown sacking of a Benedictine recluse. Evesham's face was powder-white, his lips still rather full and red, pennies pressed down his heavy eyelids, and that nose, so often wrinkled in distaste, now jutted sharp and pointed. Even in death, his full, high-cheekboned face held a hint of arrogance, despite the thick white hair being shorn close to the scalp. Corbett crouched and peered at the wound that sliced Evesham's throat from ear to ear.

'Who would do that?' demanded Roger Blandeford, chief clerk to Justice Hervey Staunton.

Corbett was tempted to reply that half of London would, whilst the other half would have clapped with glee. Instead he leaned closer, ignoring the harsh tang of the herbs in which the cadaver had been washed, and carefully scrutinising the letter 'M' carved on to Evesham's smooth forehead. He felt a chill of apprehension. 'M' for Mysterium, the hallmark of a professional assassin who'd prowled London two decades ago. A skilled killer who'd murdered for profit until Lord Walter Evesham had brought him down.

He moved to the second corpse. Ignacio Engleat had never been handsome in life; death only emphasised his ugly face and scrawny hair, the jowly mouth, the snub nose and flared nostrils, those ever-peering eyes now closed for good. Both body and face were bloated with water and, despite the herbs and washing, reeked of mud slime and river offal. Engleat had been Walter Evesham's faithful clerk and scribe; he had shadowed him in more senses than one. An arrogant, haughty man with a scornful heart and viper-like tongue, he would toady to the great but savage those weaker or more vulnerable than himself.

'Found floating in the Thames.'

Edward of England walked over. The King's face was rather pale, the furrowed lines more emphasised, the iron-grey tangle of hair uncombed. Corbett recognised the signs. Edward's lips were a bloodless line, his right eye drooped almost shut. The King was seething.

'Again the Mysterium.' Corbett pointed to the large 'M' etched on Engleat's brow.

'And these were found pinned to the two corpses.' Edward handed over two scraps of soaked vellum. The ink was blurred but the two words were clear enough: *Mysterium Rei* – the Mystery of the Thing. 'Evesham,' he hissed. 'I thought Evesham trapped that assassin?'

'If I recall,' Corbett replied, 'the Mysterium escaped. He vanished. Now, your grace, he has apparently returned with a vengeance. And this?' He moved to the third corpse.

The last cadaver was disgusting. The man had undoubtedly been hanged; his bloated face was a bluish grey. One eye had been plucked out, and the end of his nose and part of his upper lip had been gnawed away.

'Scemscale,' called Hervey Staunton, a pomander muffling his nose and mouth. Corbett looked up. 'Scemscale,' Staunton repeated. 'That's what he called himself. That's the name I used when I sentenced him to hang on the river scaffold for the turn of three tides.'

'When?'

'Oh, about a week ago.'

'His corpse,' the King intervened, 'was found lashed to that of Ignacio Engleat.'

'An ancient punishment.' Staunton was determined to show his knowledge. 'And one more's the pity, not used today. The punishment for a liar and a perjurer who sent others to their deaths by false accusation and blasphemous oaths.'

'What else?'

'The assassin is proclaiming that Engleat was also a murderer, but when, how and why? I don't know.'

'A sorry tale,' Corbett whispered.

'But not here,' murmured the King, 'not here. My lord abbot's parlour would be more fitting for our deliberations.'

Corbett agreed. The abbot's parlour proved to be a welcome relief from the haunting, dour corpse chapel. He'd been glad to be free of it, out in the clear night air, the rich smell of burning wood mingling with that of sweet incense and candle smoke. The chanting of compline echoed from the great church. On the fitful breeze faint sounds carried from the surrounding woods as darkness settled. Corbett washed his face and hands at a lavarium in the cloisters, the King constantly by his side whispering how he must stay in the abbey that night, how he wanted this malevolent business swiftly resolved. Corbett just nodded until the King fell silent, glaring at him as a lay brother led them through a labyrinth of hollow-stoned passageways to this exquisitely comfortable chamber where flames sparked and flared as the logs in the great mantled hearth cracked and split. Candlelight glowed in the sheen of oaken panelling and the long table dominated by a small nef, an intricately carved silver cog bearing the Mary and her Divine Child. Many-coloured triptychs decorated the white plaster above the gleaming panelling. The shelves of the open aumbry against the far wall displayed the precious gold and silver plate of the abbey. It was truly a place to relax after the rigours of the day.

A servant poured mulled wine, so hot each goblet was wrapped in a thick white napkin. On a small pewter plate beside it was diced spiced meat covered with breadcrumbs, to be eaten with the horn spoon provided. The King, seated at the top of the table, invited them to eat and swiftly devoured his own portion. Sir Hervey Staunton seemed reluctant, so the King pulled across his platter and quickly cleared it, sitting back in the high-backed chair with a sigh of relief as he warmed his hands around the goblet. Corbett ate carefully, nudging Ranulf with his knee to warn him not to laugh at the King. Ranulf obeyed, keeping his head down, though now and again the red-haired clerk would glance across at Staunton and Blandeford. Corbett did not like either of them; neither did Ranulf, who secretly dismissed the precious pair as 'cheeks of the same arse'.

Staunton sat in the Court of King's Bench: he was a small, furtive man with a pointed face that reminded Ranulf of a rat. His lank hair framed thin, solemn features: a small mouth, sharp nose and close-set eyes. Clean-shaven, dressed in a bottle-green cotehardie with a silver chain of office around his neck, Staunton might be considered a lowly official, but that was a dangerous conclusion, Ranulf reflected. In the scarlet silks of his office he was a truly frightening figure, a bully who would often reduce those who appeared before him to a state of nervous exhaustion. A ruthlessly ambitious man who, according to Corbett, believed only in one legal verse: *Voluntas Principis habet vigorem legis* – the will of the Prince has force of law, Staunton was a royal creature, with only one master, the Crown.

Blandeford, his scribe, was tall and slender, his olive-skinned face closely shaved, his black hair neatly cut, his clerical tonsure clear to see. His pious, gentle looks concealed a brain teeming like a beehive and a heart as hard as flint. Court gossips maintained that Blandeford, a truly vaunting clerk, would enter the Church and became a bishop. God help us all on that, Ranulf reflected. He finished his food and stared directly across at Blandeford, who sat watching him just as closely.

Edward I, now warm, his belly full, the royal right eye no longer drooping so much, sat lost in thought. Corbett cradled his own wine cup and stared at a triptych on the wall opposite. Gilt-edged and painted deftly in red, blue, green and gold, it described the death of St Benedict's sister Scholastica. He concentrated on the pious images, which soothed the harrowing memories of the day.

'My lords,' Edward tapped the table, 'it is good to be here.' He gestured at the door barred from the inside, then at the polished shutters over the small oriel window on the far wall. 'We can take close council here, so I shall begin. You know most of the sorry tale, but it becomes richer in its retelling. Twenty years ago, an assassin appeared in London. Now that city, that seething pot of dissent and rebellion, is truly the house of murder: assassins and slayers are manifold, but the Mysterium was different. He'd kill those whom the powerful of London wanted dead. His victims suffered various fates: drowning, stabbing, burning in a fire, garrotting, or the casualty of a falling wall.' The King raised a hand. 'When the corpses were found, and I believe not all were, the letter "M" was carved on the victim's forehead and upon the corpse was a scrap of parchment with the words *Mysterium Rei* – the Mystery of the Thing – an enigmatic, taunting phrase. God knows what it means; perhaps it was left to intrigue or to serve as a hallmark. Now London bubbles with enmities and rivalries of every kind: husband and wife, feuding kin, business rivals, insults given, insults suffered . . .' The King paused as Staunton lifted his hand.

'Sire, the writing on the parchment?'

'By a hand ordinary enough, on parchment that could be found anywhere. Nothing remarkable, except,' Edward added flatly, 'this was murder. The number of deaths increased; protests were lodged.'

Staunton and Blandeford murmured their agreement.

'Now.' Edward gestured around. 'All of you served in the chancery at the time. You know most of this through rumour, gossip and tittle-tattle. A murder by the gangs in London is one thing, but the Mysterium was another. Old Burnell, my chancellor, turned to a very ambitious, talented clerk, Walter Evesham. All of you must have known him. Corbett, this was in your green and salad days.' The King's glance softened. 'Before my beloved Eleanor.' His voice became choked with emotion, as it did whenever he mentioned his first wife. 'Ah well,' he whispered, 'glory days! Do you remember them, Corbett? As for you, Ranulf,' Edward half smiled, 'no, you wouldn't know any of this.'

Corbett just sat and nodded in agreement. He remembered Evesham, sharp as a knife, secretive, always busy on this and that.

'Keen-witted and cunning,' he murmured. 'Evesham was a man of many talents.'

'He certainly was,' the King agreed. 'He was born at Ingachin, a lonely manor along the Welsh March, a desolate place. His father did good service for me in Wales. Walter was the apple of his eye, a scholar. He attended the cathedral schools of Gloucester and Hereford; later the halls of Oxford and Cambridge, studying the Quadrivium and Trivium, though his special talent was logic and the law. He served in the royal levies before being schooled at the Inns of Court, where he was professed as a serjeant. He entered the royal service and did excellent work at the court of France. A true and assiduous collector of information, he had to leave Paris one step ahead of the Secretissimi, my sweet cousin Philip of France's ruthless agents, and returned to Westminster as a clerk in the Chancery of the Green Wax. He later entered the Office of the Secret Seal. I can't actually remember the details, but Burnell, my chancellor, the same who favoured you, Sir Hugh, entrusted Evesham with one task: to hunt down and trap the Mysterium.'

'He hid it well,' Corbett remarked. 'He still kept busy, busy.'

'A pretence,' Edward declared. 'I shall first move to the

conclusion. Evesham actually believed the Mysterium was a chancery clerk, a senior one. Let me explain his logic. Corbett and Staunton, you both know how all the information from home and abroad flows like a river through the offices of the chancery: trade negotiations, alliances, purchases, licences to do this or that, but also the scandal, gossip and chatter from both the court and the city. The faults and foibles of many. Which merchant is playing the two-backed beast, who frequents the stews and bath houses. Above all, the various enmities and hostilities, be it husband or wife, or one guild merchant against another.' Edward smiled at Ranulf. 'Even one clerk's rivalry with a colleague.'

'And the Mysterium used this?' Ranulf asked.

'Yes, he did,' the King agreed. 'I said I would first deal with the conclusion. Apparently the Mysterium would learn of an intense hostility, usually hatred, and send a message to one of the parties, the one he believed to be the most susceptible to his advances. All this,' he waved a hand, 'can be found in the archives of the Secret Seal. The message would be stark, something to the effect: "Your enemy is my enemy, no mystery. Your enemy can be no more, says the Mysterium. By what name is your enemy called?" Before you ask,' The King shook his head, 'the writing on the parchment could have come from a legion of sources.'

'And the same for how it was delivered,' Staunton remarked.

'Slipped into the hand or left at your lodgings,' added Blandeford, eager to follow his master.

'But surely,' Ranulf asked, 'the recipient would recognise the name Mysterium and realise what this entailed. Wouldn't someone come forward?'

'Would they?' Corbett sipped from the now cooled mulled wine. 'Very dangerous, Ranulf. A lawyer might argue that you were the Mysterium's accomplice in some guise or other, whilst God help you if something did befall your enemy.'

'Precisely!' Edward tapped the table.

'But there is something missing, isn't there?' Corbett continued. 'How could the recipient respond?'

'At the end of the message,' the King smiled, 'was a reference; for example, St Paul VI, 2. At first glance the murderer seemed to be referring to one of the Apostle's letters.'

'But he wasn't,' Ranulf exclaimed. 'It's St Paul's Cathedral and the great hanging board or hoarding in the nave. It's divided into a hundred and forty-four squares, a reference to the Apocalypse; a wall painting on either side of it depicts how many people will be saved at the Last Judgement.' He paused. Staunton and Blandeford were smiling at him as if he were a child who'd solved a riddle to which they already knew the answer.

'Let us hear it, Ranulf,' Corbett intervened. 'It's a long time since I used the great hoarding.'

'It's a hundred and forty-four squares,' Ranulf repeated, wishing the flush in his face would fade, 'twelve across and twelve down. The horizontal squares are numbered in the Arabic fashion, the vertical in the Roman. VI, 2 would be the square where these two numbers meet. You place your money in an alms box and take a scrap of parchment from a nearby dish. You then write your notice and put it in whatever square you've chosen. Everything is advertised there, be it a servant looking for employment, or someone arranging a meeting.'

'Or a murderer,' Corbett continued, 'offering up the name of their intended victim. The Mysterium would come to the cathedral and read what was placed there.' He pulled a face. 'Cunning and devious is the human heart. The great hoarding is covered in notices, whilst visitors crowd through St Paul's many entrances.'

'And there's the disguise, the cowl, the visor,' Staunton declared. 'People push and shove; who would guess murder was being planned?'

'So tempting.' Blandeford's high-pitched voice held a wistful note. 'But payment?'

'The Mysterium always demanded the same: two hundred pounds in pure gold,' replied the King. 'Again a short message pushed into the hand once the deed was done. It would list the amount as well as the time and place for payment, usually a tavern or a busy church. Another note would stipulate where the money was to be left: in an empty tankard, under a platter or in some wall niche. Who could object? The Mysterium was the assassin, but so was the person who supplied the name.'

'But the hirer could refuse payment.' Ranulf spoke up, then pulled a face. 'Though of course,' he added, 'he could be blackmailed. He'd already provided the name of his victim. The Mysterium would hold on to that and could denounce him anonymously. Suspicion would already be sharp about a rival's involvement in his enemy's murder. Such a denunciation supported by evidence, meagre though it might be, would be highly dangerous.'

'And who would refuse to pay?' Corbett declared. 'Many of the rich and powerful would see even two hundred pounds in pure gold as well worth the price. The letter "M" carved on the victim's brow would proclaim the deed to enhance the assassin's reputation. I can follow Evesham's logic. The Mysterium would have to be someone who could plumb the depths of the loathing of one person for another. He'd choose his victim very carefully. Yes, London seethes with hatred and rivalry. We clerks learn about such things. The Great Ones, as we know, hire gangs, rifflers and ribauds to confront their rivals with sword and dagger play in Cheapside. The Mysterium's method is a better, more silent way. Of course, the person who has hired the Mysterium must ensure that he is nowhere near the scene of his victim's death. Very, very clever. People might suspect, but there'd be no proof. So how did Evesham eventually trap the killer?'

'Think, Corbett,' Edward teased. 'How would you?'

'The basic premise,' Corbett replied slowly, 'is that the Mysterium knew about the affairs of the Great Ones. Yes, he could well be a clerk.' He emphasised the points with his fingers.

'*Primo*: Evesham could pretend to nourish a deep grievance against some rival, but that would founder because the Mysterium would have to murder someone, and such a crime would have sent Evesham to the scaffold. Moreover, if the Mysterium was a chancery clerk, he would quickly suspect a trap and not rise to the bait.' Corbett paused.

'*Secundo*: he could watch other clerks in the chancery, but that would be very difficult and take too much time.'

From the darkness outside, an owl hooted, long and mournful, to be answered by the strident bark of a fox.

'*Tertio?*' Staunton asked.

'*Tertio*,' Corbett announced slowly: 'I would watch. I'd ask myself who wanted a certain person dead. What was the chatter, the gossip? Now, undoubtedly that would be difficult. If you, my lord Staunton, were my enemy – though of course,' he added drily, 'you are not – people might suspect me of your murder, but suspicion is not proof. Moreover, my lord, a man like you, difficult though it is to accept, might have more than one enemy.'

Edward lowered his head. Ranulf put his face into his hands. Staunton merely smirked.

'Trial and error,' Corbett continued. 'I'd search around and listen to all the information flowing into the chancery. Remember, the Mysterium would not be paid until the deed was done and the victim identified. Therefore I'd listen to the news about all the sudden mysterious deaths amongst the Great Ones and I'd narrow the possibilities. The most opportune is a man getting rid of a rival, or, even better, his wife. If the latter occurred, the husband would ensure that he was many miles distant from the incident. He'd be able to go on oath with a host of witnesses to claim he was far away and had no hand in the murder.'

Edward laughed softly. 'You have it! A merchant, Adam Chauntoys: his wife Alice was attacked and killed in the street, the letter "M" carved on her brow. Master Chauntoys, who has now gone to his eternal reward, was, of course, absent. Witnesses could swear that he was with the Merchants of the Staple in Southampton. Rumours flew thick and fast that his wife had been entertaining young gallants while her husband was abroad. Some of these gallants were married or betrothed, so Alice had a list of enemies who would be only too eager to see her dead. Her husband, of course, acted the innocent cuckold whilst he planned his revenge.

'Evesham reasoned that if Adam was the Mysterium's accomplice, he would certainly not pay until he returned to London and viewed his wife's corpse in the coroner's court, so he decided to take a gamble. When Chauntoys arrived back from Southampton, Evesham kept him under very close scrutiny. He and his servant Ignacio Engleat asked for a comitatus of bailiffs to be ready at their beck and call, then they dogged Chauntoys' footsteps at every twist and turn, following the *soi-disant* grieving widower as he journeyed around London. Four days after his return, Chauntoys broke from his usual horarium, the daily routine he'd set himself. Cloaked and cowled, he crossed London Bridge to Southwark, but not before visiting a goldsmith in Cheapside. Evesham believed the hunt was now on. Most of the bailiffs went secretly across the river by barge; Evesham, Engleat and the rest followed Chauntoys to a spacious tavern, the Liber Albus, near the Priory of St Mary Overy. Evesham had the tavern ringed and went in. Chauntoys sat at a small closet table. Someone else was also there: Boniface Ippegrave. You remember him, Corbett?'

'A clerk in the Office of the Privy Seal. A lawyer, a bachelor of Gascon descent. Rumour had it that he was the Mysterium, but he was never brought to trial. He disappeared – yes?'

'The same,' Edward agreed. 'Anyway, on that fateful day, Evesham decided to act. The rest of the bailiffs entered the tavern and arrested both men. Now, no business had taken place, but Chauntoys could not explain why he was carrying two hundred pounds in pure gold, nor could he explain the scrap of parchment with the date, time and place along with a message telling him to leave the "mystery" on the window ledge of the closet table he'd chosen. For his part Ippegrave, a chancery clerk, could not account for why he should appear at such a tavern armed with sword and dagger. He protested his innocence, declaring that the only reason he'd come to the Liber Albus was because Chauntoys had sent him a message demanding to see him there an hour after the Angelus, for a most urgent matter affecting the King and to the great profit of Ippegrave himself. Chauntoys denied sending any such message. He claimed it wasn't in his hand, though to be true, London does have a thousand scribes for hire.'

'So why was Chauntoys there?'

'He claimed he'd come to meet a Flemish merchant over some negotiations for wool. Both he and Ippegrave were arrested and intended for Newgate. However, once they reached the city, Ippegrave, still protesting his innocence, slipped his guard and fled. The hue and cry were raised and he was pursued, but he raced through the streets and alleyways to take sanctuary in St Botulph's Cripplegate.'

'The same church . . .?' Ranulf queried.

'The same church you had to assault earlier today.' The King shrugged. 'Today, yesterday,' he sighed, 'all days seem to merge into one, but that's just the passing of the years.'

'Your memory,' Staunton flattered, 'is as sharp as ever.'

'I wish to God it was,' Edward snapped. 'Yet when I visited the chancery and read the records in the archives of the Secret Seal, everything did come back as if it happened yesterday.' He pulled himself up, leaning his elbows on the table.

'You said you'd begin with the conclusion,' Corbett queried. 'How did Evesham discover the Mysterium's method?'

'Evesham was cunning,' Edward replied 'Chauntoys was later offered a pardon, and in return for this and a heavy fine, he confessed everything. He did not know the Mysterium, but he had hired the assassin to kill his wife. From him,' Edward rapped the table, 'and only from him, did Evesham learn the Mysterium's subtle craft of murder: the messages, the great hoarding at St Paul's and the method of payment.'

'Nothing else?'

'Nothing. Chauntoys was released under heavy bail, but that came much later. At the time, Ippegrave's caskets in his lodgings at Cripplegate and the chancery were searched by a trusted clerk. More gold than he should have had was found, as well as scraps of manuscript, tags and bits of parchment bearing the names of former victims, a crude map showing where they had been found and references to the great hoarding board at St Paul's.' The King paused to drink. 'Ippegrave, sheltering in St Botulph's, was confronted with all this. He could not, or would not, explain the gold or the parchment scraps. He still protested his innocence. Evesham was hot against him. He wanted Ippegrave to be brought to trial. Ambitious and arrogant, he was determined that such a trial would be a public manifestation of his genius and skill.'

'And you, your grace?' Corbett voice was tinged with amusement. Edward hated public show unless it was to illustrate his own glory and magnificence.

'True, true,' the King agreed, 'I was not too eager. I did not wish the scandal whilst I could use the information for my own secret purposes. Believe me, Corbett, I did. Chauntoys babbled like a bairn. Many powerful lords in London were told what I had uncovered. I bluffed, I embroidered my discoveries. These city princes were advised to show their gratitude for the Crown's forbearance and mercy in many ways. Evesham had achieved a great victory. The capture of the Mysterium by a royal clerk only enhanced the power and influence of the Crown. But,' Edward smiled, 'that came much later, after Ippegrave's disappearance. At the time, Evesham was determined that St Botulph's be closely guarded. City bailiffs and men-at-arms from the Tower camped outside. Evesham and Engleat tried to persuade Ippegrave to make a full confession. So did you.' The King turned abruptly to Staunton and Blandeford. 'Were you not friends with Ippegrave?'

'Your grace,' Staunton blustered, 'we never tried to hide that. We were as surprised as any by his capture, as were you, your grace, and Chancellor Burnell. Remember, sire, Evesham was intent on garnering all the glory. He would not even allow us into the church.'

'True.' The King darted a warning look at Corbett. 'And that's a further problem.' He wiped his fingers on a napkin. 'Boniface's possessions were searched and he was confronted with the evidence but could provide no satisfactory explanation. If he'd gone on trial, he would certainly have been found guilty.'

'But he disappeared?' Corbett declared.

'Yes, and that lies at the heart of this mystery,' Edward replied. 'St Botulph's was closely guarded, every door, portal and window, but Boniface Ippegrave vanished from the face of the earth. London was scoured. Sheriffs, port-reeves and bailiffs alerted.'

'And Evesham?'

'He was beside himself with rage,' the King murmured. 'He was furious. He ordered his guards to search that church, every nook and cranny, every crevice, every aperture; nothing was left undisturbed. St Botulph's has no crypt. Evesham went up the tower, even on to the roof, yet from that day to this, nothing.' Edward paused and drank noisily from his goblet.

'Evesham was so distraught,' he continued, 'I thought he would fall ill, some malignancy of the humours. Time passed, but not a trace of Ippegrave was found. I ordered the matter be let rest. As for Evesham, I wanted to reward him. The Mysterium had been revealed and the murders stopped. Now, Evesham was a widower; he had one son, John, who later became Parson of St Botulph's.' The King shrugged. 'You know how it is. Many royal clerks acquire the right to appoint to a benefice. John Evesham wanted to become a priest, so naturally Lord Walter used his influence to secure the parish for him. However, twenty years ago, John was still a child and his father an eligible bachelor. Shortly after the Mysterium had been unmasked, Evesham married again, a rich heiress, a ward of the Crown, Clarice Pauntefroys, the daughter of a powerful merchant.' Edward was now talking as if to himself. 'My debt to Evesham was great, whilst he proved to be most skilled. He secured promotion, one chancery post after another. An expert in the Pleas of the Crown and the rights of the Exchequer, he became a justice both in Westminster and out in the shires. Two years ago he was appointed Chief Justice, but the canker was already there.' Edward gestured at Corbett. 'As you know, Sir Hugh, the Court of King's Bench receives many indictments and denunciations. About two months ago we began to receive anonymous information from the so-called Land of Cockaigne maintaining that our Chief Justice was corrupt, hand in glove with gang leaders such as Waldene and the self-styled Hubert the Monk. Now, such denunciations are commonplace; what was most singular about these was not the reference to the topsy-turvy world of Cockaigne, a scholarly citation, but how detailed the accusations were.'

'About what?' Corbett asked.

'Oh, not so much about isolated incidents.' Staunton, at Edward's request, took up the story. 'The writer from the Land of Cockaigne claimed that Evesham was too cunning a fox to inculpate himself in writing, but mentioned his secret meetings with the gang leaders Waldene and Hubert the Monk. Apparently such meetings were allegedly held in the dead of night in Lord Walter's mansion in Clothier Lane, a wealthy quarter of Cripplegate ward.'

'And the purpose of these meetings?'

'Lord Walter would receive a certain portion of all stolen goods. In return for this, when an indictment was presented against any of the gangs who did business with our Chief Justice, that indictment, for some obscure reason, would be rejected.'

'As simple as that?'

'Yes, Sir Hugh, as simple as that, but reflect.' Staunton relished the opportunity to lecture this solemn-faced clerk. 'An indictment can be rejected for many reasons before being forwarded to a jury: a mistake in law or in fact and that is the end of the matter. Lord Walter was, if anything, most skilled in the law and the beauty of its corruption, if you can call it that.' He glanced hastily at the King. 'The failed indictment has a brief reason for its rejection appended to it and that's all. We examined the schedule of indictments and found list after list of rejections against notorious rifflers, all buried on points of law. Nothing could be done about them, but the writer from the Land of Cockaigne kept referring to other matters, especially those sinister, secret meetings late at night in Evesham's mansion. A watch was kept. Four weeks ago, Blandeford and I observed two men slip through the dark and in by a postern gate. We surrounded the mansion, then forced an entrance. Lord Walter was found in his chancery chamber with Giles Waldene and Hubert the Monk. Both rifflers acted the innocent, but in Lord Walter's personal coffer we found freshly minted coins stolen from the Royal Mint in the Tower. You may remember the robbery?'

'Yes, I do.'

'As you know, Sir Hugh,' the King added bitterly, 'I hate these covens of rifflers. They disturb the peace, carry out numerous robberies, mock my authority and, above all, are used by the Great Ones of London to settle scores with each other.'

Corbett nodded sympathetically. Indeed he knew only too well. The King nursed a deep resentment, even hatred, for the merchant princes of London, with their vast profits from the wool trade. They in turn fiercely resented royal interference in what they saw as their city, they wanted to enjoy the same status and power as the self-governing communes of Florence and Venice to which they sold their precious wool.

'The evidence against Evesham was compelling, though at the

time he refused to comment,' Staunton continued. 'Why was he entertaining such wolfsheads in his own chamber at such an ungodly hour? Why did he have freshly minted gold coins in his coffer filched in a recent robbery? We believe Waldene and the Monk were responsible for that, though of course we had no proof that they had brought the gold there. Moreover,' he lifted a finger, 'that pair of rifflers, also trapped in the mire, later pleaded that if they were indicted, Evesham must also account—'

'They recognised,' Corbett intervened, 'that his grace, fearful of hideous scandal, might be prepared to gloss over the matter regarding Evesham but not as regards to them. I'm sure they would have implicated the Chief Justice.'

'Whatever those two wolfsheads decided,' the King growled, 'Evesham was finished. He'd grown arrogant as Lucifer. I confronted him in the Jerusalem Chamber at Westminster and threatened to put him on trial and seize all his chattels, including his beloved manor of Ingachin on the Welsh March. Evesham, caught red-handed, acted like a broken man. He offered to resign all his posts and retire as a recluse to the Abbey of Syon on Thames. I agreed.'

'Why here?' asked Corbett. 'Why not some other monastery?'

'Two reasons, perhaps.' The King gestured with his cup towards the door. 'Both acts of reparation. Evesham was not a prisoner, but rather a forced house guest. He was under strict instruction to assume the garb of a lay brother and never leave Syon's precincts. As I said, he may have been thinking of reparation. The lay brother in charge of the corpse chapel beneath which Evesham had his cell, you met him briefly, Brother Cuthbert. Years ago he was Cuthbert Tunstall, Parson of St Botulph's Cripplegate when Boniface

Ippegrave took sanctuary there. After Ippegrave disappeared, Evesham, in his arrogance, even though he himself held the keys of the church, blamed Parson Tunstall. He complained bitterly to the Bishop of London; more importantly, he had Tunstall confined to his house to fast on bread and water, and berated him day and night until his anger was spent. When he had finished, Tunstall was a broken man. He resigned his benefice and asked to be accepted here as a simple lay brother. According to Father Abbot, when Evesham arrived at Syon, he knelt at Tunstall's feet and asked for forgiveness. Whether it was given or not, I don't know. Abbot Serlo claimed Tunstall did not seem to care, whilst Evesham kept to himself, ate his meals and studied manuscripts from the abbey library.'

'And the second reason?'

'Ah.' Again the King pointed to the door. 'In the grounds stands an anchorite cell built near the curtain wall. Adelicia lives there, as she has for the last twenty years.'

'Adelicia?' Ranulf asked.

'Adelicia Ippegrave, beloved sister of Boniface, former chancery clerk. She lived with her brother in Cripplegate and was a parishioner of St Botulph's, a close friend I understand of Parson Tunstall. When her brother disappeared and Tunstall retired a broken man, Adelicia sold all her possessions and both bishop and abbot gave her permission to retire here as an *ancilla Domini* – handmaid of the Lord – to live the life of an anchoress.'

'How close were Cuthbert and Adelicia?' Ranulf asked. 'I mean,' he shrugged, 'some priests have their lemans, their mistresses?'

'I don't know.' The King seemed distracted. 'Adelicia publicly condemned what had happened. She constantly protested her brother's innocence and declared she would spend her life in prayer and fasting so that God would eventually make true judgement, and so it was, until yesterday.' Edward pushed himself away from the table, rose and stretched, then walked to the windows, pulled back the shutters and stared into the night. 'Yesterday was harvest time, as if the past was not buried deep enough. In Newgate, Hubert the Monk's followers believed that those of Giles Waldene would turn King's Approvers in return for a general pardon. A riot ensued. Later on that day, Ignacio Engleat, Evesham's clerk, was drinking and whoring at the Comfort of Bathsheba near Queenshithe – you've seen what happened to him. On that very evening, the same killer perhaps, crept down the steps to the cellar beneath the corpse chapel here at Syon. Somehow he eluded both Brother Cuthbert and his guard dog, Ogadon, persuaded Evesham to lift the bar on his door, entered and cut our former justice's throat. On leaving, the assassin just as mysteriously managed to lower the inside bar behind him. A true mystery, which is why,' the king turned and pointed at Corbett, 'I have summoned you here: to resolve this, to discover the truth . . .'

3

Polinator: a doggerel Latin term for undertaker

'If God had not been our protector, when the enemy rose against us, then they would have swallowed us alive . . .'

Corbett, standing in the shadowy choir stalls of Syon Abbey, joined lustily in the melodious plainchant of the good brothers of St Benedict as they sang the morning office of lauds. Ranulf, standing beside him, suppressed a smile. Corbett liked nothing better than to sing. Ranulf, bleary-eyed, quietly thanked the Lord that his master had slept through the office of matins. He glanced up. It was still early, and the light streaming through the brilliantly painted glass window above the choir remained a dull grey. The abbey church was cold, despite the fiery braziers wheeled in under the lofty rood screen. Ranulf stared around at the pinched white faces peering out of cowls. From the tops of pillars, carved woodmen, gargoyles, babewyns, angels, saints and demons smiled and glowered. Between the pillars flashes of colour shimmered from the wall frescoes, most of them scenes from the Gospels or the life of St Benedict at Subiaco and Monte Cassino.

'Don't hold the sins of our fathers against us.' The powerful chant of scores of male voices thundered like surf into the great open space created by pillars and arches, a resounding plea for God's help.

Ranulf blinked and found the place in the psalter as the choir swept to its glorious doxology: 'Glory be to the Father and to the Son . . .'

Corbett lowered the stall and sat down as the reader approached the lectern and, in a clear voice, proclaimed the reading from the Book of Daniel. A phrase caught his attention – 'Do not treat us because of the treasons we have committed against you' – and he reflected on the tangle of treasons facing him. After the meeting the night before, the King had taken him aside, finger jabbing, insisting that Corbett resolve matters and remember three important issues. First, Staunton and Blandeford had been friends of Boniface. Second, both had been approached to investigate any wrongdoing by Evesham. Third, now that the Chief Justice was dead, the case against Waldene and Hubert the Monk had collapsed, as the Crown's principal witness could never be called.

'But the riot at Newgate?' Corbett was sure the King was trying to ignore this.

Edward grimaced. 'According to what I've learnt, Waldene and Hubert were held fast in their respective pits. Like Pilate they have washed their hands of any wrongdoing. I've given orders for their immediate release.'

Then the King was gone, shouting for his escort. Blandeford and Staunton also made their farewells before following the royal household down to the quayside and the waiting barge. Corbett had immediately sought out Chanson, the Clerk of the Stables, who was responsible for their horses and pack ponies. Corbett had ensured the groom had good lodgings in the abbey guest-house before adjourning to his own sparse chamber. He had slept well, waking long before dawn. He'd washed at the lavarium and dressed in a fresh shirt, hose and leather jerkin, a welcome relief from the heavy sweaty jerkin and chainmail of the previous day.

'Master?'

Corbett glanced up. The monks were filing out. He rose, going through the rood screen into the nave, where Chanson squatted at the base of a pillar, his bobbed hair cut, as Ranulf laughingly described, as if a pudding bowl had been overturned on his head. The groom, threading his Ave beads, glanced up, the cast in his left eye giving him a constantly humorous look. Corbett clasped his shoulder, assuring him all was well and thanking him for his work the previous day. In truth Chanson loved and lived for horses and nothing else. Weapons were more dangerous to him than any opponent, whilst his singing voice, so Ranulf asserted, would make the good brothers think that the choirs of hell were mocking their plainchant.

'We'll wait for the dawn Mass,' Corbett told him. 'Stay only if you want to.'

Chanson said he would, and Corbett left him bantering with Ranulf as he turned to the grandeur of the nave, admiring its soaring pillars, darkened transepts, and the intricacies of the carved screens outside the various chantry chapels. Humming the tune of a hymn, Corbett carefully examined the paintings. One made him smile. Apollinaria, the patron saint of tooth drawers, holding the pincers and tongs of her martyrdom. Now in heaven, she was depicted dispatching help to poor unfortunates as they sat on a row of stools, each with a tooth drawer inflicting more pain than relief. An artist who suffered toothache, Corbett reflected. He walked back up into the Lady Chapel, his mind drifting back to St Botulph's. He had ringed that church and secured the doors: the main one, the sacristy door, the north door and the corpse door. The windows were narrow and high. The tower, with its plastered walls winding steps and small enclaves, held no secrets. At the top, the crenellated plat-form provided only a dizzying drop to the steep slate roof below. So, how had Boniface Ippegrave escaped? How had he managed to disappear from such a close, fast place? Corbett paused to light tapers for his wife, for their two children, Edward and Eleanor, for himself and his two companions. By the time he had finished his Ave, the Jesus bell was ringing for the dawn Mass.

Afterwards Corbett and his two companions, laughing about Chanson's singing, broke their fast over bowls of oatmeal at the ale table in the buttery before leaving the abbey precincts. The morning was dull. Clouds blocked the sun and a sharp breeze whipped their faces as they made their way out through the Galilee porch into Goose Meadow, which stretched down to the corpse chapel of St Lazarus. Already the brothers were filing out to the outlying fields and granges. Corbett heard their chanting, so strong on the morning breeze not even the cawing of a host of rooks could drown it. The grass was still frosty and wet, the feeding ground for a nearby warren of rabbits, who disappeared in darting flashes of brown and white. Ogadon, on guard outside the entrance of the chapel, close to the ledge beneath the bell, lumbered to his feet growling.

'*Pax et Bonum*,' called a voice. The old war hound collapsed, relieved that he didn't have to exert himself, as Brother Cuthbert crept out of the door. A tall, angular figure in his shabby Benedictine robe, a grey cord around his waist, stout sandals on his feet, his long neck and small, pert face gave him a bird-like look, heightened by the stiff movements of his arms, hands and legs. Corbett suspected the lay brother suffered severe inflammation of the joints. Cuthbert was old, his white hair shorn on three sides; the little on his pate displaying the tonsure. He was cheerful and welcoming enough, nodding quietly as Corbett introduced his companions, watery blue eyes crinkling in amusement when Corbett expressed regret at the death of Lord Evesham.

'You'd best come down to the pit of hell,' he said sardonically. 'My humble abode below.'

Corbett pointed to the snoring Ogadon. 'Brother, on the night Evesham was murdered?'

'The same as every night,' Cuthbert replied. 'Compline is sung. My lord abbot has excused me from that, as there are usually corpses to be washed or a recluse to be cared for. Anyway, once it is over,' he continued so breathlessly Corbett wondered if the man's wits were sound, 'a servant brings me a goblet of wine and a platter of food from the buttery. My other guests,' he gestured over his shoulder, 'are past all sustenance.'

'And Walter Evesham?'

'He had his own food brought, though much earlier than mine: a goblet of wine and a platter. The servant puts the tray on the ledge and . . .' Cuthbert pulled at the rope and glanced up as the bell clanged. 'You see, not everyone likes to enter a death house,' he whispered. 'I go up, collect the tray, then bolt the door from inside.'

'You secured the door?' Corbett exclaimed.

'Yes, yes, come in, come in.'

Corbett and Ranulf followed Cuthbert into the corpse chapel. The lay brother slammed the door shut and drew across the iron bolts at top and bottom. Corbett stared around. It was a truly chilling place now the light had faded. Shadows and shapes flittered around the macabre bundles on the mortuary tables. The only light came from the windows along one wall, nothing more than narrow apertures, their shutters flung back.

'I close the shutters and bolt the door,' Brother Cuthbert continued conversationally, 'then I am fastened in for the night. You see, Domine,' he drew back the bolts, led them out again and pointed, 'beyond the chapel, bushes and trees fringe the high wall of the abbey, lofty as that of Troy. On the outside it stands on a ramp of earth; its top is covered with sharp shards of tile and pottery. The wall has to be a good defence against the river along which flow the barges of wickedness oared by pirates and other river monsters.' Cuthbert's light blue eyes crinkled, Corbett glimpsed the intelligence and humour there. Brother Cuthbert was not just an old lay brother, but a clever man pretending to be distracted.

'And your mastiff?'

'Old Ogadon is not as fierce as he looks. He can tell friend from foe; he growls but would only roar at some footpad slipping through the night.'

Corbett smiled as Cuthbert led them back into the chapel and down the steps into the cellar. The tunnel was narrow, the timbered ceiling just above their heads. The first cell on the right, Cuthbert's own, was neat and clean. High in one corner of its whitewashed walls was a vent that allowed in a crack of light. The chamber was sparsely furnished: a cot bed draped with a black coverlet edged with silver, a stool, a table, shelves over the bed holding pots, platters and jugs. Crucifixes were nailed against the walls; robes hung on pegs, and from beneath the table peeped a small wineskin. The next cell was a storeroom. The far one, its door leaning against the wall, had been Evesham's. It was similar to Cuthbert's, but the table, pushed against the wall, was heavily stained with the justice's blood.

'Soaked it must have been,' Ranulf observed. 'His throat was cut like a pig's.'

They looked around. The coverlet and sheets on the bed had been removed, as had the jugs and pots from the shelf above it.

'Any manuscripts?' Corbett asked.

'My guest was reading Boethius' *De Consolatione Philosophiae*. It was lying on the bed so it was not stained with blood. Father Abbot had it taken back to the library.'

'Any other possessions?'

'Yes.' Cuthbert scratched his head. 'A ring or two, a cross on a chain. Abbot Serlo had them washed and sent back to Evesham's widow.'

Corbett moved to examine the door and lintel.

'Boethius!' Ranulf remarked.

'A suitable choice. The reflections of a minister who fell from

58

power, though Boethius was innocent.' Corbett turned and smiled. 'Evesham certainly wasn't, was he, Parson Tunstall?'

Cuthbert coloured slightly and glanced beyond Corbett as if staring at something else.

'That will wait, that will wait,' Corbett remarked and pushed by him to stare down at the table.

Ranulf was right. Evesham's blood must have splattered out like water, staining the surface; even the two candlesticks standing at each corner were clotted with dried blood. Corbett took a stool, sat down and stared up at Brother Cuthbert.

'Walter Evesham?'

Cuthbert glanced at Ranulf standing close to him. Corbett gestured with his head. Ranulf patted the lay brother on the shoulder and went to stand in the doorway, whilst Corbett indicated that Cuthbert sit on the end of the bed. The lay brother did so. Beads of sweat wetted his forehead, and the constant licking of lips showed his dryness. A wine toper perhaps? A man who drank to forget?

'Walter Evesham?' Corbett repeated.

'He came here weeks ago. First he sheltered in the guesthouse, then for the last month here.'

'At his request?'

'I think so. Abbot Serlo decided it was for the best. You see,' Cuthbert continued, 'this is where all who desire a recluse's life within the abbey come. To be sure,' he laughed sharply, 'a rare event. Sometimes one of the brothers simply wishes to be alone for a while.'

'Did you talk with Evesham?'

'Sir Hugh, you know I did, at least at the beginning. You've heard the story, or at least some of it. Evesham begged for my forgiveness, but if the root be tainted, so is the branch . . .'

'What do you mean?'

'Evesham was no sinner come to repentance. He was a malignant. He was born wicked, he died wicked!'

'Do you really believe that?'

'For the love of God, Sir Hugh, Evesham was caught in his own foul sin, so what does he do? Falls to his knees and assumes sackcloth, ashes, prayers, fasting, contrition and repentance.' Cuthbert's flushed face betrayed the hatred curdling within him. 'He wasn't worried about his soul or how he spent the last years of his life; he was more concerned about his neck.' The lay brother paused, licking at the froth on his lips.

Ranulf took a step forward, hand nursing the hilt of his sword.

'Keep your dagger man, your bully-boy, well away from me, Sir Hugh. I mean you no ill, I am sorry.' Cuthbert wiped his mouth on the back of his wrist. 'I am sorry I have tried so hard to hide my anger.' He struck his chest. 'My fault, my fault, I have sinned, I have sinned.' He glanced up, eyes brimming with tears. 'Sin never leaves you,' he added hoarsely. 'Like some loathsome bramble it trails the soil of your soul and its roots dig deep. Please don't think my anger is guilt. I do not want to be hauled off to some bleak prison, nor to Father Abbot, who kindly gave me shelter when I was nothing but some poor soul drifting on the winds of life.' He glared at Corbett. 'I heard how the King's hawk had arrived. They know about you, clerk, even here at Syon. Our prior says that you are ruthless in the pursuit of justice, that your soul cannot be bought and sold. Now isn't that praiseworthy in a world where souls come cheaper than apples from an orchard?'

'You claim that Evesham the recluse was in fact a hypocrite?'

'The word is yours, Sir Hugh.'

'Yes it is, and I believe you.' Corbett stretched across and touched Cuthbert's cold, wrinkled, spotted hand. 'I truly do.' He smiled. 'Evesham was caught, confronted and indicted. He turned, swift as a bird on the wing, throwing himself on the King's mercy, proclaiming himself a sinner come to repentance. Such contrition was accepted.'

'Because it was in the King's interest?' Cuthbert jibed.

'True,' Corbett agreed, 'it certainly was in the King's interest. Edward of England, the new Justinian, the great law-giver, the promulgator of statute law, the lord of parliament: to have one of his chief justices depicted in open court as corrupt? Indicted as a consorter with outlaws, a receiver of stolen goods, the lord of bribes, the master of chicanery? Oh yes, it was very much in the King's interest for Evesham to confess, to seek pardon, to hide from scrutiny, to don sackcloth and ashes and sit in the dust.'

'Until the storm blew itself out?' Cuthbert observed.

'You believe that?'

'Of course. Evesham could kneel and mutter his paternoster, thread his Ave beads and stare at the crucifix. He could eat hard bread and drink the waters of bitterness, but I believe he was secretly preparing his defence. And before you ask, Sir Hugh, God knows what that was! What secrets did he hold about others, about the King?' He leaned closer. 'Did his grace, our noble lord, wish him dead?'

'That's treason,' snapped Ranulf.

'It could still be true,' Cuthbert muttered over his shoulder. 'Your master, dagger man, is here to seek the truth; what am I supposed to do, lie? I am simply asking what the truth is. You may keep the King's Secret Seal but not his soul, Sir Hugh.'

Corbett stared at this man, whose very soul bubbled with anger. He sensed what might have happened; he had seen it before. Men and women who'd hidden and masked their own hurt, nursing it like some festering wound over the years. Then, in one hour, one moment, one heartbeat, all the bile, the bitterness, anger and hurt erupted in a violent act. Had this happened here, or worse? Was Cuthbert pointing to a darker sin? Had Edward the King decided on Evesham's death here in this lonely abbey? Corbett edged his stool closer.

'Did you kill Lord Walter Evesham, Brother?'

'Yes.' Cuthbert lifted a hand, fingers so curled with inflammation it was more like a claw. 'Yes, Sir Hugh, in my thoughts I killed him at least a score of times over the last twenty years, and I confessed as much in chapter. But in deed, in fact? No! Look at my hands, clerk, how could these fingers grasp a dagger, let alone Lord Walter's head, pulling it back for the killing stroke?'

Corbett studied that whiskered old face, eyes all troubled, those lined and furrowed cheeks.

'I swear by the sacrament that I did not kill him. I hardly spoke to him, or he to me. Evesham suspected I knew his heart. I caught his secret glances. I saw him kneel in prayer, but his visitors brought him wine that he slurped, sweetmeats he gobbled. I heard him lying on his bed quietly humming. Does a pig take to singing,

Sir Hugh? Does a cat shepherd the mice? Does the hawk protect the pigeon? I don't think so. Evesham was plotting. No,' Cuthbert shook his head, 'he wrote nothing, he said nothing. He had no manuscripts here except the ones he borrowed from the library.'

'I believe you, Brother. Now I want you to go back twenty years, to the *fons et origo* of all this. Describe to me what happened.'

The lay brother's hand went to his lips. He stared hard at Corbett, then sighed.

'In the beginning I wanted to be a Carthusian, a strict order, but they said my health was too frail.'

'You proved them wrong on that.'

'No.' Cuthbert tapped the side of his head. 'They were right. In my mind I was too frail. I became a priest, serving as a curate here and there. I recalled the words of St Francis. I tried to preach the Gospel and I lived a chaste life.' He smiled. 'That was easy, as was poverty. I truly loved my calling. No archdeacon visited to lecture me on monies missing or the company I kept or the mistress I sheltered. I was a pastor, Sir Hugh, committed to the sheep, and not just their shearing.'

Corbett caught the profound sadness of this soul.

'Eventually I was appointed Parson of St Botulph's in Cripplegate. I loved that church, my parish council, the routine of every day, until the Feast of St Irenaeus, the twenty-eighth of June in the year of Our Lord 1284. Have you ever read Irenaeus?'

Corbett shook his head.

'He said: "The things we learn in childhood become part of our soul." Outside of the Gospels I've never heard a wiser saying. Anyway, on that day, late in the afternoon, I heard the hue and cry being raised, shouts of "Harrow! Harrow!" echoing along the streets. I left the priest's house. I remember running carefully because a summer sickness had swept the ward, taking the old, the weak, the infirm, the dying. Burial plots had been dug before the summer sun became too strong and dried the ground. I did not wish to stumble into one of these. I reached the north door of the church and went in. I peered through the rood screen; a man crouched there clutching the altar. A royal clerk burst into the church, walking like God Almighty up the nave. He was booted and spurred, brandishing a sword, his face livid with anger. Evesham! The first time I'd ever met him.

'I stood my ground. A man had taken sanctuary. According to canon law, he was not to be disturbed but allowed to stay. I asked Evesham to leave. Eventually he did, but first he demanded, on my loyalty to the King, whether there was a crypt, a cellar, any secret entrance. I replied no. How many doors? I told him four. Any windows a fugitive could wriggle through? I said that was impossible. He made me swear by the sacrament that I told the truth. I did so, and he stormed off. I could hear from the noise outside that all four doors were now guarded.' Cuthbert snorted with laughter. 'They even brought rope ladders and put men up the walls and on to the roof. I went into the sanctuary, and only then did I recognise Boniface Ippegrave. I knew him by sight. He lived in the parish with his sister Adelicia. I am sure,' he added drily, 'we shall discuss her shortly. She was a close friend of mine. No, Sir Hugh, I mean close friend, a member of my parish council. I knew her brother to be a royal clerk who attended Mass in the chapels at Westminster. On the few occasions I had met him, he'd proved courteous enough. I asked him what crime he had committed, and he said none. I enquired what he was accused of. He refused to say but pleaded for me to send urgent messages to his sister. I said I would. He was in a most agitated state. He carried a knife, and according to the law of sanctuary he had to surrender this to me. I took it and left the church. Evesham searched me from head to toe. I argued that I was a cleric. He replied that so was he, whilst treason and murder were no defence. He took the knife and asked what other belongings Ippegrave held. I lied; I said nothing, except his clothes and cloak.'

'You lied?'

'I glimpsed an inkwell and quill fastened to his belt. You know the sort clerks carry?'

Corbett nodded.

'Evesham waxed hot and furious. Already the doors were closely guarded; even the graveyard, God's own acre, was cleared of children and beggars. He made me swear again by the sacrament to tell him everything Ippegrave had said. I told him. He insisted I send no message to Adelicia. I replied that I certainly would and that I'd also bring food. I sent the message but Adelicia was turned away. I remonstrated, but Evesham drove me off with threats. The food I took was examined. Evesham insisted on following me up under the rood screen to watch me hand it over. I also supplied a jakes pot. When I collected that, Evesham made me carry it through the church door and hand it over to one of his guards for disposal on the compost heap. After it was returned, he followed me when I went back into the church to place it in the sanctuary. All this happened during the afternoon and late evening of the first day. As darkness fell, a knight banneret with men-at-arms arrived.'

'Who?'

'You know him, Sir Hugh, one of the King's battle boys, Sir Ralph Sandewic, now Constable of the Tower. He must have brought at least a hundred men. Four camps ringed the church, each guarding a door. In the morning, Adelicia returned. By then Evesham's wrath had cooled. He demanded what proof she had that she was Ippegrave's sister. What token could she give? She handed over a jasper ring, a gift from her mother. Evesham took it and said he would think about it. Sir Hugh, I've never seen a man so insistent, so ruthless in the hunt. He was determined that Ippegrave would not escape. I heard him chatter to Sandewic about the coming trial. By then Boniface's coffers both at his lodgings and in Westminster had been searched. Evesham went into the church to remonstrate.'

Brother Cuthbert fell silent, eyes blinking.

'Tell me what happened.'

'From what I can remember, Evesham maintained that a great deal of gold was found in Ippegrave's coffers. More importantly, certain scraps of parchment connected with the Mysterium had been discovered. He said it was enough to indict Boniface.'

'And the fugitive?'

'He protested his innocence.' Brother Cuthbert spread his hands. 'And then it happened. On the morning of the third day, I took some food in through the corpse door. Evesham followed. I walked under the rood screen into the sanctuary. The recess at the far end beyond the high altar was empty. In my terror I dropped the tray. Evesham was beside himself. He issued strict instructions that all doors remain guarded whilst he, Engleat, Sandewic and their retinues scoured my church. Every nook and cranny, each flagstone was scrutinised, every chair, hanging, statue, altar . . . nothing! Boniface had disappeared like candle smoke, no trace, no sign. Evesham became a man at war, furious against everyone and everything. He kept the church ringed, closely guarded. For two entire days and nights the search continued. On the third, Evesham, Engleat and their horde of ruffians turned on me. I was confined to my own house, threatened and questioned. They did the same to Adelicia, then they left. I tried to return to my own life, but I had some malady of the wits. Adelicia was beside herself with grief; I tried to comfort her.'

'And you knew nothing of Boniface's alleged crime?'

'No, not at the time. I later learnt from Adelicia scraps of gossip, chatter and rumour about an assassin called the Mysterium. I asked her if she had ever suspected her brother; she only repeated what she'd already told me. How Boniface would often disappear for days on end. How he nursed some secret and at times seemed to have gold and silver well beyond his means. She suspected he was a gambler, but,' he shrugged, 'that is for her to say. You know she is also here?'

Corbett nodded.

'And the ring?' Ranulf asked.

'Ask Adelicia.' Cuthbert didn't bother to glance at Ranulf.

Corbett studied him closely. For some unknown reason the lay brother trusted him but not Ranulf, whom he dismissed as another royal clerk. But why was he talking so honestly and earnestly?

That puzzled Corbett. Was Cuthbert hoping to fend him off with only some of the truth?

'Ippegrave never said anything to you?'

Cuthbert smiled thinly, fingers playing with his lower lip.

'I did not say that, Sir Hugh. I am speaking to you openly now. Evesham is dead; he can face God's judgement. It is time; yes, it's time,' he repeated, eyes blinking furiously. 'These matters must be settled, so listen. After Evesham left, I became ill, I couldn't sleep. During the day I'd suddenly feel frightened, especially when I entered my own church. I grew full of nameless terrors and unreasoned fears. Adelicia, a poor spinster of the parish, was even more sorely oppressed. She begged me to search the church for any trace of the brother she truly loved. I dragged myself in. I couldn't find anything until I remembered Boniface's ink horn, and the Book of the Gospels that had been on the lectern. At the back of this are clear, empty pages of vellum where successive vicars and parsons have written various notes and jottings. I found something there.'

'What?'

'I think it was Ippegrave's.' Cuthbert paused. 'I have told this to no one except Adelicia.'

'What?'

'A simple entry that read: "I stand in the centre, guiltless, and point to the four corners."'

'Is that all?'

'That is all. A few months later I fell into a morbid sickness and visited the hospital at St Bartholomew's. I could not return to St Botulph's. I petitioned, I begged both my bishop and the lord abbot at Syon to allow me to retire, and so here I am.'

'And you told Adelicia about the message?' Ranulf asked.

'I did, and for what it's worth, you can ask her. A short while after I arrived here, she petitioned the bishop and abbot and followed suit.'

'As for her reasons?'

'Again, ask her.'

'You know that Walter Evesham's son eventually became Parson of St Botulph's?'

'Not immediately. There were two other parsons, old men. I believe Parson John has been at St Botulph's for the last eight years. I heard rumours about the recent troubles there. Brothers visit the city markets; they bring back both produce and gossip.' He peered at Corbett. 'There was some trouble at St Botulph's?'

'True, true.'

Cuthbert sighed. 'God knows, ever since Evesham's arrival so many years ago – or should I say Boniface seeking sanctuary there – some curse seem to have settled on that church.'

'Did Parson John ever come to visit you?'

'Yes, yes, he did quite often. A strange man! He talked little about his father, but brought the gossip of the parish. A few times he spoke about Boniface, but I think he came here as an act of kindness. Of course recently he also visited his father, though you should ask Parson John about that. You know the rule of St Benedict, Sir Hugh?'

'Not really.'

'He gave good advice. If anyone comes and asks your opinion about another, tell them to ask that person.'

'True, Brother, but I'm here to seek the truth, not opinion. Did others visit Evesham?'

'Those two limbs of Satan, Staunton and Blandeford, haughty as hell, arrogant as Lucifer. They came here with their mandates and writs, sweeping down as if they were angels of the Lord when they are really minions of . . .' He paused abruptly, 'I do not know what was said. They ordered me out as if I was some witless pigeon. I've seen men treat a dog better.'

'Who else?'

'Evesham's pretty young wife Clarice, she and her overbearing steward Richard Fink.'

'What were they like?'

'They didn't treat me ill, they simply ignored me as if I didn't exist. On such occasions I just left. Ogadon proved better company.'

'And you and Evesham,' asked Ranulf, 'never discussed what had happened at St Botulph's some twenty years ago?'

'I've told you, clerk. Evesham may have had the measure of me; I certainly had his. My silence was punishment enough. I'd survived without him for twenty years. Why should I change?'

'And on the day before he died,' Corbett asked, 'who visited him?'

Cuthbert screwed up his eyes. 'In the morning Staunton and Blandeford. After nones, the Lady Clarice and her minion.'

'What happened the night he died?' demanded Ranulf.

'Murdered, clerk; Lord Walter Evesham, former Chief Justice, was brutally murdered. Ah well, it was a normal day, ending with compline. I was alone here in my cell. I heard the bell ring and went up. It was dark; Ogadon was sleeping. I took the goblet of wine and a platter of food.'

'You've a wineskin here?'

'That's for my guests.'

'You locked yourself in that night?'

'Of course. The shutters on the corpse chapel were closed, the door bolted. Evesham was moving around his cell. I bade him good night and adjourned to my own chamber. I drank the wine, ate the sweet bread and fell asleep. When I awoke, just before first light, I went along to Evesham's cell. I peered through the grille.' He paused as Corbett rose and walked to the battered door; the grille was high, its three bars about an inch apart.

'The light is poor in here,' Cuthbert continued. 'I could see Evesham squatting at the table with his back to the door. I called out but there was no reply. I walked away, then returned. I banged on the door and shouted at him. It was still very dark, but I sensed something was wrong. I hurried as fast as I could up the stairs. The chapel was in darkness. I opened the shutters and unbolted the door. Ogadon was there.' He paused, chest heaving. 'Well, you know the rest. I hastily alerted Abbot Serlo . . .'

Corbett held up a hand. 'How do you know the chapel had remained sealed and locked?'

'Because I secured and fastened it. I had to open both shutters and doors the following morning. If you doubt me, asked Brother Odo the sacristan.' Cuthbert answered Corbett's puzzled look. 'He and his entourage walk the abbey buildings every night, ensuring all doors and windows are secure. Odo loves doing that with his retinue of acolytes, keys all a-jangle. Anyway, Abbot Serlo came here and ordered the door to be broken down.'

Corbett walked into the passageway to inspect the door. Cuthbert followed and explained how the inside bar was clasped by a great wooden screw to the thick, heavy lintel. The bar had been loosened and split, but Corbett could see how it could be raised and lowered across the door to rest in the clasp on the other side; the same device was used in many tavern chambers.

'Why are there bars on the inside and outside?' Ranulf asked. 'Was Evesham truly a prisoner?'

'Oh no.' Cuthbert shook his head. 'During the day, that door hung open. Our great sinner, brought to repentance, could, and often did, wander Goose Meadow, though he kept close to the chapel as if he found it safe. At night he lowered the inside bar and insisted I do the same with the outside one.'

'Was he frightened?' Ranulf asked. 'Did he dread the very thing that caught him out?'

'I tell you, I do not know.'

Corbett asked to examine Cuthbert's cell. The lay brother agreed and showed how a similar bar was fastened to the lintel of his door, a crude but effective device to secure the chamber from the inside. Corbett closed the door and brought the bar down. It fitted neatly into the wooden clasp on the other side.

'It was the same in Evesham's cell,' Cuthbert offered, 'and can be found in many chambers in this abbey.'

Corbett nodded, then unbarred the door and went out into the passageway, where baskets, long canes, a mattock, hoe and buckets were all neatly stacked. Cuthbert explained how he was responsible for the shrubbery along the curtain wall, as well as the small garden plot on the other side of the chapel. Corbett heard him out. Once again he asked for a list of Evesham's visitors and what happened the day before he died. The lay brother replied, adding that he'd neither seen nor heard anything unto-ward. Corbett thanked him and went back up to the chapel, Cuthbert following.

'Sir Hugh?'

Corbett turned.

'I know what you are thinking.' The lay brother hobbled closer.

'In which case,' Corbett smiled, 'you're a better man than I. So, Brother, what am I thinking?'

'That I murdered Evesham; my heart was so hot against him.'

'Oh no.' Corbett patted him on the shoulder. 'Evesham died most mysteriously, that is obvious, but I suspect that in this matter we must ignore the obvious.'

Corbett and Ranulf left the chapel, but not before they had examined the door bolts and the shutters over the windows. Everything seemed in order, no scrape, no mark or sign of violence. Corbett took a deep breath as they walked out and closed his eyes for a few heartbeats. The hunt had begun! He walked over to where Ogadon sprawled. The mastiff growled softly but now recognised there was no threat. Corbett crouched and stroked the animal's silky head, smiling at those sad red-brown eyes.

'Ogadon is placid now,' Cuthbert came alongside him, 'because he knows you. In the middle of the night, however, a stranger . . .'

Corbett rose and studied the ledge where the servitor would leave the wine cup and platter. He noticed the stains beneath and caught the piece of cord attached to the bell, which hung in its own housing. He pulled the cord; the bell clanged noisily.

'We all have to die, yet so many are frightened of the corpse house,' explained Cuthbert. 'Hence the bell. They do not want to enter the chapel, but that assassin, God's vengeance on Evesham, certainly did.'

4

Hoodman blind: blind man's bluff

Corbett half listened as he stared round. The light was stronger, and the great meadow stretching back to the abbey glistened in the sunlight. The bells of the church clanged abruptly, summoning the brothers for the day Mass. Corbett walked around the chapel; Cuthbert, trailing beside him, solemnly assured him that apart from the door and the two narrow windows, no other entrance existed. Corbett followed Ranulf into the dense line of trees, shrubs and bushes that screened the abbey grounds from the great curtain wall. He approached and examined this. It was built of sheer smooth stone at least four yards high. The top, Cuthbert reminded him, was covered with sharp fragments embedded in a barred ridge of cement. Corbett whispered to Ranulf, who nodded, smiled at Cuthbert and walked back towards the abbey. The lay brother, eyes narrowed, watched him go.

'A true clerk,' he murmured, 'hauberked and mailed. A lusty fighter, eh, Sir Hugh? Ambitious too; you can smell that from him as you would incense from a monk.'

'A good man,' Corbett replied. 'True, hot-blooded, but Ranulf has a soul as well as keen wits.'

'Why has he left?'

'To ask Father Abbot a few things, as well as to inform him that I intend to visit the Lady Adelicia.'

'Adelicia, you must understand, doesn't like royal clerks.'

'Who does?' Corbett grinned. 'We're a flock of very ambitious men, but if you could show me?'

Cuthbert led him past the chapel and up a slight rise into a thick fringe of trees and bushes. They followed a well-trodden path into a small glade, peaceful and green, with lush spring flowers already blooming. In the centre of this greenery stood a small, circular stone building of grey brick surmounted by a concave red-tiled roof. The building reminded Corbett of a dovecote. Its walls were about three yards high, and at the front, facing him, was a square window sealed with painted black shutters each perforated with eyelets; the door beside it was low and narrow. A short distance away stood a wooden table, a high-backed chair and a prie-dieu set before an ancient oak; enclosed high in the tree's massive trunk was a gilded statue of the Virgin Mary holding her Child beneath an ivory crucifix. Corbett walked around. He glimpsed a small red-brick well with a rope and a leather bucket that could be lowered by hand. A pleasant, serene place, the glade conjured up images of fairy cottages in a mythical wind-swept greenwood.

'Mistress Adelicia, you have a visitor,' Cuthbert called.

'I know, a royal clerk. How such men brighten our lives, eh? I will see him.' The voice carried strong.

'I shall leave you here,' Cuthbert murmured and walked away.

The shutters on the widow swung back, and Corbett approached. The ivory-skinned face staring back at him was smooth, narrow-featured, framed by a creamy wimple beneath the dark blue capuchin of a Benedictine nun. The eyes, however, redeemed the harshness of the woman's face; large and clear, they stared direct and frank with a hint of amusement.

'You are, sir?'

Corbett introduced himself. 'You won't come out?' he added.

'No, clerk, I feel safe here. I can and do leave, but not now. I'll listen to your questions. I know that Evesham has, thank God, gone to a higher court to answer for his sins.'

'Which are?' Corbett drew closer, and caught the sweetness of herbs and soap.

'Arrogance, cruelty, greed.'

'You know nothing of his death?'

'Of course not.'

'But you are pleased?'

'No, I am satisfied.'

'Did he ever visit you?'

'No, I wanted nothing to do with him.'

'Yet he came to this place, where you and Cuthbert Tunstall shelter?'

'Yes, clerk, sheltering from the violent tempest he caused in all our lives.'

'Yet he came to make atonement. Did he ever ask to see you?'

'Once. I refused.'

'Too little, too late?' Corbett asked.

'No, no.' Adelicia's voice turned soft. 'God save me, I'll be truthful. Brother Cuthbert and I did not believe Evesham's protestations.'

'Why not?'

'As the root, so the flower, clerk. Can a man like Evesham change so swiftly, so dramatically? I don't think you believe that either.'

'He apparently did. He came here perhaps to atone in full view of yourself and Brother Cuthbert.'

'Or to shelter,' she retorted. 'Like a ship takes refuge from a storm or a wounded wolf slinks off to some cave to lick its sores and wait for a more opportune time to return to the hunt.'

'What do you mean? What evidence do you have?'

'Nothing, clerk. You work in the chancery, in the courts of law. If you seek proof here I cannot give it. We are spiritual beings; we have faith in the things we cannot see, hear or touch. I believe Evesham was a most malignant creature.'

'You also believe that your brother, Boniface, was innocent.'

'Yes, I do.'

'So Evesham was lying?'

'No.' Doubt tinged her voice. 'He was ruthlessly ambitious. Over the years I have learnt a little about what happened. Evesham was hunting a secret assassin, a murderer. He was determined to trap his quarry. I believe, despite all that, that he truly believed Boniface was guilty. He was determined on that.'

'But?'

'I think he was mistaken.'

'Do you think Evesham realised that, I mean secretly?'

'No, clerk, I do not. Evesham was as convinced of Boniface's guilt as I am that you are here. I can see why.' Her voice faltered. 'Boniface could not truly account for being in that tavern. He did flee for sanctuary. He was secretive. He held certain scraps of manuscripts and more gold than he should have done.'

'You say secretive, yet he was your brother.'

'We lived our own lives in our narrow house in Catskin Alley off Cripplegate. I worked as a seamstress. Boniface was very much the royal clerk. I loved him dearly, but he was as elusive as a sunbeam. He was often away, and the rare times he did return, he'd be out before dawn and come back long after compline. He talked very little about what he did. He could not account for the gold and silver that sometimes bulged his purse. Other times he seemed as poor as a church mouse.'

'So you know nothing really about him or the cause of his fall?'

'Nothing at all, clerk. Sometimes I used to catch a rich smell of heavy perfume from him. Boniface, I am sure, visited the more expensive ladies of the town in the richly tapestried chambers of their own gilded world.'

'And you?'

'I was left very much on my own. I had my sewing, some books, a few friends and, of course, Parson Tunstall. He invited me on to the parish council and asked me to look after the altar cloths, vestments and all the drapery of the church.' A smile transformed her face, making it beautiful, youth-filled. 'I know what you are thinking, clerk. No, I was not his doxy, his mistress. I was his friend; he was like a brother to me. We talked, we read, we walked, we laughed together, until the darkness fell on that hideous afternoon in June some twenty years ago. I was in my chamber. One of Parson Tunstall's parishioners burst in all hot and bothered to tell me that Boniface had taken sanctuary in St Botulph's. He was accused of some ghastly crime, a hanging offence, and a royal clerk, Walter Evesham, was determined on taking him. I was beside myself, besieged by the noonday terrors. I went down to the church, but Evesham was hot as the fires of hell against Boniface. He would not let me see him. He turned me away. I pleaded with him, but his heart, if he had one, was as hard as stone. When I returned the next day, Evesham had softened a little. He asked me for some token he could show my brother. I handed over a ring, a gift from my mother. Evesham must have given it to Boniface. I never saw it again, or my brother.' She paused, head down, shoulders shaking.

Corbett stared at the window that framed this picture of misery. Adelicia sobbed a little, then raised her tear-wet face. 'Two days later I heard that Boniface had disappeared.' She lifted her mittened hands, Ave beads wrapped around her fingers. 'I swear by all that is holy, I do not know what happened to him.'

'And Evesham?'

'He was beside himself with rage. He and his minion Engleat came to my house. They bullied and threatened me with every kind of torture and punishment. They claimed I knew something.' Her voice faded. 'I did not. They did the same to Parson Tunstall. When Evesham learnt we were friends, he swept back like a summer storm with his threats and cruel sarcasm. After a while he accepted that Boniface had disappeared and left us alone, but the damage had been done.'

'Yet your brother left you a message protesting his innocence?'

'Yes, yes, he did.' Adelicia withdrew from the window. Corbett heard her move around, a coffer lid creaking open then snapping shut. She returned to the window and handed him a small scroll. 'Please,' she begged, 'it is a keepsake. I want you to read it. The good Lord has answered my prayer.'

'What prayer?'

'When Evesham had finished with us and realised that Boniface would never return, Parson Tunstall was a broken man. I was tired of life. I took a solemn vow to spend the rest of my years as an anchorite. I ask God one favour before I die.' She drew a deep breath. 'I want the truth. I want my brother vindicated. I have prayed and fasted for that. I have asked God to send his angel, and now he has. You!'

Corbett glanced up sharply.

'We tend to think that angels come in shafts of light. They also come in flesh and blood. Oh yes, I've spoken to Brother Cuthbert, which is why he has been so honest and frank with you. This is the hour. Please read what I've given you.'

Corbett wondered how honest and frank this strange couple really were. Their responses were too well rehearsed. He was sure they were only telling him half-truths, but why? He sighed. That would have to wait. He undid the crinkling yellow parchment rubbed smooth over the years. The script was clear, bold, black and stark: *I stand in the centre, guiltless, and point to the four corners.*

'Don't ask me what it means; that's Boniface. My brother was a clerk, he loved puzzles. He was also afraid of Evesham. He never wrote or sent me any loving words. Only what was on his mind, the last thing he wrote, a secret message that Evesham would never discover. I believe it is the key to Boniface's innocence. Remember it, clerk.'

Corbett handed the piece of manuscript back and stood listening. The sun was now full and strong, and wood pigeons had began their insistent cooing, chorused by the sheer lucid song of a blackbird. He breathed in the fragrance of the morning, the sweet smell of woodsmoke, fresh grass and the faint essence of oils and herbs.

'So you believe your brother was innocent?'

'Yes.' The reply came haltingly. 'Yes, I do, even though Boniface was so secretive, so furtive.'

'Mistress, his conduct was highly suspicious.'

'True. I can hardly blame Evesham for being so hot in his insistence that he was guilty.'

'And your brother's disappearance?'

'Now that is a mystery. I know St Botulph's, its every corner and cranny. Boniface could not have escaped through a window; they are too narrow, too high. No secret passageways exist; whilst every door was closely guarded.'

'And his first escape,' Corbett asked, 'when he fled to St Botulph's? If Evesham was so hot against him, how did that happen?'

'I asked Brother Cuthbert about that. It was logical. Boniface knew the runnels and alleyways of Cripplegate. He acted all stricken and stumbled. Evesham had gone on ahead, pushing aside the crowds, whilst his bailiffs escorted my brother. I understand they had another prisoner. The crowd was milling about. The bailiffs went to pick Boniface up and he suddenly broke free, fleeing through the open door of a shop, or so Brother Cuthbert learnt from parishioners who were there.'

Corbett nodded in understanding. Every day in London criminals were arrested, escaped and fled for sanctuary. It was a common hazard. The narrow streets, the alleyways and runnels, doors and gates flung open, the crowds thronging about, whilst the deep dislike of bailiffs and beadles was commonplace. Yet Boniface had fled. Was that sign of guilt? Was he a killer, a skilled, sly, secretive man who lived two lives?

'Are you finished, clerk?'

'You seem eager to be rid of me.'

'No, Sir Hugh.' Adelicia laughed. 'I sense what you are, a good man as well as a royal clerk.' She paused. 'If there is such a mixture. Yes, you are good, one who has not yet sold his soul.'

'And your brother, Boniface, did he sell his?'

'God knows, Sir Hugh. I can see, or rather sense, your mind spinning like a wheel. Was Boniface the Mysterium? What happened to him? All a great mystery,' she continued in a whisper. 'I shall think, reflect and sleep. Perhaps the ghosts of yesteryear will return. If I remember anything, I shall tell you.'

'And Brother Cuthbert, do you and he ever meet?'

'Of course we do, especially on a warm summer's evening when the sun is setting and Goose Meadow is bathed in God's glory. We sit on the grass, hold hands and remember happier days. Farewell, Sir Hugh.'

The shutters across the window closed abruptly. Corbett shrugged and walked back through the trees to meet Ranulf striding across the frost-glistening grass, clapping his hands to keep them warm and loudly assuring Corbett that Father Abbot confirmed all that Brother Cuthbert had told them. The peace and harmony of the abbey had not been disturbed, not a jot or a tittle, until Abbot Serlo had been roused after his dawn Mass with the news that Evesham would not answer any knocking.

'Gone to God,' murmured Corbett, staring up at a crow circling above him. 'Gone to God's tribunal now, Ranulf, to join Ignacio Engleat. Lord knows the indictment they'll have to answer.' He breathed out, half listening to the faint sounds of the abbey, the drifting words of a cantor, the muffled clatter of cart wheels and the peal of a handbell being rung along the cloisters. 'Ranulf, who murdered Ignacio Engleat? Who crept in here with subtle wit and cunning mind to execute Lord Evesham? Why the secrecy, why the mystery?'

'Brother Cuthbert?' Ranulf stared hard at his master. Corbett was thinking and Ranulf relished what was about to happen. The pursuit would begin with Corbett the lurcher, the staghound. He'd twist and turn like the hunter he was until his prey was trapped, penned and marked for slaughter.

'You think so?' Corbett mused. 'Possible, Ranulf. Brother Cuthbert and Adelicia could be the murderers, at least of Evesham. They certainly had good cause to hate him, and yet . . .'

'And yet what?'

Corbett's eye was caught by the twinkle of light from one of the gilded windows of the abbey church.

'Too simple,' he murmured. 'Sin is like a fox, Ranulf, it leaves a stinking trail that even the years cannot wash out or hide. A killer has now taken up that scent. Ancient sins, long-buried evil, a tangle of poisonous roots are now festering. There is a time and season under heaven for everything, or so Scripture would have us believe. The year's thawing is over, long gone, harvest beckons, vengeance time is here.'

'And so, master?'

'Look,' Corbett shook himself free of his reverie, 'we'll return to London. Ranulf, you and Chanson are off to the Comfort of Bathsheba at Queenshithe, to establish what actually did happen to Ignacio Engleat.'

'And you, master?'

'I am going back down the tunnel of the years. I'll return to the chancery, to the pouches of the Secret Seal, and see what seeds of sin I can detect there.'

The Teller of Tales, as the assassin called himself, his hooded face dirty behind its garish mask, stood on the plinth that according to the city worthies was once part of a pagan temple. He was not interested in that; he was carefully watching the great open expanse before the towering iron-clad doors of Newgate. It was a filthy, sombre building, and the stench from behind its grey-stone walls curled and wafted everywhere, an odour of dirt, despondency and despair. At the close-barred windows of the soaring towers either side of the great gate, mad, frenetic faces, hair all tangled, peered greedily out at those now assembling on the cobbled bailey before the prison. The gathering crowd cursed and shouted as they slipped and slithered on the wet offal and blood that poured from the nearby fleshers' stalls. A motley collection of rogues, cutpurses, counterfeiters, cunning men, coney-catchers, rifflers and ribauds was congregating to greet Giles Waldene and Hubert the Monk. An abrupt proclamation regarding these miscreants had been issued by the catchpoles from the steps of the Guildhall. The two riffler leaders, with no real evidence against them, were to be released immediately. Everyone recognised the truth. Lord Evesham's murder meant the Crown's case against them had collapsed, whilst no proof could be lodged that either gang-leader had been party to the recent bloody riots at the prison. In fact both rogues had been lodged deep in Newgate's pestilential pits and had nothing to do with the malefactors whose tarred and pickled heads now decorated the spikes high on the prison walls. The hour had been set. Waldene and Hubert were to be released after the bells proclaimed terce. Gossips talked of reconciliation between the two factions after the recent riot. Already a chamber had been hired for the consequent festivities in the spacious pink and black-timbered tavern the Angel's Salutation, which stood on the corner of a crooked alleyway close to the prison concourse.

The Teller of Tales had tried to divert the attention of passers-by with a spine-tingling story of the Strigoi, the undead, trooping, according to miraculous report, along the old Roman road to the north of the city. No one had really been interested; indeed neither was the Teller of Tales, for his heart was intent on murder. He'd chosen the time and place most carefully. Newgate was a surge of colour and noise. Silversmiths' apprentices paraded a gorgeous mazer to entice would-be customers to visit their masters' shops in Cheapside. Butchers yelled the price of sweet duckling, pigs and fat juicy capons. Whoremongers, taken up by the bailiffs, heads all shaven and carrying their breeches, were being paraded to the strident wailing of bagpipes towards the stocks. A night-walker who had kidnapped a child so as to enhance her begging had been fastened to a punishment post, her filthy skirts raised so that burly baileys could lash her grimy buttocks. The belled pigs of St Anthony's hospital, the only pigs allowed to wander, snuffled the piles of ordure heaped close to a horse trough. Nearby a jackanapes was being ducked for daring to pass through the Skinners' quarter saying 'meow', a public insult to that worthy guild. Once he was punished, a line of drunks and roisterers also waited to be drenched in the filthy water.

Shouts and cries, the crash of gong carts and the clip-clop of hooves drowned the prayers of the Fraternity of Salve Regina processing solemnly with bell, candle and incense to the Lady Chapel at St Mary le Bow. Merchants and aldermen garbed in glowing robes of samite and velvet lined with expensive fur, fat necks and fingers glittering with jewellery, strolled arm in arm with their plump, richly dressed wives. Market beadles shouted warnings about how the sale of charcoal was forbidden in sacks weighing less than eight bushels. The Goodmen of St Dunstan, led by a Friar of the Sack, threaded their pardon beads as they made holy pilgrimage to St Paul's to pray at the tomb of Thomas à Becket's parents. A group of knights, escorted by their pages and squires, brilliantly embroidered pennants glistening in the sharp morning light, pushed their way down towards the tourney field at Smithfield. Fripperers, dragging their handcarts piled with second-hand clothes, shouted abuse at the group as they tried to force their barrows through. Enterprising vendors were already moving amongst crowds of the poor offering mouldy bread, rancid pork, slimy veal, flat beer and stale fish to those hungry and desperate enough to eat such rotten food. The Teller of Tales watched all this and quietly rejoiced, for he knew that such clamour and bustle would help to conceal his murderous plans.

The bell in one of the Newgate towers tolled, and the ribauds noisily thronged closer to the great gates. These swung back and the riffler leaders swaggered out to the cheers and shouts of their now much-depleted followers. Waldene was a giant of a man with shaggy grey hair and beard. He was dressed in a cote-hardie of tawny damask, Lincoln-green leggings and stout Castilian boots. Hubert the Monk, balding head and shaven face all gleaming with nard, looked diminutive beside him. Hubert was dressed in a long white robe, which gave him his name, his plump feet, warmed by woollen stockings, encased in stout, thick-soled shoes. The news that these two reprobates, like Pilate and Herod, had agreed to a lasting peace had been common talk around the prison. Both gang-leaders took a generous swig from a proffered wineskin, exchanged the kiss of peace and, hands raised in greeting, moved across into the sweet, tangy darkness of the Angel's Salutation. No one really took any notice. The good citizens and honest traders gave the rifflers short shrift, whilst their followers, greeted with shouts and curses, began to drift away.

The Teller of Tales watched and smiled deep in his cowl. He adjusted his mask, got down from the plinth and, with a sack firmly gripped beneath his cloak, strolled leisurely across into the tavern. He glanced at the casks at the far end of the taproom, which were covered by gleaming planks so as to serve as a counter.

Above this, onions, cheese and bacon hung in nets from the gilded beams' exuding a spicy, mouthwatering smell. It was a spacious chamber, its narrow horn-filled windows, candles and oil-wick pots providing some light, though shadows still thronged deep enough to hide in.

The Teller of Tales sat at an overturned barrel that served as a table. Sheltered by the darkness, he ordered a blackjack of ale and watched the staircase in the far corner. Waldene and Hubert had secured a chamber off the stairwell on the first gallery. Ale and food had been carried up to this precious pair, who'd been joined by two whores, local girls so a servant declared, Mistress Robinbreast and her companion Madame Catchseed. The Teller of Tales watched as the servants in their heavy shoes of undressed leather clattered up and down. Cries of wassail echoed loudly, and the guard on the stairwell sang a drunken song. Still the Teller waited. A blind jongleur, tapping the rush-covered floor with his cane, came in and sat down, nursing his pet ferret and loudly reciting a poem about how the devil was a sibulator, a hisser, and how whistling, together with holy water sprinkled with a sprig of St John's wort, would frighten him off. The Teller of Tales ignored the newcomer. He rose to his feet, took a flask from his sack and moved to the staircase. The servitors were now back in the kitchens and sculleries, all busy for when the Angelus bell rang and local traders flocked in to break their fast. The Teller of Tales, his heart full of malice, softly climbed the stairs. The guard staggered to his feet. The Teller put down the sack and, one hand on the dagger beneath his cloak, wafted the unstoppered flask beneath the drunkard's nose.

'The best of Bordeaux,' he murmured, 'a gift from Minehost.'

'I don't think so,' the guard slurred.

'Very well.' The Teller of Tales drew closer and shoved the dagger deep, a swift killing thrust up into the heart. The guard was so drunk he could only choke and gargle as he swayed backwards and forwards. The Teller of Tales pushed him back into the shadows, watching the soul light die in those startled red-rimmed eyes. He held the dagger fast until the final blood-spluttered sigh, then withdrew it, catching the corpse, lowering it to the floor and pushing it deeper into the dark-filled recess. Then he picked up the wine flask, rapped on the door and went in.

The chamber was large. Tapers lay strewn on the polished wooden floor, coloured cloths hung pinned to the whitewashed walls. The big window wasn't shuttered; the thick piece of oil-strengthened linen across the opening had also been removed. Waldene and Hubert, deep in their cups, lounged at a table just near the window. The large four-poster bed that dominated the room had its drapes pulled back to reveal the two courtesans Robinbreast and Catchseed, naked as they were born, clasped in a drunken embrace. Waldene turned as the Teller of Tales walked across offering the flask.

'Who are you?' His voice was thick.

'A friend.' The Teller put down the sack and held up the flask. 'The richest claret from the best vineyard in St Sardos, smooth as velvet. I explained this to your guard and he let me through. More importantly, I have a plan so that all three of us can share in dead Evesham's buried treasure.'

Hubert grinned, sketched a mock blessing in the air and gestured at the Teller to draw up a stool. Waldene emptied his tankard on the floor, bawling at one of the whores to bring the goblet they were sharing. The Teller of Tales made himself comfortable. He poured claret into each of the tankards, and drained the rest into the cup Catchseed slammed down on the table in front of him. Then he raised the goblet.

'The Blackness salutes the Night,' he murmured.

The two rifflers glanced at each other, gulped one deep draught after another and sat back smacking their lips.

'Good,' purred Hubert the Monk. 'Soft and velvety. It's a long time since I've drunk such an earthly richness.'

'Bats twittering in a cave,' murmured the Teller of Tales.

Waldene, inebriated, belched and banged the table. 'What do you mean? Why the mask? What's this about Evesham's treasure?'

'Oh, I found it.' The Teller nodded. 'We must go through the Gate of Dreams where Satan waits amongst the swarming dead like some huge red wolf. Oh yes, the Angel of Death is preparing to empty the vials of God's wrath.'

'Who are you? Take off your mask!' Hubert the Monk blinked, shook his head and drank even deeper of the poisoned claret.

'I am the evoker of the spirits. I sing songs of mourning, and all around me cluster the warring wraiths of the vengeful dead.'

'I don't . . .' Waldene tried to rise but found he couldn't.

'Who . . . what?' stammered Hubert the Monk.

'You're dying,' declared the Teller of Tales. 'You cannot move, can you? You've lost the feeling in your legs. I killed your guard and mixed the deadliest hemlock with the claret, which I've not drunk. Can you,' he leaned forward, grinning at his victims, 'can

91

you move? No! Death will swiftly grip your feet, coldness in your legs. There is nothing you can do but slip into the everlasting sleep of the gathering night.' He paused as both the Monk and Waldene tried to reassert themselves.

'Certain death,' the Teller of Tales explained, 'a creeping coldness that paralyses your limbs. Dark-clouded you've become as you approach the eternal gloom.' He glanced at the two whores, who were oblivious to the vicious drama being played out around that shabby table.

'Why?' gasped Hubert.

'Why? I represent the blood-drinking ghosts. I am Boniface Ippegrave, the Vengeance of the Lord.'

Waldene tried to lurch to his feet, but knocked over a stool and collapsed. The two whores shrieked. The Teller of Tales sprang to his feet and brought a small arbalest from the sack, a wicked little crossbow, its bolt already primed, the twine pulled back. He pointed this at the whores.

'*Tace et vide*,' he hissed. 'Stay silent and watch.'

The two petrified women clung to each other as the Teller of Tales stepped back to watch the gang-leaders die, paralysed by the deadly hemlock. Then he drew his dagger and moved from one enervated victim to the other. Ignoring their coughing and groans, he etched, with the tip of his dagger, the letter 'M' on each of their foreheads. Once satisfied, he sheathed his blade, picked up the arbalest and pointed it at the two whores.

'I will not kill you. You do not deserve to die, not yet. When they come, say that Boniface Ippegrave has returned!'

5

Waelstow: the place of slaughter

Three hours later, long after the bells had tolled, Miles Fleschner, Clerk of St Botulph's in Cripplegate, nervously approached the corpse door of his parish church. Although a former coroner, he was a timid man, fearful of the horrors perpetrated in this supposedly hallowed place. St Botulph's accurately reflected the words of Scripture: 'The Abomination of the Desolation had been set up in the holy place.' The building had been desecrated by sacrilege and blasphemy, and now the Blessed Sacrament had been removed, the sanctuary lamp extinguished, the sacred vessels sealed away. No prayers could be said, no candles lit before the Virgin, no chants raised, no Mass offered until the Bishop of London purged, sanctified and reconsecrated the building as 'a Holy Place, the House of God and the Gate of Heaven'. Miles recalled memories of twenty years ago when Boniface Ippegrave had sheltered here in sanctuary before disappearing. That had been in the parish clerk's green and salad days, when he was an ambitious coroner still in the fresh spring of manhood. Now the memories drifted back like ghosts through Fleschner's tired mind. He recalled Evesham, bullying and arrogant, but no, he couldn't remember that, not here! Miles Fleschner sometimes wished he had nothing to do with this church. Was St Botulph's cursed? One parson had lost his wits and fled to an abbey. Would Parson John, all tremulous and fearful, follow suit? The parson had asked Fleschner to join him in the sacristy three hours after the sext bell. There was still work to be done: pyxes, Little Marys, chalices, monstrances and cruets to be sealed in the heavy satin-lined parish fosser; candle wax, clothes, vestments, incense, charcoal and other items to be inventoried. St Botulph's was under interdict – sealed until reconsecrated. No longer was it the home of the Seraphim, the Lords of Light, but the prowling place of demons and earthbound souls, all those poor unfortunates barbarously slain then laid out like chunks of bloodied meat along the nave.

Miles Fleschner paused under the outstretched branches of a yew tree and stared fearfully up through its ancient branches. The day was dying; soon it would be the hour of the bat, the screech-owl. He startled as he heard a sound from the church and cautiously approached the battered but rehung corpse door. Parson John had said he would leave it ajar, off the latch. Fleschner stepped around the remains of the fierce battle, pushed open the door and went into the clammy, cold darkness. Only the poor light trickling through the lancet windows pierced the gloom. The nave was a place of shifting shadows. He heard a sound and turned. A figure darted out of the door leading from the sacristy into the sanctuary.

'Who . . .?' Fleschner chilled with terror.

The figure disappeared back into the sacristy. Like a dream-walker Fleschner moved slowly forward. The sound of a door slamming shut made him start, and a sweaty fear gripped him. He wanted to turn and run. He fumbled at the dagger beneath his cloak and drew the blade. He was so nervous he could scarely put one foot in front of the other. He listened and peered around; the light was swiftly fading, the shadows lengthening from the corners where they lurked.

'Who is there?' he called out. He looked back down the church, where a slant of light lit up the great carved bowl of the baptismal font. 'Who is there?' he repeated. A groan like that of some petrified, disembodied soul echoed down the nave. Fleschner, legs shaking, sweat bathing his face, slowly climbed the sanctuary steps and glanced around, throat dry. This was his church, yet the carved, contorted face of demons, gargoyles and babewyns seemed to glare fiercely down at him. He pushed open the door to the sacristy, a dark room containing chests, stools, aumbries and the great vesting table. The air reeked strangely of wax and some other foul odour, as if a mound of refuse had been disturbed. Again the groan. He whirled around. Parson John was staring up at him in terror. Fleschner crouched down.

'Father!' He glanced in horror at the red cut on the priest's forehead.

'Release me, my feet,' gasped Parson John, pushing himself forward.

Fleschner immediately cut the bonds about the priest's ankles, then sawed at the cords around his wrists.

'I came in here, I wanted to pray for my father, I heard of his death.' Parson John kicked his ankles free of the tangled ropes. 'I was here in the sacristy when I was pushed . . .'

'Father?'

'I was pushed.' Parson John pointed to the bruises on his head and face. 'I was bound and gagged. All I saw and heard was a shadowy figure breathing noisily.'

'How did he get in?'

Parson John grasped Fleschner's shoulder. 'Miles, for the love of God, that doesn't matter. He carried a sack, which he took into the church. Then he came back. He drew his dagger and started to carve something on my forehead, then he must have heard you. He went out, came back then fled into the cemetery. I managed to break free of the gang. I must see . . .' The priest, all confused, lurched to his feet and, followed by the still trembling parish clerk, went into the sanctuary and down the nave.

Fleschner swallowed hard, his mouth dry. He had, as he later told his wife, a presentiment of evil. Some great malignancy was lurking in the gathering murk. Both men walked slowly, fearfully, their footsteps echoing ominously. Fleschner wished he'd brought a lamp or candle. When they reached the far end of the church, Parson John went towards the still battered main door, while Fleschner rested against the great bowl of the baptismal font. A strange smell pricked his nostrils. Had the font been polluted? He glanced down, then gagged in horror as he saw the two severed heads, eyes half closed, nestling at the bottom of the huge bowl.

Corbett sat in the murder chamber at the Angel's Salutation; that was what he called the room. He leaned back on the stool, eyes half closed. Across the floor, beneath the window, sprawled the corpses of Waldene and Hubert the Monk. The Friar of the

Sack, the same who'd shriven the felons executed at St Botulph's, was busy reciting the words of absolution. What did happen, Corbett wondered, to souls after death? Did the life essence of these two criminals still hover here in this chilly, dusty chamber? Did they plead for mercy? Did they wait for others to come and lead them? To what? The Friar of the Sack rose to his feet and crossed himself.

'It's done, Sir Hugh, their souls have gone to God and I must sate my appetite.'

Corbett smiled and handed over a silver piece. The friar bit the coin, grinned, sketched a blessing and went to join the rest gathered in the taproom downstairs, where the delicious details of these heinous slaying were being greedily picked at and sifted. An old beggar woman had offered to sing the song of mourning and was now doing so, the lugubrious noise echoing up the stairs. In between verses her companion, a cunning man, loudly declared that the beating heart of a mole would be sure protection against malignant chattering ghosts and offered, for a certain price, to get one for Minehost. The two whores, Robinbreast and Catchseed, were slurping their tankards of ale, smiling gratefully through their tears for the coins and free drinks offered by those who wanted to relish the gory details. Both whores wailed how the spirits of the two dead men hung close, ghosts in wolfskins. They could, they were sure, remember the details of the slaughterer, 'dark in all things', who'd slid silent as a viper into that dreadful chamber.

Corbett had questioned both the prostitutes and the others, but had learnt little except how the killer had declared himself to be Boniface Ippegrave, that he was of ragged appearance, his face 'the colour of boxwood, with a look of dark-robed night about him'. In truth the two whores were more frightened of the King's man, the royal clerk. Dressed in black, Corbett, had swept into the tavern, his heavy cloak folded over one arm, spurs jingling on his riding boots. His battle belt with its scabbarded sword and dagger made him ominous enough, but he also carried the royal warrant and wore the King's seal ring on his right hand. The whores had been deeply unsettled by the clerk's steady gaze, his black hair swept back, face all watchful, as Catchseed whispered, 'A king's hawk come to brood.'

Corbett sighed and rose to his feet, once again he examined the corpses of the two gang-leaders and that of their guard. A local physician, eyes all rheumy, nose dripping, had pronounced that Waldene and Hubert had been poisoned by a powerful infusion of hemlock. Corbett picked up the empty flask and sniffed the top; it still smelled of rich claret. The wine could have been bought at any vintner's. He turned and glanced at the corpse of the ugly ruffian sprawled on the bed. The great open wound in the guard's left side was now a thickening soggy mess. The physician had declared all three deaths unlawful, collected his coin and stomped off. Corbett tapped the hilt of his sword and turned as the door opened and Ranulf came in. He glanced at the cadavers and whistled under his breath.

'So it's true: Waldene, the Monk and one of their guards all gone to Heaven's bench. The King will be pleased. Who will mourn their passing?'

'Those who hired them,' Corbett replied, 'that tribe of serpents in the city who use such dagger men to ladle out the evil stored in their own baleful hearts.'

'Master, you're angry.'

'No, Ranulf, my apologies, I'm confused, puzzled. Why all this? Why now? It was so easily done,' he mused. 'Waldene and Hubert left Newgate; their release was well known, as it was that both malefactors would come across here to cry wassail and toast their freedom. They hired a chamber, two ladies of the town, a jug of ale and a platter of cold meat and bread. According to the whores downstairs, this cowled, cloaked stranger entered. He caused no disturbance, silently knifing their guard. Waldene and Hubert, deep in their cups, thought he'd been allowed in.' Corbett tapped the flask. 'He brought this Bordeaux with a strong infusion of powerful hemlock. He mentioned something about Evesham's treasure. He poured the claret, watched the poison swiftly paralyse his victims, carved his murderous mark on their forehead, announced that he was Boniface Ippegrave, threatened the whores and left.' He paused. 'Boniface Ippegrave,' he repeated.

'Did you know Ippegrave, master?'

'Not really. I remember him as short, good-looking, neat and precise, with sharp eyes. Yes, that's it.' Corbett chewed the corner of his lip. 'Now I remember. Yes . . .' He wagged a finger as his memory was pricked.

'Master?'

'Dark reddish hair, rather singular, though that was twenty years ago.'

'Do you think he has returned?'

'Perhaps, why not? After all, he was a royal clerk.' Corbett grinned, then stepped closer and touched Ranulf gently on the cheek with a gauntleted finger. 'Resourceful, ambitious. Anyway, the Comfort of Bathsheba?'

'Ignacio Engleat went there and then on to a tavern, the Halls of Purgatory. He drank deep and fell asleep. Someone, nobody knows who, helped him out,' Ranulf shrugged, 'hauled him off to his death. The tavern was very busy. The servants were only too pleased to see a drunk go.' He paused at a tap on the door; it opened and Minehost, face all concerned, bustled in.

'Sir Hugh, my lord,' he gestured, 'downstairs there's a creature, Lapwing he calls himself. He wishes words with you, as does Parson John of St Botulph's. He is here with Miles Fleschner, his parish clerk.'

Corbett raised his eyes heavenwards and gestured at Ranulf to follow. At the door he paused, crossed himself and pointed to the bloody mayhem on the far side of the chamber.

'Minehost, the coroner and the ward catchpole will deal with those. Now, sir?'

The men were waiting for him in the taproom below. Lapwing, neatly dressed in a bottle-green cote-hardie, leggings and soft brown boots, was playing with the clasp of his dark blue cloak. A man of sharp but calm wit, Corbett thought. He had shaved his face and his hair was cropped close above his ears. Corbett went to speak to him, but Lapwing winked and pointed to a table in a shadowy recess where Parson John and Fleschner were greedily gulping wine.

'I heard about the tumult,' Lapwing whispered, 'and hurried here. Parson John arrived close behind me; he is almost out of his wits.'

Corbett nodded, and approached the parson's table, settling himself on a stool.

'Parson John?' Corbett touched the priest's arm. 'My condolences on your father's death.'

'Blood here, blood everywhere,' murmured the parson, pushing his face forward. He looked ill and unshaven, and Corbett glimpsed the bloody line on his forehead. Fleschner was even more agitated, sitting back in the shadows, grasping his goblet as a child would a cup. Corbett let them drink and stared around. Minehost had wisely moved the two whores and their small spellbound audience into the scullery. The day's trading had not yet ceased and the taproom was deserted except for a blind jongleur humming a lullaby to his pet ferret.

'Parson John, why are you here? Tell me what has happened.'

The priest did so, words gushing out as he described the horrors perpetrated in his church. Corbett listened intently, comforted that Ranulf stood behind him. Here in this darkened tavern where savage murder had struck, another tale of terror was unfolding. He concealed his own spurts of fear, which pricked both his mind and his heart with their sheer coldness. As he listened to Parson John, he recognised that in the labyrinth of mysteries stretching before him prowled an assassin, a midnight soul. The hunt was on, dreadful and dark. The creeping flame of sudden slaughter would flicker around him. The twisted roots of long-buried sin would draw fresh sap and thrust up. The parson eventually finished and sat staring, mouth gaping in shock.

'I took the heads,' he mumbled. 'I placed them in a sack, which I left in the sanctuary. What should we . . .?' He glanced up fearfully.

'The heads?' Ranulf hissed. 'You recognised them?'

'Of course! My stepmother, my father's second wife, Clarice, and her steward, the controller of her household, Richard Fink.'

'Why should they die?'

'I don't know,' Parson John wailed. 'I must go there, I must see.'

Corbett pressed the agitated priest on the back of his hand.

'You agreed to meet Master Fleschner about the third hour after midday in the sacristy of St Botulph's?' Parson John nodded.

'We had certain business,' mumbled the parish clerk.

'You, Parson John, went into the sacristy. Your attacker followed you from outside. You were knocked to the floor, bruised, bound and gagged.' The priest nodded. 'Your assailant then went into the church with his bag and, for his own devilish reasons, placed the severed heads in the font. He returned to you, drew his dagger and was probably about to carve the letter "M" on your forehead?'

'Yes,' Parson John gasped, 'but thank God Miles opened the corpse door. My attacker went out of the sacristy as if to flee through the church, but came back and left by the outside door of the sacristy, which leads into the poor man's lot and on to the priest's house.'

'What did he look like?' Ranulf asked.

'He was cowled and visored. He whispered rather than talked; his clothes smelt rancid.'

'What did he say?' Ranulf demanded.

Parson John glanced wearily up.

'That he was Boniface Ippegrave come again to seek vengeance against Evesham and all his kin. Sir Hugh, why are we staying here? My stepmother, Richard Fink?'

'Their home?'

'Off Clothiers Lane in Cripplegate, near the old wall. We'd best . . .'

Corbett agreed and got to his feet.

'May I come?' Lapwing pushed his way by Ranulf.

'Yes, you may,' retorted Corbett. 'Indeed, sir, I wish to have close words with you sometime.' He had already made his decision. Tomorrow he would summon a special commission of oyer and terminer, so that all involved in this dire business could answer on oath, but until then . . .

Corbett took his leave of Minehost and, with Ranulf and the rest following, left the Angel's Salutation. He brushed aside the quack offering to cure worms in the ears with a poultice of fennel, plantain and mutton fat. Other tradesmen were just as insistent. The light was fading. The market bell would soon sound, the bailiffs would blow their horns and trading would cease, but until then, the stallholders and their apprentices were desperate to entice would-be customers. The air was bitterly cold, the mud and ordure beneath their feet hardening under a coating of ice. Troublemakers, all roped together, were being taken to the cage in Cheapside. A madman, manacled by his friends, was baying at the overcast sky as he was led across to a local church to be chained to the rood screen in the hope that his overnight stay before the Lord would cure his lunacy. A relic-seller offered to reveal the hand of a saint on which a finger would curl and point at the guilty. However, if the faithful were not interested in that, perhaps a scrap of unicorn blessed by St Ninias, a sure protection against poison? Only a little beggar boy seemed interested.

The crowds were thinning, and they scrambled quickly out of Corbett's way. The citizens of the night along the runnels and alleyways were already being alerted. King's men were on the prowl and no one dared impede the stride of these grim-faced clerks, hands grasping the hilts of their swords. People recognised Parson John and Fleschner and called out greetings, but only the parish clerk replied, lifting a tremulous hand in acknowledgement.

Corbett walked on, wary of the slippery trackways and narrow alleys leading off either side, where night-walkers and dark-prowlers gathered waiting for dusk. Shouts of abuse echoed. Doors slammed, shutters rattled. The foul smells of the cesspit faded abruptly as they passed a perfumer's shop, where jars of *Manus Christi*, rosewater and ambergris stood unstoppered on the lowered shop fronts. Behind these the apprentices were busy with the perfume pans, and their delicious fragrances teased Corbett's nostrils, recalling images of Lady Maeve. He stood aside as a little boy dressed in a black gown scurried by, ringing a skilla to warn people about the approach of a priest, head and shoulders covered by a red-gold cape, carrying the viaticum. Corbett knelt as he hurried on by to some sickbed, then rose and walked on.

The entrance to Clothiers Lane was blocked when he reached it by a litter carried by four priests chanting the *Libera me* psalms; inside, a leper, dressed in his shroud, hands sheathed in leather gloves, rattled a clapper warning all to step aside. Once they were gone, Corbett waved Parson John on and they went up the well-cobbled street. On either side rose the stately mansions of the very wealthy, each in its own grounds and bounded by high curtain walls, above which peeked red-slated roofs and pink-plastered, black-timbered fronts. Parson John hurried to a magnificent gate leading to one of these mansions, where a watchman stood gossiping with two young women. Once he realised who Corbett was, the watchman hurriedly explained how the women were kitchen scullions who, with other servants, had arrived after the Angelus bell to find all the doors and shutters closed and no light burning.

'We were under strict instruction to knock and wait,' one of the scullions declared. 'We knocked and waited but no one came down.'

Corbett nodded, pushed open the gate and went along the white-stone path, which skirted hedges, shrubs and garden plots, to broad stone steps leading up to a splendid porch and a gleaming black door. He pulled the bell rope, then lifted the iron clasp carved in the shape of a helmet. This he brought down time and again, listening to the sound echoing through the house. Behind him Parson John mumbled and whimpered. Corbett glanced up. All the shutters remained closed. He went round to a postern door and tried the latch. It pulled open, and he entered the paved kitchen and scullery area. A tidy place, all swept and clean, yet arid and empty, bereft of light and warmth. The only sign that it had been recently used was a huge cutting board with bread and cheese on the fleshing table. Lapwing was eager to explore further, but Ranulf, who felt the brooding menace of this house, drew sword and dagger and told them all to stay, as he followed Corbett across the well-scrubbed flagstones. He sensed dullness, a harsh emptiness that frayed the mind and agitated the soul.

They entered the long hall. Polished oaken furniture and precious items gleamed in the poor light, and their footsteps were dulled by the thick turkey rugs strewn on the floor. Corbett glimpsed triptychs, small figurines, statues in niches, the gold and silver thread of tapestries; a place of comfort that concealed its own silent, macabre secrets. They went out into the vestibule, up the staircase and along the narrow gallery. A door hung half open. Corbett pushed this back and went into the master bedchamber. One window was unshuttered, and the meagre light revealed a gruesome scene: two naked corpses, headless, the woman's sprawled across the bed, the man's lying just within the doorway. Their life-blood, now thick and drying, had drenched both bed and furniture, as well as soaking the thick woollen rugs on the floor. Corbett covered his nose at the rotten stench and stared around this once exquisite chamber.

'Tristan and Isolde!' he murmured. 'Evesham was gone, locked up in Syon. Mistress Clarice and Master Fink decided to play the two-backed beast. Servants were dismissed and told when to return. Clarice and Fink thought they were alone and safe. Instead their nemesis arrived; he came in the same way we did.' He walked across, removed the hard linen covering the casement window, leaned out and took a deep breath of cold air. Then he turned back and studied the two blood-smeared cadavers. The cuts on both necks were ragged, the top of Fink's chest a mottled bluish red.

'The assassin entered swiftly,' Corbett surmised. 'The two lovers were disturbed.' He gestured at Fink's corpse, its sagging belly, the thickening flesh around shoulders and chest. 'Fink was no warrior, but he tried to defend himself and his lover.' He crouched down and pointed to the bruising on the upper chest. 'Fink tried to resist. The assassin, probably armed with a short two-headed axe, knocked him away. I wager Fink's head is also badly bruised.' He rose and smeared the blood with the toe of his boot, then tapped at the deep cuts on the wooden floor. 'Fink was stunned. The assassin turned on Clarice; shocked and terrified, she tried to move, but again, a blow to her head. Afterwards the assassin severed each at the neck, put the heads in a sack and left. At least I think that's what happened.' He stood, eyes closed, imagining the sequence of events, then opened his eyes and returned to the window.

'The day's dying,' he remarked. 'There is nothing more I can do, not now. Ranulf, summon the coroner's bailiffs; have the cadavers removed to the death house at St Margaret's-on-the-Heath.' He whispered a requiem and crossed himself. 'Afterwards, go to St Botulph's and collect the heads. They'll be bruised and I am sure will have the letter "M" carved on the foreheads. Take them to the—' He suddenly noticed the piece of yellowing parchment lying on top of a small coffer. He picked it up. It was well used, the script clear in a bluish-green ink.

'*Mysterium Rei* – the Mystery of the Thing?' asked Ranulf.

'Aye . . .' Corbett pushed the scrap into his belt pouch and pressed a hand against a crucifix nailed to the wall. 'And with the Lord's good help I will solve the mystery and send this murderer to the scaffold. Ranulf, once you've finished with the dead, quicken the living. Go to the writ chamber in the Chancery of the Green Wax and issue a summons to everyone: Lapwing,' Corbett chewed his lip, 'Brother Cuthbert, Mistress Adelicia.' He waved a hand. 'Even those recluses must obey the King's writ and attend to God's business. Oh yes,' he smiled thinly, 'Staunton and Blandeford, that precious pair. Parson John, Miles Fleschner. Afterwards, seek out any bailiff involved in the arrest of Boniface Ippegrave. Tell Chanson to help you. Talk to Sandewic; he may have names.'

'And the time and place?'

'After the sext bell tomorrow in the oyer and terminer chamber at Westminster. I want them all there, on oath, to see what calm I can impose on this bloody chaos.'

6

Murdrum: murder

Corbett, muffled in his cloak, sat at the great chancery table in the Office of the Secret Seal, deep in the labyrinth of galleries, passageways and chambers on the second floor of the rambling, ancient palace of Westminster. The lowered candelabra of beeswax lights illuminated the ox-blood Cordovan leather table top and the manuscripts Corbett had neatly laid out. He slouched in the quilted high-backed chair and stared around. Braziers crackled against the cold seeping like a mist through the shuttered windows. Lantern horns brightened the corners as well as the aumbries, coffers and chests stacked around the chamber. The flickering light caught the glint of a silver crucifix and shimmered in the vivid colours of the glorious tapestry, a gift from the King's allies in Flanders, which proclaimed the story of the Archangel Raphael from the Book of Tobit. A shadowy shape flittered across the pool of light and disappeared through the slightly ajar door.

'Good hunting Footpad,' Corbett called; the great tomcat, the scourge of vermin, prowled like Death itself along the narrow wintry galleries, ready to pounce on any wandering mouse or rat.

Elsewhere, Footpad's lieutenant Assassin was also on the hunt. Corbett half listened. The old timbers and woodwork of the palace creaked and groaned. Sentry calls carried on the late-night air, whilst the persistent chilling breeze rattled the shutters. A place of ghosts, Corbett reflected. He got to his feet, stretched and moved to a small mullioned glass window, its panes decorated with heraldic motifs, where he peered down at the juddering light from cressets flaring in their holdings as well as the makeshift fires of the sentries. Westminster was now quiet. Some claimed how, after dark, the palace became too silent and all the ghosts of yesteryear returned. Clerks who'd spent their lives in their narrow chambers and ignored the call to worship God. Priests who had flocked to the palace to collect fat benefices and comfortable sinecures but failed to offer masses for the stipends received. Those killed in the constant brawls and affrays in Westminster's many taverns, ale houses and brothels, which did such lively business for the court. These were joined by the spectres of those who'd died in sanctuary, the refuge for outlaws and wolfsheads in the great meadow that separated the Abbey of Westminster from the palace, their shades mingling with those who'd been hanged outside the great gate of the abbey. Corbett smiled. Despite the legends, he preferred Westminster after dark, at peace from the constant clatter and chatter of the day.

He returned to his chair. It was very warm in here, and he was glad to be out of the cold, away from that dreadful chamber in Evesham's house. He and Ranulf had informed Parson John about what had happened. The priest said he could not bear to view the corpses. Indeed, he began to shiver and cry so woefully that

Fleschner had to take him back to St Botulph's. Lapwing had kept his distance. Once Corbett had announced the dire news, the mysterious clerk declared that he wished to leave. Corbett had grasped the man by the cloak and warned that he would soon receive a writ of summons and must accept it. Lapwing had simply shrugged and slipped away. Corbett then re-entered that macabre house and carefully searched it, yet apart from the gruesome slaughter in the bedchamber, nothing else had been disturbed. No sign of forced caskets, chests or coffers, no violence anywhere. The killer had slipped like the Angel of Death through that mansion, where the two lovers had considered they were safe, with no servants, no one to report on their illicit tryst.

'And no manuscripts,' he mused loudly. 'Evesham's chancery chamber was as empty as a poor man's pantry.'

He picked up his goblet of mulled wine and sipped carefully. He must sleep and prepare for tomorrow, yet he was vexed, for he could make little sense nor impose any real order on the bloody swirl of events. He pulled across the various manuscripts culled from the pouches and coffers of the Secret Seal. He had read Evesham's report on his hunt and capture of Ippegrave. The King's summation of events had been accurate; only one extra detail stood out. Evesham had explained how he was so surprised at Boniface being the Mysterium that he had bound neither him nor the merchant Chauntoys when they were brought across the bridge from Southwark. As he had rightly argued, Ippegrave was a clerk in minor orders accused but not condemned. For the rest, the account provided no new information nor offered any further evidence. Evesham described how Boniface had escaped, taken sanctuary in St Botulph's and was not allowed out. How his sister had approached with a ring that Evesham claimed he handed over to her brother. He detailed how closely guarded the church had been, every door and window, and could not explain his quarry's escape. A list of depositions from bailiffs and others who had guarded St Botulph's all confirmed this mystery.

Corbett pulled across another pouch. He'd broken the seal and examined its contents, found in Boniface's lodgings as well as his iron-bound coffer here in the chancery. The items had been listed by a clerk, Rastall. Corbett smiled. He remembered old Rastall, grim and abrasive but as clear and honest as the day. He had led the search of Boniface's personal belongings; he would have scrupulously ensured that nothing had been deliberately placed there to incriminate the fugitive clerk, and had declared as much in a small memorandum sewn to the contents. The list of gold and silver found, now long spent by the exchequer, was considerable. Corbett whistled under his breath. It was certainly more than any chancery clerk could earn in a year. He examined with interest the message found on Boniface the day he was arrested. Written anonymously in faded ink, the writ gave the time and place, with the added advice that Boniface's presence at the Liber Albus would be of great profit to both himself and the King.

'That could have been written by anyone,' he murmured aloud.

The rest of the items included a rough sketch map of London, or at least the area around St Paul's, Cheapside, Aldgate, Cripplegate and Farringdon. Crosses had been etched in red. According to the memorandum drawn up by Rastall, the map, definitely the work of Boniface himself, marked some of the murders carried out by the Mysterium. A second sheaf consisted of faded scraps bearing the same macabre message the assassin had pinned to the corpses of his victims: *Mysterium Rei* – the Mystery of the Thing. Corbett held one of these up; undoubtedly they had been sent to the chancery by the coroners and sheriffs who'd attended the victim's corpses. Boniface had apparently collected them, but why? More important was a piece of parchment with the words 'St Paul' scrawled above a square roughly divided into columns, twelve across and twelve down. According to Rastall, the document had been found in Boniface's coffer and was certainly in his hand. Corbett tapped the table, muttering to himself. Evesham had revealed the Mysterium's murderous method only after he had arrested both Ippegrave and the merchant Chauntoys. Only did then did he deduce, supported by Chauntoys' full confession, how the Mysterium chose his victims and demanded payment.

'But that was after the event!' Corbett exclaimed to himself. 'So how did Boniface know about St Paul's?'

He couldn't have done, he reasoned, unless he truly was the Mysterium. Yet he had protested his innocence to his sister and to others. He'd written that puzzle about being guiltless, standing in the centre and pointing to the four corners; what did that mean? An enigmatic riddle to protect himself? Was Boniface a liar and an assassin who'd managed to escape and had now returned to exact vengeance?

Corbett blew on his mittened fingers and extended his hands over the nearby chafing dish, then picked up a parchment that Rastall had again confirmed was written in Boniface's hand. The lettering was neat and precise, as if the author had carefully reflected

Paul Doherty

before scribbling each word. The entries were elliptical: *Hervey Staunton, Blandeford? Clerks? Messengers to St Paul's Cross?* Then beneath this, *Walter Evesham? Ignacio Engleat? Clerks in the city?* Corbett moved the manuscript around and glimpsed a sketch in the far right-hand corner: two letters, 'B' and 'M', separated by a heart pierced with an arrow. Was that a mere jotting? Some long-lost love of Boniface's? He picked up the last piece of parchment. Grey and faded, it bore a list of names beginning with 'Emma', then others that sparked Corbett's memory though he couldn't place them: Odo Furnival, Stephen Bassetlawe, William Rescales. Beneath this the letters

A, B, C,
D, E, F,
G, H, I

A flurry of noise followed by a creak in the gallery outside made him start. Footpad or Assassin had struck! He settled in his chair, allowing the exhaustion to seep in. When, he wondered, would he strike at this cunning killer? The piece of parchment slipped from his fingers and, eyes growing heavy, he drifted into sleep.

Adelicia Ippegrave started awake. She'd been dreaming about walking through the moon-washed woodland of the abbey searching for Boniface. She was worried about the tapping that seemed to follow her. Pulling herself up on the cot bed, she realised the noise was coming from the shuttered window of

114

her anker house. She picked up the small crucifix from the rough-hewn table beside her bed and crossed herself with it, whispering a prayer to St Michael against the prowlers of the dark. Then she drew a deep breath, took a tinder and lit the fat tallow candle in the lantern horn. Again the tapping on the shutters.

'Adelicia,' hissed a voice, 'Adelicia, *pax et bonum*.'

She moved across, opened the shutters and stood back. A rush of icy night air made her snatch up her mantle and wrap it about her shoulders. She stared into the blackness.

'Who are you?'

'Why, sister, your sweet brother Boniface.'

Adelicia caught her breath and sat down clumsily on a stool. 'I don't believe you!' she gasped. 'Show yourself.'

'It's best not, not the way I am now.'

'Then how—' Adelicia flinched as something sparkling was tossed lightly through the window. She scrabbled on the ground and picked up the circle of gold with its jasper stone.

'Your ring.' The voice was low, slightly mocking. 'Your ring,' it repeated. 'Mother's ring. You sent it to me.'

Adelicia held the ring fast as tears pricked her eyes. 'If you are Boniface, where have you been? Why have you come back now? Why didn't—'

'The past is closed, sealed, Adelicia. No going back down amongst the dead men. My hour has come, vengeance is here.'

'For what?'

'Sins reeking of malice and evil.'

'But you said the past is sealed.'

'So it is, except for sin. Its blossoms bloom rich and thick, they have to be culled.'

'Are you the Mysterium?'

'Yes.'

'But you protested your innocence. You claimed to be guilt-less, standing in the centre, pointing to the four corners. You wrote—'

'That was then,' came the whisper.

'Did you . . .' Adelicia's mouth went dry, 'kill Evesham and the others? Dreadful deaths. Even more, I've heard news from the city. I have been summoned by the royal clerk . . .'

'Dogs nosing the muck,' taunted the voice. 'What do we have to do with royal clerks, Adelicia?'

'Boniface, how did you escape?'

'I will answer that if you answer me.'

'What?'

'When you came to see me, when I was in sanctuary at St Botulph's, did Evesham,' the voice thrilled with hatred, 'did Evesham, that limb of Satan, ask about a woman called Beatrice?'

'No,' whispered Adelicia, 'but later, when you escaped, he and Engleat came to our house. They searched it from cellar to garret, but of course—'

'I never kept anything there; well not much, did I, sister?'

'No, no.'

'And Evesham, what did he ask?'

'He screamed at me about a woman Boniface, if that is who you are. Yes, he gave her name, Beatrice, that's all. And now my question: how did you escape?'

'Sister, I simply walked through the door.'

'But that's . . .' Adelicia hastened to the window and gripped the rough wooden sill. She stared bleakly into the darkness, but her visitor had gone.

'I don't understand.' Hervey Staunton, Justice in King's Bench, tightened his vair-lined cloak, then leaned over and rapped the dark green leather covering of the judgement bench in the chamber of oyer and terminer just off the great hall of Westminster. 'I don't understand,' he sniffed, glancing quickly at his companion Blandeford, who also sat swathed in a costly robe, face all peevish.

Ranulf leaned back in his high chair and stared around the comfortable lofty chamber. The walls were half covered in gleaming linen panelling, the pinkish-coloured plaster above adorned with paintings, cloths and triptychs all showing the same theme of justice, be it Daniel defending Susannah or Solomon deciding over the ownership of a child. He then glanced quickly at Chanson, Clerk of the Stables, now acting as court usher, sitting on a stool near the door. Outside, two burly men-at-arms, resplendent in their blue and gold scarlet livery, were ready to provide assistance.

Ranulf smiled to himself when Staunton repeated his question. 'Master Long-Face', as Ranulf secretly called Corbett, seemed oblivious to everything except the sheets of parchment before him. He wondered if he should intervene. He leaned forward, but Corbett, quick as a cat, gently tapped the table, a sign to remain silent. Ranulf rearranged his writing tray, its ink pots of red, blue and green still warm to the touch, the sharpened quills gleaming like knives ready to be grasped, the smooth creamy parchment stretched out under the weights carved in the shape of grimacing gargoyles. The inquisition would soon begin, but Corbett was determined to emphasise his authority over these two arrogant officials.

Corbett glanced up. He touched one of the two heavy candelabras, then his commission next to the crucifix, brushing this with his fingers before moving to the hilt of his sword lying with its point towards Staunton, his fingers finally resting on his seal. All these symbols of office should remind this precious pair that although they exercised the law, they were not above it. Staunton's persistent questioning and objections faded into silence.

In the yard below, a crier announced the removal of a corpse to a chapel. A voice began to bellow the 'Requiem Aeternam'. Corbett waited for silence, staring down at the parchment, lips murmuring as if reciting a prayer. Ranulf watched. He would remember all this when Fortune's wheel turned and he himself had to preside, to carry out judgement. He dreamed dreams. He fully understood the rancorous emotions that seethed through the chancery and palace: Evesham's ambition, the cunning secrecy of Boniface Ippegrave, the arrogance of Staunton and Blandeford. The chancery was a ladder, slippery and dangerous, but for the agile and keen-witted it was a passage to the highest office in the land. Ranulf, with or without Corbett's help, was determined to climb that ladder. He now understood the rules of the game. True, he was not a clerk from the halls of Oxford or Cambridge. He was a sharp, abrasive denizen from the city of the night, but so what? The only thing that mattered was the

King. Edward's will was law, and Ranulf was a King's man heart and soul.

One thing he did not understand, could not comprehend, was Corbett, a true enigma, a puzzle. Even Edward the King was baffled by old Master Longface. Ranulf could plumb the depths of Staunton's arrogance when summoned to answer questions. Blandeford was no different. The corridors of Westminster were full of clerks and judges, justices and officials just like them, all intent on pleasing the King and carrying out his will, though only those who did it successfully were noticed and rewarded. Corbett was different. Was that why Edward, with increasing frequency, took Ranulf aside to sit with him on the ale bench in the royal quarters and share a tankard or blackjack of ale? Ranulf always understood the drift of the King's words. What would happen if the King wanted something but Corbett didn't? What the King desired had the force of law. Ranulf accepted this; he just wished he could understand his master.

Corbett was a highly successful clerk, yet he was so monkish. He loved his wife deeply and refused to attend the various suppers, banquets and parties organised by the court. He was more absorbed in the liturgy and ritual of the Church, and drew strength from these, firm in his insistence that chaos must be controlled through right law and prepared to vigorously enter the most violent affrays to enforce this. He was locked in his own prayer chamber; in the world but not of it, part of the world yet distant from it. A clerk who fervently believed in the Church and the law, and that without these the world, wicked though it was, would be infinitely worse.

'We are waiting, Sir Hugh?' Staunton declared wearily.

Corbett's head came up. 'Of course you are, my lord. I too am waiting. The King is waiting, God is waiting. You are not here to parry words with me, or debate the finer points of the law, but to answer certain questions under oath.' He gestured to where Chanson sat near the door, next to him the lectern holding the Book of the Gospels. 'You have both taken the oath?'

'Of course,' Staunton and Blandeford chorused.

'Then you know the punishment for perjury?'

'Sir Hugh!'

'I am just reminding you, my lords.' Corbett sifted through the parchments and sat back in his chair, staring up at the raftered ceiling. 'Very well then, we'll go back twenty years. Both of you were chancery clerks, specialising in the affairs of the city, dealing with the Great Ones at the Guildhall?'

'Of course,' Staunton snapped. 'We still are. You know that, Sir Hugh. We hold our commissions for matters affecting the city and the rights of the King in London.'

'Very good, very good,' Corbett murmured. 'Then let's go back to the murders by the Mysterium. You knew nothing of them?'

'Of course not.'

'Did you know Boniface Ippegrave?'

'Naturally.'

'Were you his friend? Some people, including his grace, claim you were.'

'Some people are wrong, though not the King. He has now been apprised of the full facts. Ippegrave was an acquaintance, a man we liked,' Staunton shrugged, 'but nothing special. He was not, how can I put it, of our household. We did not consort with him at night. We did not sup or revel with him till the early hours.'

'No, no, I am sure you did not. So can you explain why, in his scribblings, Boniface Ippegrave should mention your names?'

'Why not?' Blandeford blurted out before Staunton could stop him. 'Why shouldn't he scribble down our names? I know what you are talking about, Sir Hugh, I have seen the same scraps of parchment.'

'You have?' Corbett leaned forward.

Blandeford looked as if he was going to bluster, but Staunton, acting the serene judge, held up a hand. 'Sir Hugh, Sir Hugh, when the Mysterium was unmasked and Boniface Ippegrave disappeared, everyone was fascinated by the details. We knew that Ippegrave's chancery pouches were being emptied and the evidence collated. Master Blandeford and I, like many others, sifted through it. You must have done the same.'

Corbett smiled, narrowing his eyes.

'I was young and tender then, Sir Hugh,' Staunton purred, 'more concerned with the business before me than with what had happened. Oh, of course I remember the rumours, the scandal. We picked at what morsels we could, but everything else was hushed, hidden away like the pyx in a tabernacle.' He pulled a face. 'As for our names being on that list, who knows. Did Ippegrave suspect us?'

'Of what?'

'God knows,' came the bland reply. 'Perhaps,' he shrugged, 'we were intended victims.'

'So, on your oath, you know nothing of those matters?'

'What his grace the King has already told you covers everything we knew.'

'Very good, very good.' Corbett wiped his mouth on the back of his hand. 'And so we move forward twenty years. My lord Staunton, Master Blandeford, you have both prospered well, waxed wealthy and powerful under the King's protection. Of course your relationship with the city has deepened and become more, how can I put it, enriched.'

'What are you implying?' Blandeford accused.

'I am implying nothing,' Corbett snapped. 'That is the situation. Walter Evesham was Chief Justice in King's Bench. You, my lord Staunton, are a judge, whilst Master Blandeford here is your senior clerk, a minor justice who one day hopes to join you in your pre-eminence – true?'

Staunton nodded, watching Corbett carefully.

'Now,' Corbett chewed the corner of his lip, 'your mandate is to keep an eye on the city merchants, the powerful ones, those the King loves to tax and often does, those with whom he clashes. What happened regarding Evesham? How did his fall begin?'

'We received information, anonymous messages, that our chief justice was no Angel of Light,' Staunton replied tersely. 'This information, so the writer claimed, came from the Land of Cockaigne, another word for nonsense, except that such testimony maintained that Evesham was hand in glove with two leading gang members: Giles Waldene and Hubert the Monk.'

'And how was this information given to you?'

'By letters delivered at Westminster, left with this clerk or that.'

'You have examples? You have brought the documents? I would like to see them.'

'Of course.' Staunton snapped his fingers, and Blandeford leaned down and picked up a small sack. He handed this to Corbett, who undid the knot at the neck and emptied the contents on to the table. The scraps of parchment were all about the same size. The vellum was of poor quality; the writing was large, in dark blue ink. Corbett sifted amongst them even as he realised they could have been written by any scribe, scribbler or clerk at the chancery. Nevertheless the information they contained was striking: allegations that on this indictment or that, Lord Walter Evesham had shown great favour to either Waldene or Hubert the Monk, members of their gangs being released without charge or trial. Corbett quickly calculated that there must be at least ten or twelve such pieces of parchment. Most contained the same kind of information, with names and dates. He organised them into a pile and, ignoring Staunton's protests, gave them over to Ranulf, who was busy transcribing Corbett's questions and the answers he received. Ranulf picked up an empty bag off the floor, put the documents in it, tied it securely and placed it in a coffer on the small table beside him. Staunton made to protest.

'Don't.' Corbett lifted a hand. 'My lord, you know the law. This is a commission of oyer and terminer. I will take whatever evidence I require.'

'You will return them?'

'When I have finished.' Corbett lifted his arms and leaned his elbows on the arms of his chair. 'Of course you received more information.' He held out a hand. 'I will have that too.'

Again Staunton nodded, and Blandeford handed over more scraps of parchment. These were different, providing the times and dates of nocturnal meetings between Walter Evesham and the two gang leaders at Evesham's mansion in Clothiers Lane. Corbett studied them sifting amongst them.

'At first we couldn't believe it,' Staunton murmured, 'but then we brought the information to the King. We organised a watch and, as you know, entered Walter Evesham's house and found him deep in conversation with the two riffler leaders. There was the question of gold that had been stolen from the mint. The King decided that Evesham, Waldene and Hubert the Monk should be committed for trial. He hoped to execute all three as a warning to the rest. Evesham threw himself on the King's mercy. He promised a full confession that would detail everything.'

'Did you get one?' asked Ranulf.

'No, Evesham's murder ended all that. However,' Staunton sighed, 'the information at least gave us the power to arrest and detain Waldene and Hubert's gangs. We thought it best to keep the leaders separate from their followers. They were all placed in Newgate and would have later gone on trial in Westminster Hall, but of course, Evesham's murder frustrated all this. His detailed confession would have been vital, but once he was dead, the King had no choice but to free the two gang leaders.' Staunton shrugged. 'Ostensibly they had done no wrong. Evesham was holding the stolen gold; there was no evidence linking them to it. They maintained the pretence that they had been summoned by Evesham to his house, and how could they refuse the King's chief justice?'

'Yes, yes, I understand all that,' Corbett waved his hand, 'but this Land of Cockaigne? Do you know its author, the spy who gave you such information?'

'Sir Hugh, if we did, we would tell you.'

'But you do have other information?' Corbett insisted. 'Waiting outside is the clerk who rejoices in the name of Lapwing as well as a string of other aliases as long as anyone's arm.' He paused as Staunton shifted uneasily in his seat.

'My lord,' Corbett sighed, 'am I to drag it out from you word for word, letter by letter? Lapwing is your man, isn't he? You are on oath.'

Staunton glanced at Blandeford, who simply stared down at his hands.

'Answer the question.' Ranulf lifted his head. 'My lord, I am waiting for your answer, an answer that is on oath.'

'There is no need to talk to me like that, clerk.'

'There's every need,' Corbett replied. 'We are not here to while away the time. I want the truth. The man known as Lapwing is a beneficed clerk. He knows Latin and Norman French. He is well dressed, courteous and educated. He is or was your spy. Yes or no?'

'Yes.'

'Then tell me about him. I want the truth.' Corbett rapped the table. 'He was caught in the company of those at St Botulph's who were tried and executed as traitors and felons, and produced a writ signed by the King saying that what the bearer of that document had done, he had done for the good of the kingdom and the welfare of the Crown. That document was witnessed by both of you. So, we have Lapwing, who is your man, yes or no?'

'I have said yes.'

'And what is his real name? What is his provenance?'

Staunton closed his eyes and sighed.

'Answer!' Ranulf demanded sharply.

The judge opened his eyes and glared at Ranulf across the table.

'I shall remember you, sir.'

'And I shall not forget you, sir. Please answer.'

'Do so,' Corbett murmured, 'for the love of God, either here, or I can have the men-at-arms outside put you in chains. We shall then go to the King's palace at Sheen, where this mummery will be repeated. Lapwing?'

'Lapwing is a clerk,' Staunton replied. 'As you know, his real name is Stephen Escolier. He was educated in the halls of Oxford. He entered the household of the Bishop of Winchester and served abroad. Last autumn, around Michaelmas, he returned to London and took lodgings in Mitre Street, where he lives with his mother. The reason he returned to London is that she is ailing and he needs to look after her. He approached me for service, for employment, a benefice, a sinecure, anything I could give him. Despite the letters from the Bishop of Winchester, I was unable to help, but then Escolier, or Lapwing as he calls himself, made me an offer. He told me that he had a secret grievance against Giles Waldene and Hubert the Monk, and offered to become a member of their coven and betray whatever he discovered. Now as you can appreciate, that was a dangerous enterprise, yet the clerk impressed me: he was razor-witted, intelligent and observant. I agreed, and Escolier became Lapwing, a wandering scholar with a ready tongue and a sharp knife. He joined Waldene's

coven and soon established a cordial relationship with that repro-
bate. Lapwing can read and write, Waldene could not, so he
was glad to acquire such a skilled and enterprising clerk. Lapwing
gave us information about what mischief was being planned and
plotted: abductions, assaults, but above all, who amongst our
so-called city fathers was hiring Waldene. I paid him well.'
Staunton spread his hands. 'You must also appreciate that he
only worked for me for a short while. Evesham's fate actually
hindered us bringing such work to a successful conclusion.' He
shrugged. 'A few more months and we'd have had enough
evidence to indict many of the gang leaders in London ten times
over.'

'But he was not your spy in the Land of Cockaigne, the one
who gave you information about how Evesham protected Waldene
and Hubert the Monk's followers.'

'No.'

'And you are certain he did not provide you with information
about their secret meetings at night?'

'No. I have asked him about that. He replied that he would
have loved to have done so but such information did not fall into
his hands.'

'But when Waldene and Hubert the Monk's followers were
arrested and lodged in Newgate, Lapwing was not taken up?'

'Of course not. He carried that small roll of parchment that
he showed you. No king's officer would have dared touch him.'

'And yet he was found with them in the graveyard of St
Botulph's.'

'Yes, he had visited Waldene in prison. When the riot broke

out, he heard about the criminals escaping to St Botulph's and went there. A keeper from Newgate recognised him near the lych-gate. Lapwing was seized and had to continue the pretence.'

'Had to?'

'Sir Hugh, he was our spy. He hoped to acquire more information about what had happened. Of course the criminals who sheltered in St Botulph's had no chance of surviving. Lapwing was arrested, but he made sure he was one of the last to be brought before you, and only then did he produce his letter. You of course had to release him.'

Corbett glanced through his sheaf of papers. 'Let me go back to Evesham. You visited him at Syon?'

'Of course we did. Evesham may have become a recluse, a hermit, a man turned to God, but the King was insistent that he should answer our questions.'

'And did he? What questions did you ask?' demanded Ranulf.

Staunton dismissed him with a flicker of his eyes and turned back to Corbett. 'We visited Syon Abbey on a number of occasions. We asked Walter Evesham about certain matters in the city, but he replied that he had become "lost in God" and had no remembrance about what had happened. He did not wish to discuss anything he'd done except confess that he had sinned against God and the King. Remember, Sir Hugh, Walter Evesham was one of us,' he glanced disdainfully at Ranulf, 'an Oxford clerk, skilled in logic and debate. He could argue with the best; in the end he told us very little.'

'Do you think his repentance was genuine?'

'Of course not! Walter Evesham may have proclaimed he was

trying to save his soul, but I suspect he was desperately trying to save his neck.'

'Do you think he intended to stay in Syon until his natural death?'

'I cannot speculate on what that viper of a man was plotting, but yes, he may have intended that.' Staunton leaned forward. 'Sir Hugh, I do not like the way you are talking to me. Am I a suspect? Do you think that I, or Master Blandeford here, have Evesham's blood on our hands?'

'Why not?' Corbett whispered. 'Why not? We are royal clerks, not God's angels. Lord Evesham was proved to be a felon. Boniface Ippegrave was proved to be a felon. It is possible that you and Master Blandeford secretly entered Syon Abbey and executed Evesham for your own mysterious purposes.'

'How dare you!' Blandeford blustered.

'Merely a hypothesis,' Corbett remarked. 'You may say not probable, but I say it's possible. You could have also, on that same evening, gone down to Queenshithe, taken Ignacio Engleat out and murdered him. Both of you are mailed clerks,' he continued quietly. 'You have fought in the King's armies in Wales and in Scotland as I have. You have killed men as I have. You could have entered the tavern of the Angel's Salutation and executed Waldene and Hubert the Monk. It is possible. You could have visited Walter Evesham's house, and decapitated Richard Fink and the Lady Clarice. All things are possible and therefore probable.'

'This is ridiculous,' Staunton protested. He made to rise, but then sat back as Ranulf also moved in his seat.

'My lord,' Corbett tapped the table, 'don't you understand?

Can't you see? We are all on trial. Walter Evesham was Chief Justice in King's Bench, yet he was an ally, a close friend, of two of the greatest rogues in the city. He twisted and perverted justice. He profited from robberies. If that happened in the green wood, what might happen in the dry? So yes, my lord, you are a suspect, as is Master Blandeford, as is everybody in this chamber. How far has such corruption spread, how deep does it reach?'

'I have told the truth,' Staunton said flatly.

'Oh my lord, I am sure you have.' Corbett smiled. 'I will go on oath that you have told me the truth, but you've not told me the full truth, and for that we may have to question you both again. Now go.' He waved a hand and returned to his papers as Staunton and Blandeford rose noisily, pushed back their chairs and, muttering amongst themselves, left the chamber.

'Sir Hugh, you have upset them.'

'Master Ranulf, I intended to. Both of them are ambitious and very ruthless men.'

'Ruthless enough to murder?'

Corbett turned to face Ranulf squarely. 'Yes, my friend, to murder. They are King's men. There's something here,' he gestured vaguely, 'something I cannot form into an idea, an emotion, a feeling, a suspicion. The King has a hand in these matters, but why, where and how I don't really know. Enough of speculation. Let's question the mysterious Lapwing.'

7

Barrator: a corrupt official

The young clerk came swaggering in. He paused just inside the chamber to place a hand on the Book of the Gospels and recite the oath, reading swiftly from the piece of parchment Chanson gave him. Then he walked forward and, without being invited, sat down on one of the chairs. He crossed his legs, playing with the ring on his finger, staring now at Ranulf then back at Corbett.

'Master Escolier, known as Lapwing,' Corbett jabbed a finger at him, 'you were lucky enough not to lose your head at St Botulph's.'

'Sir Hugh, all my life I have been fortunate. It's not the first time, and I doubt if it will be the last, that I have risked losing my head.'

'Clever-mouthed,' Ranulf declared, 'but you'll answer our questions truthfully. You've taken an oath. You can still hang or be crushed to death for perjury.'

'Have I said I won't answer? Ask your questions, whatever you wish.'

'Why did you go to the Angel's Salutation?' Corbett demanded.

'I heard the news, rumours about Giles Waldene and Hubert the Monk being murdered. Of course I wanted to know.'

'Why?'

'I hated them.'

'Ah yes, your masters Hervey Staunton and Master Blandeford claimed you had some grievance against the rifflers.'

'That's correct, Sir Hugh. Many years ago my father was a prosperous merchant, a chandler. He sold precious wax both to the city and abroad.' Lapwing spread his hands. 'What Waldene and Hubert did was simply demand that he pay them a tax, a sort of protection. My father protested. They assaulted him grievously and wrecked his shop. I never forgot.'

'And where do you live now?'

'In Mitre Street, a small house with my mother.'

'And before that?'

'I went to school at St Paul's, then on to the halls of Oxford. Afterwards I took employment with his grace the Bishop of Winchester. I served him well and long, but I had to leave because my mother is ailing. The bishop gave me letters of testimony and I returned to London. I tried to seek employment here and there, but as you know, it is difficult. I approached my lord Staunton, but he could not give me a benefice or office. I later discovered how Waldene and Hubert the Monk had waxed fat and powerful. I told Staunton that I would join their coven and betray them. I would have loved nothing better than to see both of them hang from the Elms in Smithfield.'

'And were you not afraid?' Ranulf asked. 'I mean, a clerk from the household of the Bishop of Winchester mingling with wolfsheads?'

'Master Ranulf, like you I have worn armour. I have stood in the battle line in Scotland and Gascony. The letters of his grace the Bishop of Winchester will attest to that. I am not afraid of the cut and thrust. I've seen more bloodshed in my life than others do in many lifetimes. It did not concern me. Moreover, I had grievances against both those rogues.'

'And so you joined Giles Waldene's coven. He accepted you?'

'Of course! I am literate, I can write, I can read. I represented myself as a former priest who had to flee from his benefice in Lincolnshire because of certain crimes. How I could sin with the best of them. Waldene accepted me. I sat high in his councils. What information I learnt I passed on to my lord Staunton. I just wish I'd had more time.'

'But you knew nothing of Waldene or Hubert the Monk's relationship with Walter Evesham, the chief justice?'

'I did not. I now understand there was another spy, someone who described himself as being from the Land of Cockaigne, but I knew nothing of that.'

'And the prison riot?' Corbett asked. 'You visited the coven in Newgate?'

'Yes.'

'Why?'

'I wanted to maintain the fable that I was their ally, worried about what might have happened to my friends. I told them I'd escaped the clutches of the sheriffs' men. They didn't realise I secretly carried a letter that provides me with all the protection of the Crown.'

'And when was this?'

Lapwing blinked, and his lips tightened. You're lying, Corbett thought, you are not telling the full truth.

'When was this?' Ranulf barked.

'Shortly before the riot. I continued to pose as one of them. I did not see Waldene; he was held in one of the pits. I brought wine, bread and fruit for his followers. I chattered with them, I assure you, nothing of importance.'

'And that is all?'

'I have told you, that is all.'

'So why did you join the other criminals and felons in the cemetery of St Botulph's?'

'The Chief Justice's disgrace came as a surprise to me. I hoped to learn more information that could tie Waldene and Evesham more closely together. I didn't. The following day, hearing of the riot and the consequent escape, I went down to St Botulph's. By sheer chance, a mere accident, I was recognised and taken prisoner. I maintained my pretence till I appeared before you.'

'What now, Master Clerk?' Corbett asked. 'What will you do?'

'I hope to gain from what I've achieved. Lord Staunton might well appoint me to his household or secure some other benefice for me.'

Corbett sat back in his chair.

'You know, Master Escolier, Lapwing or whatever you call yourself, I am half minded to put you in irons and send you back to Newgate.'

'Sir Hugh, why? What crime have I committed?'

'Like your masters,' Corbett replied, 'you haven't told a lie, or I don't think you have; you just haven't told me the full truth. You are far too glib, sir! The words trip off your tongue like a well-rehearsed speech, some lesson learnt by rote in the halls of Oxford. To put it bluntly, I do not trust you. I think you know more about the villainy that has occurred than you reveal. You are, by your own admission, a mailed clerk. You've served in the King's armies. It's possible that you entered the Halls of Purgatory, took Ignacio Engleat out and murdered him at Queenshithe. It's possible that you entered the grounds at Syon Abbey and executed Walter Evesham. It's possible that you entered the Angel's Salutation and slaughtered two men you nurse deep grievances against. Finally it's possible that you entered Walter Evesham's house and, for reasons known only to your-self, decapitated Clarice, our former justice's second wife, and her lover Richard Fink.'

'All things are possible, Sir Hugh, but there again, why should I? My only interest was Waldene and Hubert the Monk.'

'I don't deny that,' Corbett retorted. 'What I want to estab-lish is what role you may have had in these other horrid deaths. So, sir, you reside with your mother in Mitre Street. Well, do not go far, and wait to be summoned again.'

Lapwing left. Corbett picked up a quill and began to sharpen it with a small paper knife.

'You don't believe him, master?'

'Far too glib, pretty-tongued, sharp-witted, but one thing he cannot hide.' Corbett smiled at his companion. 'His hair.'

'Yes, master?'

'His hair,' Corbett murmured, 'dark-flamed red like that of Boniface Ippegrave.'

'Which means?'

'I don't know, Ranulf, it's something we have return to. Let's deal with the others.'

Ralph Sandewic and an old bailiff named Osbert bustled in next to take the oath. Sandewic was gruff, rushing through his words; he then had to walk back to help Osbert recite them, bellowing at the man to keep his hand on the Book of the Gospels. Once they were seated, Corbett bowed towards Sandewic. He liked the old constable. Absolutely fearless in battle; Sandewic had only one weakness: he believed that the King sat on God's right hand, so what Edward wanted could never be wrong. Nevertheless, he was honest and blunt. He could no more tell a lie than a pigeon could sing plainchant. Dressed in his half-armour, the veteran glared at Ranulf, who found it deeply amusing that the Guardian of the Tower was garbed as if expecting attack at any moment. He had even whispered to Corbett how 'The constable must go to bed armoured and his lady wife must surely protest at the sharp chain mail and the spurs on his boots.' This morning, however, Ranulf kept his head down and his face impassive, and when he did have to grin, he brought up a hand to hide his mouth. Corbett decided to move matters swiftly.

'I am asking you a great favour, Master Constable: go back twenty years to the arrest of Boniface Ippegrave. Were you there?'

'No I wasn't, but Osbert was. He was a bailiff in Cripplegate ward and was taken up in the posse organised by Walter Evesham to go across to a certain tavern in Southwark.' Sandewic turned and poked Osbert in the chest. 'Well, tell them, you're on oath, tell them what happened.'

Corbett, however, was still distracted. He was not satisfied with the answers he'd received from Staunton or Lapwing. He held up a hand for silence.

'Chanson,' he called, 'hasten now. Go out after Staunton, Blandeford and the creature who calls himself Lapwing. Tell them I am not finished with them. I have further questions; they are to return here and wait.'

Chanson leapt to his feet and left, slamming the door behind him so hard that Osbert startled in alarm. Corbett smiled at the bailiff.

'Now, sir, you still hold office?'

'No, I'm well past my sixtieth year. I can't run or chase villains as I used to.'

'Twenty years ago,' Corbett said quietly, 'you were part of a comitatus, a posse,' he explained, 'summoned by Walter Evesham, who later became Chief Justice in the Court of King's Bench. You remember it?'

'Oh yes, sir, I was a bailiff in Cripplegate ward. We had to muster outside St Botulph's Church and Evesham joined us there. Some of us went by barge and others followed him across London Bridge. We were told to assemble outside a tavern.' He screwed his eyes up. 'The Liber Albus, that's what it was called. It was a bright summer morning, very quiet. Evesham and his henchman, an arrogant clerk . . .'

'Engleat?'

'Yes, sir, that's right, Engleat. They went into the tavern. We heard shouts and cries. Engleat came out and summoned us in. The taproom was fairly deserted. You know Southwark, sir, it only comes alive at night. The clerk Boniface Ippegrave was there. He looked startled. In a window-seat enclosure sat a prosperous-looking merchant. Evesham had confronted both men.'

'Can you recall precisely what happened?' Corbett pleaded. 'It's very important.'

'Yes, sir, I was at the front. Ippegrave had surrendered his sword and so had the merchant. Evesham asked the merchant what he was doing in a Southwark tavern. The man was beside himself with fright; he was trembling, face pale as a ghost. He kept plucking at his cloak and looking towards the door. He could give no honest explanation.'

'And the clerk Boniface?'

'He produced a piece of parchment and handed it over. Evesham read it. If I remember rightly, it was simply a message that if Ippegrave came to the Liber Albus tavern in Southwark at a certain hour, it would be of great profit to both himself and the King.'

Corbett nodded; he'd seen such a scrap in the archives of the Secret Seal.

'Then what?'

'Both Boniface and the merchant were searched. Apart from that note and some coins, nothing else was found on the clerk, but the merchant carried a heavy purse of gold. I remember Evesham weighing it in his hand. He declared that both men were under arrest and they were to accompany him to Newgate. I think it was Newgate.'

'Not to Westminster?' Corbett asked.

'No, sir, it was definitely to Newgate, or the Fleet. I am sure it was Newgate. So we left.'

'Did Evesham bind his prisoners?' Ranulf asked.

'I offered to do that, but Boniface objected and so did the merchant. They maintained that whatever they were being accused of, they had not been indicted. Evesham accepted this; after all, he had a heavy guard. Some of my companions went back by barge, and the rest followed Evesham and Engleat across London Bridge. We ringed the two prisoners.'

'How did they behave?'

'Both men were crestfallen, rather frightened; they no longer protested. The merchant glared at Boniface but he seemed locked in his own thoughts. We left the bridge and made our way along Thames Street and up towards St Paul's. As we reached Milk Street, neither prisoner offering resistance, the crowd surged around us, and that is when it happened. Boniface appeared to slip, going down on one knee.'

'Who was next to him?'

'I don't know, sir. At one time he and Evesham were walking by themselves. Anyway, there was confusion. You know what it's like, we bailiffs are not liked. There were catcalls, some refuse thrown. Apprentices darted in trying to sell things. There were beggars, cunning men, street prowlers, pimps and their whores, people who revel in a commotion. As I said, Boniface went down on one knee as if he'd slipped, and suddenly he was gone, fast as a whippet. He snaked through the line of bailiffs into the crowd, and you can imagine what happened.'

Corbett nodded. People always felt sorry for a prisoner, hence escape was common.

'The hue and cry were raised.' Osbert paused.

'Continue,' Corbett demanded.

'Well, we cried, "Harrow! Harrow!" and tried to pursue, but of course our path was blocked. Boniface was a fairly young man, swift on his feet. He went down an alleyway and disappeared. We followed and caught sight of him. He was fleeing across St Botulph's cemetery, then he entered the church.' Osbert shrugged. 'We knew the law. We didn't want to be excommunicated. A man who has taken sanctuary has taken sanctuary. Our job was finished.'

'And Evesham?'

'He organised the pursuit. When Boniface reached St Botulph's he was beside himself with rage. He tongue-lashed us for being incompetent, cursed us and said he wished he'd bound both captives.'

'And the merchant?' Ranulf asked.

'Oh, he tried to escape in the confusion, but he was seized, bound and safely lodged in Newgate.'

'And at St Botulph's?' asked Corbett. 'What happened there, apart from Evesham cursing and shouting?'

'He told us not to disperse but to guard the four doors, the main one, the corpse door, the Galilee porch on the north side and the sacristy door. We examined the windows in both the tower and the church itself; these were too narrow for any man to push himself through. We thought this was an ordinary case of sanctuary. The fugitive would stay there for forty days then either flee, give himself up or agree to be taken to the nearest port and sent to foreign parts, if he survived the walk.' The old man ran a finger around his mouth and smacked his lips.

Corbett whispered to Ranulf, who rose, filled a wine cup and handed it over. Osbert smiled, raised it in a toast and took a deep gulp.

'Evesham?'

'Evesham and Engleat were like men possessed, and only then did we realise that the fugitive was such an important prisoner. The two of them went into the church. By then the priest had appeared, and he made it very clear that Boniface Ippegrave had taken sanctuary and that whilst he remained in the church, Evesham and Engleat must do nothing about it. Then . . .' Osbert turned and gestured at Sandewic, who snatched the wine cup from the former bailiff and finished the wine, smacking his lips and grinning at Corbett before taking up the story.

'I was at the Tower. I received a message from Evesham that an important prisoner had fled for sanctuary, so I brought guards, some soldiers and archers as well as a few market beadles I collected on the way. Sir Hugh, we ringed that church. A mouse couldn't leave. All four doors were carefully guarded. We even got ladders and put people on the roof. We inspected the tower, whilst the priest assured us that no secret passageway, crypt or cellar existed.'

'And who approached the church?'

'I think you know, Sir Hugh.'

'Boniface's sister?'

'But she was refused entry,' Sandewic replied.

'Anyone else?'

'Your two colleagues, Lord Staunton and Master Blandeford.'

By the sly grin on Sandewic's face, Corbett could see that the constable had no love for either of them.

'They also wanted to see Boniface, but Evesham was hot and choleric. He said it was none of their business and no one could see the prisoner. Apart from Evesham and Engleat, the only person allowed in was Parson Tunstall, who brought food or took out the jakes pot to be emptied. No one else entered. On the morning of the third day, Evesham followed the priest into the church, and they found that Boniface had disappeared. And to answer your next question, Sir Hugh, I don't know how, when or why. I've never seen the likes before, a man vanishing off the face of God's earth.'

'You're sure each door was guarded?'

'Sir Hugh, the cemetery of St Botulph's thronged with armed men. Evesham had sent letters to the King; by then royal men-at-arms and hobelars had joined us.'

'It's a sprawling cemetery, isn't it?' Corbett mused. He paused as Chanson slipped back through the door, nodded and sat down on his stool.

'Yes, it is, but I repeat, no one left that church.' Sandewic turned and watched Ranulf's sharpened quill pen skimming across the creamy surface of the vellum.

'Master Osbert,' Corbett smiled, 'I am very grateful for your attention to these matters. Is there anything else you can remember that might help solve this mystery?'

The old man shook his head.

'Tell me, Sir Ralph,' Corbett continued, 'after the recent affray in Newgate, the escaped prisoners took refuge at St Botulph's. Why did they choose that church?'

The constable blew his lips out. 'Sir Hugh, I don't know. One of the reasons people take sanctuary there is that it is strong as a castle. There are no secret entrances and it is well fortified and easy to defend, as we found to our cost.'

Corbett agreed and thanked both Sandewic and Osbert. He waited until the door closed behind them and then banged the table in exasperation.

'Chanson,' he raised his voice, 'tell Lord Staunton, Master Blandeford and Lapwing I want words with them.'

A short while later all three entered. Staunton, gathering his cloak about him, brimmed with rage at being summoned back. Corbett ignored this, not even offering them a chair.

'Sir Hugh, I thought we were finished?'

'My lord, I am not finished. When I am finished I will tell you. I have now established,' Corbett pointed at Lapwing, 'that this clerk works for you, yes?'

Staunton nodded. Corbett glanced quickly at Lapwing, who stood confident and poised. Could he be a killer with his own private grievances? wondered Corbett.

'Sir Hugh, what do you want with us?' Staunton asked.

'This is what I want,' Corbett retorted. 'Tell me about the night you surprised Evesham with Waldene and Hubert the Monk.'

'As I said, we kept Lord Evesham's house under close scrutiny. Waldene and the Monk were seen to enter. We simply watched and waited for another occasion when they entered, and then we followed.'

'Were you admitted?'

'No we forced the door. Master Blandeford drew his sword and demanded a servant take us immediately to Lord Walter. He did so. We found him in his chancery room with Waldene and the other rogue.'

'And what happened then?'

'Lord Evesham blustered and flustered, but there was little he could do. He was caught red-handed. The gold he held was stolen. He could not explain its presence there. Naturally he had no choice but to deny that the two rifflers had brought it.'

'You say you caught him in his chancery room.' Corbett rose to his feet. 'And what happened then? The two riffler leaders were taken to Newgate – yes?'

Staunton, eyes watchful, nodded.

'And Lord Walter?'

'He was confined to his house until the King was informed, then he'd be taken to where his grace wished.'

'So you left him there?'

'Yes.'

'His papers, his manuscripts, his household books, his secret memoranda, didn't you seize them?' Corbett glanced quickly at Blandeford, who swallowed nervously and refused to meet his gaze. Lapwing stood half smiling to himself. 'Well?' Corbett turned back to Staunton. 'My lord, you had just arrested a Chief Justice of King's Bench. He was consorting with well-known outlaws and wolfsheads. I can understand that he'd be confined to his own house under a strong guard, but surely the documents and memoranda, everything in that chamber, could have been of use to you? Why didn't you seize them?'

'We tried to, later.'

'But not immediately?'

'No, Sir Hugh, we did not.'

'And what happened to all those documents and memoranda?

Don't tell me! Lord Evesham had a fireplace in his chancery room, not to mention braziers, and when you returned, everything had been burnt, yes?'

Staunton nodded. Corbett breathed out noisily.

'Did you tell Evesham to burn all his manuscripts, his papers? An act of kindness by one judge to another? Or did the King himself give you such a commission? After all, the less scandal, the better.'

Staunton shrugged. 'I cannot answer for the King, Sir Hugh, you must ask him yourself. We made a mistake, we thought it would be safe, and yes, when we returned, Evesham had burnt his manuscripts.'

'You told the King?'

'Of course. His grace simply said that it was a mistake. Evesham was still finished, his career destroyed. We had all the evidence we needed.'

Corbett nodded and walked over to Lapwing. 'And you, sir?' He tapped him on the chest. 'You visited Newgate just before the riot broke out. Did you tell Waldene's followers that Hubert the Monk might turn King's evidence, or vice versa?'

Lapwing held Corbett's gaze. 'I've told the truth. I acted a part, nothing else.'

'And when they did escape, those violent, desperate men, who told them to go to St Botulph's?'

'I don't know. Perhaps they could have answered that. However, Sir Hugh, you put them on trial and dispatched them to execution. I cannot answer for what their evil wits or nasty souls plotted. I've told the truth.'

'Have you?' Corbett declared. 'Have you really? I don't think any of you gentlemen have told the truth. You may not have told a lie, but . . .' He turned away, waving his hand in dismissal. 'I may summon you again.' He walked back behind the table. Even as Chanson ushered Staunton and the rest through the door, he could hear the justice's protests and complaints. He slouched back in his chair.

'There's nothing, is there, master?' Ranulf whispered, leaning over. 'Nothing at all.'

'Oh yes there is. Let's question Brother Cuthbert and Adelicia.'

'Together?' Ranulf demanded.

'Oh yes, together.'

Brother Cuthbert, garbed in his black Benedictine robe, shuffled in, Adelicia behind him. Corbett was immediately struck by how tall, purposeful and energetic the woman was. She was dressed in a dark blue gown like that of a nun, a veil about her head, her face almost hidden by the gleaming white coif beneath. She was graceful in all her movements. She smiled, bowed at Corbett and took her seat, helping Brother Cuthbert into his. The former parson of St Botulph's sat down with a sigh, head slightly back, staring at Corbett from under heavy-lidded eyes.

'You've taken the oath,' Corbett began gently, 'and now I want you to tell me the truth.'

'But we have,' Adelicia murmured. 'We have spoken the truth. Sir Hugh, I have something else to tell you. Last night, or rather in the early hours of this morning, I was disturbed by a stranger who tapped on the shutters of my anker house.' As she swiftly told Corbett what had happened, Ranulf's pen raced across the surface of the parchment, taking down in his own neat cipher everything she said.

'Do you think it was your brother?' Corbett asked.

'Sir Hugh.' Adelicia brought her hands from beneath the folds of her gown, stretched across and put the jasper-stone ring on the table. 'He gave me that. Last time I saw that ring was when I gave it to Evesham, who promised to hand it to my brother.'

'And did he?' Corbett asked.

'Yes, he did,' declared Brother Cuthbert. 'I brought Boniface's food. On one occasion I found him examining that ring. He'd slipped it on to his finger. Sir Hugh, it must have been him; Boniface Ippegrave must have escaped. Now he's returned to wreak vengeance.'

'One thing at a time . . .' Corbett paused at the tolling of a bell. He felt a slight thrill of excitement. Nothing was embedded in rock. Many of the stories he'd heard were lies, a twisting of the truth. Perhaps it was time to shake the edifice to reveal the sham.

'Brother Cuthbert, on the night Evesham died, you would have us believe that everything was calm and serene, harmonious as ever.'

'As well as it could be,' Brother Cuthbert half joked.

'Apparently, when you retired, Evesham was in his cell, its door closed and barred both inside and out. Ogadon your guard dog was resting at his post. Then a macabre miracle occurred. Someone managed to go through either a locked door or a barred shutter, then down the steps of that chapel. He or she did not disturb you, but persuaded Evesham to open the door of his chamber. The assassin followed Evesham in, cut his throat and left just as silently and mysteriously locking the door behind him.' Corbett rested his elbows on the table. 'Brother Cuthbert, Mistress Adelicia, you are good-hearted people, the evidence will support that. Nonetheless, if you think I believe such a fabulous story, then you insult me. It's impossible.'

Adelicia glanced quickly at Brother Cuthbert, who just shook his head and stared down, fiddling with the cord of his robe.

'I don't believe you,' Corbett declared, then paused because Ranulf, in his surprise, had dropped his quill. He busily picked up another, sharpening its point with a puzzled look at his master.

'I believe you two love each other,' Corbett continued softly. 'You always have, you always will. Brother Cuthbert, when you were parson at St Botulph's, you and Adelicia became hand-fast friends, two hearts united, two souls one. In other circumstances, in another place at another time, you would have become man and wife.' He smiled sadly. 'I understand that. There's nothing in Scripture that says a priest cannot fall in love with a woman. Evesham shattered all that, didn't he? He hounded Adelicia's brother into oblivion, then he tortured both of you, not with pincers or hot irons but with allegations and accusations. I do wonder if in your hearts, both of you regard what happened at St Botulph's twenty years ago as punishment for what you thought was an unchaste attraction.'

'We were never lovers,' Brother Cuthbert retorted, staring full at Corbett. 'You have the truth. I have taken an oath. I am a celibate priest. I met Adelicia and we fell deeply in love. God knows what might have happened, though God knows what actually did.

You're correct, Master Clerk. Evesham shattered our lives. I truly believed it was God's punishment on me.'

'I argued against that,' declared Adelicia. 'I said it wasn't possible. On reflection,' she smiled thinly, colouring with embarrassment, 'I know what you are thinking, clerk: just another priest with his leman, his mistress. We were never that. Nevertheless we loved each other as passionately as any man does his wife, or wife her husband.'

'So,' Corbett continued, 'Brother Cuthbert, you left St Botulph's and became a recluse at Syon Abbey. Adelicia, of course, after Boniface's disappearance, decided that she had no choice but to follow. I would say before God that you've lived chaste lives, but as the years passed, I am sure that you often met under the cover of night, deep in those woods. Perhaps you'd take a flagon of wine, goblets. In cold weather a muffler with hot coals. You'd sit and talk about what was and what might have been, true?'

Cuthbert nodded.

'And then,' Corbett declared, 'Evesham arrived at Syon Abbey; Satan re-entered your lives. The man who had wrecked everything was now your closest neighbour. Your midnight trysts occurred more often. On the night Evesham was murdered, you, Brother Cuthbert, left the death chapel and went to meet the only woman you have ever loved.'

Cuthbert put his face in his hands and began to sob quietly. Adelicia leaned over and caressed him on the shoulder, just a light touch yet it told Corbett everything.

'What did happen?' Ranulf asked sharply.

'I left the chapel.' Cuthbert lifted his tear-stained face. 'I took a small wineskin, two cups. Adelicia was to bring some coals to warm our fingers. I wore a heavy cloak and cowl, mittens on my hands. There's a log in the forest where we used to sit and stare up. We could study the night sky. You're right, clerk, we used to talk about the past, about God's will, about this and that, everything under the moon. On the night in question when I came back I found Ogadon fast asleep. I could tell by the way he was lying that he'd been fed some meat laced with a sleeping potion. I crossed the chapel and went down the steps. Evesham's door was open; his body lay sprawled over his desk, blood everywhere. I never touched anything; I simply closed the door. I did not wish to alarm Adelicia, so I didn't tell her what had happened until later.'

'How did you lower the bar on the inside?'

'Oh, simple enough. There's a grille high in the wood. Those rods in the passageway? I simply threaded one through and pushed the bar down; the rest was as you found it. How did you know?'

'Logic,' Corbett replied. 'How could anyone get past a guard dog, never disturb you, persuade Evesham to open his door, murder him then bar the door from the inside and leave without being noticed? Oh yes, it's a puzzle that fascinated me, but there again, before you become locked in a mystery you look for the obvious way out, and that was the only solution. But you see,' Corbett moved in the chair, 'what I must consider is another possibility. On that night, Brother Cuthbert, did you invite Mistress Adelicia down to the cellars beneath that chapel and both of you murder a man who, by your own admission, had shattered your lives?'

'Never!'

Corbett glanced sharply at Adelicia.

'Never!' she repeated, yet she refused to hold his gaze.

'Tell me, Brother,' Corbett toyed with the manuscripts lying before him, 'on your oath now. Did Evesham ever confess anything to you that might explain his own death or the events of twenty years ago?'

'On that, Sir Hugh, I have told the truth. I hardly spoke to him; he rarely spoke to me. I could not stand the man's stink, his stare, his touch. If I had my way I would have driven him from the abbey.'

'And Adelicia, did you at any time approach Evesham and question him?'

'No.' This time her tone was more precise. 'I would never approach such a man. Sir Hugh, we did not murder him.'

'You say that.' Ranulf spoke up. 'Brother Cuthbert, your fingers are pained with the rheums, yet you secured that door sure enough.'

'Oh, it was painful,' declared Cuthbert. 'But I was so startled to find Evesham dead, all I wanted to do was close that door, seal it off and present it as a mystery. Of course I realised people might think that I had murdered him, but there was no proof, no evidence, and don't forget, clerk,' he tapped the side of his head, 'up here I know I am innocent. I did not carry out what I would have loved to have done.'

'Surely,' Adelicia declared, 'if we, or one of us, murdered Evesham, are we not therefore responsible for the other dreadful deaths? Engleat, the two riffler leaders executed in a London tavern, the disgusting murders of Mistress Clarice and her steward Richard Fink? Oh yes, clerk, we've heard the rumours! The good brothers of the abbey are full of the chatter from the city. They may live the lives of monks, but they take a deep interest in the affairs of the world.'

'To be blunt, mistress,' Corbett smiled, 'I watched you come into this room. You are not old, you're strong, it's possible you could have committed those murders or assisted someone else to do them. I will ask both of you again: is there anything you can tell me, on oath, that would help my investigation?'

They replied that there was not.

'And you, Mistress Adelicia. This midnight conversation with a stranger claiming to be your brother, Boniface. He questioned you about a certain Beatrice; do you know who she was?'

'No.'

'Did your brother ever mention a woman called Beatrice?'

'Never.'

Corbett sat back in his chair. 'In which case, I thank you. You may return to the abbey, where, if I need to, I will visit you again. One final question.' He picked up a piece of parchment. 'Boniface Ippegrave wrote a riddle at the back of the Book of the Gospels in St Botulph's: "I stand in the centre guiltless and point to the four corners"; you gave that to Mistress Adelicia?'

'Yes.'

'Do either of you know what he meant?'

Both chorused: 'No.'

Too swift, too glib, Corbett thought, but he lifted his hand. 'You may go. I wish you a safe journey.'

8

Ribaudaille: camp-followers, the dispossessed

'How did you . . .'? asked Ranulf as the door closed behind them.

'Logic, Ranulf.' Corbett chewed the corner of his lip. 'It's the only feasible answer. If two people really love each other and live in such close proximity, they will meet, and only death will stop that. I suspect they see each other quite regularly – oh, nothing wrong, like two children sitting whispering in the dark.' He paused. 'They've not told me the full truth. Oh no, Brother Cuthbert is far too curt. He watches me intently. He dreads a certain question, but for the life of me I don't know what. Well,' he called, 'Chanson, bring in Parson John and Master Fleschner.'

The two men entered the room, swore the oath and took their seats. Parson John had shaved his face, though the bruises and marks still looked angry and there were dark rings around his eyes. Both men looked calmer, more composed than the day before, though the priest remained agitated, moving on the seat, playing with the folds of his robe. Master Fleschner on the other hand seemed half asleep. Corbett wondered if he had taken a deep-bowled goblet of wine to help him through the questioning.

'I thank you for coming here,' Corbett began. 'Both of you have sworn the oath. You must realise how important this is and what penalties perjury carries. I know that you witnessed yesterday heinous and gruesome sins, but with your help I can solve these mysteries and bring the malefactor to justice. Now, Master Fleschner, I understand you are parish clerk at St Botulph's and have been—'

'For at least twenty-five years. I was also coroner in the ward, though I gave that up about ten years ago. I became tired of viewing corpses, gashed and garrotted, their heads caved in, limbs missing, dragged from the river or some rubbish heap covered in slime. There is more to life than death.'

'Did you know Boniface Ippegrave?'

'No, I didn't. I had nothing to do with the affray of twenty years ago. I was busy elsewhere.'

'But you knew the parish priest, now Brother Cuthbert, a recluse in Syon Abbey?'

'Of course.'

'And his friendship with Mistress Adelicia?'

'I heard rumours, but that was tavern gossip, market chatter. I cannot help you with anything on that.'

Corbett stared hard at this peevish-faced man with his wispy moustache and beard. He was undoubtedly timid, yet he was too quick for one so nervous.

'And the affray at St Botulph's when the malefactors broke out of Newgate?'

'Again, Sir Hugh, I know nothing of that. You summoned me to take down the proceedings of their trial in the church; what I know, you know.'

'Tell me, Master Fleschner.' Ranulf spoke up, putting down his pen. 'Are you aware of any secret entrance to or from St Botulph's church? After all, you are the parish clerk.'

'No. If there is one it is very secret and very well concealed. I was born and raised in Cripplegate. I know of no secret passageway.'

'And the attack on Parson John?'

'I've told you what happened. Parson John asked me to meet him around the third hour after the sext bell. He told me he would leave the corpse door off the latch. I approached St Botulph's. I heard a sound and went in. I saw a shadow come darting into the sanctuary, then it disappeared back into the sacristy. I heard a groan. I went across, entered the sacristy and found Parson John bound, though he'd broken free of the gag. I helped free him.'

'On the same night Lord Evesham was murdered,' Corbett continued, 'Ignacio Engleat his clerk was barbarously slain at Queenshithe. Where were you, Master Fleschner?'

'At home with my lady wife like any good citizen should be.' Fleschner tugged at his robe. 'Why, Sir Hugh, do you think I'm an assassin, a man like me?'

'And where were you,' Corbett insisted, 'yesterday around midday, when Giles Waldene and Hubert the Monk were executed in the Angel's Salutation?'

Fleschner closed his eyes and leaned back slightly. 'I was busy on my own affairs. I was in Cheapside looking at the stalls.'

'Do you have witnesses to that?' Ranulf barked. 'Witnesses who could swear to it?'

'Of course not, of course not,' Fleschner flustered.

'Perhaps earlier in the day?' Ranulf insisted. 'When Mistress Clarice and Richard Fink were so cruelly slain at their house in Clothiers Lane.'

'This is preposterous, ridiculous! I'm no assassin. I could no more wield an axe—'

'Who said it was an axe?'

'It must have been.' Fleschner threw his hands out. 'It must have been an axe to sever their heads.'

Corbett noticed how flushed the clerk's face had become. He decided to leave him and turn to Parson John, who now sat like a man half asleep, just staring at the wall above Corbett's head as if fascinated by the tapestry depicting Christ in judgement on the Last Day.

'Parson John, tell me about yourself.'

'You know who I am, Sir Hugh. I am the not so illustrious son of the very illustrious Lord Walter Evesham, once Chief Justice in the Court of King's Bench. My mother died when I was three or four years of age, an accident in the street, I don't know.' He continued without a pause. 'You are going to ask me about my father. The honest truth is, Sir Hugh,' he stared hard at the clerk, 'I didn't know my father. He was always busy with this or that. I knew nothing about his affairs. I was a disappointment to him. He wanted me to become a knight banneret at the King's court. I was sent to school at St Paul's. I studied logic and theology in the halls of Cambridge and then I was sent to be a squire in the Bigod household in Norfolk. The old earl blithely informed my father that I could no more hold a sword than a frog could fly. I told my father, when he confronted me, that I did not wish to be a liveried killer. I wanted to be a priest. Of course, my father, with all his influence, secured that. I finished my studies, this time in the schools at Oxford, and was ordained by the Bishop of London. I served as a curate in parishes south of the river, and then my father, because he was a great lord and a figure of authority in Cripplegate, obtained my appointment as Parson of St Botulph's. Again, I must make it very clear: I did not know my father.'

'Did you know his second wife, Clarice?'

'She was a kind, pretty, flirtatious woman. I was never close to her nor she to me. As I said, I spent most of my life away from the family home. Father didn't object and neither did I. Sir Hugh, I know nothing of the affray involving Boniface Ippegrave that took place twenty years ago. I was not in Cripplegate but in Norfolk, and as for the rioters who broke out of Newgate, you saw what happened. They attacked my church, they killed my parishioners. They turned God's house into a slaughter shed.' He paused.

Corbett sat back in his chair. He'd fought in Wales and Scotland and he recognised that Parson John appeared fey-witted with shock. He sat slightly twisted, reciting his words as if by rote.

'As for where I was and what I was doing,' the priest blurted out, 'when all these horrid murders took place, I was in the priest's house preparing for the next day.'

'And yesterday?'

'The same. Master Fleschner here will bear witness. I planned to meet him in the afternoon to draw up inventories of our church goods. Sir Hugh, God knows I would love to assist, but I cannot.'

'And now?' Ranulf asked. 'I mean, St Botulph's lies under

interdict. The Mass cannot be offered there, prayers cannot be said, and the church is closed.'

'Why, clerk, I will follow Brother Cuthbert and petition Abbot Serlo to allow me to shelter at Syon. Not to become a recluse, just to think, pray and wait until this storm blows over and peace and harmony have returned.' He got to his feet. 'Sir Hugh, if you have more questions I'll answer them, but the afternoon is drawing on and the evening will soon be here. I have things to do. I do not wish to stay in the priest's house for much longer. Is Master Fleschner free to return with me? You know where I will be.'

Corbett nodded. 'Very good, Father, for the time being we have finished.'

He watched both men leave. Chanson closed the door behind them, then looked expectantly at his master.

'Sir Hugh, will there be any more?' Chanson, although his great love was for horses, liked nothing better than to sit and watch his master twist and turn after his quarry; as he'd remarked to Ranulf, it was better than watching a hawk on the wing.

Corbett pushed back his chair and rose to his feet. He waited until Ranulf finished writing, then walked to one of the small windows, pulled back the shutters and stared out. The light was fading; bells and horns were sounding.

'What do we do now, Sir Hugh? Who else is there to question?'

Corbett gazed into the gathering darkness. 'Who else is there?' He spoke as if to himself. 'Waldene and Hubert the Monk are dead. Mistress Clarice and her lover Richard Fink lie next to them in the corpse house. Evesham's papers are either hidden in the

King's secret coffers or have been destroyed by fire. Tell me, Ranulf, of all the people named in this hideous tale, whom have we overlooked?'

'The merchant Chauntoys,' Ranulf replied. 'The one whom Boniface met at the Liber Albus in Southwark.'

'You heard the King: Chauntoys has long gone to God.'

'But he may have married again.'

Corbett turned and smiled. 'Very good, Ranulf. Seek out any family. Discover if there is anyone who could perhaps add a little more to this twisted tale. And now . . .' He returned to his chair and picked up his cloak. 'I'll try to meditate on what I have listened to and what I have learnt. Perhaps I'll walk across to the abbey and join the good brothers for vespers. Afterwards we'll meet back here, take our supper and weave together all the different strands we've plucked.'

'Stomach worms gnaw at me,' Chanson wailed. 'I'm hungry!'

'We could go to one of the taverns,' Ranulf offered. 'There's the Catch a Penny, or the Gate Hangs Well. Or I could,' he joked, 'get bachelor's fare.'

'Which is?' Corbett asked.

'Bread, cheese and kippers from a slattern.'

Corbett pulled a face. 'No, the palace kitchens will serve a good platter. The King is returning from Sheen, where he's been hunting, so the cooks will be well prepared.' He clasped Chanson's shoulder. 'Calm the wolf in your belly, we'll feed it soon enough.'

'And you, master?' Ranulf asked.

'As I said, I will join the good brothers at their vespers. You'll come?'

Chanson pulled a face and nursed his stomach. Ranulf gestured at the parchment still strewn across the table.

'In which case . . .' Corbett smiled and left them.

The antechamber was cold, the brazier full of spent ash. Servants had snuffed the candles, and only one cresset flame danced in the chilly breeze. Corbett went along the ancient wood-lined gallery to his own chancery office, where he sifted amongst documents received: sealed pouches and parcels containing reports, letters, memoranda and billae from spies, merchants, wandering scholars, friars, envoys at foreign courts, agents in Paris, Rome and Bruges, all forwarding the chatter of the various courts. Pulling the candelabra closer, he went swiftly through them. When he had finished, he snuffed the candle. There was nothing of note, nothing that could not wait. He rose, left the chamber and went down into a small garden enclosure. The light was fading fast but a wheeled brazier crackled beside a turf seat near a reed-ringed pond all calm under its skin of ice. Corbett sat down and pulled his cloak about him. The incense strewn over the charcoal fragranced the air. He relaxed, loosened his sword-belt and stared up at the sky. The stars were so clear and glittering. Words, images and memories from the recent questioning seethed through his mind; the various faces, gestures and mannerisms. What had he missed? What could he pursue? He was still perplexed. Certain mysteries, such as how Evesham had been so cunningly murdered, had been resolved, but that created other problems. Was Cuthbert the killer? Was Adelicia his accomplice? They certainly had good reason to cut the former chief justice's throat.

Corbett got to his feet, tightened his sword-belt and re-entered the palace. Lost in his own thoughts, he wandered the galleries, passing through a vestibule where he noticed a group of the knight bannerets from the royal household in their resplendent livery. They clustered around one of the King's jesters, a dwarf who was entertaining them with a droll story about a maiden, a knight and a certain chastity belt. The dwarf, a born mimic, played the various roles, provoking guffaws of laughter from these royal bully-boys, 'knighted rifflers' as Corbett secretly called them, killers who loved nothing better than the clash of battle and the song of the sword. He left the palace grounds and crossed the great waste area that separated the royal house from the abbey, its towers, buttresses and cornices soaring up like a majestic hymn in stone against the evening sky. Bells sounded, their clanging trailing away, an early warning to the brothers that vespers would soon begin.

Corbett became more alert. He was about to enter the Sanctuary, a different world to the opulence of the court and the hallowed atmosphere of the abbey. Smells drifted. The odour of wood smoke, crackling charcoal and roasting meats mingled with the stench of sweat and ordure, all the stinks of the citizens of the night. Campfires glowed. Dark shapes darted about. Donkeys brayed over the clucking of chickens and the harsh cry of geese. A sow lumbered by chased by two ragged children. Corbett threw back his cloak and, hand resting on the hilt of his sword, crossed the small footbridge spanning a narrow ditch. He went through the half-broken gate of the palisade and entered the Sanctuary proper, an eerie underworld, a man-made Hades for those who lived in the twilight, well away from the glare of the law. Rifflers and robbers, prowlers of the night, cheats and cunning men,

outlaws and wolfsheads, murderers and assassins, pimps and prostitutes of every kind, all sheltered here. The Sanctuary was supposedly holy ground that, by tradition and law, was well beyond the
power of courts, the sheriffs and their bailiffs. In truth it was a
place of permanent dusk where, as one preacher described it,
'unholy lusts' had free play.

All around Corbett stretched the makeshift huts, bothies and
fires of the Brotherhood of the Cowl. Weasel faces glared up at
him. Ladybirds from their nagging houses, strumpets and whores
sauntered up dressed in their tawdry finery, hips swaying, hair
and faces garishly painted. Corbett strolled on. Ranulf constantly
warned him about walking so carelessly through what he termed
the hog-grabbers, piss prophets and toad-eaters who sheltered
here. Corbett did not care. Most of these children of the dark
were hen-hearted, fearful of a royal clerk. Why should they accost
him and so give the King, his sheriffs and justices good reason to
sweep through this meadow of misery with fire and sword? More
importantly, Corbett had spread the word through Ranulf and
Chanson that anyone who brought him information about the
recent riot at Newgate and all the horrid deaths in the city would
be amply rewarded. He wondered if he'd be approached.

He passed a group of gamblers taking wages on how many
would hang tomorrow, execution morning, on the gibbet outside
the great abbey gate. A man dressed garishly as a woman swept
by in a cloud of cheap perfume, face all hideous in its coating of
paste. This grotesque provoked jeers, laughter and curses from
the gamblers, before they lost interest and returned to their game.
Deep in the camp, two hellcat women were preparing to fight,

stripped to their under-tunics, pennies gripped in their hands to stop them scratching. They circled each other close to a roaring bonfire. When Corbett entered the pool of light, the raucous shouting ebbed away and a few curses were flung.

Corbett passed safely on up the slight incline and across the monks' cemetery, which stretched to the south door of the abbey. A lay brother allowed him in and he walked through the small porch, glancing quickly at the human skin nailed to the door leading into the chapter house. He crossed himself and murmured a prayer, wishing fervently that the King would listen to his plea and that of the good brothers that the skin be taken down. It belonged to Richard Puddlicott, a felon recently taken in a wheelbarrow to the abbey scaffold and hanged for robbing, with the help of certain monks, the royal treasure stored in the great crypt beneath the chapter house. The King had insisted that Puddlicott's corpse be flayed and this grisly symbol of royal anger hang there as a warning until it rotted.

'It frightens me,' whispered the lay brother standing behind Corbett. 'They say his ghost prowls here along with all the other dark men.'

Corbett turned and smiled at him.

'But angels also tread here, yes, Brother?' He carried on, turning right into the cloisters, where a group of novices stood gapemouthed around one of the high desks illumined by glowing candles. The ancient scribe perched on his writing stool was relaying the horrors of hell as described in the legend of St Brendan, which he was busily transcribing. In a voice powerful but sepulchral the old monk described how across the river of death swirled a wind stinking of bitumen, sulphur and pitch, mingled with the stench of roasting human flesh. On the shores of hell clustered woods where the only trees were tall poppies and deadly nightshade from the branches of which hung a host of bats. The ground beneath bristled with swords and stakes whilst over these flew birds fierce as flaming firebrands. Corbett, who'd paused to listen, wondered about those souls whose cadavers he'd recently inspected – were they journeying through such a living nightmare?

He passed on into the great soaring nave. Torches, candles and lanterns glowed to make it a place of creeping shadows through which peered the carved and painted faces of the holy, the ugly and the demonic. He approached the sanctuary, where the majestic oaken choir stalls gleamed in the glow of freshly lit candles. Each tongue of flame shimmered in the precious cloths, jewels and ornaments that decorated the royal tombs either side of the high altar. The air was fragrant with perfumed incense smoke, the eerie silence broken by the shuffling of sandalled feet as two long lines of black-cowled monks filed into the stalls. It was too late for Corbett to join them, so instead he squatted just within the rood screen and watched the drama unfold. The monks took their positions in the stalls, psalters at the ready; the lector and cantor went to their places. A small handbell was rung and vespers began with its usual impassioned plea: 'Oh God, come to our aid. Oh Lord, make haste to help us.'

Corbett closed his eyes. He needed such help if he was to clear the cloying murk gathering around him and bring to justice a most sinister killer.

*   *   *

In the chamber of oyer and terminer, Ranulf still sat at the chancery desk sifting amongst the papers. Chanson had wandered off. Ranulf paused as the royal choir, gathered in the small chapel below, rehearsed a song for some banquet or feast. He listened intently to the words:

> My song is in sighing,
> My soul in longing,
> Till I see thee my King,
> So fair in thy shining.

He glanced up as the door abruptly opened and Edward the King slipped in. Ranulf made to rise, but the King gestured at him to sit. Wrapped in a heavy military cloak, spurs jingling on his hunting boots, Edward strode across and sat in Corbett's chair, turning slightly to stare at Ranulf, the amber-flecked eyes in his dark leathery face scrutinising the clerk as if searching his soul. The King's iron-grey hair was all a-tangle, though the greying moustache and beard were neatly clipped. He smelled of rosewater, sweat and leather. Ranulf made to speak, but the King held up a hand for silence as he waited for a certain line of the choir's song: 'I want nothing but only thee.' Then he let his hand drop, grinned and leaned a little closer.

'Do you, Ranulf-atte-Newgate, Clerk in the Chancery of Green Wax, desire nothing but the King's will?'

'If it go not against God's law or my conscience.' Ranulf quoted Corbett's common axiom.

'You learn well, Ranulf.' The King pointed to the stack of parchment. 'And this business, tell me now . . .'

Ranulf did so, swiftly listing what had happened, and empha-
sising Corbett's questions about the murderous mysteries
confronting them. Edward listened intently, saying nothing, though
now and again he would glance swiftly around as if fearful of an
eavesdropper. Once Ranulf was finished, the king slouched in his
chair, eyes half closed.

'I was hunting today,' he remarked, 'out on the moorlands north
of Sheen. Good weather for it, Ranulf. I flew Roncesvalles, my
favourite peregrine. Sickly he was, or so I think, wouldn't listen
to my voice. I've had a wax image of him sent to Becket's shrine
in Canterbury. Our martyred archbishop was a keen falconer;
he'll help. I'll make an offering.' Edward turned in a creak of
leather to face Ranulf. 'A king's hawk is swift and dangerous. It
can see and do what the King cannot, but,' he picked at his teeth,
'it is still a royal hawk. It brings down the quail and the herring
not for itself but for the King, remember that! This business . . .'
He rose to his feet. 'I want no public clamour, Ranulf; the least
said, the soonest mended.' He grinned. 'Yes, Waldene and Hubert
the Monk are dead. Good, that's how I like it! All dispatched to
be judged by God, clean and quiet. I prefer to hang people by
the purse rather than the neck; remember that as well. Do not
forget,' he leaned down and pressed a finger against the clerk's
lips, 'the King's will is paramount.'

'You'll say the same to Sir Hugh, your grace?'

'No, Ranulf, I said it just for you. You do understand?'

'Yes, your grace.'

'Good.' For a moment Edward's eyes turned sad. 'I can't say
that to Hugh. God knows, Ranulf, he's a better man than you,

and as the Lord is my witness, certainly a better one than I.' And spinning on his heel, the King left as quietly as he'd entered.

In the darkened abbey, Corbett was becoming restless. The words of the psalm echoed powerful and sombre.

> Lions surround me,
> Greedy for human prey,
> Their teeth like spears and barbs.
> Their tongues like sharpened swords.

He blessed himself, got to his feet and left, hurrying back along the cloisters. He could not understand his own anxiety; he knew only that he was restless, impatient to make some progress in the mysteries confronting him. He left the abbey, following the winding path through the monks' cemetery and into the Sanctuary, where he strolled purposefully, sword and dagger drawn, the glint of the steel sending the creatures of the night scuttling out of his path. He'd almost reached the far gate when he heard his name called. He whirled round, lifting sword and dagger up as a figure stepped out of the gloom.

'I mean no ill, Sir Hugh. I heard your proclamation.' The voice was low, almost cultured.

Corbett moved forward.

'I'll not talk to you here, sir. You'd best follow me.' The Sanctuary man seemed reluctant.

'Don't worry.' Corbett smiled through the darkness. 'You have my word as Keeper of the King's Secret Seal that no harm will befall you. If we can do business then we shall; if not, you will be allowed to return safely here. The choice is yours. Follow me.'

He led the way into the vestibule of the palace, where he turned and surveyed the wolfshead who had followed him. The man was of moderate height, with lank, greasy hair, face pitted with scars, beard and moustache stained with food. His clothing, a cote-hardie, leggings and boots, was scuffed and dirty, his fingernails thick with black, though the eyes he rubbed were sharp and alert. Corbett sat on a stone bench just within the door and indicated for the stranger to join him.

'What's your name?'

The man remained standing.

'You may sit down,' Corbett declared.

The man sighed and did so. Corbett tried to ignore the offensive smell.

'They call me Mouseman.'

'Why?'

'Because there is not a door, chest or coffer I cannot enter. I was baptised Edmund Arrowsmith at the font of the abbey church in St Albans.'

'And now you're utlegatum,' Corbett declared, 'beyond the law. Yes? Picking locks when you shouldn't have done?'

'Only one,' Mouseman retorted in clipped tones. 'I worked at the Abbey at St Albans. The prior owed me money. He refused to pay.'

'So you went back in the dead of night, opened the coffer and paid yourself.'

'In a word, lord, yes.' Mouseman's eyes crinkled in amusement.

'But I was a skilled tradesman, I served my apprenticeship. I had a wife and family.'

'How long ago did this happen?'

'Oh, at least two summers. Sometimes I went back, but on one occasion I was nearly caught, so never again. The Prior of St Albans would love to hang me from his gibbet.'

'Have you been tried before the King's justices?'

'They haven't caught me yet, lord.'

'So what do you want now?'

'A full pardon, some money, a belly full of food and permission to return to St Albans and live in peace.'

'So pleads everyone who lives in Sanctuary,' Corbett joked. 'How can you earn it?'

'Lord, I drifted into London. I became involved in this mischief and that. Eventually I joined the coven of Hubert the Monk. He needed a locksmith like me. Parish coffers wait to be riffled. I had no choice. Hubert said that if I didn't work for him, he'd hand me over to the sheriff's men. So it was either steal or be hanged for stealing. I chose the former.'

Corbett stared hard. There was something about the man's voice, his steady gaze, the certainty with which he held himself that reassured the clerk. Edmund Arrowsmith, also known as the Mouseman, was good-hearted, a desperate man eager to break free from the trap in which he found himself.

'Just tell me then,' Corbett said quietly. 'I may not give you a pardon, yet you'll have coin enough to buy a full belly of food. No lies, though.'

'I heard about your offer to anybody who could provide

information about the riot at Newgate or the deaths of Waldene and Hubert the Monk. Oh yes, we heard about them in Sanctuary – there's been some rejoicing. Waldene and the Monk were feared, not liked. They were bully-boys, well protected by . . . well, how can I put it . . .?'

'Lord Evesham?'

'And others. The city sheriffs often took bribes to look the other way.'

'And you are going to claim to be the innocent in all this.'

'My lord, I never said that. I've done my share of mischief but I was rounded up with the rest.'

'How did that happen?'

'Well, when Waldene and Hubert the Monk were arrested, the sheriffs decided to make a full sweep. It's easy enough to catch us. We assemble at various taverns or inns, and of course, rewards and bribes were offered.'

Corbett quietly agreed that was the way of the world. Once a gang-leader fell, his followers were vulnerable to capture or betrayal.

'So we all ended up in Newgate.' Mouseman stretched out his legs, knocking the broken heel of one of his boots against a paving stone. 'We weren't given much to eat or drink. Waldene and Hubert were moved from the Common Side and put in the pits; a living death, lord?'

'Certainly.'

'Very few survive,' Mouseman continued. 'You're usually dead of gaol fever within a week, a month at the very most. Now, on the morning before the riot took place, rumours swept the gaol that Waldene was going to be pardoned and that it would be extended to his followers on condition they turned King's Approver.'

'You mean they would all turn King's Approver?'

'Yes, lord. They'd go in front of the justices, take an oath, and where possible convict Hubert the Monk and his followers. We would all have ended up dancing from the gibbet outside Westminster or at the Elms. Feelings began to run high. I don't know how, but weapons were found, knives and clubs. We were marshalled in just before the noonday bell to receive our food, the usual slops and platter of dirt, and that's when the riot began. We found doors unlocked and burst through into the great yard. A postern gate was prised open. We fled into the city, but,' Mouseman held his hand up, 'there was also a whisper, a rumour, that we should all assemble at St Botulph's Cripplegate.'

'Why that church?'

'We were told it had a secret passageway that would take us out of the city and away from the sheriff's men. They said—'

'Who's they?'

'The people who passed the rumours. They claimed it would give us at least a day's start ahead of the bailiffs.'

'Why didn't you go there?'

'Lord, I may be an outlaw but I'm no fool. My companions were bloodthirsty men. I knew it would end violently.'

'There was something else, wasn't there?'

'Yes, my lord. The escape seemed so well planned. I'd been a member of the Monk's coven for at least a year. I'd heard of riots at Newgate, prisoners escaping, but that one? So many were involved, and the way clubs and knives appeared, the ease whereby doors and gates were forced . . . I suspected a trap. Moreover, once we broke free, Waldene and Hubert's men began to attack citizens, fresh crimes that would certainly not go unpunished. I decided it was best to slip away. I fled to Sanctuary here at Westminster, and since then no one has troubled me.'

Corbett leaned back against the stone and stared up at a gargoyle's face, a monkey with devil's horns; next to it was a jester, bauble and stick in one hand, eyes protuberant, lips parted in a carved stone grin. Mouseman's news confirmed his own suspicions. Waldene and Hubert the Monk had been moved to the pits to die and then their followers had been deliberately agitated. Somehow or other they were given weapons and easy passage out, as well as false information that a secret passageway from St Botulph's would take them to freedom. Or was it false?

'Well, my lord, what have I earned?'

'Mouseman, you are well named. There's many a door you can enter, and you've just entered by the most narrow one.' Corbett patted the man on the shoulder. 'Welcome to the light.' He opened his purse, and took out a silver coin and a wax cast of his seal. 'For your comfort,' he advised. 'Tomorrow, around the bell for sext, present yourself at the Chancery Chamber of the Green Wax, give your full name, show them the seal and ask for Ranulf-atte-Newgate.'

'I've heard of him.'

'He will prepare the necessary letters. Then, Edmund Arrowsmith, also known as Mouseman, I suggest you visit a barber. Have your head and face shaved, buy some new clothes and, once your pardon is sealed, go back to St Albans and live in peace.' He patted the outlaw on the shoulder and, with his thanks ringing in his ears, escorted him out of the palace back down the path to the Sanctuary. Mouseman was about to step out of the light when he turned abruptly.

'Evesham?' he called out. 'The judge who proved to be a bigger sinner than all of us?'

'What about him?'

'We heard of his death. According to rumour, Waldene and Hubert the Monk were deeply troubled.'

'Why is that?' Corbett followed him into the night air.

'Apparently they had been comrades of Evesham for many a year and a day. People said it was time all three of them fell, that's all,' and Mouseman disappeared into the darkness.

9

Lyam hound: a bloodhound

Corbett hurried back up the stairs and along the gallery to the oyer and terminer chamber, where Chanson was sitting just within the door gnawing a piece of bread filched from the kitchens. He chewed the crust like some angry dog. Ranulf was laughing at him while sorting out the manuscripts on the table. He immediately told Corbett about the King's visit. Corbett stood chewing the corner of his lip, studying Ranulf intently. His comrade nourished burning ambitions, which Edward was always eager to exploit.

'Is that all, Ranulf?' he asked.

'Why yes, Sir Hugh. The King seemed in good humour,' Ranulf replied evasively. 'Why do you ask?'

'And there was never anyone more given to double-dealing than he,' Corbett murmured.

'Master?'

'Oh, just a line from Scripture about one of Israel's kings. Now, the Mouseman . . .' Corbett swiftly told them what he'd learnt, impressing upon Ranulf that when the Mouseman appeared at the Chancery of the Green Wax the following day, he was to be given every help and assistance. Ranulf assured him that he would be. Corbett then sent Chanson down to the kitchen with his seal, asking the cooks to provide them with what he called 'a feast for the King's good servants'. A short while later Chanson returned with two servants trailing behind him bearing trays carrying pots of hot quail covered in a spicy sauce, dishes of vegetables, small white rolls in napkins to keep them warm, pots of butter and a flagon of the best claret with three goblets. Ranulf had cleared the chancery table, pulling back the leather cover, and Corbett ushered Chanson to his seat, saying that it was time they feasted like princes. They ate and drank in silence. Now and again Ranulf would ask a question about what the Mouseman had said, but Corbett just shrugged and said that they would have to wait and see if his information fitted with the rest. Corbett ate and drank slowly. The more he'd reflected during his time in the abbey, the more he believed the roots of this mystery lay with Evesham and the events of twenty years ago. Yet where should he begin to dig? How could he delve deep and unmask an evil that had lain dormant for decades until abruptly manifesting itself in horrid murder?

Once they'd finished their supper, Chanson offered to take the platters and goblets down to the kitchen. Knowing that the groom wanted to sit and gossip with the other clerks of the kitchen and stable, Corbett let him go. Then he and Ranulf washed their hands at the lavarium and prepared the chancery table. Ranulf sat in Corbett's chair, whilst Sir Hugh walked up and down trying to marshal his thoughts.

'The beginning . . .' He paused. 'What do we have here, Ranulf? The *Mysterium Rei* – the Mystery of the Thing. It's well named.

Over twenty years ago a murderer prowled London, a professional assassin who carried out crimes on behalf of the rich and powerful. The Mysterium would remove undesirables, individuals the Great Ones wanted dead: a business rival, or a wife who'd served her purpose. He seemed to enjoy his work. He didn't just kill silently, he left his own message. Why such revelling in heinous sin?'

Ranulf paused in his writing and lifted his head. 'You're saying he could have worked more secretly?'

'Instead he had to boast, to proclaim. I detect a relish, a deep pleasure in what he did, a pride in his bloody handiwork. Most murderers kill stealthily; the Mysterium was arrogant, openly baiting judges, sheriffs and the Crown itself. According to what we know, Burnell the old chancellor hired an ambitious clerk, Walter Evesham, with his faithful lieutenant Ignacio Engleat, to trap the Mysterium. Evesham dedicated all his energies to the task. He must have studied the killer very closely. We now know how the Mysterium worked, but at the time, Evesham didn't. What he did was watch and wait, sitting like some spider in the chancery listening for news from the city. One day he was fortunate. A merchant's wife was murdered. The Mysterium left his taunting message, and although merchant Chauntoys might be suspected, he could go on oath that when his wife was killed he was elsewhere. Evesham's logic was brilliantly simple. He waited for that merchant to return to London and brought him under close scrutiny. For a while Chauntoys acted the role of the grieving widower, but one day, like a fox hidden in the brambles, he decided to break cover. He went to the Liber Albus in Southwark, Evesham followed and lo and behold, in the same tavern, he found the clerk Boniface Ippegrave.'

'Why was Evesham,' Ranulf interrupted 'and therefore Chancellor Burnell, so trusting in his belief that the Mysterium was a chancery clerk?'

'You heard the King, Ranulf; the chancery receives all kinds of gossip: who hates whom, rivalries, animosities, husband and wife at each other's throats.'

'True, master, but so does the Guildhall and its clerks. Why was Evesham so insistent that the Mysterium must be a chancery clerk?'

Corbett paused in his pacing. 'You are right,' he conceded. 'Clerks in the Guildhall also hear the gossip of the city, but that will have to wait. To return to what actually happened. Evesham arrests both Boniface and Chauntoys. The merchant acts guilty; he cannot really explain why he is there. More importantly, he is carrying a heavy purse of gold, an amount he would not take to a Southwark tavern unless he truly had to. Above all he holds a scrap of parchment informing him where to leave that gold. Chauntoys blusters but his guilt is obvious. Boniface, however, carries only a message that could have been scrawled by anyone, saying how his presence in that particular tavern at that hour would be for the greater profit of both himself and the King.

'Evesham believes he has been successful. He has taken a comitatus with him. Some bailiffs return by barge across the river, others escort Chauntoys and Boniface over London Bridge and up towards Newgate. Now we don't know exactly what happened. Boniface is simply under arrest; he has not been indicted, and also because he is a clerk, he is not chained or bound. He escapes and flees to St Botulph's, where he claims sanctuary.'

'Is St Botulph's the nearest church?' Ranulf asked.

'I don't think so, but Boniface knew the church and its parson; perhaps he thought he'd be safer there. You heard Sandewic: St Botulph's is a secure place. Anyway, Evesham is beside himself with rage. He surrounds that church, allows no one to enter except himself, Engleat and the priest. Others visit, Staunton and Blandeford, but they are turned away. Adelicia also approaches. Evesham demands some token of recognition. Adelicia hands over her mother's ring, which, according to Cuthbert, Evesham definitely gave to Boniface, because he saw him studying it. Sandewic at the Tower has been alerted, and St Botulph's, its four doors in particular, is circled in a ring of steel. Nonetheless, on the third morning, when Evesham and Parson Tunstall enter, Boniface has vanished and hasn't been seen since, either alive or dead.'

'Could Mouseman be correct about a secret passageway?' Ranulf asked, pausing as Chanson came back through the door. The clerk of the stables slumped down on a stool, crossed his arms and promptly fell asleep. Ranulf grinned and winked at his master.

'Such a rumour would certainly solve the problem,' Corbett conceded, 'but according to what we know, I doubt if there is any such passageway. What we do know is that Evesham was furious. He berated Parson Cuthbert and Adelicia, but they could not help. Brother Cuthbert, a broken man, retires as a recluse to Syon Abbey. A short while later, Adelicia, distraught by what has happened, takes the veil as an anchorite to pray for justice.'

'And Boniface?'

'He protests his innocence from the moment of capture to that enigmatic message he left in the Book of the Gospels at St Botulph's: "I stand in the centre guiltless and point to the four corners." Nevertheless,' Corbett continued, 'whatever his excuse, he was found in that Southwark tavern. Now he may well have escaped; he may have returned. He allegedly visited his sister Adelicia and gave her their mother's ring. However, if he has truly returned, he has now changed his plea to guilty.'

'Do you think he was?' Ranulf glanced up.

'Well,' Corbett sighed, 'there was the gold, and those scraps of evidence found in his chancery chamber. The old clerk Rastall, who was no one's fool, detected nothing left there to incriminate him. The great hoarding at St Paul's? How did Boniface learn about that? Evesham only discovered the method the Mysterium used when Chauntoys confessed in return for his life, so that is most damning. Then there's the crude map of London showing where some of the murders took place.'

'That still does not make him the Mysterium,' Ranulf declared.

'True,' Corbett admitted, 'but there are those other lists of names, Staunton and Blandeford, and that final scrap of parchment with the name of a woman, Emma, followed by Odo Furnival, Stephen Bassetlawe, William Rescales. Who were those? I also wonder what the enigmatic "B" and "M" means, or that square containing the first nine letters of the alphabet. Scraps,' he murmured, 'from twenty years ago.' He sat down on a stool. 'Let's go back to Adelicia's mysterious midnight visitor. Was it Boniface? And why the interest in the woman Beatrice; her name has never appeared before.' He shook his head. 'The mysteries of twenty years ago, like those of the present, are impenetrable. I am anxious, Ranulf. Is this one mystery we may just have to leave?'

Ranulf smiled. 'We have not yet finished. Let's continue.'

'True,' Corbett agreed. 'So, item – Evesham: why was he in unholy alliance with Waldene and Hubert? For God's sake, a chief justice of King's Bench. And who betrayed him? Who was this writer from the Land of Cockaigne?'

'The clerk Lapwing?'

'Lapwing was definitely Staunton's spy, but he openly admits he had no knowledge of Cockaigne. We will return to Lapwing later; let's concentrate on Evesham. He is disgraced and resigns from his offices. The King allows him to destroy all his records – a great tragedy; those manuscripts might have helped us. Our noble judge then leaves his house, his pretty wife, faithless though she was, his status and wealth, to hide in Syon Abbey as a hermit. He chooses a place close to two people whose lives he has destroyed, Cuthbert and Adelicia.' Corbett paused.

'Item – what really happened in the Chapel of St Lazarus at Syon Abbey? We know that Cuthbert and Adelicia met secretly. The murderer must also have known this, but how? Once Brother Cuthbert was occupied elsewhere, the assassin went down into that cell. Evesham did not resist but allowed him in; he must have done. The assassin kills Evesham and leaves. Only later does Cuthbert, whatever he told us, with the help of Adelicia, cover up the crime by posing another mystery, which, they hoped, couldn't be solved. Our assassin, however, is still determined. On the same evening he deals out gruesome death to Ignacio Engleat, and then disappears for a while.' Corbett took a drink from his goblet, swirling the wine around his mouth. In front of him flickered the shadow of his quarry. He loved being in pursuit of an assassin, and despite all his anxieties was determined to catch him.

'Master?'

'Item – the Newgate riot. What was really being planned? Waldene and Hubert were lowered into the pits, a living death. Who agitated their followers with the rumour that some of them were about to turn King's evidence? Who supplied them with weapons? Who fed them the lie that if they fled to St Botulph's, they'd find safety through a secret passage out of that church?'

'Master, there still might be one.'

'I doubt it,' Corbett retorted. 'And so we move on. Item – who killed Waldene and Hubert? Why? Why were Evesham's widow Clarice and her steward Richard Fink so barbarously murdered? Why did the assassin leave their heads in the baptismal bowl at St Botulph's? And why the attack on Parson John?'

'Because he was Evesham's son; the same reason Clarice and Fink were killed,' Ranulf observed. 'Whilst Waldene and Hubert were his allies.'

'True, true.' Corbett nodded. 'And so we move to other conundrums. Is Boniface Ippegrave really alive and bent on murderous slaughter? If not, who has assumed his name and identity. Brother Cuthbert? Parson John?'

'Look at Cuthbert's hands,' Ranulf pointed out. 'Could he hold a knife? Parson John is as timid as a rabbit pursued by a fox. He was bound and gagged at St Botulph's.'

'What about Staunton and Blandeford? Their names pepper this story,' continued Corbett. 'They run like a refrain through this murderous tale. They are mentioned in Boniface's lists; they were clerks who dealt with the city. Staunton, now a judge, negotiates directly with the Great Ones at the Guildhall. They were the officials who received the information to indict Evesham. Nor must we forget their creature Lapwing, our wandering clerk who has returned to London to look after his ageing, ailing mother. He offered his services to our worthy colleagues to spy on Waldene and Hubert.' Corbett watched Ranulf's pen flicker over the surface of the manuscript. 'Round and round,' he murmured, 'and there's the other matter, the King's great interest in this. Ranulf, what does it all mean? Where can we look? Evesham's personal records have been destroyed. I suspect that any found in the chancery are not worth a pot of bird seed. Strange . . .' Corbett paused. 'So little evidence has remained. In the chancery there's Evesham's full, self-congratulatory report but little else. The most interesting evidence is what was actually found in Boniface's coffer, which was kept and preserved because of the thoroughness of old Rastall. Apart from that, both Evesham and his papers have been removed for ever. We cannot question his widow or her steward, whilst I doubt the other servants know very much. Cuthbert acts very warily; he remains a closed book, which, at this moment in time, I cannot open. Parson John may tell us something. Adelicia may have a few more items or scraps about Boniface,' he added. 'But we don't really know if Boniface is alive or dead. Someone may have just assumed his name. Are any of the people we've mentioned the murderer, or has one of them hired a professional killer? I am not even sure about his grace the King and his role in these matters.'

'You could go to Newgate,' Ranulf offered. 'You could question the keeper.'

'I doubt it, Ranulf. I suspect what happened at Newgate is now well hidden.'

'What do you mean, master?'

'I have a suspicion, deep in my heart, that the riot at Newgate was what the King wanted.'

'Master, you have no proof!'

'I have admitted that, Ranulf. What if Waldene and Hubert had died in the pit, of gaol fever, as hundreds do every year? What if their gangs were destroyed by royal archers?'

'But they were.'

'Precisely, Ranulf. We destroyed both covens, we executed them, but Evesham's death meant there was no case against Waldene and Hubert. The King couldn't very well bring them to trial, which he didn't really want to for fear of further scandal, nor could he detain that precious pair without trial and so create more public furore. He had to release them. He could not prove they had done any wrong with Evesham, whilst they were certainly not involved in the riot. This, in turn, begs another question. What if some royal executioner was responsible for what happened in the Angel's Salutation?'

'You're saying the King is involved in murder?'

'I know Edward.' Corbett ran a finger around the rim of his goblet. 'A prince devoted to the law but one who wishes to keep things silent, hidden. Ah well.' He drummed his hands on the tabletop. 'Ranulf, stay in the chancery and go back through the records. Look for anything you can discover on Evesham,

Blandeford, Staunton, Hubert the Monk, Waldene — it may be laborious, but,' he pointed to the now snoring Chanson, 'he can help. First of all find out about Chauntoys, the merchant arrested with Boniface in the Southwark tavern. Perhaps he left a widow. She may be able to help. In the meantime I will wait for a mistake. All murderers are arrogant, proud as Satan. They invariably do something that betrays them, the Judas kiss of their own malevolence, a mistake, an error that traps them.'

'And you hope our assassin will do this?'

'Yes I do, Ranulf. There are three paths to follow here. First, what happened twenty years ago. Second, the recent deaths of Evesham and Engleat. Both murders are understandable in the sense that both scoundrels must have made enemies. What I cannot understand, and this is our third path, are the deaths of Waldene and Hubert, Clarice and Richard Fink.'

'What do you mean?'

'Were those four people killed to silence them, as an act of revenge, or both? Remember, Ranulf, the assassin took great pains and dangerous risks in executing them.' Corbett paused, narrowing his eyes. 'True, I might regret this, but I wish he would strike again, make a mistake, something we can seize on, something out of the ordinary, a possible key to all these mysteries. Finally there is the question that keeps nagging my mind, gnawing away at my heart, one that would take us back to the very beginning.'

'Which is, master?'

'For the sake of argument, what if Boniface Ippegrave was completely and utterly innocent?'

'I can follow your logic,' Ranulf conceded ruefully. 'But if Boniface wasn't the Mysterium, who was? Who is?'

'I've no evidence, no proof, nothing at all,' Corbett murmured, 'but something tells me to start there. I want to see things the way Boniface Ippegrave may have seen them. Perhaps that's the best way forward . . .'

Miles Fleschner, Clerk of St Botulph's, left the priest house of his parish church and hurried through the narrow, dark, emptying streets. He paused at a tavern, the Scarlet Wyvern, and hurriedly drank a tankard of strong ale and wolfed down a platter of bread and cheese. All replete and refreshed, he then unsheathed his dagger and hurried out into the night-bound street. A river mist curled and trailed along the narrow alleys and lanes leading down to the Thames, but Fleschner was comfortable enough. The taverns were still busy, their half-opened doors and shutters allowing out shafts of light. Now and again he'd catch glimpses of the merry, boisterous life within. A tavern master stood beside a leather tank of live fish positioned near the entrance so that customers could choose one for their own dish. On the floor nearby a slattern placed a trancher smeared with bird lime, a lighted candle in the middle, to attract and kill flies and other insects. On the hook of the door hung garments belonging to customers who still owed monies for drinks, waiting to be redeemed. The slattern glanced up and smiled; Fleschner nodded in acknowledgement and hurried on. In truth, he thought, he should be sheltering in such a warm tavern, or, better still, be back in his own narrow house in Cripplegate, toasting his toes before a roaring fire and savouring the odours of cooked goose, yet he had to do this. He must return to Westminster, seek out that royal clerk and confess everything. It was best that way. He had been in turmoil ever since Evesham's death. Old sins had been dragged up, ancient doors unlocked, dark memories stirred. Evil deeds were waiting to be purged, confessed and atoned for. Fleschner was determined on that.

The parish clerk reached the narrow approaches to Thames Street. A hog-caller was blocking the way; loud and angry, he was shouting abuse at a singing clerk, who was desperately trying to organise his small choir outside a tavern. A group of mourners had also become involved in the tumult as they tried to negotiate a path for a corpse sewn in its deerskin shroud and laid out on a long, two-wheeled funeral cart. Despite the turmoil, Fleschner found the dancing torchlight, the shouts, the very presence of these people comforting. He slipped by them down a needle-thin runnel, holding out his dagger, a warning to any night-walker lurking in the recesses of the walls soaring up on either side. He also watched the ground underfoot, pitted and rutted, strewn with every kind of filth, which exuded a rancid smell despite the scattering of saltpetre.

He safely reached Thames Street and sighed in relief. Dung carts were still out clearing the heaps of dirty offal over which cats and rats fought, whilst kites and other scavenger birds floated above them, sinister shadows in the fading light. Fleschner was aware of the hot sweat drying on him. He'd done well. He'd overcome his fears. He had taken Parson John back to the deserted priest house, putting the anguished man to bed, giving him a cup of wine laced with the opiate the priest had brought from a cupboard. He had left him on his cot bed in that narrow chamber muttering about sin and the devil, and had then made a decision about his own doubts and suspicions, the anxieties he nourished. Corbett would surely listen to him.

Fleschner glanced along Thames Street. People moved, flitting shapes in the poor light. He was nearly there. He'd get to the river steps at Queenshithe, hire a barge and make his way up to Westminster. Night or not, he'd seek Corbett out like a penitent would a shriving priest and confess all. He crossed Thames Street and hastened down another runnel. It was then he heard a sound behind him and made to turn, but it was too late. A crashing blow to his head sent him spinning to the ground.

When he awoke, Fleschner throbbed with pain. He was bruised and cold and he realised that some time had passed. Blood trickled down his face. He tried to speak but he couldn't. It was as if his tongue was clipped by a brooch. He went to move his hands but they were bound, his ankles too. He blinked. Again a trickle of blood snaked down his nose; the cut on his forehead was very sore. He startled and gagged as a rat slithered across his legs and disappeared into the darkness, and the full horror of what was happening swept through him. He recalled Parson John bound and gagged, the bloody cut to his forehead. That 'M' was already inscribed on his own skin. A shape moved out of the darkness.

'Please,' Fleschner pleaded, 'for the love of God.'

'Too late,' hissed a voice. 'Too little, too late. Vengeance has come, Master Fleschner, tribulation time!'

His captor gripped him by the back of his cloak, and he was dragged further down the runnel and forced up on to a barrel

187

against the wall, where a noose was looped around his neck. He realised with horror that the other end was slung over an iron bracket high on the wall. He screamed as the barrel was kicked from beneath him, and jerked and struggled frantically, but the noose tightened swiftly around his throat.

When at last Fleschner's body stopped twitching and trembling, his murderer, who had watched fascinated, pinned a scrap of parchment to the dead man's cloak and disappeared into the night.

Hugh Corbett knelt beside Fleschner's corpse, drew his dagger and sawed at the noose still tight around the dead man's throat. The coarse rope had squeezed tight, scoring the skin. The mottled face was hideously covered with a light frost, which caught the sheer horror of violent death. Corbett closed his eyes, crossed himself and murmured the requiem. He felt sorry for this poor, fussy man, seized in the dead of night and executed like some common felon. He gazed up at the iron bracket from which a length of rough oiled cordage still dangled.

'What a place to die,' he murmured. He stared along the filthy alleyway running down to the river-soaked quayside of Queenshithe. It was still early in the morning; a mist curled, the light remained a dull grey. A short distance away a group of women huddled around Fleschner's widow, who was sobbing uncontrollably. Corbett could hear their words of comfort. He glanced up at the bailiff, face almost hidden by the cowl of his heavy cloak.

'This is all you found?' he asked.

'Yes, sir, doing my morning watch. Usually very quiet, nothing but cats, rats and the occasional drunken sailor with his whore. At first I thought my eyes were deceiving me. I just saw him, cloak fluttering, body swaying in the river breeze, so I came over.'

Corbett tried to ignore Fleschner's horrid face. He unpinned the scrap of parchment and stared at those words scrawled in blue-green ink: *Mysterium Rei – the Mystery of the Thing*. He put this into his wallet, then rose and walked across to the group of women. They were a desolate sight, wrapped in heavy cloaks, hoods protecting their pallid faces against the biting river wind. They were all comforting Mistress Fleschner, a plain-faced woman, her red-rimmed eyes still full of shock at her husband's sudden, brutal death. Corbett grasped her gloved hand. When he introduced himself and offered his condolences, Mistress Fleschner abruptly withdrew her hand.

'Sir, royal clerks have never brought me or mine good fortune.'

'Mistress, I am sorry to hear that. What do you mean?'

'Evesham.' She spat the word out. 'Master Miles has never been the same since he visited our home.'

'When was this?'

Mistress Fleschner swallowed hard, dabbing her eyes. 'Years ago, when Evesham's villainy was green and fresh. He visited us often. No, sir, I don't know why. Master Miles never said. I tried to discover but he remained tight-lipped, so why should I worry? Soon afterwards he resigned his office as coroner. I was pleased; no more sitting over corpses dragged from the river or horribly murdered. He could spend more time with me. He was happy to be parish clerk at St Botulph's. I thought that was where he was last night. I know he was with Parson John. He must have comforted and looked after him. I thought he would come straight home afterwards or send me a message, but oh no, and now . . .' She burst into tears and crept back amongst the other women.

Corbett bowed and walked over to where the bailiff, now joined by his companions, was organising the removal of the corpse. He stared at the pitiful remains of Miles Fleschner being bundled on to a makeshift stretcher and covered with a piece of rough sacking. The chatter amongst the bailiffs was that Fleschner had been murdered by footpads who'd decided to mock their victim by hanging him from the iron bracket. Corbett knew different, but why? What had Fleschner to do with the other deaths? He glanced back to where Mistress Fleschner was still being fussed by the other women. They would accompany her husband's remains to the corpse house of the nearest church. He glanced beyond them at the mist boiling over the river. Queenshithe was coming to life. Figures trailed here and there, the odd shout, the rattle of a wheelbarrow, the clatter of a cart. The city would soon be wakening. He heard a sob and glanced pitifully at Mistress Fleschner as she knelt and placed her hands on the covered corpse of her husband. He recalled her words. Had Fleschner been killed not because of any connection with St Botulph's but because he was once coroner in Cripplegate? Was that the reason? Had the assassin made a mistake at last?

Corbett studied the bailiffs and chose the youngest, a bright lad. He drew him away from the rest and handed over a seal cast and a coin, then gripped the young man by his shoulder.

'Your name?'

'John, sir, John-atte-Somerhill.'

'Well, John-atte-Somerhill,' Corbett smiled, 'I want you to memorise this.' He pressed the bailiff's hand. 'Take a wherry to Westminster. Show this seal to any guard or bailiff who tries to stop you. Ask for Ranulf-atte-Newgate, Clerk in the Chancery of the Green Wax.' He made the bailiff repeat the name and title. 'You'll find him busy already. Show him the seal and ask him to go to the archives at the Guildhall. He is to ask for all the coroner rolls from when Master Miles Fleschner was coroner in Cripplegate. Do you understand that?' He made the young man repeat it, and once he was satisfied, let him go.

Corbett made his farewells of the rest and walked back up the lane towards Cheapside. The previous evening Ranulf had scoured the chancery records and discovered that the widow of the merchant arrested with Boniface in Southwark still lived in a splendid mansion in Milk Street off Cheapside. She must know something. Although hungry and unshaven, Corbett felt almost elated. Fleschner's murder, he reasoned, was another move forward across this murderous chessboard, for it opened the door to other paths. Corbett was determined to follow these.

He glanced around. The city was stirring. Whores and pimps, topers and cunning men, all the creatures of the night were scuttling back into the dark. Doors were being opened, lanterns doused, buckets emptied into the sewer channels running down the centre of the streets. Apprentices and slatterns, faces heavy with sleep, were busy fetching water, buying milk from the carriers or hurrying through the murky lanes to the bakers and cookshops where the ovens and spits had been fired. A multitude of odours seeped through the misty morning air. Bells rang.

Carts and barrows were on the move. Horses and donkeys brayed. People called out greetings. Sheriff's men were roughly organising the night-walkers, drunks and whores caught breaking the curfew, herding them up to the stocks. The bells of St Paul's boomed out their summons to the Jesus Mass. Corbett decided to attend. He went through the great gates, past the noisy Sanctuary, where wolfsheads were scrambling across the high wall one step ahead of the greedy clutches of bailiffs and bounty-hunters. At the Great Cross in the centre of the cemetery, a city herald was proclaiming how a certain corner in Lothbury, where a Scottish traitor had been executed on a movable gallows, was not a holy site, a martyr's shrine. The gibbet, the herald bellowed, had been burnt, whilst gong carts would deposit a load of filth on the spot. Any citizen who insisted on regarding that place as sacred would be viewed as outside the protection of both the Crown and Holy Mother Church.

Corbett went in through the 'Si Quis' door, where lawyers and scribes were beginning to gather, for the nave of St Paul's was truly a place of business rather than a house of prayer. The church was gloomy, lit fitfully by dancing torch and candle flame. Corbett moved up under the carved rood screen with its stark depiction of the crucified Christ. The sanctuary mass was about to begin. He knelt by a pillar and watched the old priest unfold the dramatic enactment of Christ's passion and death. The Book of Gospels was passed around to be kissed before the Eucharist. Corbett tried to concentrate on the liturgy, but memories, images, scraps of conversations milled around in his tired brain, sharpening his impatience with the task in hand. As soon as Mass was finished, he left and broke his fast at a cookshop on a pastry filled with fresh spiced mince and a cup of wine to warm his belly, then made his way leisurely through the colourful bustle towards Milk Street.

10

Embracery: corruption of a public official

The hour was still early. The market horn had yet to sound, and traders were busy setting up stalls. Corbett, slipping and slithering on the icy trackway, decided that the merchant's widow, the Lady Idola, would perhaps not be ready to receive him, so he continued up into Cripplegate, through the narrow runnels and under the lychgate of St Botulph's. The bleak church tower brooded over the ghostly mist-hung cemetery, where the branches of ancient yew trees curled and twisted, stretching out over the countless tombs and graves, their crumbling headstones and crosses an eloquent testimony to the forgotten dead. The great front door of the church was barred and shuttered, the steps leading up to it blackened and stained by the furious battle recently fought there. Corbett followed the line of the building along the north side, up through an open wicket gate to the two-storey priest house. Its front door, ancient and tar-stained, hung slightly open on its thick leather hinges.

'Parson John?' Corbett called. There was no answer. He entered the flagstoned kitchen and scullery, a neat, tidy place with its scrubbed table, simple benches and aumbries, cooking pots stacked on the shelves above the mantle. It was bitterly cold; the brazier and small hearth both brimmed with grey ash.

'Parson John?' Corbett moved into what must be the solar, a sparse room, its whitewashed walls decorated with a crucifix and a few coloured cloths. A chancery table and chair stood in the far corner; above these ranged shelves filled with calfskin-covered books. A lectern, a high chest and some small coffers and caskets were the only other furnishings. He called the priest's name again, then went up the stairs built into the corner and pushed open the door at the top.

Parson John sat on the edge of his bed, fully clothed, head in his hands. He glanced up bleary-eyed as Corbett entered. The chamber stank of stale sweat and wine. Corbett noticed the flagon on the small table beside the bed. The light was poor, the window still shuttered. He went across and opened it, then picked up the lantern horn from a carved chest beneath the sill and stood over the priest. Parson John just stared back. He looked pitiful, dirty and unshaven, his lips stained with wine.

'I know, clerk,' he slurred. 'A bailiff came here, a raucous fellow muttering about how poor Fleschner is dead, hung like a rat down at Queenshithe.' He clambered to his feet, breath heavy with wine. 'I cannot stay here, I'll never come back.' He rubbed his eyes and stared at Corbett. 'Why are you here?' he asked.

'As you said, poor Fleschner. What happened yesterday?'

'Very little,' mumbled the priest. 'We left Westminster. Fleschner brought me here. He put me to bed. He added an opiate to the wine and I fell into a deep sleep. I woke in the middle of the night, so cold! I fetched more wine, drank it and slept again until the bailiff came.'

'What will you do now?'

'Sir Hugh, I am going to go out and fill my belly with good food. Afterwards I will seek out some barber in a warm, comfortable spot. He'll shave my face and cut my hair. I'll come back here to pack my bundles and books then go to seek shelter at Syon Abbey as my late, but not lamented, father did.'

'Listen,' Corbett said. 'Fleschner found the heads of your stepmother and her steward in the baptismal bowl at the back of your church. Why do you think they were left there of all places?'

'I don't know,' muttered the priest. 'I truly don't.'

'And why should the assassin murder Fleschner and leave his demonic insult? What had Fleschner to do with events some twenty years ago?'

'Sir Hugh, Sir Hugh.' Parson John wailed like a child. 'Let me go to Syon. Let me rest, let me think, then I . . .' He paused, mouth gaping at a sound from below.

Corbett pressed a finger against the priest's lips, then undid the clasps of his own cloak and drew both sword and dagger. Through the half-open door he glimpsed a shadow shift at the bottom of the stairs. He hurled himself out, crashing down the stairs. The intruder fled, but stumbled over the step leading back into the kitchen, sprawling and twisting, hand going for his own dagger. Corbett went and stood over him, the tip of his sword pressed against the man's chest. Leaning down, he pushed back the cowl, undoing the muffler across the man's mouth.

'Ah, Lapwing, you steal like a thief into Parson John's house.' He gestured with his sword for the intruder to get up. Lapwing did so, scrambling to his feet, eyes and face no longer merry.

'Like a thief!' Corbett repeated, aware of Parson John coming down the stairs behind him.

'What are you doing here?'

'I heard the herald's proclamation in Cheapside about Master Fleschner being found hanged down at Queenshithe. I thought I should visit Parson John to see if there was anything I could do.'

'Is there, Parson John?' asked Corbett over his shoulder. The priest came up beside him and smiled at the intruder. Corbett wondered if there was a friendship between these two. 'Parson John?' he snapped.

'He could help me pack. As I said, Sir Hugh, I must fill my belly, wash, shave and leave for Syon Abbey. There's no crime in entering a priest's house to help a friend.'

'Is Parson John your friend?'

'After the Newgate riot,' Lapwing gestured with his head towards the church, 'when I was falsely arrested, I came here. Parson John was kind. I have a debt to repay.'

'In which case, sirs, I leave you to it. However,' Corbett tapped the clerk's shoulder with his sword, 'do not leave your lodgings in this city. If I send for you, or visit you, you must be there.'

Lapwing, his composure regained, shrugged nonchalantly, and Corbett left St Botulph's, making his way once more towards Milk Street. Tinkers were selling ribbons and other geegaws, and one of these showed him to Lady Idola's house. Corbett knocked on the door, and a maid answered. Corbett showed her the seals and demanded entrance. The slattern was about to protest, but he leaned closer and touched her under the chin.

'Don't worry my pretty,' he whispered. 'I'm on king's business. I need to see Lady Idola now, so I do not want to be told she is otherwise engaged or shopping. The morning is cold. I am sure she is in her chamber.'

A short while later, he was shown up the stairs into a beautiful, elegant room. The bottom half of its walls were covered in gleaming wainscoting; above this hung heraldic devices, embroidered cloths, triptychs and paintings. It was furnished with gleaming settles, chairs and stools, and smelled fragrantly of the herbs and spices sprinkled over the great log fire spluttering in the mantled hearth. Lady Idola, an imperious old woman, was sitting on a throne-like chair swathed in robes, her sandalled feet on a rest before a fire. She was supping from a goblet of mulled wine, in her lap a silver tray of sweetmeats. She looked Corbett up and down, received his introductions and waved him to the smaller chair beside her.

'Well, Sir Hugh, I've heard of you. What are you here for?' Her bright button-black eyes studied his face. 'You look cold and pinched. Have you eaten?'

Corbett smiled and nodded.

'Would you like some wine?'

He shook his head.

'Well, clerk, what is your business? Oh, by the way . . .' She popped another delicacy into her mouth and slurped noisily from the goblet. 'I am expecting other visitors.'

'Lady Idola, I will not keep you long. You were married to the merchant Adam Chauntoys; I think you know his history.'

'Let me tell you, clerk,' she settled herself more comfortably, 'I sit here nursing my memories. Oh yes, I know all about my late husband's . . . how can I put it . . . dealings with the King.'

'Which were?'

'Master Chauntoys was first married to Lady Alice, daughter of Sir Walter Plumpton. Lady Alice was born of a wealthy family; she was well educated but had the morals of an alley cat. She brought my late husband a large and generous dowry. He thought that the ceremony at the church door, the binding of hands and the swearing of eternal love, meant that Lady Alice would change her ways, but she did not. There wasn't a young man in Cheapside who, if he caught her eye, didn't share her bed. My husband put up with such strumpet behaviour for at least five years of their marriage. She gave him no son. He suspected she took medicine or potions to prevent herself conceiving. He did consider seeking an annulment from the Church. Of course Lady Alice's family were powerful, and would fight such a slight to their honour, whilst Master Chauntoys was advised by canon lawyers that no grounds existed for annulment. The years passed. What should have been love turned into a deep, languishing hatred between them. My husband decided to go to Southampton on business. While he was absent, his wife was attacked by street brawlers and killed.'

'But that wasn't the truth of it,' declared Corbett. 'Your husband had been communicating with a murderer, a professional assassin known as the Mysterium. An agreement was reached that whilst Master Chauntoys was absent on business, Lady Alice would be killed. This was accomplished. The Mysterium then demanded payment. Your husband was told to go to a tavern, the Liber Albus in Southwark, bringing the blood money with him. However, neither your husband nor the Mysterium realised they were being hunted by a chancery clerk named Walter Evesham.' Corbett paused at the rude sound Idola made with her lips. 'Did you ever meet Walter Evesham?'

'I knew of him, sir, and I've heard what has happened. Evesham has received his just deserts, disgraced, dismissed and murdered, all richly deserved.'

'Why, mistress?'

'He destroyed my husband. If it hadn't been for his grace the King, Master Chauntoys would have ended his days on the common gallows at Smithfield.'

'Evesham was simply doing his duty.'

'He relished it.'

'What did your husband say about it?'

'I married my husband about a year after Lady Alice's death. He was still very prosperous and eager to begin again. I accepted his proposal. I thought I could make him happy.'

'And did you?'

'We were more friends than lovers, a relationship resting on the firm foundations of fidelity and common sense. My husband, however was broken by Evesham's discovery, and of course he had to face the truth. He was indeed party to his first wife's murder. During the last year of his life he began to describe what really happened. I shall talk about him rather than the Lady Alice's many sins. She's gone to God and can answer for herself. My husband was desperately unhappy with her. He received a message, pushed into his hand, saying that his enemy was also the enemy of the anonymous sender, and if my husband wanted, that enemy could be no more. At the bottom of this scrap of parchment was a reference to St Paul, with two numbers. My husband, being a merchant, knew what that meant: the great hoarding at St Paul's. Provoked, shamed by his wife as a public cuckold, Master Chauntoys decided to rid himself of her. He placed her name in the numbered square of the hoarding, and a short while later he received a message.'

'How was that delivered?'

'Again pushed into his hand. Sir Hugh, you are a royal clerk. You know how it is. My husband would attend the Guildhall; people would present petitions to him, as they would to you. This time the scrap of parchment simply had one name: Lady Alice. If my husband agreed to confirm that, he was to place her name in the stipulated square on the hoarding at St Paul's. So he did. Oh yes,' Lady Idola pointed her finger, 'he did have business with the Merchants of the Staple in Southampton, and during his absence, Lady Alice was apparently attacked in the streets and killed. When he returned to London, he received another message with a reference to St Paul's; when he went there, he found a note giving the time and place, the amount of money and where he was to leave it. My husband, to put it bluntly, was very relieved to be rid of Lady Alice. He hastened across to Southwark and waited in that tavern.'

'Did he recognise anyone who came in?'

'No he did not. The clerk Boniface Ippegrave, the man later accused of being the Mysterium, entered. He seemed—'

Corbett held up a hand. 'Lady Idola, I must ask you to be precise. What did your husband actually say about him?'

'I truly will,' she snapped. 'According to my husband, Boniface Ippegrave looked very confused, staring around, hand on his dagger. He kept glancing at a scrap of parchment. My husband did wonder if he was the Mysterium, but then Walter Evesham, followed by his creature Engleat and others, burst into the tavern. My husband and Boniface Ippegrave were seized. Adam could not defend himself. He held that scrap of parchment and a considerable amount of gold.'

'But Boniface Ippegrave?'

'He seemed totally shocked, very surprised, but then . . .'

'But then what?'

'My husband, of course, was similarly distraught. He was under arrest. He knew what he had done. He faced the gallows. He glanced across at Ippegrave, but he had been taken aside by Evesham and they were deep in discussion. They all left the tavern, crossed London Bridge and walked up towards Cheapside, and my husband realised they were going to Newgate. Evesham was close to Ippegrave. Adam saw them argue, then Ippegrave apparently crouched down. The bailiffs stopped. The crowd milling around was hostile. It was then that Boniface Ippegrave escaped.

'My husband was lodged in Newgate. He expected to go on trial, but then he received an offer of a pardon. If he confessed everything, divulged secrets about the machinations of the Guildhall and paid a most considerable fine, he'd be released. He agreed.'

'How was this done?'

'Evesham visited him in Newgate. He berated him, threatened

him with torture and said he would ensure he'd hang very slowly at Smithfield. Then the King intervened. I understand his grace,' Lady Idola's words were tinged with sarcasm, 'was concerned to discover how the Mysterium worked, and we all know the King.' She bowed. 'He is more interested in good silver and valuable information than in seeing a man dangle on the gallows.

'After his release, my husband lived quietly. Sir Hugh, he did great wrong, but he was sorely provoked. He later went on pilgrimage to Canterbury. He crept to the cross every Good Friday. He was shrived, forgiven his sins, and did penance, but in the end he was a broken man. Only in the last year of his life did he begin to talk.'

'Lady Idola, did he remark on anything extraordinary or remarkable about the day he was arrested?'

'Yes, my husband learnt, as we all did, about Boniface Ippegrave: how he took sanctuary at St Botulph's, his later disappearance . . .'

'And?'

'To put it bluntly, he did not believe Boniface Ippegrave was the Mysterium.'

'Why?'

'Think, Sir Hugh. My husband is sheltering in a tavern. He is there to pay an assassin, and has brought a considerable amount of gold. Boniface Ippegrave enters, but he does not act the resolute killer. Instead he stares around like some lost child who doesn't know why he is there. True, he glanced at my husband, but then he looked away.' Lady Idola leaned forward to fill her cup.

Corbett stretched his hands out towards the fire. He felt a horrid chill, a cold creeping up his back, a sense of dread cloying his soul. What had been a mere suspicion hardened into fact. Was the very root of this mystery wrong? He closed his eyes and tried to imagine the scene. If Boniface was the assassin, why hadn't he moved directly to seize the gold and flee? He opened his eyes.

'Lady Idola, can you remember if your husband described the tavern as busy or empty?'

'Oh, it was fairly empty, being mid-morning. He noticed only Boniface Ippegrave.'

Corbett nodded, pushed back the chair and got to his feet. He bowed.

'Lady Idola, I thank you.'

'You seem confused, Sir Hugh.'

'Mistress, I am, and only God can clear the chaos in my mind.'

Corbett swept back into Westminster like a hungry lion. He threw open the door of the chancery chamber and strode in, startling Ranulf and Chanson.

'Have the coroners' rolls arrived yet?' he demanded, clapping his hands. 'Ranulf, I need them now.'

'Sir Hugh, I received your message. I've sent to the Guildhall; they'll be here shortly. I've also dealt with Mouseman,' Ranulf added quickly. 'He came here demanding his pardon. I have never seen a man so happy. He's taken lodgings while he prepares to return to St Albans.'

Corbett pointed at Ranulf. 'What the Mouseman said may be important.'

'What's the matter, master?'

'A faint suspicion, Ranulf, though it's no more than feathers in the wind. What we must do, to quote Scripture, is build our house on rock. I think I have found that rock. In the meantime,' he gestured round, 'make this place warm and lighted. I am going to return to my own chamber. I shall wash, change and go down to the kitchens. Let me know when the coroners' rolls have arrived, then we'll begin.'

The hour candle had burnt two more rings when Corbett returned to the chancery chamber to find his table heaped with rolls of manuscripts. They were arranged according to each regnal year. Fleschner had been coroner for about ten years before the capture of Boniface Ippegrave, and a host of entries were entered under his name, each giving the barest details of the crimes committed: the date, the place, the name of the victim, possible suspects and the outcome. Corbett and Ranulf worked steadily through the lists, and the abbey bells were tolling their dusk warning before Ranulf suddenly rapped the table.

'Master, look at this.'

Corbett hurried across. Ranulf moved the oil lamp, repositioned the roll and pointed to a four-line entry for Candlemas 1280: Emma Evesham, wife of Walter Evesham, clerk, killed by unknown assailants just after dusk on the corner of Amen Court as she was returning from the almshouses. No suspects were listed. Corbett caught his breath. A further sentence explained how Emma's maid Beatrice had also been with her; she had apparently escaped and could not be traced. The coroner's conclusion was that Emma Evesham had died 'an unnatural death other than her natural one'.

'Emma Evesham,' breathed Corbett, 'killed in a street attack like so many others, what, about four years before the Mysterium was unmasked? And this maid Beatrice, who seems to have just disappeared? Was she party to the attack? Or was she abducted and later killed?'

Ranulf simply pulled a face.

Corbett could hardly contain his excitement. He went to his own chancery pouches and drew out the scraps of parchment taken from Boniface Ippegrave. He sifted amongst these and found the one with the list of names: Emma, Furnival, Bassetlawe and Rescales. This he handed to Ranulf.

'Take great care of this. Go down to the exchequer and main chancery. Tell the clerks there to stop everything and search the records for these other names: anything to do with them. Once you have organised that, go to Evesham's mansion in Clothiers Lane; talk to the maid, servants, neighbours, anyone, the cat, the dog, the pigeons.'

'Master?' Ranulf could see that Sir Hugh was excited, agitated, as he always was when a problem was about to unravel.

'Try and trace,' Corbett insisted, 'an old servant, a maid, a nurse, anyone who knew Emma Evesham, who served in her household twenty-four years ago. There must be someone,' he mused.

'And you, master, you'll take to wandering?'

'Ranulf, I confess,' Corbett struck his breast in mock sorrow, 'I'm agitated and confused but I'm also hungry. I am going to eat and drink, adjourn to my own narrow room and reflect. Rouse me when you have made progress.'

He left the chamber, but instead of going down to the palace kitchens, he slipped into the exquisite, incensed-filled chancery chapel. He loved this little jewel of a chamber, an exquisitely furnished house of prayer with dark oaken wainscoting covering most of the walls, its floor tiled with the original design of a map of the world with Jerusalem at the centre. Prie-dieus with velvet padded kneelers ranged before an altar of carved porphyry. In the centre of this stood a pure gold crucifix flanked by candles of the same precious metal. Above the altar, against the backdrop of a luxurious Bruges tapestry depicting the Marriage at Cana, a silver-gilt sanctuary lamp glowed fiery red beside a jewel-encrusted pyx holding the Sacrament. Corbett crossed himself, knelt at a prie-dieu and quietly intoned the 'Veni Creator Spiritus' – 'Come Holy Spirit'. When he reached the line 'If you take your hand away, nothing good in man will stay, all his good is turned to ill', he closed his eyes. What he was about to confront was certainly devoid of God's righteousness, brimming with the rottenness of sin, a corruption that had engulfed other souls over the years. He was about to enter the Garden of Midnight Souls, cross the Meadows of Murder, and there, sheltering in the shadows darker than night, lurked a true son of Cain.

When Corbett had finished his prayer, he blessed himself and rose, then crossed to the small Lady Chapel to the left of the altar, a simple recess holding a carved statue of Our Lady of Walsingham. There he lit three tapers, for his wife and children, blessed himself at the water stoup and left to make his way to the palace kitchens.

The kitchens, a range of buildings around a cobbled yard, were frenetically busy. The fleshing tables just inside the door were awash with the blood of deer, rabbit, pig and lamb. Quails, pheasants, larks and pigeons hung on hooks by their throats, drenching the floor beneath with their gore. Fires built up with dried pine logs blazed like the fury of hell. Cooks and spit boys, bathed in sweat, basted chunks of meat with oil and herbs. Bakers wailed about their pastry and sweetmeats being ruined. Chamberlains supervised the washing of royal cups, dishes and platters in vats of steaming water. Dogs and cats nosed the floor and fought over scraps. Stewards and comptrollers watched the stores being opened, the wine casks broached, the precious plate and cups being carried in. All this busy activity was directed at the huge door leading to the covered gallery stretching towards the King's banqueting chamber.

Corbett slipped through the bustle. He begged a cup of wine and a piece of freshly roasted quail meat, which tasted delicious, then he went and sat on an ale bench just within the doorway, chewing quietly and enjoying the warm glow of the wine and the soft sweet meat. He was tempted to stay, eat some more, but his eyes were growing heavy, and he did not want to fall asleep in public. He retreated from the confusion and went back to his own chamber. There he took off his sword-belt, kicked off his boots, wrapped his cloak about him, stretched out on the cot bed and fell into a deep sleep, only woken by Ranulf shaking him vigorously.

'Master?'The clerk crouched down. 'Master, you've got to wake up, it's well past compline. You've been asleep for hours. We have news.'

Corbett, still half asleep, pulled himself up and swung his legs off the bed. Ranulf went across, fetched a stool and sat opposite him.

'What news?' Corbett asked.

'Those three names . . .' Ranulf paused as Corbett took a tinder and lit the small candelabra on the bedside table. He pulled both table and candelabra closer towards him.

'The three names, Ranulf?'

'All senior clerks of the chancery, old men. They died rather mysteriously in the eighth and ninth year of the present king's reign.'

'Mysteriously?'

'One at a time. Their deaths,' Ranulf shrugged, 'were seen simply as accidents, but it's strange that Boniface Ippegrave should list their names. Rescales fell down the steps of the old turret tower – you know where the chancery records are stored. He was an old man, the light was poor, he stumbled and broke his neck. Furnival? Well, he liked his wine and often drank deep at night. He also liked the river; his corpse was fished from the Thames close to King's Steps. The verdict was that he was so inebriated he must have missed his footing and fallen into the water.'

'And Bassetlawe?'

'He died rather quietly, sitting at the buttery table enjoying a tankard of ale and some bread and cheese. He was found with his head on his arm as if asleep, but his heart had failed. Master, you don't think they were accidents?'

'A month ago I would have said they were.' Corbett pulled his boots towards him, put them on and got to his feet, picking up his sword-belt. He rearranged his cloak. 'There's something else?'

'Yes, master.' Ranulf snuffed the candle and followed Corbett out of the chamber into the cold passageway outside. Only then did Corbett, glancing through a window, realise how long he'd slept.

'I went to Evesham's house and made diligent enquiries, and sure enough, I was given the name of Elizabeth Vavasour, a sort of maid and nurse to Lady Emma. When she retired, Evesham used his influence to obtain a corrody for her, a pension at St Catherine's by the Tower. I went there and spoke to the master of the hospital, who introduced me to Elizabeth. I told her she must come to the chancery chamber after compline this evening, that it was urgent, King's business.'

'Did she object?'

'Far from it. She was looking forward to a journey upriver, even if it was through the icy blackness of night.' Ranulf grinned. 'Be careful, master, she chatters like a sparrow on a branch. She is full of praise for Sir Walter Evesham, loudly proclaiming that she'll brook no ill against him. She'll be here soon.'

By the time Corbett reached his chancery chamber, washed his hands and face, prepared his table and instructed Ranulf and Chanson what to do, Elizabeth Vavasour had arrived. Two bargemen had escorted her through the palace corridors, and by the look on their faces, Corbett realised that they were more than happy to hand over their passenger. Elizabeth Vavasour not only chattered like a sparrow, she looked like one, her small nut-brown face framed by a white wimple above the grey garb of the hospital of St Catherine's. Despite her age, she moved quickly, plumping herself down on a stool, her little black eyes darting around the candlelit chamber before coming to rest on Corbett.

'So you're Sir Hugh, I've heard of you. You must have known my master?'

'Slightly.'

'He was a good man, Sir Hugh. I know he made mistakes,' she leaned across the table, her voice falling to a conspiratorial whisper, 'but he was good, very good indeed.'

'Tell me, Mistress Elizabeth, you worked for Lord Walter and Lady Emma?'

'Oh yes, your grace.'

Corbett glanced sharply at Ranulf and Chanson standing behind the old lady, a threatening glance against their laughter.

'Oh yes, your grace,' she repeated, 'I worked for them for many years. I was hired by Lady Emma when she first married Sir Walter. He was very ambitious, determined to rise high in the royal service. Sometimes he did not feel at home with the other clerks, but he soon won the King's favour.'

'And the Lady Emma?'

'She was quiet, very pious, engaged in good works.'

'And their marriage, it was happy?'

Mistress Elizabeth's eyes rounded, lips pursed. 'Of course, Lord Walter was devoted to her.'

'There was another woman, Beatrice, Lady Emma's maid?'

'Oh, her!' Mistress Elizabeth snorted, and turned slightly, glancing at Corbett out of the corner of her eye. 'She had airs and graces, a rather haughty young woman. She kept herself to herself. I think there was bad blood between her and Lord Walter, though I never knew the reason. Sir Hugh, I was quite happy with my own little tasks. There was the usual chatter, but in the main, it was a happy household.'

Corbett studied this old woman. She was telling the truth. Walter Evesham had looked after her and made sure that in her old age she'd never starve. He had provided her with a comfortable, warm chamber at St Catherine's, all the food she could eat and the delicious gossip of other retired retainers.

'And Lady Emma's death?'

'Oh, sir, an evening like this. Lady Emma and Beatrice went out late in the afternoon. They were taking Mary loaves to the almshouses somewhere near the old Roman wall. Darkness had fallen. Lady Emma was courageous. She had Beatrice with her, so there was no link boy or guard. We don't really know what happened; the attackers were never arrested. Beatrice fled, but Lady Emma was beaten to the ground, her head staved in, her money, goods and all the jewellery she wore taken.'

'And Lord Walter?'

'He was overcome with grief. He locked himself in his chamber for days and refused to come out. He didn't eat or drink. We organised her funeral at St Botulph's.'

'And this Beatrice?'

'Lord Walter scoured London, and her name was proclaimed at St Paul's Cross. The mayor, sheriffs and bailiffs were all advised, but she had vanished, disappeared off the face of God's earth. And of course, Sir Hugh, as you know, life goes on. Look at me, I'm a widow four times over! Oh yes, met my husbands at the church door and within a few years followed their coffins in. Surely the Good Book is true in what it says: life is changed not taken away.'

Corbett glanced up. Ranulf had turned his back and walked away, shoulders shaking.

'Well,' Mistress Elizabeth blinked, 'two years after Lady Emma's death, Sir Walter married again, the Lady Clarice. She was a hussy.

I didn't like her. By then I was growing too frail for heavy duties. Lord Walter said he would give me safe, comfortable lodgings, and so he did, God bless his name. Now, Sir Hugh, if you have finished, I would like to go back, if possible by barge. I know it's dark, but the lantern horns are bright and those bargemen are so kind and attentive, they listen to every word I say. I must be back soon. There's a special supper tonight. Cook has offered lampreys cooked in a rich sauce with soft white bread. Oh, every time I eat, every night I press my head against a feather-filled bolster, I always praise Sir Walter, and say a prayer for him. Terrible what happened, wasn't it, Sir Hugh?'

Corbett nodded. 'Mistress Elizabeth, I can see that you're very busy.' He got to his feet and, taking a silver piece out of his purse, stretched across and placed it in her vein-streaked hand. 'Please take that, buy some comforts for yourself. I thank you. God bless you, mistress.'

11

Luparius: a wolf-hunter

Mistress Elizabeth, still chattering, allowed Chanson to escort her out of the chamber. Corbett sat down and heaved a sigh. 'Ranulf,' he glanced up, 'when Chanson returns, go about your business. You must be hungry. One final thing, send a courier to Cripplegate ward, find out who holds the keys to St Botulph's and have them brought here.'

When Ranulf had left, Corbett paced the chamber for a while. He shifted the brazier close to his desk, moving candles and lamps to create a pool of light and warmth, and settled himself. He tried to imagine being Ippegrave, so close and secretive, then smiled: he was that already. Yet in truth, Boniface had been different from him, a bachelor with a doting sister and a secret lover whose name began with M. Corbett smoothed the piece of vellum in front of him, dipped his quill pen in the ink and began to write.

Item: This mysterious Beatrice, Emma Evesham's maid, had been present when her mistress was attacked and murdered. Was the assault simply a bloody street affray and Emma Evesham the wrong woman in the wrong place at the wrong time? Or was it a planned assault? Was Beatrice party to it? And what had happened to her? Was she killed and her corpse taken elsewhere? Evesham and Coroner Fleschner appeared to have searched for this elusive maid but discovered no trace of her alive or dead. So did Beatrice flee, but where? To whom? Why? Was she abducted and still alive? Again why? What had happened to her?

Item: Why had Boniface collected some of those horrid messages left on the corpses of the Mysterium's victims? What was he searching for?

Item: How had Boniface been able to discover the secret machinations of the Mysterium and his use of the great hoarding at St Paul's? Evesham had only established the truth of that after he had trapped the merchant Chauntoys and Boniface in Southwark.

Item: Why had Boniface listed Emma alongside other victims of mysterious death? She was certainly murdered, but there was no real proof that Bassetlawe, Furnival and Rescales had been. All three deaths could have been accidents, the verdict recorded at the time.

Item: Why had Boniface listed other clerks, Blandeford, Staunton, Evesham and Engleat? For what purpose?

Item: Boniface had protested his innocence. What was that phrase he'd scrawled on the page of the Book of the Gospels at St Botulph's: 'I stand in the centre guiltless and point to the four corners.' What did it mean?

Item: Why did Evesham and others believe the Mysterium was a chancery clerk? Who had reached that conclusion? Why not a scribe at the Guildhall?

Item: Why did the Mysterium always leave that mocking message,

'*Mysterium Rei* – the Mystery of the Thing', on the corpses of his victims?

Item: Evesham, Engleat, Waldene, Hubert the Monk, Clarice, Richard Fink and now Fleschner had all been killed within a short period of time by the same killer: why? What linked all these victims to this bloody mysterious mayhem?

Item: Nevertheless, there were incidents that seemed out of harmony with this murderous pattern. The writer from the Land of Cockaigne, who was he? The riot at Newgate: who had really caused both that and the furious fight at St Botulph's?

Item: If Boniface was innocent and, for sake of argument, had survived, why had he returned to his sister to proclaim that he was carrying out vengeance? Why his interest in the woman Beatrice?

Corbett put his pen down. He felt lost, unable to form a rock-hard conclusion on which to construct a thesis that would match the evidence. He rose, paced the chamber, ate some of the stale food left on Chanson's platter and returned to his chair. He dozed for a while and startled as the door latch rattled and Staunton and Blandeford strode in. Corbett immediately grasped the hilt of his knife. Both men looked sinister in their heavy cloaks and deep cowls, more like monkish rats than judge and clerk. They parted to go around the table, walking swiftly towards Corbett, who, hand still on his dagger, rose to his feet. Staunton stopped abruptly, drew a set of keys out of the pocket of his cloak and waved these tauntingly in Corbett's face.

'We were coming to see you, Sir Hugh. We found the catch-pole from Cripplegate wandering the galleries below. One of the guards stopped him. He was demanding to see you, so we took his keys. I gather,' he smirked, 'your companions Ranulf and Chanson are savouring the joys of a nearby tavern.'

'They have worked hard.' Corbett grasped the heavy bunch of keys and slammed then down on the desk. 'So these are the keys to St Botulph's?'

'So the catchpole said.'

'And you, sirs, what do you want?'

Staunton, uninvited, sat down on a chair; Blandeford pulled a stool up close.

'We've heard rumours, Sir Hugh. You seem to be concentrating on events of twenty years ago rather than—'

'I dig for the roots,' Corbett intervened, asserting himself. He did not like the arrogance of these two men, who seemed slightly menacing in the shifting shadows. 'Tell me,' he sat down, 'Boniface Ippegrave put your names on a list.'

'So?' Staunton pushed back the deep cowl from over his head.

'Were you suspected of being the Mysterium?'

'What do you mean? What are you implying? How dare you . . .'

'Oh, I dare.' Corbett laughed. 'And I would dare again. Listen, Evesham believed the Mysterium was a chancery clerk, someone like us, party to the chatter of both city and court.'

'That's logical,' Staunton conceded.

'I disagree.' Corbett crossed his arms and leaned closer, holding Staunton's arrogant stare. 'Learned judge, it is not logical. What about the clerks at the Guildhall, or even those of the merchants?'

'What are you implying?'

'Who first raised the possibility that the Mysterium must be a

217

chancery clerk?' Corbett glanced down the floor, waiting for the answer. Outside, the strengthening night breeze rattled the shutters, the icy draught seeping in making the timbers of the ancient palace creak.

'I don't know,' Staunton blustered. 'I cannot remember. Old Chancellor Burnell was beside himself. An assassin was loose in the city, hired by the great merchants to settle scores with their enemies. The Mysterium was taunting the authority of the law. You know how the King would regard that, especially in London. Burnell turned to his clerks for advice and help; that's how I suspect the conclusion was reached that the Mysterium was a chancery official.' Staunton rose abruptly. 'Sir Hugh, we simply came to give our greetings.'

'No you didn't.' Corbett also stood up. 'You came to give me a bunch of keys and pry on what I'm doing. Why, sirs, are you reporting to the King? Or are you worried about your clerk Lapwing? I hold you responsible for him.' He wagged a finger in Staunton's face. 'I must have close words with Lapwing on a number of matters. Now, sirs, unless you have further information for me . . .'

He ushered them to the door and closed it quietly behind them, drawing across the bolts. If Staunton and Blandeford could wander in here . . . Corbett felt uneasy. Why had those sly courtiers visited him? Did they also suspect something was wrong with the accepted story about Ippegrave? He heard a scratching at the door. He drew back the bolts and allowed the two cats through. They immediately went and sprawled near one of the braziers. 'I wish I could do that.' Corbett smiled. He crouched beside them, stroking them softly. 'You've been hunting and I think you've killed, whilst I'm still prowling in the dark. Now, my two fine sirs, you're more welcome than the other two who've just left, but what do they want? What are they frightened of? What are they concerned about?' He stared at the fiery mess in the charcoal brazier. 'What if . . .' He rose and returned to his chair. 'What if Boniface Ippegrave was not the Mysterium? Then who was?'

Corbett pulled across the crude copy he'd made of Boniface's diagram of the first nine letters of the alphabet:

$$A \quad B \quad C$$
$$D \quad E \quad F$$
$$G \quad H \quad I$$

He was concentrating so hard, his eyes grew heavy and he dozed for a while. He started awake at a cry from the yard below, followed by the sound of swords being drawn. He hastened to the window, pulled back the shutters and stared down at the serjeant-at-arms and liveried guards standing in a pool of torch-light.

'What is it?' he called.

The serjeant-at-arms, shading his eyes, gazed up.

'Is that you, Sir Hugh?'

'Yes.'

'I thought so, all the other chambers are in darkness. Sir Hugh, it's nothing. We thought there was an intruder, but it's only the shadows, perhaps some dog. One of our lads is missing his sweetheart. He imagines many things.'

Corbett smiled at the laughter this caused, then raised his hand and closed the shutters. Nevertheless, despite the cheery words, he felt uneasy. A prickling fear as if he was walking down some night-filled alleyway. He might be in this sealed chamber warmed and lit by glowing coals and leaping tongues of candle flame, where wall tapestries glowed colour and crucifixes and statues glinted in the jittering light, and yet . . . Guards patrolled downstairs, and he had his own sword-belt within reach, but Corbett sensed Murder was prowling, a demon deep in the shadows like some scuttling, ravenous rat. An assassin was loose. Whether it was the Mysterium or not was immaterial; this was a killer who struck swiftly and savagely with a keen eye to his own advantage.

Corbett sat down and picked up the scrap of parchment with the square of letters.

'I stand in the centre,' he whispered. 'That is the E. I point to the four corners: A, C, G, I.' He wrote out the four letters, rearranging them several times but could still make no sense of it. 'I should be back at Leighton,' he whispered. 'God knows, Maeve, I miss you so much. I'm tired. I want to sleep.'

He thought of Staunton of Westminster, of himself, Corbett of Leighton, of Boniface of Cripplegate, Blandeford of the Guildhall, the way people defined themselves by the place they called home. He glanced down at the letter E and those in the four corners and his mouth went dry. He rummaged amongst his papers and found what he was looking for. He studied it carefully, then went back to those four letters.

'The Land of Cockaigne,' he whispered. 'The world turned topsy-turvy, the hunted becomes the hunter, the righteous the wicked.' He snatched up a piece of parchment, took a pen and listed the evidence.

Item: The Mysterium was a chancery clerk.

Item: The Mysterium used the great hoarding at St Paul's.

Item: The Mysterium gloated about his work.

Item: The Mysterium's murderous campaign ended with Boniface Ippegrave's disappearance.

Item: Boniface Ippegrave maintained his innocence until now.

'No, no,' he murmured, and crossed out 'until now'. 'Go back,' he told himself. 'Go back twenty years and stay there. That's where the truth is.'

Item: The Mysterium – Boniface Ippegrave – was captured red-handed with his accomplice in that tavern in Southwark.

Item: Only after that did Walter Evesham claim he knew how the Mysterium carried out his dreadful crimes.

Item: Boniface Ippegrave was taken into custody but escaped.

Item: Boniface Ippegrave remained in sanctuary for two days at St Botulph's. No one visited him except the parson, Evesham and Engleat. He received his mother's ring from his sister and scrawled his proclamation of innocence on a page of the Book of the Gospels.

Item: On the third day, Boniface Ippegrave disappeared, but how?

Corbett glanced up. 'I think I know,' he whispered fiercely. 'Yes, I'm sure I do, but how does it all fit?'

He rose and paced the chamber, lost in thought, trying to track down the assassin who'd prowled the city some twenty years ago. He kept returning to the table, fingering the scraps of parchment, scribbling down notes. He was certain that he had a hypothesis, but how could he link it to present events? He gathered his cloak about him, wheeled the brazier closer to his chair and sat down. Staring into the sparkling coals, sifting the evidence, his eyes grew heavy again. He fell asleep, and when he woke, the light outside was greying. He went to the garderobe, then returned and washed himself at the lavarium, and as he dried his hands and face, he glimpsed the ring of keys to St Botulph's. He had to go there.

'St Botulph's,' he exclaimed. 'You are truly a house of secrets! I need to search you to test my hypothesis.'

He sat and wrote a short letter to Ranulf, then another to Sir Ralph Sandewic at the Tower. Dressing quickly and preparing himself, he went out along the gallery and down to the bailey. The early morning was bitterly cold; a river mist still hung heavy. Torches glowed. Muffled sounds echoed through the murky gloom. Corbett loosened his sword in its scabbard. Danger threatened, he sensed it. It was always so. The hunt was on! The assassin, clever and subtle, must have realised Corbett had not given up. The killer would ponder his own survival. What chance did he have? If Corbett closed and trapped him for such heinous crimes, a hideous punishment awaited, being forced up a ladder to slowly strangle to death on a Smithfield scaffold. Corbett murmured a prayer for help.

'It is your face I seek, O Lord, hide not your face. Do not dismiss your poor servant in anger, for you have been my saving help.'

He felt the church keys weighing heavily in the pocket of his cloak. He would not go there alone. Nightmare memories warned him against that!

'*Aux aide! Aux aide!*' he shouted in Norman French, and was immediately answered by the rattle of armour as the serjeant-at-arms and two archers came hurrying through the mist.

'Sir Hugh, what is the matter?'

'Nothing.' Corbett grasped the serjeant's shoulder. 'Nothing for now, but listen.' He handed over the two letters. 'Send one of your archers to my colleague Ranulf-atte-Newgate; rouse him wherever he is. The other to Sir Ralph Sandewic at the Tower. Both are urgent dispatches. You,' he pointed at a bearded archer whose hood almost covered his face, 'are to come with me to St Botulph's, where we'll meet the rest.'

A short while later, Corbett and the archer, who introduced himself as Griffyths from South Wales, clambered into a wherry near King's Steps. The two bargemen pushed away, hugging the bank along the misty, choppy river. Corbett sat in the stern, the archer beside him. Griffyths wanted to talk, but Corbett remained lost in his own thoughts, so the archer turned his attention to the bargemen, engaging them in good-natured banter, loudly asking if Englishmen did have tails and was it true that one Welshman was worth at least a dozen English? Corbett half listened. The river was shrouded in mist, bitterly cold, and very little could be seen except for the lantern lights of ships and torches flaring along the bank. Here and there scaffolds rose, grim spectacles, some decorated with corpses, others empty, awaiting what would be offered later in the day. Corbett recalled Fleschner hanging from that iron bracket, Waldene and Hubert the Monk slaughtered in the tavern chamber. All these squalid deaths were surely linked to what happened twenty years ago, but for the moment, Corbett did not want to speculate further. St Botulph's would hold the key.

They disembarked at Queenshithe and made their way up through the still empty streets. The mist was like a veil, abruptly parting to reveal hideous sights. Beggars, faces distorted, their bodies displaying horrid wounds, scuttled out on all fours on their makeshift little carts, hands gripping wooden pegs as they clattered across the cobbles whining for alms. Corbett disbursed some pennies and moved on. Whores and their pimps still searched for customers. Night-walkers and dark-dwellers gathered at the mouths of alleyways and watched the two men pass. The icy weather had hardened the track beneath their feet, but the stench was still offensive, and Corbett glanced away at the sight of mangled corpses of cats and dogs struck down by carts. Occasionally a troop of bailiffs crossed their path pursuing a malefactor, their cries of 'Harrow! Harrow!' muffled by the mist. Griffyths had now found his tongue again and inveighed stridently against the night-walkers, dismissing them as 'a dirty, everlastingly gruesome assembly, not a Christian amongst them, with their base dark faces, nothing more than swift, ravening demons'.

Corbett smiled to himself. The Welshman was most eloquent in his dismissal of all they saw.

'This is,' Griffyths declared, 'the most hideous depths of hell, Sir Hugh. I'd give a year's wage to be back in the loveliness of South Wales.'

Corbett didn't answer. He remembered the 'loveliness' of South

Wales! Trees clustered together, the light barely piercing them, the grass underneath slippery. He recalled waiting with men-at-arms and archers for the Welsh bowmen with all their hideous skill to appear and loose their shafts, a rain of death clattering against their armour before disappearing as swiftly . . .

'You've served in Wales, Sir Hugh?'

'Of course.'

'And you never met the Mouldwarp? He is an ugly-coloured, dismal, lurking character with a hump. He wears a ragged thread-bare cloak and his every limb is blacker than a blacksmith's.'

Corbett paused and put a hand on the archer's shoulder.

'Griffyths, we are going to a place more ominous and threatening than any monster prowling the woods of South Wales or, indeed, any night-walker on these streets. I bid you say your prayers.'

'St Botulph's?' Griffyths refused to be abashed. 'I know of it, sir. I've heard the stories. I was there at the battle. All kinds of legends flourish about it being haunted, a place where people disappear. Is that true, Sir Hugh?'

Corbett sighed, tapped the archer on the shoulder and led him on. 'Listen, Griffyths, what I want you to do is guard me and watch that church. Now, this monster from the Welsh woods, have *you* ever met him?'

He allowed Griffyths to chatter as they made their way through the streets, until eventually they reached St Botulph's. Here the Welsh archer fell silent. The heavy mist thinned to reveal the gnarled yew trees and crumbling cluster of tombs. The church itself looked silent and forbidding. No beacon light glowed in its steeple, no sound carried. God's acre was strangely empty, as if the beggars and the other dispossessed who usually sheltered there had recognised the sinister atmosphere and fled. Griffyths threw back his cloak, hand on the hilt of his sword, muttering prayers in Welsh. He pointed to the main door and whispered something about the recent battle. Corbett patted him on the shoulder and led him into the trees, along the path to the corpse door. Griffyths abruptly paused, one hand on Corbett's arm.

'Sir Hugh, did you hear that?'

Corbett stared into the mist closing behind them.

'What?'

'A footfall, something snuffling.' He forced a smile. 'Like the Mouldwarp.'

'Ghosts.' Corbett smiled, tapping the archer's broad forehead. 'Ghosts in here, Griffyths.'

He brought out the keys and eventually found the correct one. The corpse door creaked open and they entered the nave. A musty, damp smell seeped out of the chilly blackness to greet them. Corbett, recalling where the sconce torches were positioned, took out a tinder and moved to the left, feeling along the wall. Griffyths followed, muttering incantations against the Evil One, his boots slithering over the paving stones. Corbett lit a torch and used it to fire the others. The flickering flames created a ghostly atmosphere along that cavernous nave with its fat rounded pillars and shadow-filled aisles. The light picked up the vivid wall paintings proclaiming the story of Man's fall from Paradise and his constant battle against the powers of hell. Painted faces, scowling, angry, beseeching, lovely and ugly, celestial and demonic, peered out as

Corbett, followed by a now subdued Griffyths holding a sconce torch, made his way round that haunted church, carefully inspecting everything. He confided to Griffyths that they might have to wait for the full light of day, though he was certain no secret cellar, recess, crypt, tunnel or passageway existed. The church grew bitterly cold. Griffyths voiced his unease as they went up into the sanctuary towards the sacristy. Corbett teased his companion, promising that they would soon break their fast before a roaring fire in some nearby tavern. He unlocked the sacristy door, then went back into the church, where a thought occurred to him He returned to the sacristy and stared down at the place where Parson John must have been assaulted and bound. A sound echoed from the church.

'Griffyths?' exclaimed Corbett.

The archer slipped out into the sanctuary. Corbett loosened his own sword, then startled at a clatter. He stepped out of the sacristy and immediately retreated. The church was dark, the sconce torches doused. He peered round the lintel of the door. Only one cresset still flamed.

'Griffyths?' he shouted. A click alarmed him, and he threw himself down even as a crossbow bolt whirled like some angry wasp above his head. He slammed shut the door to the sanctuary, pushing across the rusty bolts at top and bottom, then unlocked the door to the outside and hastened into the mist-strewn poor man's lot, the burial ground for strangers lying to the north side of the church. Hot sweat cooling in the freezing air, he slammed the door shut and fumbled with the keys but couldn't find the correct one. He slipped the bunch into the pocket of his cloak

and drew both sword and dagger, edging out across the waste-
land trying to control his panic. This was his nightmare, one that
had haunted him ever since he had fought in Wales, whether it
was here in this graveyard or in some lonely copse or filthy alleyway.
He was facing death, hunted by an assassin hungry for slaughter.

Slipping and slithering on the icy ground. he made his way
around wooden crosses, stumbling over mounds, ruts and holes.
A sound forced him to stop and turn. A shape moved in the mist.
Corbett crouched. He glimpsed a mongrel scavenging at the dead
underneath their thin layer of dirt. The dog turned, a bone between
its jaws. Corbett lunged with his sword, and the dog yelped and
fled. Immediately a crossbow bolt hissed through the air to smash
against a headstone. Corbett stared back at the church. He'd made
a mistake: he'd have been safer inside. He took a deep breath and
whispered a prayer. The mist was thinning, the light strengthening, but he was not safe. St Botulph's, now seen as accursed,
was desolate; very few would enter here. His attacker, armed
with a crossbow, would simply hunt him down, drive him into a
trap or wait for a mistake.

A low growl made him turn swiftly, and in doing so he struck
one of the wooden crosses, which snapped and broke. Corbett
however could only stare in horror at the huge mastiff, belly low
to the ground, creeping towards him. He kept still, recognising
the breed. Royal levies had used them in Wales and Scotland: a
war dog with a spiked collar to protect its thick, muscular throat,
the hound had been trained to hunt silently. The assassin had
released it to track Corbett down, flush him out and, if he stood
still or tried to defend himself, attack. The mastiff growled again,

huge cruel jaws slightly open, sharp, tufted ears going back, black eyes intent on its prey. Corbett stepped to the right. The dog, muscular flanks quivering, halted, eyes intent on him. A twig snapped. The assassin was also creeping forward. Corbett crouched down and caught the pungent smell from the freshly dug burial mound over which the fallen cross lay. He recognised the odour of the unadulterated heavy lime used by the grave-diggers. He dropped his sword. The soil was hard, the lime lay loosely strewn. He collected a brimming handful in his gauntleted hand. The war hound half rose, and Corbett lunged, throwing the lime at that great ugly head just as the dog charged. The lime, a congealed mess, hit the hound as it sprang. Corbett moved swiftly to one side. The dog had misjudged its leap, and Corbett scored it with the tip of his dagger. The hound turned in a swirl of muscular black flesh but then broke its stride, confused by the ugly knife wound to its flank as well as the lime burning its eyes, nostrils and mouth. Its great head went back as the lime scorched deeper, and Corbett lurched forward and, grasping his sword, drove it deep into the dog's exposed throat. The hound rolled in agony on to its side.

Corbett moved swiftly at a half-crouch back to the sacristy door. A bolt winged dangerously close, but he reached the door and hurled himself inside. He scrambled up and pushed one bolt home, then raced out of the sacristy through the sanctuary, down the steps and across to the corpse door, which he slammed shut. Hands trembling, he snatched out the bunch of keys, finding the correct one as a hideous yelping echoed from outside. Then he sank to the ground, pressing his sweat-soaked face against the icy-cold flagstones. He heard the sacristy door rattle, then silence. He waited. A short while later the door beside him shook violently. Corbett pulled himself up.

'God damn you,' he shouted. 'Go down to hell, you and your killer dog.' He stood up and waited again. Nothing. Swaying on his feet, he kicked aside his sword, dagger and keys and stumbled over to where Griffyths lay in a widening pool of blood. He pushed aside the archer's fallen sword, turned the corpse over and groaned. Griffyths' face was smeared with blood, which had gushed from both nose and mouth. The crossbow bolt was embedded so deeply in the archer's chest it was almost hidden, except for the feathers on the end of the wicked-looking quarrel. Corbett knelt and made the sign of the cross on the man's forehead and whispered the 'De Profundis'. Hands clasped, he prayed that the Welshman's faithful soul would journey unchallenged into the realm of light. Then he sat back on his heels, glancing round this hateful church. He recognised what had happened. The murderer, that hideous assassin, had been hunting him. The serjeant-at-arms at Westminster had been wrong. Some evil killer had gone there to spy Corbett out. He'd withdrawn to lurk in the shadows, then pursued him and Griffyths to this desolate church. The assassin must have left the war hound quiet outside, followed them in through the corpse door, doused the torches and waited. Griffyths simply walked to his death. If Corbett had not been so fortunate, he would have met his out in that ghostly cemetery.

Corbett stumbled to his feet and went down the church to the small cask of holy water beside the baptismal bowl. He took off the lid and filled the ladle inside, then took it back and dripped the water over Griffyths' corpse.

'It's the best I can do for the moment,' he murmured. 'I can do no more.' He tossed the ladle to the ground and went across to the Lady Chapel, pausing on the steps leading into it. He'd noticed how one of the flagstones was smooth, recently replaced, but apart from that, he'd observed nothing untoward in this ghost-filled church.

'It should be burnt,' he murmured. 'If I had my way, I would burn this house of blood and build anew.'

12

Caitiff: a cowardly, wicked being

'Master? Master?' Ranulf's voice echoed, followed by a pounding on the corpse door. 'Sir Hugh!'

Corbett hurried across and unlocked the door. Ranulf almost knocked him aside as he strode into the church followed by Chanson.

'Master, what's happened here? We've been to the north door. There's a war dog lying outside, its throat slashed.' He glanced across at Griffyths' corpse and hurried over. '*Jesu miserere*,' he murmured. 'Sir Hugh, what happened here?'

Corbett swayed on his feet, and Ranulf caught him.

'Come,' he whispered hoarsely. 'Chanson, tell Sir Ralph to stay outside. He is not to come in here, not yet.' He lowered Corbett to the ground, leaning his master back against the church wall.

For a while Corbett fought the urge to be sick, to retch, to vomit out the tension he felt. At last he felt better.

'Apart from the war dog you saw nothing else?' he asked.

'A crossbow bolt in the sacristy door.'

Corbett told him what had happened. Ranulf, crouching beside him, listened intently.

'You shouldn't have come . . .' he said when Corbett had finished.

'Don't lecture me, don't preach. Griffyths has gone to God, and I think this mystery is clearing. Look,' Corbett clambered to his feet, 'first Sir Ralph.'

They went out into the cemetery, where the constable had already set up camp beneath the yew trees. His men had collected dry bracken and were starting a fire. Sandewic rose as Corbett approached.

'Sir Ralph, I am pleased you're here.' Corbett grasped Sandewic's hand and led him away, Ranulf and Chanson following.

Corbett pithily described what had happened.

'The war hound is dead,' Ranulf commented. 'The lime did terrible damage to its throat and eyes. Its owner put the beast out of its misery with a mercy cut.'

'And who is its owner?' Corbett paused as starlings burst out from a nearby tree.

'Boniface perhaps? He's returned and is lurking in hiding. I've heard of such assassins . . .' Ranulf's voice trailed away. He was concerned about Corbett, his lack of colour, the nervous twitch to his eyes and lips.

'We could scout the entire ward,' Sandewic grumbled, 'but what good would that do? Sir Hugh, what do you want with me? You asked for a comitatus . . .?'

Corbett stared up at the church tower. He must be done with this. He wanted to warm himself before a fire, but the ghosts were gathering about him. Somewhere here, in this churchyard, lay the rotting corpse of Boniface Ippegrave, a good clerk, a man of integrity. His flesh must have long decayed but his soul, like some tongue of flame hungry for dry wood, surely demanded justice.

'Sir Hugh?'

Corbett smiled, stretched across and pulled up Chanson's cowl. The Clerk of the Stables looked surprised.

'Pull it tighter,' Corbett ordered. 'Ranulf, do up your cloak and cover your head with the hood.' He turned to the constable. 'Divide your men. You must place a close guard around the church.' He paused as the corpse door opened and two of Sandewic's men brought out Griffyths' body shrouded under the archer's cloak.

'Sir Ralph, before we begin, send poor Griffyths' remains to the corpse house near the King's Chapel at Westminster.'

'And for the rest?'

'Divide your comitatus. Guard the north door, sacristy door, front door and corpse door. Tell your guards that they must not allow Chanson out of St Botulph's.'

'But they don't know him.'

Corbett pointed to Ranulf. 'Our cloaks are Benedictine black, Chanson's is Lincoln green. He must not leave. Do you understand?'

Sandewic grinned, shrugged and sauntered off. He knew Corbett of old. The clerk could be capricious and eccentric yet ruthless in his pursuit of the truth.

'Well, Chanson?' Corbett tapped the surprised groom on the shoulder. 'Go on, enter the church. Oh, Sir Ralph,' he called. The constable turned. 'Chanson will pretend to be in sanctuary. No one except Ranulf and myself may visit him, you understand?'

The constable raised a hand.

'Go into the church, Chanson.' Corbett gestured at the corpse door. 'Sit on the sanctuary steps.'

'Master, this is a place of blood.'

'You can always sing,' teased Ranulf. 'Sir Hugh, what is this?'

'I will show you how Boniface disappeared. Do you remember Adelicia's night visitor, the prowler in the woods? He claimed to be Boniface. When asked how he disappeared from St Botulph's, he replied that he simply walked through the door. Whoever he was, that stranger was telling the truth, as we shall prove.'

Corbett ushered the reluctant Chanson into the church and closed the door, then he and Ranulf went round checking on all the other doors. A small group of Sandewic's archers had assembled near the still battered front porch, but Corbett, now recovering from the attack, laughingly reassured them that if Chanson did escape, it would not be through there.

Once Griffyths' corpse had been honourably removed and Sandewic's men were in place, Corbett and Ranulf went in and out of the various doors muffled and cowled in their heavy cloaks. Sandewic, taking up his command at the north door, watched fascinated. The grizzled constable was already relishing the story he would tell the King next time they were in their cups. On one occasion Corbett paused to inspect the corpse of the war hound, which Sandewic's men had sprawled across an old tombstone. On another, Sandewic, at Corbett's invitation, followed them as near as he could into the church and listened to Corbett and Ranulf trying to cheer the disconsolate Chanson. The clerks would then separate to wander in and out of the church or across the sprawling cemetery. At last Corbett approached Sandewic.

'Master Constable, your prisoner has escaped!'

Sandewic, muttering curses, stormed through the corpse door and stared around in surprise.

'It's empty!' he shouted. 'Sir Hugh, where is your clerk? Where's Chanson?' He went back shouting the groom's name, his voice echoing vainly through that sombre church.

'Go on,' Corbett urged, 'bring your men in. Search this church from door to door, every crevice, nook and cranny. See if you can find Chanson.'

Sandewic, baffled, did as he was told. The bells of other churches were ringing out the hours before he came back shaking his head.

'He's disappeared,' he exclaimed, 'just like Boniface Ippegrave did. Sir Hugh, is he hiding here?'

'I will tell you,' Corbett took off his gauntlets, 'but not here. Sir Ralph, tell your lieutenant to lock the church and take your men back for a blackjack of ale at the Tower. You, my friend,' he touched the constable's whiskered face, 'will join me and my companions in the most cheerful tavern we can find.'

A short while later, closeted in a partitioned area to the left of the great roaring fire in the taproom of the Golden Thistle, Corbett finished the last morsels of his delicious venison. He cleaned his horn spoon, slipped it back into his belt pouch, grasped his blackjack of ale and sat back. The tavern was small, clean and sweet-smelling, a stark contrast to that icy, ghostly church and cemetery. He waited for his companions, equally ravenous, to finish their own food before toasting them with his tankard. Sandewic kept staring at Chanson, shaking his head in disbelief. He was brimming with questions about how the clerk had disappeared from St Botulph's. Chanson had been waiting for them here, crouched on a stool next to the spit boy, advising him how to baste the pork with mingled spices that gave the taproom its mouth-watering aromas.

'Sir Ralph, I'll tell you in a while,' began Corbett, 'but first I want to go back twenty years.' The rest, nursing their tankards, listened intently. Corbett closed his eyes, then opened them and smiled around. 'Boniface Ippegrave was not the Mysterium; Walter Evesham was.'

'Never!' Sandewic exclaimed. 'Walter Evesham may have been a rogue, but a professional assassin . . . He was the one—'

'Yes, Sir Ralph, he was the one who trapped Boniface Ippegrave. He committed him into custody but allowed him to escape to sanctuary at St Botulph's. Let me explain. Sir Ralph, you have fought in Wales and Scotland. Soldiers kill because they have to, because they are frightened or to defend themselves. Sometimes, sodden with ale or blood lust, they can commit horrible crimes, but in the main, most people don't want to kill for the sake of it. However, whilst serving with the King's troops I – and I am sure you too, Sir Ralph – came across those who love the smell of blood. They take to killing as a bird to flying. They enjoy it. They relish it. I remember one serjeant-at-arms who loved to hang Welsh prisoners taken in battle. He'd kick them off the scaffold, closely savour their every struggle and watch the life light fade in their eyes. No one was safe from him, women, children, even those of his own kind who refused to carry out his orders. I believe Evesham was of similar ilk. I have a friend, a physician,' Corbett sipped from his tankard, 'at St Bartholomew's in Smithfield.

One night, while sharing a jug of ale with him, he talked about such men, who appear to have two souls, conflicting personalities. Like the old Roman god Janus, they glance either way at the same time. They can be charming, intelligent, courteous, but change their circumstances and they become angry, homicidal, violent and vengeful. I believe Walter Evesham was one of these, two souls in one body: the upright judge, the faithful clerk, but beneath that a killer, a murderer, someone who relished mayhem. A soul who'd have liked nothing better than to see the world burning, and he certainly did his best to achieve that.' He paused and drew a deep breath.

'Evesham was born on the Welsh March at the manor of Ingachin. He served in the royal levies in Wales, where his appetite for blood was probably whetted. He journeyed to London. A mailed clerk, he soon secured employment in the chancery at Westminster. He was lonely but he was ambitious, hungry for power. He was attracted to both the law and its opposite, the very mayhem it tries to control. He was also a man in a hurry. I suspect that from the very beginning he mixed with the underworld, the wolfsheads and outlaws. It would be so easy. I recently walked from the palace to the abbey, passing through the Sanctuary, which shelters men who would do anything for a favour or a silver coin. Evesham recognised that and relished it. I am also certain that in those early days he met those limbs of Satan – what Ranulf would describe as two cheeks of the same arse – Giles Waldene and Hubert the Monk. They too were beginning their career of lawlessness. A friendship developed between this pair and the royal clerk, but more of that in a while.'

'Those three names,' Ranulf asked, 'Bassetlawe, Furnival and Rescales?'

'I suspect, though I have no evidence, that Evesham killed them. The coroner ruled that they died natural deaths. Of course all three were bachelors, old men; who would care? Evesham did. He saw them as obstacles to his promotion, so all three went into the dark. Evesham also moved in courtly circles, where he met his darling Clarice, but he was already married to Emma. Now there is nothing like a marriage to help a good man up the slippery ladder of preferment. Evesham, although he had a child by the Lady Emma, found his first marriage irksome. A rising star in the court and chancery, he wanted to begin again. Lady Emma and her maid Beatrice were out doing good, visiting the almshouses, when they were attacked.'

'By Waldene and Hubert?'

'I suspect so. I have no proof, not yet. Lady Emma died in that violent affray. Fleschner, Coroner of Cripplegate at the time, hastily dismissed the incident in four lines. I suspect that both he and his inquiry were controlled, or rather hindered, by Evesham. Emma's death, lamentable indeed, was dismissed as just another hideous street attack. Was the finger of suspicion pointed at the mysterious Beatrice, who simply disappeared? I don't know – not yet. Walter Evesham acted the grieving husband, throwing his hands in the air, wailing and moaning, pleading to the King for justice. Secretly, though, he rejoiced. He was now the lonely widower, free to go hunting for a more profitable dowry. Even more important,' Corbett placed his tankard back on the table, 'an unholy pact had been created between Evesham, Waldene and Hubert the

Monk. They were hand in glove in their villainy. At the same time Evesham was very able, erudite and skilled. He soon won the attention of old Burnell, the chancellor, but he wanted more. You see, he just didn't kill for profit. He murdered because he enjoyed it. I cannot plumb the machinations of his dark soul, but he wanted to taunt both the very Crown and the lord he served, and so the Mysterium emerged.

'Now, London is a seething pot of intrigue, murderous mayhem and unrest. Intense rivalries divide the Guilds, the merchants, the city fathers. The Great Ones at the Guildhall are not above using the likes of Waldene and Hubert the Monk for swordplay in Cheapside or elsewhere. However, if a merchant hires a dagger man, and that dagger man is caught, he will confess all. Evesham was cunning and subtle. He would approach a merchant and send him a short, curt message: "Your enemy is my enemy. St Paul's VI, 2" or something similar. Of course the merchant or city father concerned would be intrigued. It might take some time to work out the reference to St Paul, but we all know about the great hoarding. Perhaps Evesham then sent another message explaining in greater detail what he was offering: the removal of a rival, a wife, someone who threatened his client. Let us say the merchant concerned agreed—'

'But master, one of those merchants could have gone to Burnell or the King.'

'Perhaps they did, but I doubt it. Nobody wants to be associated with killing, not openly. Nobody wants to admit that their rivalry with someone or their hatred for another person has turned murderous. Evesham may have been wicked, but he was a shrewd observer of human frailty. He'd scrutinise his client very closely. Someone like the merchant Chauntoys, full of resentment at being cuckolded. Down he'd go to St Paul's and place the name of his enemy in that square. Then he would wait for Evesham to kill, or have killed, the chosen victim.'

'Do you think,' Sandewic observed, fascinated by Corbett's revelation, 'that those two miscreants Waldene and Hubert the Monk were party to such slayings?'

'They were certainly involved in Lady Emma's death, I'm sure of it. Mouseman claimed that Evesham and the two gang-leaders had been friends and allies for many a day.'

'And Engleat?' Ranulf asked.

'Evesham's faithful shadow? Of course, and indeed, once a murder has been committed, everyone involved is party to it, an accomplice; they too can go to the scaffold. Participation ensures silence and silence is taken as consent.'

'And the tag?' Ranulf asked. '*Mysterium Rei* – the Mystery of the Thing?'

'Oh, that was Evesham. He was boasting. He couldn't stop proclaiming how clever he was, how subtle. Ranulf, how many murderers have we trapped because they all share that one sin, the arrogance of Lucifer? They glory in what they've done because they see themselves as almost God-like, being able to dispense life and death at a whim.' Corbett paused, crossing his arms. 'Nor must we forget that Evesham liked the rich things of life: an elegant mansion, costly tapestries from Bruges, oaken furniture, the exquisite furnishings of the best craftsmen. He would revel in opulent robes, the finest food and wine. Moreover, he would use the profits of his murderous affrays to ease his way even further along the passageways of power into the heart of the chancery, the court and the Guildhall. Just think – and I am sure it happened – how many suppers he would host, banquets he would arrange, costly gifts for this bishop or that lord, presents to leading citizens, even our noble King. Evesham had a great deal to gain and very little to lose. After all, who would suspect such an upright, loyal, skilled clerk? True, someone like Engleat, Giles Waldene or Hubert the Monk might be tempted to turn King's Approver and seek a reward, or even blackmail Evesham, but that would be highly dangerous.'

'They were all members of the same pack, weren't they?' Chanson spoke up. 'Like wild dogs that roam the streets.'

'Precisely, Chanson. They were probably terrified of Evesham. They were also his accomplices. What would they have to gain through betrayal? If Evesham went down, so would they. I am sure they were generously rewarded for their murderous cooperation. So the Mysterium emerges in the city as a skilled assassin. You can just imagine how Evesham would enjoy himself, relishing the prospect of living a secret life. The humble clerk from the lonely manor on the Welsh March now a leading luminary at Westminster. Of course, he must have known that sooner or later the Crown would intervene. Burnell wanted the assassin trapped. Only then would Evesham consider that the Mysterium had served his purpose and it was time for him to disappear.

'Burnell made careful enquiry amongst the clerks of the chancery, looking for someone to track the Mysterium down. Boniface Ippegrave became devoted to the task. I am not too sure why.'

Corbett unfolded his arms and sighed heavily. 'I have as yet no evidence for this. In the schools of Oxford my hypothesis would be rejected as mere speculation. Somehow, and as yet I cannot explain why, Ippegrave concluded that the Mysterium was a chancery clerk. He listed suspects, men such as Staunton and Blandeford, ambitious young officials, but he also began to look very carefully at Walter Evesham. He kept his own records, some of which have undoubtedly been destroyed, but fragments remain. On one list are the names of fellow clerks, on another Evesham's possible victims: Emma, Bassetlawe, Furnival, Rescales. He brought Evesham under closer scrutiny, and Evesham, no fool, recognised the danger. Boniface Ippegrave had to be dealt with. Already the rumour was circulating in the chancery that the Mysterium might be a clerk at Westminster. Who started that? Boniface, Evesham? I don't really know, but Evesham was intent on silencing Ippegrave once and for all and at the same time bringing the Mysterium's murderous foray to a satisfactory close.'

'Evesham would like that, wouldn't he?' Ranulf intervened. 'He would find it amusing, clever and subtle to rid himself of a dangerous rival, bring the Mysterium's career to an end and then be hailed as the person responsible for it.'

'True, Ranulf, and it was so easy to accomplish. Walter Evesham sends the merchant Chauntoys a message. He kills Chauntoys' wife, then sets up both lure and trap. He orders Chauntoys to bring payment to the Liber Albus and at the same time hires some scrivener in the city to send a note to Boniface Ippegrave to the effect that his presence at a certain time in that same tavern would be of great profit to himself and the King. Boniface rose to the bait; he might even have thought he would learn vital information about the Mysterium.' Corbett paused to drink from his tankard.

'We all know what happened next. The merchant and Ippegrave are arrested and brought across the river into London. Now Ippegrave may have suspected Evesham, but Evesham played a very subtle trick. Chauntoys' widow informed me how surprised Boniface seemed, as well as about hushed conversations between Evesham and his quarry. I believe Evesham told Ippegrave that he didn't really believe he was guilty, that he would provide the opportunity for him to escape and he should take sanctuary in St Botulph's until this matter was cleared up and the mystery resolved.'

'Would Boniface believe that?' Ranulf asked.

'Why not? If he was taken to Newgate, what further opportunity would he have to establish his innocence? Would he even survive such a pestilential place? If he could lodge in St Botulph's, his own parish church, close to his sister, something might be done. I am sure Evesham had a number of choices open to him. If Boniface hadn't escaped, something else would have happened. So Ippegrave flees to St Botulph's and takes sanctuary. Evesham acts like virtue outraged, the honest royal official, furious at his prisoner's escape. He summons the watch, as well as troops from the Tower. He has the church surrounded, every door and window closely guarded. No one, not even Adelicia, is allowed to see Boniface; only the parson, who brings the sanctuary man food and looks after his basic needs.'

'But the ring Adelicia brought?' Ranulf asked.

'Yes, the ring. Again I can't answer that, not yet. You see,' he continued, grasping his blackjack and taking a generous mouthful, 'Evesham and Engleat had decided that Boniface Ippegrave must not leave that church alive. Perhaps when Boniface first escaped he was in a panic, fearful. Now he had had time to think. Only God knows what happened in that church, what hushed conversations took place. Boniface certainly realised the pressing danger.'

'Couldn't he have appealed to Parson Cuthbert?' Ranulf asked.

'What could he say? What proof could he offer? Any counter-allegation made against Evesham would be dismissed as a guilty person trying to pass the blame elsewhere. What Boniface did was open the Book of the Gospels and write that riddle. Remember what he inscribed: "I stand in the centre guiltless and point to the four corners." At the time neither Cuthbert nor Adelicia knew what he meant. However, when I sifted amongst Boniface's papers I came across a scrap of parchment, a square of letters: ABC DEF GHI. It's one of those puzzles much loved by clerks and scholars. Now, again I have no evidence, but if Boniface claims he was standing in the centre, that's the letter E. Was he implying that Evesham was the Mysterium? He reinforces that by saying "I point to the four corners", where the letters are AC GI. As they stand, these don't mean much, but all four letters appear in Ingachin, Evesham's manor, the birthplace he was so proud of. I am Corbett of Leighton, there's Adelicia of Cripplegate, Sandewic of the Tower and, of course, Evesham of Ingachin. Boniface was leaving some sort of warning to whoever might find it. You must remember that he was fearful and apprehensive.'

'So what happened next?' asked Sandewic.

Corbett held his hands up. 'Again this is conjecture. Boniface must have been truly desperate. The evidence against him could appear truly damning.' He emphasised each point on his fingers. 'He could provide no acceptable explanation for his presence with Chauntoys in the Liber Albus. He had escaped and sought sanctuary. Eventually he would have to leave the protection of Holy Mother Church and face the hideous risk of capture or being killed. I suspect that once again he was offered the chance to flee. There was a risk, but it was one that I, and I suspect all of you, would have taken. He had done all he could by voicing his suspicions on the page of that Book of the Gospels.'

'But his suspicions were about Evesham,' Ranulf insisted. 'Why should Boniface trust him?'

'Perhaps Evesham assured him that all he wanted was for Boniface to flee, disappear. Or,' Corbett paused, 'did Evesham use Engleat? Whatever, Evesham, or maybe just Engleat by himself, revealed a plan for Boniface to escape by night. Now imagine it. Darkness falls. Engleat enters the church, bringing with him Evesham's cloak, and tells Boniface a farrago of lies about wanting to help. The solution is so simple. They will walk out through a different door from the one Engleat entered by. Let us say Engleat entered by the north door. He collects Ippegrave, gives him Evesham's cloak and they leave by the corpse door. Who cares? It is dark. All the guards would see is Engleat, and someone they think is Evesham, all cloaked and cowled, leaving the church. Why should they challenge them? Master Evesham had been hot in his detention of Boniface, the last thing those guards expected would be for the very men who'd organised Ippegrave's arrest and then so stringently blockaded the church to be helping their prisoner to escape. Such duplicity, surely, Master Constable, would be beyond your guards' comprehension?'

'True, true,' Sandewic agreed, 'and like this morning we simply had to watch for a fugitive dressed in a Lincoln-green cloak trying to escape. Two men, muffled and cowled, leaving in the dead of night would pass unnoticed. Moreover, the guards were accustomed to seeing Evesham and Engleat together, as we were you and Master Ranulf. We would never dream that such duplicity was being played out.' The constable shook his head. 'So simple,' he murmured, 'so very, very simple, yet so clever.' He cradled his blackjack of ale and whistled under his breath. 'Of course,' he half smiled, 'the guards would be tired, sprawling by their fire. Darkness had fallen. The door opens, unlocked by Engleat, and two men walk out. Engleat assures the guards that all is well and the two figures stride into the night.' Sandewic snapped his fingers. 'All over in a few heartbeats, no longer than it would take to gabble an Ave.' He pointed at Corbett. 'You did the same with Chanson this morning, didn't you? We were all looking for a man dressed in a Lincoln-green cloak.'

'Of course,' Corbett agreed. 'Ranulf and I entered St Botulph's. Ranulf gave Chanson a black cloak to cover his own. Chanson and I left by one door, Ranulf by another. Who'd notice? Who really cared if Ranulf was no longer wearing a cloak? The guards recognised him as my faithful lieutenant, so why challenge him? Such a ploy would be even easier in the dead of night, with cloaks pulled tight, deep cowls shrouding heads and faces.' He paused. 'I know Boniface must have been suspicious, but he was already trapped. Why shouldn't he seize an opportunity to escape? I don't really understand how it actually happened. Perhaps Engleat depicted himself as an angel of light. Chanson here left for a warm tavern, but Boniface was hurried to his death. You can imagine Engleat and Boniface passing quietly and quickly through that cemetery. The assassins, probably Waldene and Hubert, springing up from the ground, knives glittering. It would be over so quickly. St Botulph's cemetery is a sprawling place. Boniface is knocked to the ground by a blow to the back of his head, then his throat is cut. Remember, it was summer. Cuthbert has told us how graves had been dug before the sun baked the ground too hard. Boniface's corpse was tumbled into one of these, then dirt was thrown over it. One corpse amongst many. Who would even think? Somewhere in God's acre, poor Boniface's remains have turned to dust. Our Lady be my witness, I wouldn't even know where to begin my search for them.'

'Yet if Evesham was still alive,' Sandewic declared, 'what you allege would not be enough to convict him before King's Bench.'

'True,' Corbett conceded, 'it's all conjecture, surmise, but it's the only logical conclusion I can reach. Evesham of course was a sinner to the bone, a killer to his very heart. He never changed. He let the dust settle after Ippegrave's disappearance. After all, he was now very wealthy. He'd won the personal attention of the King and was promoted. A great future lay before him. Naturally the Mysterium couldn't return, but Evesham did, like a dog to its vomit. He was caught in the toils of sin. He liked to live the noble judge in the light of day and the thief, the rogue, the outlaw once darkness fell.'

'But if you are correct,' Ranulf interviewed, 'and Boniface

Ippegrave was murdered at St Botulph's, then who visited his sister? The ring he produced? How do you explain that, Sir Hugh? How do you account for the murders of Evesham's wife Clarice, Richard Fink, Waldene, Hubert the Monk and Fleschner the coroner?'

'I don't know,' Corbett sighed, 'not yet. Waldene and Hubert were killed possibly because of their involvement in Lady Emma's murder, and the same is true of Fleschner. He was coroner at the time she was slain.' He chewed his lip. 'All I can say is that the killer seems absolutely determined to annihilate Evesham and all his coven. I believe Engleat, Waldene, the Monk and Fleschner were all caught up in Evesham's web of wickedness. I still can't understand why Clarice and Richard Fink were so barbarously murdered and their heads left in the baptismal bowl at St Botulph's.' He sighed. 'I don't think I will ever secure hard evidence. We are going to have to trap this killer another way. Now look,' he turned to Chanson, 'you are to take writs, sworn out by Ranulf and sealed with green wax, to Brother Cuthbert, Adelicia and Parson John at Syon Abbey. They are to present themselves at the third hour, early tomorrow morning, in St Botulph's church. Once you have delivered the summons, the same applies to Staunton and Blandeford. They too must be brought in. Sir Ralph,' he pointed at the constable, 'in the early hours you are to visit the clerk Lapwing. You are to take both him and his mother from their house in Mitre Street and bring them to St Botulph's under close guard. Ranulf, once you have the writs sworn out, I want that church cleaned, a judgment table and chairs set up, benches, stools and wheeled braziers. Bring some warmth to that benighted place, for tomorrow I shall hold court there.'

'At St Botulph's?' Ranulf exclaimed.

'Why not?' Corbett declared. 'Is it not customary for judges to sit where the actual crime has been committed? Why go to Westminster? Now,' he gestured to a tap boy, 'your presence this morning saved me. I just regret it didn't save poor Griffyths. So before we part, one further blackjack of ale to warm our stomachs and gladden our hearts. Gentlemen,' he raised his almost empty tankard, 'to tomorrow's hunt . . .'

Later on, Corbett lay on the bed in the chamber he had hired at the Golden Thistle. A comfortable room, warmed by the kitchen and scullery below, it was sparse but clean and tidy. Corbett, having removed his boots, sword-belt and cloak, sprawled staring up at the brightly covered tester. He was still puzzled and confused.

'Some of this mystery,' he murmured, 'yes some of it is understandable, but the rest . . .' He still faced the vexed question he had not voiced to his companions when they'd met below. Whoever had committed these hideous murders knew everything that had happened twenty years ago. Corbett was sure of that, but who could it be? He had his suspicions but no evidence; that would have to wait until tomorrow.

13

Ingenium: a poacher's trap

At the third hour the following day, Corbett's court of oyer and terminer opened at the foot of the sanctuary steps beneath the great rood screen of St Botulph's. Corbett openly wondered where Ranulf had spent the previous day, the Clerk of the Green Wax being absent until very late. Only as they broke their fast after attending the dawn Mass did he admit that he had spent a considerable amount of time establishing where those summoned had actually been when Corbett had been attacked.

'I went to Syon to investigate our three recluses. Brother Cuthbert and Adelicia claimed they were in their separate cells, though God knows if that's the truth. Parson John, however, was not in his. He'd felt unwell and was admitted to the infirmary. Its keeper stoutly maintained that he remained there until yesterday evening. As for Staunton and Blandeford, well,' Ranulf pulled a face, 'very difficult to establish where they were, so busy were they about their duties, visiting friends, doing business at the Guildhall and elsewhere.'

'And Master Lapwing?'

'He claims he was at home with his sickly mother, who as you will discover is not so poorly.'

Corbett stared down the church, to where those summoned sat on benches around the roaring braziers.

'They have every luxury,' Ranulf murmured. 'The church is now warm.' He pointed to a side table bearing jugs of mulled wine, platters of bread and dried meat. 'They can eat and drink to their hearts' content.'

'Did they object?'

'Staunton and Blandeford were their usual arrogant selves. They'd heard about the attack on you and were curious. Well, is everything ready, master, the way you want it?'

'Yes,' Corbett replied. 'Yes it is, thank you.'

Ranulf had borrowed the great table from a nearby tavern. It was cleaned and washed, and on it was stretched Corbett's commission with its blood-red seals next to a Book of the Gospels. Close to this stood ink pots, a tray of quills, pumice stones and fresh sheets of the finest vellum. Corbett stared at these. He'd been through the records, and sensed there was a way forward. He'd have to gamble, as he had before, on his secret adversary's malicious arrogance. If he could exploit that, perhaps his opponent would make a mistake. He closed his eyes, whispered a prayer then rose and walked down the nave to meet those summoned.

Staunton and Blandeford looked as sleek and proud as ever, glistening faces framed by vair-lined hoods, the gold and silver clasps of their cloaks glittering in the light of the torches and the host of candles Ranulf had lit.

'Good morning, Sir Hugh. We heard rumours of an assault on

you, the King's own clerk!' Staunton shook his head in disbelief, while Blandeford tutted under his breath. Corbett held their gaze. They were not one whit concerned, but nursed their smugness as they did their goblets of hot posset. 'You'll not keep us long, Sir Hugh?' Staunton jibed. 'We too have business.'

'Not long,' Corbett retorted. 'Not long!'

'God save you, Sir Hugh,' declared Parson John, pushing back his hood.

Corbett smiled at the anxious-faced priest. Despite what he'd suffered, Parson John certainly looked better, clear-eyed, face shaved, more composed. On either side of him sat Brother Cuthbert, bleary-eyed and half asleep, and Adelicia, pale-faced and tense. Corbett nodded at them and wondered if they had spent the night together discussing what was happening. Parson John must have told them about the bloody mayhem in and around St Botulph's.

'Sir Hugh, may I introduce . . .'

Corbett turned to greet Lapwing, all strident and alert in his tawny cote-hardie and black leggings, a heavy mantle of costly sarcanet about his shoulders.

'Master Escolier.' Corbett clasped his hand and glanced at the lady seated behind Lapwing. She didn't rise, but proffered a slender snow-white hand. Corbett bowed, kissed her fingertips then grasped her hand, the skin warm, smooth, soft as silk. He caught the look of slight alarm in her cold blue eyes and noticed the wisps of faded blonde hair beneath the tight wimple framing her lovely face: skin like alabaster, smiling full lips, high cheekbones unadorned by any paints or paste. She was truly beautiful, even though she was dressed in sombre grey like some nun from the Convent of Minoresses.

'Sir Hugh, my mother.'

'Mistress?' Corbett asked.

'Mistress Isabella.' Her voice was cultivated, her Norman French precise. 'Sir Hugh, I am Isabella Escolier.'

'Are you really, my lady?' Corbett gripped her hand tighter, again he glimpsed her alarm. 'If that is so,' he whispered, 'I am honoured to greet you. I assure you, I will not keep you long.' He let go of her hand, bowed and walked back up the nave to the judgement table.

Sandewic, who'd also been sworn in as a justice, entered the church, huffing and puffing, clapping his hands against the cold. Ranulf called everyone to order, and those summoned lined up and swore the oath. Corbett took his seat and the proceedings began. Staunton and Blandeford were invited forward. Corbett treated them curtly.

'I only have a few questions for you, sirs. I would like your measured replies.'

'Yes, Sir Hugh?'

'Who first suggested that the Mysterium might be a chancery clerk?'

Staunton made to reply, but Corbett held up his hand.

'Think,' he insisted. 'Was it Evesham or someone else?'

Staunton opened his mouth, then sighed noisily. 'Sir Hugh, to be honest I thought it was Evesham, but Blandeford and I have discussed this. Perhaps it was Boniface Ippegrave.'

'And Ippegrave, what was his attitude to Evesham?'

Again silence. Blandeford made to reply, but Staunton grasped his arm and answered instead.

'Ippegrave became very curious about Evesham. He began to ask questions, you know, observations, remarks . . .'

'Why?' Corbett insisted. 'The truth!'

'Now that you ask,' Staunton had lost his arrogance, 'Ippegrave appeared to know a great deal about Evesham. He asked questions as if to clarify certain matters.'

'Such as?'

'Oh, his service in Wales, his work in the chancery, who had died, how Evesham was progressing, general questions. In truth I became intrigued. Ippegrave asked me in confidence . . .'

'But you eventually told Evesham?'

'Of course I did. You know why, Sir Hugh. Westminster is a small, narrow world, I was intrigued. I simply informed him about Ippegrave's curiosity.'

'And what was Evesham's reply?' Ranulf asked.

Staunton refused to acknowledge Ranulf, but stared hard at Corbett.

'If I remember correctly, Sir Hugh, he dismissed it laughingly.'

'And Burnell?' Corbett insisted. 'Chancellor Burnell, did he really appoint Evesham to hunt the Mysterium?'

Staunton, no fool, recognised that Corbett was trying to lead him.

'You clear the fog of years, Sir Hugh. Burnell asked for help; Evesham responded.' He flailed a hand. 'Perhaps Ippegrave did as well. I'm not too sure, that's all I can say.'

Staunton and Blandeford, now dismissed, flounced out eager

to escape the rigour of Corbett's questions. Brother Cuthbert and Adelicia came next, sitting on their stools like sinners waiting for absolution. Corbett decided not to question their relationship or what they may have been discussing but immediately took both of them back to events twenty years ago.

'Mistress Adelicia,' he began, 'did your brother have a lover, a leman, a confidante?'

'He may have.'

'Did he?' Corbett insisted.

'Yes,' Adelicia retorted. 'Yes, I think he did. Sometimes I could smell perfume on him.' She pulled a face. 'He seemed like a man in love but he was so secretive.'

'And his gold?'

'I've told you, I don't know. He may have gambled, he played hazard.'

'Brother Cuthbert?'

The lay brother refused to meet Corbett's gaze.

'Brother Cuthbert, you were once a priest. You exercised the faculties of shriving and absolution.'

Cuthbert began to tremble.

'Tell me, Brother. Boniface Ippegrave was *in periculo mortis*, in fear of death. He took sanctuary in your church. He was a good man but he recognised he might die soon. At such a time a man's thoughts turn to his soul, to judgement, to life everlasting. In a word, Brother, did you hear Boniface Ippegrave's confession?'

Brother Cuthbert, eyes brimming with tears, grasped Adelicia's arm. Sandewic, slouched in the chair next to Corbett, pulled himself up. Ranulf forgot his transcribing. Even Chanson on guard further down the nave walked closer as he caught the tension of confrontation. The others, grouped around the braziers, although they could not hear what was being said, fell silent, looking over their shoulders expectantly.

'Well, Brother Cuthbert, did you hear Ippegrave's confession?'

'Yes.'

'I know canon law, Brother,' Corbett continued. 'You cannot, under pain of eternal damnation, reveal what was told to you in confession, but let me ask you questions. Do you believe Boniface Ippegrave was innocent?' He tried to curb his excitement; the answer might provide evidence that the hypothesis he'd created was true. 'Brother, do you believe he was innocent?'

'Yes, yes, I do. Boniface Ippegrave had committed many sins, but not murder.'

'And what do you think of Evesham?' Corbett asked. 'I mean generally, from what you know?'

'Evesham was the devil incarnate, a man bound up in sin. His death was justly deserved.'

'But not just because of the way he treated you or Adelicia afterwards. More because of what Boniface Ippegrave told you in confession. Yes?'

Brother Cuthbert blinked nervously and nodded.

'Do you think, Brother, I mean outside of confession, that Boniface Ippegrave had a lover?'

Brother Cuthbert closed his eyes, opened his mouth and licked his lips.

'Please, Brother,' Corbett pleaded. 'I asked you not what was said in confession but what you think.'

'I believe he had a lover, a woman he truly cared for. I asked him if I could send her a message, but he replied no, that she would hear what had happened and act accordingly.'

'Do you know what he meant by that?'

'No, Sir Hugh, but I had the impression that she would flee.'

'When was this confession made?' Sandewic asked. 'I mean, with Evesham watching you so closely?'

'I took food and the jakes pot in.' Cuthbert smiled thinly. 'Evesham could not enter the sanctuary. Boniface hid at the far end, beyond the high altar. It does not take too long, in such circumstances, for a penitent to whisper a list of sins, protest his innocence over others and receive general absolution. He shrugged. 'To be honest, the confession came piecemeal during Boniface's second day in sanctuary, whenever I tended to him. A whisper here, a whisper there. I could recite the absolution later.'

'And Brother, after listening to that confession, I simply ask your opinion, not what you heard. Coroner Fleschner, who wielded authority in Cripplegate, did you have a high regard for him?'

Again Brother Cuthbert grasped Adelicia's arm and stared hard at her. Corbett realised that whatever this priest had heard in confession, he'd already hinted the same to this woman.

'I heard things, Sir Hugh, things that were of public interest. Later on, I met Master Fleschner and told him how in my view he had no right to act as coroner, that he was Evesham's creature. He was a weak man, Sir Hugh, but still good. I suspect he knew what I was hinting at.'

'Which was?'

Brother Cuthbert shook his head. 'You push me too far. You recognise the seal of confession. I cannot break that.'

'Very well.' Corbett paused. 'Let me phrase the question another way. Emma Evesham was killed in a street assault. Coroner Fleschner investigated the murder. No real conclusion was drawn. What do you think of that, Brother?'

Cuthbert smiled weakly. He realised where Corbett was leading him.

'I would say, Sir Hugh, that Coroner Fleschner should have investigated such an assault more stringently, searched for suspects, but he did not.'

'Why do you think that was?'

'Because of Evesham, that devil incarnate.'

'When Evesham took refuge at Syon Abbey, did you ever discuss these matters with him?'

'Sir Hugh, I have told you the truth about that. I could hardly look at him, let alone talk to him. I knew what he truly was and so do you. What was the use of lecturing him? He was an evil man who did evil things.'

'And you, Adelicia, you brought your mother's ring to St Botulph's but Evesham took it off you?'

'I have told you that.'

'We know from Brother Cuthbert that Evesham handed that ring over to Boniface Ippegrave. What happened to it then?'

'Boniface must have kept it,' Adelicia retorted. 'My midnight visitor handed it back to me. Perhaps my brother is still alive.'

'Mistress,' Corbett stared sadly at her, 'your midnight visitor was definitely not your brother. It would be cruel to hold out any hope that you will see him this side of heaven.' He rose, came around the table and, crouching beside Adelicia, clasped her hand as he told her about his conclusions. How Boniface had been lured to this church, taken out in the dark and murdered. Once he'd finished, Adelicia sat, head bowed, quietly sobbing.

'God save you, mistress,' Corbett whispered, 'but I can't even tell you where he is buried.'

'Then who?' Adelicia lifted her tear-stained face. 'Who approached me in the dead of night? How did he get that ring?'

'I am sure your brother's corpse was stripped of any possessions or valuables. Evesham and his assassins would have seen to that. No mark of recognition would be found. One of them must have taken it, but who, or how your mysterious midnight visitor acquired it, I don't know, not yet.'

'Hell's foul fiend!' Brother Cuthbert grated. 'Evesham was a midnight soul. Now that you have told us the truth, Sir Hugh, I can reveal a little more.' He swallowed hard, one rheumatic hand going to his unshaven cheek. 'Boniface truly believed the Mysterium was a chancery clerk, but he was not certain. At one time he even suspected Staunton,' Cuthbert crossed himself. 'What you say is correct, in parts. Boniface, however, found it difficult to accept that Evesham, who could be so very charming, was an assassin, a man who'd killed his wife and any rivals in the chancery.'

'So?'

'Engleat,' whispered Cuthbert. 'Boniface wondered if Engleat was the Mysterium.'

'But what was the logic to that?'

'Think, Sir Hugh. Engleat rose with Evesham. When Evesham

260

fell, so did Engleat. Did he clear rivals out of Evesham's path? So that where his master went he could follow? Reflect.' Brother Cuthbert pointed at Ranulf. 'Have you not made him? Does he not ride high in your retinue? Engleat was no different. Did he arrange the killing of Emma? Did he see her as a rival, an obstacle for his master? When Boniface was arrested in Southwark he whispered such suspicions to Evesham, who then allowed him to escape to safe sanctuary here.'

'Of course.' Corbett rose and stared down the church. 'Of course that makes sense!'

'What does?' Sandewic barked. 'Sir Hugh, I cannot hear such whisperings.'

'My apologies.' Corbett went and sat down behind the table. 'Imagine Evesham taking Ippegrave into the city. Ippegrave hotly but quietly hisses his own suspicions. Evesham appears to co-operate, but already a plan is forming. Boniface Ippegrave must be depicted as the Mysterium and killed, either fleeing the law or by accident. What he certainly does not want is Ippegrave appearing before King's Bench to voice his allegations.' Corbett spread his hands. 'We'll never know what plots curled and weaved in Evesham's brain, busy as a box of worms, except for one decision. Boniface Ippegrave was marked down for sudden death. Evesham allowed him to escape from the comitatus to demonstrate his good will. Later he entered the sanctuary of St Botulph's, a demon disguised as an angel of light, and lured Boniface out into the dark where the assassins clustered. Yes,' Corbett tapped the table, 'I can imagine him accepting Boniface's allegations, whispering how he must escape until the matter was investigated. He may even have suspected you were hearing Boniface's confession, but why should he care? You could not reveal what was said under the seal of confession, which in fact would only assist Evesham in persuading Boniface to escape from St Botulph's and the supposedly malign influence of Longleat. An escape that would play directly into Evesham's hands. Boniface would be publicly depicted as a guilty fugitive, but in truth he was taken out for summary execution and silenced for ever.'

Corbett stared down the nave. Cuthbert's allegations made sense. Evesham's actions possessed their own deadly logic. Engleat could easily be depicted as the wicked servant with a will of his own. He glanced quickly at Ranulf. Did the clerk nurse his own secret ambitions? Would his friendship for Corbett withstand the allure of power? Would all the years of comradeship be one day weighed in the balance and found wanting? Boniface had pursued his quarry but then made a fatal mistake: unable to accept Evesham's true wickedness, he'd turned on Engleat.

'But that square of letters?' Ranulf insisted.

'We thought of that.' Brother Cuthbert gathered the knotted cord around his waist. 'Adelicia and I have discussed it many a time. We could see how Boniface reached his conclusion. Engleat was the child of a Gascon squire and a Spanish woman who came to England in the retinue of Eleanor of Castile. The corners of the square hold the letters A,C,G and I. They are contained in the title of Evesham's manor, but they are also part of Engleat's first name, Ignacio.'

'Whilst the E,' Ranulf murmured, 'could stand for Engleat as well as Evesham.'

'But, in the end,' declared Corbett, 'it was all a lie.'

'Yes,' Brother Cuthbert conceded mournfully. 'Evesham was the root and the cause of all this evil. He let Engleat take the blame to achieve what he wanted, Boniface's death.'

Cuthbert grasped Adelicia's hand. 'We have discussed this over the years. After Evesham came to Syon, whenever I could I fled from St Lazarus' Chapel. I wanted to be nowhere near him. I was not interested in talking to such a malevolent man.'

'And the killer must have known this,' Ranulf remarked.

'Yes.'

'What,' Corbett asked, 'did Evesham intend by taking refuge there?'

'Certainly not repentance or absolution!' Adelicia snapped.

'I think he was waiting,' Brother Cuthbert murmured.

'For what?'

'I don't know. The King, perhaps, to change, to relent, I cannot say. I had so little to do with him.'

'Brother Cuthbert, you heard Boniface's confession. Did he ever mention a woman called Beatrice?'

The lay brother became agitated. 'Sir Hugh, Sir Hugh,' he pleaded. 'You keep pressing me. You know canon law: to break the seal of confession warrants instant excommunication. The same penalty is levelled against those who persuade a priest to break it.'

'But you have discussed the same with Adelicia?'

'Only when she asks questions that reveal that she knew the truth.'

'Which is?' Ranulf asked harshly.

'I cannot, I will not break the seal of confession,' Brother Cuthbert murmured. 'But yes, I will tell you for other reasons. There was a woman, Beatrice, in Boniface's life but I don't know who she was. He confessed his sins; on one occasion I think he was going to ask me to take a message to her, but then,' he shook his head and turned away, 'he made no further mention of it.'

'And the reason you are telling us this now?' Ranulf demanded.

'Some time later, just before I left for Syon, I was here in this church, listening to confessions, giving absolution. You know how it is. I sit with my back to the prie-dieu where those who want the sacrament kneel and whisper their sins. A woman came but she did not ask for confession; instead she demanded what I knew about Boniface Ippegrave. I was going to turn round, but she pleaded with me not to, pointing out that it would be to no avail, since she was cowled and visored. She said that all she wanted was the truth. What had happened to Boniface Ippegrave? She said her name was Beatrice. Hadn't Boniface mentioned her to me? I think she told me that as reassurance, to convince me of her own good faith. She had a lovely voice. I smelled her fragrant perfume. I could not help her. I declared before God that Boniface Ippegrave had taken sanctuary here then disappeared. I dared not tell her my suspicions and so she left. Sir Hugh, I know what you are going to say. Why didn't I tell you this before? Because it was all caught up in the sacrament of absolution, and in the end, what proof do I have that it is the truth? Not much. According to the law, Boniface Ippegrave was a felon who disappeared. How many lawyers in the King's court would cry over him or plead for justice on his behalf?'

'Tell me then,' Corbett asked, 'as a priest, a man who has the power to consecrate the bread and wine into Christ's body and blood, have you, on solemn oath, ever discussed this with anyone apart from the Lady Adelicia?'

'Never!' Brother Cuthbert retorted. 'Not even with my own confessor.'

'Is there,' Ranulf demanded, 'anything else you know that could help us?'

'Nothing. I don't know how Evesham died. I don't know why he came to Syon. All I can say, and not because Adelicia is his sister, is that I shall go to my grave claiming that Boniface Ippegrave was innocent.' He leaned forward. 'And you, Sir Hugh, have our most grateful thanks. If you can see this matter through . . .'

'If I see this matter through,' Corbett retorted, 'I will ensure that a pardon is issued clearing Boniface Ippegrave of any crime, though God knows what good that will do in this vale of tears.'

'It will help me, Sir Hugh,' whispered Adelicia. 'It will show me that God's justice can be done, even if it is through a King's clerk . . .'

Parson John came next. He sat composed on the stool fingering a small ring of Ave beads. Corbett asked what he knew about his father's death. The priest held up a hand. 'Sir Hugh, nothing, nothing, about his death or his crimes.'

'Then listen.' And in short, pithy sentences, Corbett described his conclusions. Parson John sat dull-eyed, mouth gaping. He did not exclaim or cry out, but rocked himself backwards and forwards, face in his hands.

'Did you know any of this?' Ranulf demanded.

Parson John took his hands away. 'For the love of God,' he

wailed, 'how could I? I was a mere child when my mother died, then I was sent away. Ippegrave, Waldene, Hubert the Monk, Engleat, who are these to me? Who'd come and tell me the truth, that my father, a leading justice in King's Bench, was as foul a felon as any strangled at Smithfield, that he'd murdered rivals at Westminster as well as my beloved mother?'

'You never suspected?'

'In the name of all that's holy, why should I suspect anything when the King himself did not know? My mother?' Parson John fought back the tears. 'I was told she had been killed in an attack by felons, wolfsheads.'

'Was mention ever made of a woman named Beatrice, your mother's maid?'

Parson John screwed up his eyes. 'Yes, yes, but she disappeared at the time. People did not know what had happened to her. My father mentioned that she'd been abducted. Sir Hugh, my father was so busy about his many affairs that he'd very little time for me. I ask you again, how could I know all this? I knew nothing, I know nothing,' he added flatly.

'True, true,' Corbett replied. 'And these recent killings?'

Parson John touched the scar on his forehead. 'Someone, Sir Hugh, who, rightly or wrongly, wages unholy war on my father and all his kin.'

'Did Fleschner ever discuss your father?'

'Fleschner was a good but very weak man. Like me he feared my father, but he hardly ever spoke of him.'

'You know he was guilty of looking the other way regarding your mother's death.'

'Yes, so you told me, but that would be Fleschner's way. He was hardly going to confess such a sin to me, was he?'

Corbett smiled in agreement.

'I owe Fleschner my life,' Parson John whispered. 'He rescued me here in this hideous church.' He began to mumble, and Corbett dismissed him, eager for Lapwing and his mother, Mistress Isabella, to take their seats. He gestured at this subtle clerk.

'Master Lapwing, or Master Stephen Escolier, or whatever you like to call yourself, we do have questions about that riot in Newgate.'

'Which are?' The reply was impudent, delivered in an arrogant tone.

'You went there,' Corbett said, 'you spread the rumours that one of the gang was to turn King's Approver and accuse the other. A riot ensued.' He leaned across the table. 'No one here gives a fig about such wolfsheads, but they broke out and killed innocents, the King's loyal, law-abiding subjects.' He jabbed a finger. 'You also spun the tale that St Botulph's would be a secure refuge with a secret passageway to safety. In truth all you did was bring about the total destruction of those felons, as well as the savage murder of innocents, men hacked down, women raped and abused.'

'If I did what you claim, sir, I was acting on the King's orders. What these felons did, however, is a matter for their own consciences.'

'Mistress Isabella,' Corbett turned to the woman, 'we were told you were sickly, yet you look comely and healthy enough.'

'I was very ill with fever last Advent. Indeed, I feared death was so close I went to receive my Christmas shriving at St Paul's, but yes, I am better, particularly now that my son has returned. Sir Hugh, he is a royal clerk, but what do I have to do with this business?'

'Yes, yes.' Corbett lowered his head to hide his excitement. He was sure, he was certain. 'What do you, Mistress Beatrice, have to do with this business?'

'Nothing!' The woman's hand flew to her lips. 'I am sorry,' she stammered, 'you startled me.'

'Of course I did,' Corbett replied. 'Let me see now. Isabella Escolier, so the son, so the mother. You were once called Mathilda? Yes? Or some other name beginning with M, but the one given you at the baptismal font was Beatrice. Twenty years ago you were maid to Emma Evesham, wife to Sir Walter, now deceased. You were with her when she was attacked in the streets. What happened to you afterwards, well, I don't know the details, but one thing is certain. You became the leman, the mistress, perhaps even the wife of the chancery clerk Boniface Ippegrave, and this,' Corbett pointed at Lapwing, 'is your son, the child you had by Boniface.' His raised voice alerted those clustered further down the nave. Parson John, Brother Cuthbert and Adelicia left their stools and were staring back up the church. Corbett waved at them to sit.

'Oh yes,' he insisted, 'Beatrice who became Mathilda. Boniface was so in love with you, he scrawled the first letter of your new name against his, separated by a heart, the mark of lovers.'

'I don't know what you are talking about,' spluttered Lapwing, all the arrogant certainty drained from his face. 'Sir Hugh, how can you say that about my mother?'

'Very easily,' Sandewic snarled. 'You and your mother are on solemn pledge before the King's commissioners. Lying on oath is perjury, and she can hang for that, as can you, sir.'

'I'm a clerk.'

'You're still a liar,' taunted Ranulf, hiding his own surprise. Sir Hugh had kept all this well hidden.

'You're wondering how I know?' Corbett asked. 'Stare around this church, Mistress Beatrice. Name me one person who knew exactly what happened twenty years ago, and I mean exactly. Staunton or Blandeford? They were only spectators. Parson John? A mere child. Brother Cuthbert and Adelicia? Broken by a man you hated deeply.' Corbett pointed at her. 'I believe only you know the truth, mistress. Now this is what will happen if you continue to lie. You will be confined to Newgate, and your son will tell you what a foul pit that is. It has a great cobbled yard, the stones of which are particularly sharp and pointed. You will be stretched out on your back and a door will be placed over you, then weights, increasingly heavy, will be loaded on to that. You'll be pressed until you confess the truth.'

'I am innocent.'

'You are not innocent,' Corbett countered. 'You know the secrets behind all the murderous frenzy that plagues this church.'

'I do not.'

'Or at least some of those secrets,' Corbett continued remorselessly. 'One thing is certain, mistress, you are not going to leave this church wiping your mouth on the back of your hand and claiming you know nothing when indeed you do. Moreover, I'll make careful investigation. Oh, it may take a week, two weeks, a month perhaps, but eventually,' his voice rose, 'you will be depicted as the liar you truly are and your son as the killer he is.'

'That's not true!' Lapwing protested

'It is, according to the evidence,' Corbett retorted. 'Someone in this church knew what happened twenty years ago. Your mother did and she passed that information to you. Take a mirror, Master Lapwing, look into it. I knew your father vaguely. I remember the colour of his hair. You have the same; that's what made me wonder about young Lapwing flapping like a busy bird around all this. Sir Ralph, call your guards and have Mistress Beatrice taken into custody. She'll spend the rest of the day in Newgate and be pressed tomorrow morning.'

'It's true,' Lapwing blurted out. 'It's true.' He stilled his mother's protests with his hand, holding Corbett's gaze. 'Mother, I know what he'll do. He'll pursue us like some lurcher after a hare. He'll urge you to confess. He'll inflict pain. It doesn't really matter what happens as long as he gets the truth, so tell him I'm no killer, no assassin.'

'I think you are,' Corbett retorted, 'and I shall prove that according to the law, but you've saved your mother from being pressed. So, Mistress Beatrice,' he shifted his gaze, 'the truth, every morsel of it!'

14

Maindefer: hand of iron

'I was born Beatrice Sturmy,' she began, 'a clothier's daughter. I knew the Lady Emma before her marriage. After she became hand-fast to Sir Walter, she invited me to be her maid. I accepted. She was gracious, kind and sweet-natured. I entered her household.'

'And the marriage?'

'Lady Emma seemed happy enough. She became pregnant and bore Sir Walter a son.'

'Did you know about Evesham's secret life, his nefarious activities under the cloak of night?'

'Sir Hugh, I knew very little. Sir Walter was always smiling, though I would use the word smirking. He could be free with his hands. I often glimpsed him staring hotly at me. On one occasion he tried to seduce me, but I pushed him away. I threatened to tell his wife but I never did, I hadn't the heart. She seemed happy enough. Sir Walter always gave the impression that he'd married beneath him, but that was part of his sneering attitude. He liked to show how clever and subtle he was, how highly regarded in the chancery at Westminster.

'Lady Emma and I were often invited to this banquet or that, and it was at one of these that I met Boniface Ippegrave. He was a good clerk, Sir Hugh; who knows, he may have risen to the same high position as yourself. He was clever, industrious, witty and kind. He had a passion for gambling, but he was good at it. On one occasion he took me aside and showed me his winnings, a heavy purse of gold.'

'And you believed him?'

'Yes, I did, as I have always believed that he was no killer. I knew Boniface Ippegrave. I slept with him. He had a good heart and a pure soul; he was a man of honour, someone dedicated to the truth. That is why I am confessing now, not because I am frightened of pain or disgrace.' She leaned over and squeezed her son's arm. 'It is also the time for the truth. I made one hideous mistake, as did the Lady Emma. We never really understood the depths of Evesham's wickedness. Oh, I wondered about him, but I always put it down to chancery business, why he would slip out after dark for this secret meeting or that, why night-walkers visited the house.'

'You mean the likes of Giles Waldene and Hubert the Monk?'

'Yes, on a number of occasions I saw them in his company. I wasn't supposed to, but after his attempted seduction, I kept a very sharp eye on Evesham and all his doings.'

'But you never knew his true relationship with them?'

'Never! Don't you, sir,' she asked archly, 'have your own confidants amongst the wolfsheads and outlaws of Westminster? I thought Walter Evesham had the same.'

'Until when?'

'Until the day my mistress was killed. We went to visit an almshouse. As I said, Lady Emma had a kind heart. She always protested that she had more than enough and was ever prepared to share the rest with the poor. Darkness was falling, a mist-hung evening. We were hurrying along a runnel when I heard Lady Evesham's name called. She turned, pushing back her hood, then they were on us, daggers flashing. They were cowled and visored, but I recognised the bottom half of Hubert the Monk's ugly face.'

'How did you escape?'

'Because of Lady Emma. I was surprised, Sir Hugh. I knew she was kind, but on that evening she also showed her brave heart. She told me to flee, and God forgive me, I did, a sin that has always haunted me. My mistress was kneeling down, and both men were standing over her. As I said, it was misty, the light was poor. I was only a slip of a girl. I panicked and fled into the night.' She paused. 'Even as I ran, I realised Evesham might have had a hand in that attack; those men were waiting for us. I had some silver on me, I took a wherry downriver to Westminster. Boniface was there. I told him what had happened. At first he refused to believe me, but when the news seeped through of Lady Evesham's death, he hid me away and our relationship began. Boniface was just and true. At first I thought I could hide until Evesham forgot me. Then the Mysterium emerged and the murders began. Boniface would come home and discuss the problem with me. He believed the assassin must be a high-ranking clerk, someone who sifted the gossip of the city. He cast his net wide and far.' She smiled thinly. 'Do you know, Sir Hugh, he even mentioned you. He called you the silent one, who always watched and said very little, a junior clerk with great promise.'

'I served then in the Chancery of the Green Wax. Mistress, do continue.'

'Boniface brought Evesham under close scrutiny. He was clever; he would slip out at night and began to see and hear things about Evesham. Yet strange as it is, he had a liking for the man. Engleat, though, he called an evil presence, Evesham's malevolent shadow.' She paused.

'Mistress?'

'God forgive me. I encouraged him in such thoughts. When I served Lady Emma, Engleat was like a malignant shadow forever hovering about. A viper of a man who seemed to have no love for women except, according to household rumour, the costliest strumpets in Cheapside.'

'Evesham, Engleat, they must have searched for you?'

'Boniface was clever. He openly lodged with his sister but he hired secret lodgings for me in Paternoster Row. Because of what he earned, as well as his gambling, he was able to furnish good chambers, warm and snug. You guessed correctly. I assumed another name, Mathilda. I was always very skilled with the needle and I made good silver as a seamstress. Time passed. Boniface became busy on this task or that, but what he called Evesham's web truly fascinated him. He came to realise that Evesham seemed to exercise power and influence well beyond Westminster. He couldn't really decide between Engleat and Evesham; was it an unholy alliance? Was Evesham really innocent of any wrongdoing? Was Engleat the guilty one? Or did Evesham just turn a blind eye to his companion's malice? He played with the problem as any scholar would a vexed question of logic, constructing puzzles, composing verses—'

'I stand in the centre, guiltless,' Corbett interrupted, 'and point to the four corners.'

'Yes, yes,' Beatrice replied, 'that was one of them. Boniface, however, was determined on one conclusion. He truly believed that through Evesham and Engleat he could unmask the Mysterium. He never really told me the details, though he listed names, possibilities. He kept going back to the death of Lady Evesham and those involved. He believed Coroner Fleschner could have done more, and wondered if that official was in the pay of, or being blackmailed by, Engleat, Evesham or both of them. In the days before Boniface's death—'

'So you were certain that he was killed?' Corbett asked.

'Boniface would never desert me. In those last days he became frenetically busy, so absorbed with the problem I did not tell him I was enceinte, expecting a child. Then it happened. Rumours swept the ward about how Boniface Ippegrave, arrested in Southwark, had fled to St Botulph's in Cripplegate. I wanted to visit him, but he had warned me to be very wary, especially of Engleat. I did come down here but the church was closely guarded by soldiers and bailiffs. I became frightened and went into hiding, and then Boniface disappeared. Oh, I heard the rumours, the gossip and the chatter, which over the weeks gradually faded. In my heart I knew Boniface was dead. If he had survived, if he had escaped, he would have come back to me.' Her voice shook. I grew deeply concerned for myself,' she stretched across and grasped Lapwing's arm, 'and for my unborn child. I fled to a distant kinswoman in Winchester, where Stephen was born. I took yet another name and professed to be a widow, and an old wool merchant, wealthy and kind, asked for my hand in marriage. He accepted Stephen as his own, educated him, sent him to the schools then on to the halls of Oxford . . .'

'Do you think,' Ranulf demanded, 'that Evesham suspected Boniface was sheltering you? Was that another reason he turned on him?'

'Perhaps,' Beatrice murmured, 'but what danger would I be to Evesham? A maid who'd fled when her mistress was murdered.'

'So tell me, mistress,' Corbett intervened. 'You are on oath. I ask you, on your loyalty to the King, have you ever told any other living person apart from your son what you have just confessed to me?'

'No,' she replied flatly. 'I wish to God I could say I had. I know what you are going to conclude, Sir Hugh.'

'Stephen Escolier,' Corbett's voice turned hard, 'also known as the Lapwing. You are young, energetic and skilled. You had the motive and the strength to kill Sir Walter Evesham, his henchman Engleat, Waldene and Hubert the Monk. Coroner Fleschner was also guilty of crimes against your mother, so he too died. Clarice, Evesham's second wife, you viewed as guilty by association with Evesham. You killed her and the man who tried to protect her, Richard Fink. You also entered this church and tried to slay Evesham's son, Parson John. On occasions you took your father's name, on others you aped the Mysterium, the assassin your father hunted. The evidence against you weighs heavy. Can you give me any reason why I should not arraign you for murder before King's Bench?'

'No, no,' whimpered Beatrice, 'no, it can't be!'

'Mistress, who else knew what you did? Either your son is guilty, or both of you are. Remember, you've still to account for your own conduct in escaping the murderous attack upon your former mistress Lady Emma.'

'I know, I know,' Beatrice whispered. 'To quote the psalm, that sin is always before me. I knew that one day I would have to pay a terrible price.'

'Master Stephen,' Corbett rose to his feet, 'how say you?'

The accused clerk, face pale and taut, just stared back. He opened his mouth, but then closed it and stared beseechingly at his mother.

'Sir Ralph?'

Sandewic leapt to this feet, shouting orders at the guards near the door. Lapwing broke from his fear.

'They deserved it!' he screamed, lunging at Corbett. Chanson came up behind and grasped him by the shoulder, and Ranulf ran around the table and helped him pull Lapwing back.

'They deserved it!' Lapwing screamed again. 'They killed my father, and given the opportunity they would have killed me. God's judgement was visited on them and they died for their sins. I have no regrets, do you hear, king's clerk?' He licked the froth from his lips. 'But I'm also innocent,' he moaned.

'You face many charges.' Corbett approached and tapped him on the chest. 'One hideous murder after another, then there's the affray at Newgate and the poor innocents who died in and around this church. You have a great deal to answer for.' He grasped Lapwing's wrist between his hands. 'Do you think,' he hissed, 'that because you are a clerk you can claim benefit of clergy, that your powerful friends Staunton and Blandeford will help you? I tell you this, sir,' he ignored the piteous sobbing from Beatrice, who sat crumpled on a stool, 'you will never be a free man. Sir Ralph, have your guards take Master Lapwing to the Tower. Lodge him in the keep.'

'And his mother?' asked the constable.

Corbett crouched beside Beatrice, pulling her hands away from her face. 'Mistress, the case against your son presses sorely hard, as it does against you. You may return to your lodgings. If you attempt to flee, that will be taken as a sign not only of your own guilt but also your son's. If you're captured fleeing you could be hanged out of hand. Do you understand me? You must know the law and its penalties.'

Beatrice, face ghostly white, stared back, eyes shocked, lips trembling.

'Master Sandewic, have someone escort Mistress Beatrice back to her lodgings. Lapwing, you're for the Tower. Perhaps the King's questioners can elicit the truth from you.'

'I'll not be put to the torture,' Lapwing whispered.

'What you have done,' Corbett intervened swiftly, 'is a matter for the courts. Now take him away.'

Lapwing, recovered from his shock, tried to break free of his guards, shouting curses at Corbett before turning tearfully to his mother, who, escorted by two archers, trailed sorrowfully behind. The procession left the church, the door slamming shut behind them. Sandewic grabbed his sword-belt and cloak from one of his henchmen and fastened these on, asking Corbett if the business was finished. He replied that it was, and was making to go down the nave when Ranulf plucked him by the sleeve.

'The evidence against Lapwing weighs heavy. His own mother's confession was damning enough. After all, who else knew?' He pointed down the nave. 'They certainly didn't.'

Corbett nodded, eager to join the remaining three. They'd watched the drama unfold and were now staring expectantly towards him.

'Sir Hugh?'

'Yes, Ranulf?'

'Lapwing had no war dog. You never mentioned that murderous assault on you.'

'Think.' Corbett walked back. 'Think, Ranulf.' He raised his voice so that it echoed through the hollow church. 'Lapwing was as accustomed to dealing with the wolfsheads and outlaws in the Sanctuaries at Westminster and White Friars as we are. In this city you can hire killers by the dozen. I am sure he did that. Thank God he failed. I'd be grateful,' he gestured around, 'if you'd douse the braziers, the lights and candles. Lock this church behind me.'

'I'll do it, and then . . .'

'And then what, Ranulf?'

'Certain business in the city.' Ranulf smiled, eager to evade Corbett's hard glance. 'We should celebrate, Sir Hugh. You'll return to Leighton Manor?'

'In a while,' Corbett retorted. 'When this is truly finished.'

He walked down the nave to where Brother Cuthbert stood with Adelicia resting on his arm. Parson John beside them raised his hand in blessing.

'Sir Hugh,' asked the priest, 'is it true? We've heard some of it. Will Master Lapwing be indicted for these hideous murders?'

'He'll certainly go before King's Bench.'

'And his mother?' Brother Cuthbert asked.

'She too will face charges.' Corbett walked across and extended his hand for Parson John to grasp. The priest's grip was limp, fingers cold. 'I'm sorry,' Corbett murmured, holding his gaze. 'Your mother being brutally murdered. I tell you this, sir, the woman who calls herself Mistress Beatrice has a great deal to answer for.'

'Could she have been an accomplice?' Parson John asked.

'Certainly,' Corbett replied, 'and I assure you, when Master Lapwing goes on trial in Westminster Hall, you will all be there to hear the evidence.'

Beatrice Escolier dug her needle into the intricately brocaded cover, then lifted her head and stared around the small but comfortable solar of her narrow house in Mitre Street. She pushed away the footstool and spread her hands to catch the warmth from the fire burning merrily in its covered hearth. She stared at the carved faces of the woodwoses that decorated the mantel and wondered about Sir Hugh Corbett, so clever, so cunning, yet, like an arrow launched true and straight, aiming for its mark. In many ways he reminded Beatrice of Boniface, single-minded and determined. She stared across at the shuttered window. Another day had passed. Despite what Corbett had said, nothing had happened. Here she was in a warm, sweet-smelling chamber whilst Stephen languished in some cold dungeon in the Tower. She'd pleaded for him, wanted to visit him, but Corbett had proved obdurate. She must stay here and wait.

Beatrice sighed, rose and lit the lantern horn on the flat top of the black oaken chest, then the candles on their spigots. Tongues of flame glowed greedily, shooting up to catch the glitter from the cups, ewers, mazers and silver platters on the shelves, the mother-of-pearl wall crucifix as well as the gold and silver threads of the tapestries covering the walls. She moved back to the chair before the fire, her hand grazing the psalter on the small table next to it. Perhaps she should pray. She moved a candlestick, took up the psalter and turned to her favourite prayer, the Benedictus of Simeon. She always admired the exquisite, minutely jewelled painting that decorated the capital B. The young clerk depicted there in his green cote-hardie and white leggings, standing in a stall holding a breviary, always reminded her of Boniface.

Beatrice began to cry quietly. She settled back in the chair, giving way to her memories and the cloying heat. If she half closed her eyes in this chamber of dappled light, she might catch her beloved staring at her as he always did with that lovely smile. She closed her eyes then startled at the knocking on the front door. She picked up a candlestick and went out into the icy passageway, the cold from the flagstones seeping through the soft warmth of her buskins.

'Who's there?' she called.

'Mistress, it's only Parson John. I've come to ensure all is well, to show I bear no ill favour.'

Beatrice bit her lip, pulled back the bolts at top and bottom and opened the door. The light was swiftly fading. Parson John, muffled in a great cloak, stamped his feet, pulled down the muffler from his mouth and smiled as he showed her the small stoppered flask in his right hand. 'Mistress, I am freezing, but this is rich claret, the best from the vineyards of Gascony. Heated with a burning poker and sprinkled with some crushed apple and nutmeg, it would make a heart-warming posset.'

'Come in, Father, come in.'

The priest passed by her and she closed the door.

'You've bolted it?' he asked.

'No, Father.' Beatrice smiled. 'Now you're here that's protection enough. Do . . .' She gestured at the door to the solar. 'Go in and warm yourself.' She bustled in after him, pulling out a stool so the priest could sit by the fire. Parson John undid his cloak, pulled off his gloves and sat down, hands towards the heat.

'Mistress,' he smiled, 'unstopper the flask, let's drink some warmth.'

She hastened to obey, taking down two pewter goblets from the shelf above the mantle. She placed these on the table, broke the seal of the flask and filled both cups, then busied herself thrusting two narrow pokers into the burning logs, before going towards the scullery to search for her nutmeg sprinkler. She was almost there when the door to the solar opened and she whirled round with a start. Sir Hugh Corbett, followed by his two henchmen, Ranulf and Chanson, entered. Parson John sprang to his feet.

'Sir Hugh, I never heard you . . .'

'You were not supposed to.' Corbett pressed the priest's shoulder, forcing him to retake his seat. 'Ranulf, help Mistress Beatrice make us all comfortable.' He gestured at the quilted seat. 'I'll sit here, next to our good Parson John.' His voice, rich with sarcasm, made the priest turn abruptly. 'Oh, by the way,' Corbett pointed at the belt around the priest's waist with its long sheathed dagger, 'unbuckle that, sir.'

Parson John obeyed. Corbett took the belt and placed it on the other side of his chair. Ranulf had pulled up another stool so that he could sit on the parson's right. Chanson, armed with a small arbalest, stayed near the door. Corbett sniffed the air appreciatively.

'Sweet herbs, good meat and fine wine.' He picked up the flask. 'You brought this, Parson John?'

'Yes, a gift to share with Mistress Beatrice. I wish to comfort her.'

'I was about to make a posset,' Beatrice snapped peevishly from where she stood next to the door to the small scullery.

'Why waste such good wine on a posset?' Corbett picked up one of the goblets and thrust it at the priest. 'Drink.' His smile faded. 'Drink!' he repeated.

Parson John, face all tense, just stared back.

'Drink,' whispered Ranulf, bringing up the dagger concealed in his hand. He pricked the priest under the chin with its point, and Beatrice gave a small scream of protest, which died as Parson John pushed the goblet away.

'I don't feel like wine, Sir Hugh, not now. I should leave . . .'

Again Ranulf's dagger came up.

'Mistress,' Corbett warned, 'do not even think of drinking such a gift. I am sure it's poisoned, death-bearing.' He clapped Parson

John on the shoulder. 'You are in so many ways your father's true son. You came here as a wolf in sheep's clothing to finish the game, to kill the last person on your murderous list.'

'Lapwing is the murderer.' Parson John retorted. 'Lapwing is in the Tower for his crimes?'

'And he can stay there,' Corbett retorted. 'Master Escolier has a great deal to answer for, unless his grace the King decides otherwise, and I think he might. Certain questions about the riot in Newgate have to be put to him, but as for what happened recently in St Botulph's, that, in the main, was mummery. I recognised that something was wrong. Lapwing always denied he was the writer from the Land of Cockaigne.'

'What?'

'Oh don't act the innocent. There are so many unresolved questions. I never really understood why Lapwing should kill Mistress Clarice and her lover Richard Fink.'

'I don't—'

'I asked myself one constant question,' Corbett continued softly. 'Who knew the truth about Evesham's evil doings? Most likely Mistress Beatrice. She, in turn, admitted that the only person she ever told was her son, the clerk who calls himself Lapwing. She was not lying. She simply overlooked one important fact, a sin that has haunted her over the years.' Corbett glanced at Beatrice. 'Isn't that true, mistress?' He didn't wait for an answer, but turned back to the priest, watching those eyes dart and shift like those of all murderers did when they searched for a path out of the trap opening before them. 'She was with your mother the night she was murdered. Only a slip of a girl, Mistress Beatrice fled, your mother died. She was always haunted by a deep sense of guilt, which harrowed her soul. Now last Advent, in preparation for Christmas, Beatrice made a full confession. You recall the occasion, surely, Parson John? The Dean of St Paul's, as is customary, invites the citizens of London to receive absolution. Priests gather from all over the city. They sit the length and breadth of the nave behind curtained screens so that penitents, ashamed of what they have to confess, can whisper their sins anonymously. Now, as often in life, chance or God's own grace can create the most extraordinary coincidences. Mistress Beatrice went to confess her sins at St Paul's. She did so in great detail and told the priest everything: the murder of Emma Evesham, her own flight, her suspicions about Sir Walter, his possible connivance in his wife's death, his evil alliance with the likes of Waldene and Hubert the Monk. Most importantly, she still felt she was a coward who'd betrayed her mistress.'

'She did not confess to me.'

'Oh Parson John, I think she did. There's no evidence for that,' Corbett tapped the wine, 'except this, your one and only terrible mistake. True?' He pulled himself up in the chair. 'I did suspect you, despite your fearful, tremulous way. You always had a story, an excuse for being elsewhere when these hideous deeds were committed.' He lifted a hand. 'Except for one, which was too glib, too smooth.'

'What do you mean?' Parson John protested.

'That attack on you in St Botulph's.' Corbett paused as Beatrice went into the scullery and brought back a stool to sit on and watch fascinated. 'According to you, Parson John, your attacker entered the sacristy by the outside door. You were struck down and bound.'

'Sir Hugh, I was bruised, you saw the marks on my face.'

'No, no,' Corbett countered, 'they were caused during your struggle with Master Fink. We'll leave that for a while. You were not struck down. You did not wander into St Botulph's. You went into that church as a murderer with the severed heads of your victims Clarice and Master Fink. You placed those in that font as a rejection of everything you once believed in. You then went back into the sacristy and waited for Master Fleschner. You'd invited him at a certain time to act as your witness; he was as much your victim as anyone else. You had the ropes ready in a tangle to slip over your ankles and wrists. It's easily done. When Master Fleschner came to your rescue, he would not notice, not poor, nervous Fleschner in that cold, desolate sacristy, desperate to free the hapless Parson John. You certainly prepared well.' Corbett leaned over and touched the small, fading scar on Parson John's forehead. 'You'd even cut yourself, as if the assassin had marked you down for death and was about to carve the letter M.

'Of course it was all a charade, based on false logic. First, Master Fleschner claimed that as he entered the church, the assassin came out of the sacristy door, then fled back in. Why should he do that? His best path of escape was through the outer door and into the tangled, overgrown cemetery. Why come into the church except to create the illusion that there were two people in the sacristy? You, the victim, and your supposed assailant. Master Fleschner was a nervous man, you described him as such. He would take his time to cross and creep up the sanctuary steps into the sacristy. Time enough for you to pose as the victim. You wrapped the tangle of ropes around your ankles and wrists.' Corbett paused. 'What did it matter anyway? Master Fleschner didn't notice anything untoward. Yet your account was further flawed. Fleschner found you bound, the letter M about to be carved on your forehead. Why didn't the assassin take the next logical step and kill you, draw a knife across your throat in a heartbeat of breath? Why did this ruthless killer spare his victim, Evesham's own son, all trussed up for the killing? Why leave you as a possible witness against him?' Corbett shrugged. 'Except, of course, that you were providing a subtle defence against any allegation levelled about yourself.'

Parson John didn't answer. He sat more relaxed, lips parted eyes half closed, staring into the fire. Corbett wondered about the man's wits. Did he care about what was happening? Had the revelations about his father murdering his mother crushed his soul?

'Then there's Mistress Adelicia's midnight visitor out in the woods at Syon; more of that later, though it must have been you. Again a matter of logic. You asked after a woman called Beatrice. You demanded to know if Evesham had sought such information from Adelicia twenty years ago, just after Boniface's disappearance.'

'I am sorry?' interrupted Parson John, his face all haughty. 'What do you mean, clerk?'

'Why, priest, when I held court in St Botulph's, I looked around and quietly asked myself who would pose such a question. Staunton or Blandeford? No, they fish in other stew ponds. Parson Cuthbert? Why should he dissimulate? Adelicia would soon have recognised him. Master Lapwing? But he knew all about Beatrice. That left you, a murderer wondering if your list of victims was complete. Sometime after you heard Mistress Beatrice's confession, you must have visited the Guildhall and read the coroner's roll, Master's Fleschner's entry regarding your mother's death and her maid's disappearance. You must have wondered, as I did, about Beatrice's role in that hideous affair. Was she an accomplice? How had she escaped? Where was she? Above all, did she have any guilt regarding your mother's death?' Corbett paused. 'Oh yes, you certainly heard Beatrice's confession. By the way, where was your mother buried?'

Parson John just swallowed hard, staring unflinchingly into the fire.

'Let me tell you,' Corbett continued. He glanced across at Ranulf, who gazed curiously back. The clerk had been busy about his own enquiries, whilst his master had kept what he was plotting very close to his heart. All Corbett had asked him to do was to keep Mistress Beatrice's house under tight scrutiny and immediately alert him, at a nearby tavern, if she received any visitors.

'You know where my mother lies buried,' Parson John broke in harshly.

'Of course I do.' Corbett replied. 'In St Botulph's, beneath the flagstones leading to the Lady Chapel. I am sure Walter Evesham placed a stone there extolling your mother's virtues whilst lamenting his own sad loss. Once you'd heard Beatrice's confession, you regarded that carving as a devilish lie. You had the stone pulled up and replaced with something smoother. No one would really notice. After all, grave memorials are soon forgotten, but not by you, not with memories fresh with the truth about your mother's gruesome fate. Oh yes, you removed that stone. In your mind, it represented everything you hated about your father.' Corbett paused, gathering his thoughts.

'You constantly protested that you knew nothing about your father's affairs, but that was a lie. You knew everything, which was why you became a priest, wasn't it? You rejected your father's world. You knew the filth he waded through, his friends, his double-dealing, his duplicity, his treachery, perhaps his love of disorder. A father knows a son, a son knows a father. It wouldn't be hard for you to bring your father under scrutiny, to visit him in the guise of a friendly, loving son whilst keeping your eyes and ears alert. You found out about his meetings with the likes of Waldene and Hubert the Monk. You heard rumours about the way he favoured members of their covens, and so you posed as the writer from the Land of Cockaigne. A suitable choice, the world turned upside down.' Corbett leaned across and touched the priest. 'Parson John, I fully understand your anger, your hatred, your desire for revenge. It was what you did that makes me your adversary. At first you struck at your father's reputation. You sent those letters to Staunton and Blandeford, one piece of evidence after another so the King was forced to act and your father was caught red-handed with Waldene and Hubert the Monk. That must have been a great source of satisfaction to you.'

Parson John grinned, as if savouring some secret joke.

'Waldene and Hubert the Monk were lodged in Newgate, but your father surprised everyone. He didn't try to defend his reputation; he simply threw himself on the King's mercy. He underwent a Damascus road conversion and became the tired, broken recluse of Syon Abbey. In truth, you knew your father, as did Brother Cuthbert. Walter Evesham simply wanted time and space to reflect, to plot, to seek a way back. You were determined that he would never walk that path. You went to Syon Abbey. You visited Brother Cuthbert and Adelicia in your pastoral guise, but then you returned to spy out the land. You discovered, as I did, that the two of them would often meet at night. Brother Cuthbert would leave the Chapel of St Lazarus and go into the woods to be with the one true love of his life. They would sit and discuss the past, revelling in each other's company. You simply waited for your opportunity, and then you struck.'

15

Holm-gang: a fight to the death between
two adversaries on a small island

'My visits to Syon Abbey are well recorded,' Parson John protested.

'No, priest. I am not talking about you entering the main gate, talking to the prior, the abbot, the guest master or the almoner, but about other times. How you came back hooded and visored, armed for war in the dead of night, bringing a ladder, scaling those walls, hiding in the undergrowth.'

'Brother Cuthbert is sharp enough, as is his war dog.'

'Nonsense. Ogadon is an old dog who would recognise you and offer no challenge. Just in case, you'd bring some delicacy laced with an opiate so that Ogadon would flop down and sink into the deepest slumber. That's what happened the night you murdered your father.'

'I was at St Botulph's,' Parson John declared. 'Remember, clerk, the riot at Newgate? My church was sacked and pillaged, my parishioners slaughtered.'

'Were you really?' Corbett countered. 'Who says? All was chaos and confusion. I recall meeting you the following morning –

nothing more. Indeed, what happened at St Botulph's would only intensify your determination to mete out justice. As far as everyone else was concerned, Parson John, shocked and distraught at what was happening, was sheltering in his priest's house or had sought sanctuary elsewhere. You were in fact hastening through the dark to Syon Abbey. You entered the grounds. Brother Cuthbert was gone, Ogadon sleeping, and you helped him to remain so. You entered the mortuary chapel, going down the steps to your father's cell. He would greet you, curious, perhaps even surprised, but not threatened, not by his son who'd given up the world of arms to be a priest. I can only imagine his arrogance, his mocking condescension. He invited you into his cell. You simply waited for him to sit down and then you struck, a blade across his throat, cutting it open, letting the blood splash out. On that night you helped yourself to the jewellery, the few possessions your father had taken with him. You were searching for a certain ring, weren't you?'

'How would I know about that?'

'Oh come, priest, the story about what happened at St Botulph's is well known. It's something you could have learnt over the years, I mean about Adelicia's ring. It would certainly be an item your father would keep close. Once you'd killed Sir Walter, you took the ring and left. Sometimes circumstances conspire against us, other times in our favour. Brother Cuthbert returned to find Sir Walter murdered and became involved in a great deal of mummery to cloak the murder in deep mystery in order to protect himself, so that he wouldn't have to answer questions about where he was when Sir Walter was slain.'

'I did all this?' Parson John jibed. 'And no one noticed?'

'I have walked the grounds of Syon Abbey, they're deserted. The curtain wall is very close to the river. Someone like yourself, young, able and strong, could hire a small boat, go along the bank, remove the ladder you've concealed there and climb over the wall. Sentries don't patrol. Ogadon knows you. Brother Cuthbert often leaves the Chapel of St Lazarus to visit Adelicia. You did the same the night you went to see Adelicia, slipping through the woods determined to establish who this Beatrice was. However, to return to the night your father was murdered.' Corbett glanced quickly back at the doorway. Chanson stood on guard, the arbalest primed. Ranulf was as vigilant as ever. Beatrice sat on her stool, gaping in astonishment at what she was hearing. 'You also struck at Engleat. He was a much easier quarry. Engleat was in his cups. He'd been to a brothel. Tired and drunk, he sat slumped in that taproom. You entered, hooded and masked. The tavern was busy, who would notice, who would care? Engleat, drunk and fuddled in his wits, was helped through the door, down to that lonely, filthy alleyway, where he was prepared for execution, lashed to the hanged man, before being rolled into the river.'

Corbett started as the priest fished beneath his robe, but all he brought out was a small string of Ave beads, which he started threading through his fingers.

'I did say,' Corbett remarked, 'that sometimes circumstances conspire in our favour, sometimes against. What you had not plotted or planned for was the riot at Newgate and the followers of Waldene and Hubert the Monk breaking out. Now that was the work of Master Lapwing, and he must answer for it. You could have been killed but you weren't; perhaps you viewed your survival as justification for your actions. You had already decided on the deaths of Waldene and the Monk, and to put it bluntly, their heads were presented to you on a plate. The King was forced to release them for lack of evidence following your father's murder. It was well known that they were going to celebrate in the Angel's Salutation. You simply waited, chose your moment and struck. Armed and disguised, you entered that tavern, climbed the stairs, killed their guard then confronted them. Both riffler leaders were fuddled in their cups. They took the poisoned wine and you watched them die. You carved the "M" on their foreheads, threatened the whores and left.'

'I could have been apprehended, seen.'

'Not really. Your head and face were hidden behind a mask and a deep cowl. Anyway, who'd really care about Giles Waldene and Hubert the Monk? I don't think the line of mourners at their funerals was a long one. You were fully intent on finishing your murderous business as swiftly as possible. I'm not too sure about the events as they happened, but either before you killed those two rogues or shortly afterwards, you visited Mistress Clarice and Richard Fink in their great mansion. You must have suspected Lady Clarice's loose morals, her relationship with Fink. You'd certainly have discovered how they were most reluctant for their servants to stay. That helped your cause; it certainly struck me as suspicious. Who would know that the house was deserted? Moreover, when I entered, I detected no signs of disturbance or robbery. That's because you knew your way in. You went up those stairs knowing what you'd find. You reached the bedchamber. Fink was alarmed, he met you as you entered the room. Blows were struck . . .'

'I'm a priest, I have no skill——'

'Nonsense,' Corbett retorted. 'You trained as a battle squire in Norfolk's household. More importantly, you are full of hate and anger. You were determined that Clarice would die. Why should such a woman benefit from your mother's death? You're brutal. Fink bruises you, but he is knocked to the ground. Clarice, terrified, is next. She too is struck. Both lie stunned. You carry out your next grisly task. You mark their foreheads, then decapitate them. The love chamber is now awash with blood. You place the heads in a leather sack, hasten back down the stairs and out into the streets. Disguised, you walk back to St Botulph's, where you carry out the charade I described before.' Corbett paused. 'I wondered why the severed heads were placed in the baptismal font. I realise now. When someone enters the Church, they're baptised, initiated into the Community of the Faithful. You were rejecting that, weren't you? You wanted to desecrate everything you believed in. The heads are tossed there and you go into the sacristy to wait for Master Fleschner. A busy day, priest. You must have been satisfied. You'd almost finished your task; only the woman Beatrice remained.'

'Master clerk.' Parson John's voice was almost a drawl. Corbett noticed how he brushed his mouth with his fingers. 'You were attacked in St Botulph's.' He sniffed. 'Are you blaming me for that? I have no war dog. Skilled I may be with a battleaxe or sword, but——'

'Who said you used a battleaxe?' Corbett asked.

'Skilled I may be,' Parson John almost smiled, 'but an abarlest, a war dog?'

'Hush now!' Ranulf used his hand to force the priest to look at him. 'Parson John, across the river in Southwark, around the Sanctuary at Westminster or out near White Friars I could hire killers by the dozen. That's what you did. It's easily done, in some darkened shadowy corner, coins exchanged . . .'

'You gave the assassin my name and description,' Corbett accused. 'You told him I resided at Westminster. He waited there and followed me to St Botulph's and struck when he could. Poor Griffyths, a soldier doing his duty, was killed and sent unshriven to God. You did the same to Fleschner. He never suspected that the lamb he was tending was really a ravenous wolf. He took you back to the priest's house. You wanted a goblet of wine with an opiate to help you sleep. You drank nothing of the sort. Fleschner left and you followed him down to Queenshithe. You attacked him in some filthy alleyway, knocked him on the head, marked him with your murderous sign and hanged him from a street bracket. You are very good at acting the frightened, cowed priest, alienated from his father, not knowing what was happening. You knew everything. You're a redoubtable man, Parson John. A killer, but still redoubtable, ruthless and ferocious. You missed your calling. I've served with the likes of you in Wales and along the Northern March. God knows,' he whispered, 'you had cause enough to turn, but why follow the same path as your father, as Waldene and Hubert the Monk?'

'I'm still asking for evidence, Sir Hugh.' Parson John slipped down in the chair, stretching as if he were listening to a good story. 'And even if you collect enough evidence, I'm still a priest, I'll claim benefit of clergy.' Again he passed his hand before his mouth. Corbett looked down. The chain had been broken, beads lay scattered in the priest's lap. Parson John followed his gaze. 'Oh, don't worry, clerk, I have already decided my way. I know what you are going to say. The King would never put me on trial. He wouldn't want such a scandal voiced the length and breadth of his kingdom. As for being a priest, that wouldn't save me from some filthy dungeon, walled up, living on bread and water, to become the plaything of gaolers, or committed to a lonely monastery and the vicious spite of its father abbot. No, no.' He gestured over his shoulder at Ranulf. 'Or taken into custody by some royal bully-boy, to be harassed and tortured. After all, there's my name, isn't there? I like to be called Parson John, but I'd be hated as the son of Evesham, a murderer like my father.'

Corbett stretched out and picked up a bead from the priest's lap. 'What are these? You've eaten some?'

'Of course I have,' the priest replied. 'Abrin seed; they use it in Venice. You're given one if you are accused of a crime. If you're innocent you survive, if you're guilty you die. The trick is that if you swallow the seed it simply passes through you; the hard shell cannot be digested. If you chew it, as I have, it is a fairly pain-less death, not now, but soon.' He clutched his stomach and started forward. 'I'll not challenge what you've said. I hated my father from the very beginning. I wanted to be different. That is why I became a priest. I knew about his wickedness, his nefarious doings, his alliances, but I never plotted against him, not until I heard that woman's confession. Then, like a puzzle, pieces fell into place.

Things I'd seen and heard. Suspicions, whispers, rumours all became fact. I really did like Brother Cuthbert and Mistress Adelicia. I often visited them. They were two people who truly loved each other. They used to talk about what happened at St Botulph's. From them I got the description of that ring, my first real suspicion, as I'd seen a similar ring hidden away in my father's casket. I'd let that pass, but once I learnt the truth, everything died. How could I believe in God the Father when my own father had murdered my mother, a loving, sweet woman? What was the use of candlelight, prayers, the Mass, incense, blessings, holy water? It's all a pretence: blackness here, blackness beyond. I couldn't care.

'It is as you say. I thought, I reflected. I went to the Guildhall on business. I took down the coroner's rolls. I saw the entry about my mother. I wondered what had happened to Mistress Beatrice, then I waited. It was so simple. I kept my father's house under close watch at night; he always worked under the cover of dark. He only believed in one verse from the Scriptures: "live for the day", and he certainly did that. He was attracted to wickedness like a bird to flying. I was the writer from the Land of Cockaigne. I like that description; it suited my world turned upside down. I betrayed him to Staunton and Blandeford and then my father fled to Syon Abbey. I knew what he was doing. He'd lurk there, he'd think and plot, then he'd crawl back into the sunlight, offer some pact with the King, negotiate his way back to preferment. He'd betray anybody for that, do anything. So I struck.

'I knew that Brother Cuthbert used to meet Adelicia, that was as obvious as the sun rises. It was so easy to go along the river by boat, climb the wall and just wait. It is as you described. The murderous affray at St Botulph's? I took that as a sign.' He paused, swallowing hard, staring up at the ceiling. 'First my father, or the creature who called himself that. I cut his throat without a whisper of guilt. Engleat the drunkard deserved his fate. The same for the rest. Who would miss Waldene, Hubert the Monk, Clarice the adulteress? My father chose well. I suspect she was playing the two-backed beast with Master Fink long before my father fell from grace. I swept into that house like God's anger. Up the stairs I strode. Fink was fat and flabby. I knocked him aside. I was their executioner, Corbett. Fleschner, all timorous and pleading? He looked the other way when my mother died; he must have known but he never told me, my faithful parish clerk.' Parson John wiped his mouth.

'I realised, as you did, that my father was the Mysterium. I reached the truth. It was only fitting for me to assume the Mysterium's mantle in my pursuit of justice.' The priest had gone pale, beads of sweat glistening on his brow, but he managed to smile at Corbett. 'Very subtle and very clever, aren't you, clerk? You suspected me but you didn't have the evidence. You fed me, baited me like a fish about how Mistress Beatrice might have had a hand in my own mother's murder.' He paused, gripping his stomach, bending forward, gargling at the back of his throat. Mistress Beatrice sprang to her feet, fingers to her lips. Corbett made a sign with his hand, and she stayed where she was. Parson John lifted his face, now ghastly, eyes straining against the pain. 'How did you do it?' he said.

'I went to see her,' Corbett replied. 'She assured me she'd told no other man, so I simply asked her another question. Had she at her shriving ever confessed what she called her secret sin, fleeing when her mistress died? I thought she might have done, and she had. She told me how she was shriven last Advent at St Paul's. I made a few enquiries, but even before that, I nursed suspicions about you, a deep unease.' He gripped the priest's arm. 'You're dying, Parson John.'

'I'm dying, Corbett. For God's sake let me go in peace. You condemn me, but if there is a light beyond, if there is judgement before some tribunal, I'll plead my cause.' He glanced watery-eyed at Corbett and gasped at the pain. 'I was a good priest, clerk, I truly was. I rejected everything my father did, everything he was, until I heard that woman's confession, then my world fell apart. Do you know what it's like to suddenly realise that everything you believe in is a lie? There's no justice, there's no right? You told me once how we are all murderers. We kill each other in our thoughts. Men like my father must be brought down by men like me or you. They are made by the sword. They die by the sword. They live bad lives, they die bad deaths. Tell me, Corbett, who amongst those I killed was innocent?' He paused, a white spittle dripping from his lips. 'That attack in St Botulph's when the prisoners of Newgate barred themselves in? Look at the innocents who died there – why, Corbett? Look at my poor mother going out to an almshouse, doing good, slaughtered like some wandering pig in the streets.' He leaned back in the chair. 'I've said enough,' he gasped. 'Leave me.' His fingers fluttered. 'Leave me . . .'

'We'll not leave you,' Corbett replied. 'We'll stay with you. We'll watch you go, priest, and I shall murmur a prayer that God in his mercy will show you some favour.' He gestured with his hand at the others to remain silent. Parson John became lost in his own world of pain. He made no attempt to talk, but sat hunched in the chair, hands on his belly, coughing and spluttering as the white spittle thickened around his lips. Abruptly he jerked, head back, heels kicking the ground, then he gave a great sigh and sagged, head drooping, eyes half open.

'I didn't believe.' Mistress Beatrice rose to her feet and came round to stare down at the priest. 'I truly didn't believe that God's justice would wait so long. Sir Hugh, why did he take his life?'

'Because he was correct, mistress.' Corbett pressed a hand against the dead priest's neck; already the skin was cold and clammy and he could feel no life pulse. 'His life was finished when he heard your confession about his mother. After that, a blackness descended, a deep, dark night of the soul. He lived for one reason and one reason only, to wreak hideous revenge. Once he achieved that, what else was there? Go back to being a priest, to shriving people's sins and offering Mass in reparation for all our wicked-ness? Parson John's world had collapsed. He would have killed you and then continued to murder anyone associated with his father or his father's nefarious schemes until he was either caught or killed.' Corbett rose. 'Mistress Beatrice, I thank you. As for your son, Parson John is right about that too: innocents died at St Botulph's; that riot was deliberately caused.'

'Clerks,' Beatrice murmured, 'all royal clerks are ambitious, following the King's will, seeking the King's favour, his gold, the status and power he can confer. That's the root cause of all this, Sir Hugh.'

'I don't think so.' Corbett struck his breast. 'We all have it in us, mistress, a desire for power, to lord it over others, to make our presence felt. Ah well,' he gave a deep sigh, 'Ranulf, have the corpse removed to some death house at a local church. Tell the priest to bless the corpse, arrange for a requiem Mass to be said, bury his body in the poor man's lot. That's the best I can do.'

'And you, Sir Hugh, you will go to Westminster?'

Corbett picked up the priest's belt and placed it on the chair he'd just vacated. 'You'll come with me, Ranulf. We must have words with the King.'

'First I'll remove the corpse, I'll even say a prayer for him. He did us all a favour, certainly the King. His grace will be pleased at such a silent death, no scandal, no public outcry, no trial. But before I join you at Westminster, I have certain business to complete.'

'What business?' Corbett asked sharply.

Ranulf refused to meet his gaze. 'Master, you have your tasks and I have mine.'

Ranulf-atte-Newgate entered the Bowels of Hell, a tavern deep in the labyrinth of the needle-thin alleyways and runnels around White Friars. He paused just within the doorway, threw back his cloak and adjusted his war belt so that all could see the sword and dagger in their brocaded scabbards. Then he glanced around and smiled.

'Home from home,' he murmured, 'sweet memories of my youth.'

The taproom of the Bowels of Hell was spacious and dark, a

true hiding place for the counterfeits, cranks, cunning men, forgers, outlaws and wolfsheads from the nearby Sanctuary. They all clustered here in the juddering light of the squat, rancid-smelling tallow candles, a garish, motley gang of London's underworld, all dressed in their tawdry finery, consorting with the bawds in their strumpet rags and shiny cheap jewellery. No one looked directly at Ranulf. They all recognised Corbett's fighting man, his dagger-boy, a dangerous character made even more so by the ring he wore and the chain around his neck. They glanced quickly at him, then returned to their business, quietly praying that they weren't his.

The clerk stood for a while, then moved over to the counter, a long board laid over a row of casks. Minehost, a former pirate in the Thames estuary who, as he often boasted, had escaped the scaffold on at least two occasions by murmuring the first line of Psalm 50, moved to present him with a tankard of his finest ale.

'Brewed with pigshit,' Ranulf murmured, pushing it away. 'You'll not have me fuddled, sir.' He plucked at Minehost's bloodstained apron. 'I've talked to Mouseman. He's lodged in a chamber at Westminster. He awaits his pardon being sealed by the chancellor.'

'And?' Minehost's fat, sweaty face creased into a smile.

'He mentioned a dog-man, a dagger-lad with a war hound.'

'Never heard of him.'

Ranulf plucked at the apron again. 'Very good,' he hissed, 'then I'll be gone, but . . .' His smile faded and he paused at the screeching of some whore as she was thrown to the floor and her skirts pulled back.

'But what?' Minehost asked.

'I'll be back with a comitatus.' Ranulf pulled a face, moving his head from side to side. 'I'm not too sure when, but late one night we will break in here. We'll arrest all law-breakers and those who shelter them. I'll try to be fair and careful.' He moved his arm swiftly, knocking over one of the candles. 'Sorry!' He picked it up. 'I'll really try and make sure we are careful. I mean that no fire breaks out, that the bailiffs don't plunder here or the treasure you've undoubtedly hidden away in the cellars below.' Ranulf shrugged. 'And, of course I'll do my best to protect you personally.'

'Over there.' Minehost supped from the tankard he'd just offered. 'In the far corner. He's sitting facing you. He has a scar across his face.'

Ranulf smiled and swaggered across the ill-lit taproom, shoving aside bawds and pimps, boots scuffing the strewn rushes now turned to a mushy mess. From the cellar below echoed the raucous shouts of gamblers wagering on the cock fight about to begin. He reached the corner, picked up a fallen stool and pushed his way through to the great squat tun that served as a table. He took out his own dice and cup from his wallet and grinned cheekily at the gamblers.

'Good evening, my lords,' he intoned, 'and a finer collection I've not seen, even on the execution cart bound for the Elms.'

The gamblers, their unshaven faces betraying their nervousness, peered back warily from hoods and cowls. The man sitting opposite, with a greyish scar running from his left eye right across his face, hastily scooped up the few silver coins, hands disappearing beneath the table. Ranulf just shrugged and shook his own dice.

'Call a number.' He smiled at the dog-man. 'You go first!'

'I don't want to gamble. I have no silver.'

'You have a war hound. Choose a number.' Ranulf rolled the dice. 'Seven!' he exclaimed and rolled again. 'Eight.' He picked up the dice. 'My number's higher. I've won your dog.'

'I didn't wager it.'

'Why, where is it?'

'I don't have one.'

'You did have,' Ranulf grinned, 'but you had to kill it in St Botulph's cemetery . . .'

The dog-man's knife hand came out above the table. Ranulf was swifter, a clean straight thrust into his opponent's throat. The dog-man choked, gagged and spluttered, hands beating the air.

'You tried to kill my friend, my master,' and pressing again on the dagger, Ranulf watched the soul-light in those dark eyes fade before withdrawing his blade. The dog-man, coughing blood, collapsed over the table, sending tankards and platters hurtling to the floor. The hubbub in the tavern immediately stilled. Ranulf rose, leaned over, wiped his blade on the shoulder of the dead assassin, pocketed his dice and stared down at the other gamblers, who sat hands gripping whatever weapons they carried.

'*Pax et bonum.*' Ranulf smiled and leaned down. 'You'll agree, sirs, won't you, it was self-defence?'

'As clear as day,' agreed a gaunt-faced rogue to Ranulf's right. 'I'll take any oath that it's the truth. We all would, wouldn't we?' His companions, eager to plunder their dead companion, nodded vigorously in agreement.

'So it is.' Ranulf re-sheathed his dagger. 'There truly is honour amongst thieves. Gentlemen, I bid you good night.'

Edward the King considered it to be a very good night as he lounged in front of the great hearth-fire in the Jerusalem Chamber at Westminster. The King gulped his claret and stared appreciatively at Corbett, who sat on a chair opposite. Edward was about to smile but stiffened. Corbett was looking at him strangely. He recognised that look, unblinking, as if the Keeper of the King's Secret Seal was trying to probe the royal soul, demand an answer to some nagging question.

'Hugh,' the King lifted his goblet in toast, 'you are indeed a good and faithful servant. I listened to your report and my heart leapt with joy. Evesham and Engleat are gone – no prattling there – Waldene and Hubert dispatched to hell, their gangs broken, a warning to those Great Ones in the Guildhall. Arrogant peacocks with a host of kites and ravens at their beck and call.' Edward loosened the braids of his quilted jerkin. 'All gone,' he murmured. 'I'll confiscate Evesham's house and his treasures. More importantly, Parson John. Thank God, thank God for what he did. There'll be no trial, no scandal, no trumpeting abroad.' Edward wanted Corbett out. He felt uncomfortable. 'Now, Hugh, there's a strange business in Kent, a haunted manor house where—'

'Sire?'

'Hugh?' Edward curbed his growing nervousness.

'Why did you allow Evesham to burn his manuscripts?'

'What use were they?'

'Did they contain secrets harmful to you?'

'Possibly, but I wouldn't know, would I.' The King grinned. 'They were secret.'

'And what did you really plan for Evesham, sire? A long stay in Syon, then he'd turn King's Approver, reveal all the wickedness about the city, the Great Ones at the Guildhall? And why did you ask me to investigate? Did you suspect that Staunton and Blandeford had murdered Evesham after seizing some of his records? Knowing that precious pair, I'd have their chambers searched for any information hurtful to you. Did you, did they, always entertain suspicions about Boniface Ippegrave's guilt?'

Edward bared his teeth in a smile.

'And that riot in Newgate? Staunton and Blandeford's work through their creature Lapwing? You separated the gangs from their leaders. Master Lapwing agitated them, spreading the lie that one coven was about to turn King's evidence. Why weren't the prisoners lodged in the Tower? Was the keeper of Newgate told to look the other way? Did he have his secret orders? Lapwing plotted well. He spread a mess of lies about how St Botulph's could be fortified, that it had a secret passageway out. You wanted to destroy those gangs, separate them from their leaders, and shatter Waldene and the Monk's power. Perhaps they too, if they survived the pits, could be persuaded to sing the same hymn as Evesham, but Evesham's murder foiled all that. How could you threaten those two coven leaders if your principal witness was dead? More importantly, Waldene and the Monk, when they were released, were no longer powerful, their retinues annihilated. Whatever, you arranged that riot. The two gangs, caught in open rebellion, would face summary justice, a warning to all the other covens and dagger-men in the city.'

Edward noisily tapped his fingers against the quilted arm of his chair.

'Lapwing,' Corbett insisted, 'he provoked that riot. So did Staunton and Blandeford. In the end, sire, you achieved what you planned: the total destruction of two of London's most violent gangs. But Lapwing should pay for what he did, as should Staunton and Blandeford.'

'Lapwing is to be released,' the King snapped, 'and restored to office. Staunton and Blandeford are good, faithful servants of the Crown.'

'Innocents died that day,' Corbett continued as if talking to himself, 'poor men and women hastening about their God-given lives. Some were going to the stalls, others to church to pray. They were slaughtered like pigs, the women raped and abused.'

'Sir Hugh . . .'

Corbett slipped the chancery ring off his finger and took off the delicate silver chain around his neck. He placed these carefully on a nearby footstool and rose.

'I'll not be going to Kent, sire.'

'Hugh?'

'I have resigned from office. I am tired, sick at heart and weary. This is finished and so am I. It's time for me to be gone.'

'Hugh, for the love of God, don't leave me. Not you.' Edward slammed down his goblet and sprang to his feet, fingers tapping the hilt of his dagger.

'Really,' Corbett smiled thinly, 'will it come to that one day?

Sire, I bid you good night.' He turned and walked out of the chamber, letting the door slam shut on Edward's shouts.

Ranulf, waiting outside, sprang to his feet.

'Sir Hugh?' He stared anxiously at his master's grim face. The door to the Jerusalem Chamber was flung open and Edward stormed out.

'Hugh, please!'

'Master?'

Corbett ignored the King. He clasped Ranulf on the shoulder.

'As you said, old friend, you have your tasks, I have mine. You know where I am going; you may follow if you wish.'

Edward grasped his arm, but Corbett shook him off, not even bothering to look at him. Then he started purposefully down the darkening gallery, the King's passionate pleading echoing after him.

Author's Note

The Mysterium is of course a work of fiction, but it is based very firmly on events that did occur during the reign of Edward I. All the elements mentioned here figure prominently in the tumultuous history of medieval London: the wealthy merchants, their links to the underworld and its powerful gangs ever ready to answer their masters' call. Edward I never trusted Londoners, and Sir Ralph Sandewic, Constable of the Tower, is a real historical figure who kept strict watch on England's capital city from its Tower. Riots and escapes from Newgate were common, escaped felons often took sanctuary only to be violently seized and immediately decapitated.

Edward I did pride himself on his love of the law, though when it came to it, he honoured it more in the breach than the observance. Sir Walter Evesham is based on a true historical character, Chief Justice Sir Thomas de Weyland, who fell from grace and fled to sanctuary. The legal system of Edward I and the violent underworld it tried to control is described in very great detail in my non-fiction work, *The Great Crown Jewel Robbery of 1303*, which also explains why human skin was left pinned to a door in Westminster Abbey!

Paul Doherty
January, 2010
www.paulcdoherty.com